THE SPIKE

ARNAUD de BORCHGRAVE AND ROBERT MOSS

AVON
PUBLISHERS OF BARD, CAMELOT AND DISCUS BOOKS

AVON BOOKS
A division of
The Hearst Corporation
959 Eighth Avenue
New York, New York 10019

The Crown Publishers, Inc. edition contains the following Library of Congress Cataloging in Publication Data:

de Borchgrave, Arnaud.
The spike.
I. Moss, Robert, 1946– joint author.
II. Title.

First Avon Printing, May, 1981

AVON TRADEMARK REG. U.S. PAT. OFF. AND IN
OTHER COUNTRIES, MARCA REGISTRADA,
HECHO EN U.S.A.

Printed in the U.S.A.

To Alexandra and Katrina

May 1967

1

JAMMED AGAINST THE BIG BELL TOWER by the press of students around him in the middle of Sproul Plaza, Bob Hockney stared up into the belly of the helicopter that had blacked out the sun. It looked like a fat blowfly about to settle on their heads.

Across the plaza Tom Flack, small, dark, and pixielike, was hopping about on the wide steps of the student center, trying to make himself audible above the whir of the chopper blades. Flack was a radical guru on the Berkeley campus. He had helped organize the occupation of a plot of vacant land that became "People's Park," a liberated zone where the flower people could play music, grow pot, and make love. When the authorities tried to reclaim the land and put up a hurricane fence around it, Flack and his friends pulled the fence down. The Governor had to send in the National Guard with tanks and helicopters. Tom Flack had ideas on how to deal with the National Guard. He advised female students to hand out oranges to the Guardsmen during demonstrations as a gesture of goodwill. The oranges had been spiked with LSD.

Now two more choppers were visible above the first. Tom Flack shook his fist at them, abandoning his speech on how the university had been co-opted by the defense establishment because of its dependence on contracts from the Pentagon and the CIA.

Bob Hockney, a lanky, good-looking political science major, twenty-two years old, agreed with most of what Flack had been saying. He now passed a hand through his dark wavy hair, worn moderately long. One of his professors, he knew, was engaged in a CIA-funded research project on the effects of urban overcrowding on modern society, and would sometimes regale his classes with accounts of the latest upheavals inside the city of rats he had con-

2

structed in a special laboratory. Herded together in more and more confined pens, the rats developed neurotic symptoms, indulged in orgies, warred with each other, and finally turned cannibal. Professor Milorad Yankovich did not appear to doubt that there was an exact analogy between the behavior of his rats and that of twentieth-century man.

The three helicopters hovered overhead in delta formation.

"What are they going to do?" the shapely girl standing next to Hockney asked nervously. The downdraft from the chopper blades blew her long blonde hair across Hockney's mouth and chin. He playfully stroked it back into place.

"The Governor thinks we're in Vietnam," Hockney murmured.

From his perch in front of the student center, Tom Flack sensed the need to rally his forces.

"Hey, Hey, LBJ," he bellowed into his microphone. The amplifiers were not working properly, but the crowd got the message.

"How many kids d'you kill today?" The students took up the chorus.

Hockney mouthed the words without speaking. He was embarrassed by slogans. That was one reason he had stayed on the fringes of the antiwar movement. He took part, but he didn't shout—just as he smoked grass at the occasional beach party, but wasn't into the heavy stuff. His reserve infuriated some of his friends, who accused him of treating the revolution as a spectator sport. In the same spirit, he had turned down an invitation to spend his summer vacation helping Castro's revolution by cutting sugarcane. The girl in wire-rimmed glasses who was setting up the trip had called him "a bourgeois East Coast asshole." Hockney suspected that the people who took causes *that* seriously were, at bottom, not serious at all.

Hockney watched the arms of a Guardsman reach out through the open door of the nearest helicopter, dumping small black pellets into the mass of students. Flyshit, Hockney thought for an instant, before the first tear gas grenade exploded in midair.

A girl's scream knifed through the chanting.

3

"My God!" exclaimed the blonde standing next to Hockney. "We *are* in Vietnam. The Governor's bombing us!"

The girl edged away from him, trying to push her way through the crowd toward Sproul Hall, the administration building. But the bodies were too tightly packed for her to move more than a couple of steps, and the ebb and flow of students trying to run in all directions from the gas flung her back violently against Hockney's chest. He toppled backward and would have fallen but for the soft wall of bodies behind. As he helped the girl to steady herself, he found that his hand was cupping one of her full breasts. They both laughed.

"Stay cool." Tom Flack's voice crackled over the microphone. "If you've got a handkerchief, spit on it and hold it over your nose and mouth. If you haven't got a handkerchief, use your shirt. That'll slow down the effect of the gas."

Hockney's eyes were stinging. The girl's were red and streaming and she started to cough. He eased a handkerchief out of the tight pocket of his jeans, moistened it with his tongue, and clamped it over her face.

"It's okay," Hockney said. "I brushed my teeth this morning."

As the students who were farthest away from the bell tower took cover in the student center and the cafeteria, the crowd in the middle of the plaza began to break up. Hockney took the girl's hand and pulled her behind him as he shouldered his way, spluttering, in the direction of Tom Flack. Overhead, tear gas grenades were still tumbling out of the sky.

"It could be worse," Hockney joked to the girl. "Next time, the Governor will try napalm."

Tom Flack, excited and angry, looked as if he were dancing a jig as he yelled out his war chants to the formless, thinning crowd.

"Ho, Ho, Ho Chi Minh!" Flack's voice rose to a shriek.

This time, Hockney joined in the ragged chorus. It was no longer just a question of solidarity—of showing support for the way his friends felt about the war. The Governor's assault on Sproul Plaza was a personal affront to him. Halfway to the student center, Hockney was already thinking up some graphic phrases he could use to describe the scene in the next issue of the *Berkeley Barb*. The more savage the methods employed by the Governor to smash the antiwar movement, he thought, the faster the movement would grow. Middle America would not let its kids be treated like Vietnamese peasants.

Inside the cafeteria, Tom Flack's supporters were equipping themselves with buckets of water and bunches of rags.

"Let's get out of here," Hockney said to the girl. She had by now drunk a Coke, and stopped coughing.

They started walking back to the old brown-shingled house in North Side, on a street lined with oaks and eucalyptus trees, that Hockney shared with three other students.

A second demonstration seemed to be taking place on the road that led to Dwinelle Hall, the ugly, sprawling building where Hockney's political science courses were held. Twenty or thirty students were shouting abuse at a man in a dark suit. Hockney recognized the widow's peak and taut, thin-lipped features of Milorad Yankovich.

"It's my professor," he explained to the girl. "Let's see what's going on."

Hockney had skipped Yankovich's lecture on the origins of the cold war in order to go to the demonstration. The professor, he learned now, had canceled his lecture halfway through, when all but two of his students had peeled off to see what was going on in Sproul Plaza. "We might as well join the party," Yankovich had said. Although he was a Yugoslav émigré who had only recently become a naturalized American, Yankovich prided himself on being liberated from reflex anti-Communist attitudes. He had written a book on the eventual convergence of the capitalist and Communist systems, and had prepared a speech for the President on the need to build bridges to the East through trade. He regarded himself as a liberal and bitterly resented the fact that the campus radicals made him out to be a Dr. Strangelove. He made it known in private that he

5

thought the Vietnam war was a disastrous mistake because it had divided America. But he refused to condemn the war in public on the grounds that America's credibility as a world power was at issue. To some of his students, this was a further example of his cynicism and hypocrisy. Yankovich had considered giving up teaching and devoting himself to research or a government consultancy. The trouble with American students, in his opinion, was that they thought they knew everything before they attended a single class.

Hockney had noticed that Yankovich's Serbian accent thickened when he was distressed. The professor now sounded like a stage foreigner as he tried to defend himself against a hostile group that interrupted his every remark with shouts of "CIA."

"No, I do *not* approve of the Governor's methods," Yankovich was insisting. "But neither do I approve of trying to provoke the authorities into using tear gas on campus."

"Is that the view of the CIA, Yanko?" someone challenged him.

"I don't know why you all get so excited about government contracts," the professor said. "You wouldn't be getting an education without government money."

"I don't call CIA brainwashing an education," the same heckler responded.

Hockney watched the exchange with distaste. Yankovich's accusers had a point. He believed that defense establishment contracts were corrupting the universities. And he himself had been the subject of a tentative approach by a CIA recruiter on campus. But abusing professors was not the way to change things. At times, Hockney was appalled by the bad manners of his contemporaries. As he watched, some of the more aggressive students started to jostle Yankovich.

"Hey, you guys," Hockney called out. "There's a fight with the cops going on down Telegraph Avenue." It was a perfectly plausible suggestion. The frequent follow-up to a big demonstration was a bout of trashing—setting fire to garbage cans down the main boulevard—which usually brought the police out in force. Yankovich's tormentors began to drift away.

Yankovich's relief was mixed with embarrassment; he felt he had badly lost face. Instead of thanking Hockney, he merely cleared his throat and said, "The problem is that some of your friends think they already own the world."

"It could do with a change of ownership," Hockney observed. "See you."

In the shingled house in North Side, Hockney opened a bottle of California red. The blonde, as he had guessed already, had no sexual inhibitions. As they lounged on the bed smoking after making love, Hockney played with the damp triangle of hair between her legs.

"I don't even remember what you said your name was," he reflected aloud.

"I never liked my name anyway."

Hockney didn't pursue it. "You know," he said solemnly, "we're not going to be students forever."

"I don't know about that." She stubbed out her cigarette and put her hand on his penis, feeling it harden again under her touch. "I don't think I'll ever pass my exams. What are you going to do—I mean, after you graduate?"

Hockney closed his eyes, thinking of another girl, back on the East Coast. He was instantly rigid. Then he felt lips and teeth moving gently along him. Julia had never done that.

"I want to see things and write about them," he said without opening his eyes. The statement sounded astonishingly mild. Tom Flack would call him a shitass spectator. "Tom Flack," he continued, "has got it all wrong. You don't stop the war or beat the police state by pissing on the National Guard or trashing Telegraph Avenue. You do it by *explaining* things to people—the things the government doesn't want us to know."

The girl hauled herself up the bed and straddled him.

"I'm going to be a reporter," Hockney announced, gasping slightly, but still intent on the idea he wanted to get across.

"I'm going to be . . . ah . . . the greatest reporter in America," he emphasized.

"Mmmm." The girl's groan had nothing to do with Hockney's declaration of intent.

Two weeks after graduation, Admiral Tennant Hockney was watching the television news in his study and affecting total disinterest in the imminent homecoming of his only son. His wife, Patricia, leaned over his studded leather armchair, a martini in her hand, repeating the same questions she had been asking for the last two weeks. The Admiral did not allow them to divert his attention from the football scores for one second.

"Why didn't Bob let us go to his graduation?"

The Admiral grunted.

"He didn't even *call* me after graduation. Is it those antiwar radicals? Is that what's disturbing him?"

"Mmmph."

After almost thirty years of marriage, Admiral Hockney knew that conversation with his wife did not have to be a dialogue. All she needed was an echo chamber. In any case, he had no satisfactory answers to her questions. He was fully aware of the rift that had opened between them and their son, but he was also fully convinced that it was not his doing. He had not tried to stop Bob from going to Berkeley instead of an East Coast college. Their discussions about Vietnam had never become quarrels. When Bob raised the subject, the Admiral had quietly declined to debate the morality of his own job in naval intelligence at the Pentagon. Admiral Hockney was resigned to the fact that his generation had lost control of the next and that his son was a prisoner of the prevailing political mood among the young. Still, it galled him to imagine Bob parading with the draft card burners; that was not in the Hockney style.

Outside on the porch, Julia Cummings stood framed in the doorway of the wide house on Rockwood Parkway that the Hockney family had occupied since the Admiral had been recalled from the naval mission in Paris. She watched the sun turn the color of blood oranges as it sank behind the trees. The wind had picked up again at the end of the long summer day. It toyed with the hem of Julia's pale turquoise dress, lifting it, making her feel naked under the light fabric. She folded her arms over the gentle swell of her breasts and tossed her head so that her long auburn hair floated free.

At nineteen, Julia had the clear, translucent skin of a child. The last rays picked out the flecks of gold in her forest green eyes, set deep in the delicate oval face. Her slightly parted lips gave her the look of expectancy, and seemed to anticipate the smile she was saving for Robert Hockney.

"He'll come," said a voice behind her. It was Julia's brother, Perry.

"Will you talk to Bob?" she said.

"Sure I'll talk to him." Cummings was conscious that, in many ways, he had been as much of a big brother to Bob Hockney as to his kid sister. Cummings and Hockney had grown up side by side, the offspring of Washington officialdom—his father in the State Department, Hockney's in Defense. There had been only a few intermissions before Bob had gone away to the West Coast. The difference was that Perry Cummings, three years older, had never worn his hair long or demonstrated against the war, and was already a wage-earning adult with a science degree working (probably to Bob's disgust) in the Pentagon, two floors up from the Admiral.

Cummings looked the part of a government clerk who was still waiting for an office with a window; his prematurely bald pate had the gray pallor of a man twice his age. His steel-rimmed glasses gave him an air of intolerance.

The places had been set for dinner before Hockney's dented red convertible clanked to a halt in the drive. Hockney jumped out, tall—almost as tall as the Admiral, who stood six foot four in his bare feet—and bronzed from the California sun.

Julia ran down to greet him. "You still taste of salt," she murmured when she had drawn breath after a tender, lingering kiss.

"And you smell of jasmine," Hockney said, letting his head rest for a moment against her perfumed neck.

She seemed so fragile, Hockney thought, compared with

9

the girls he had known at Berkeley, to whom jumping in and out of bed was as natural as jumping in and out of the pool. He put his arm carefully around her waist to lead her into the house.

The family meal started ominously, with a trivial accident that was nonetheless unprecedented at the Admiral's well-ordered table. Admiral Hockney's orderly, conscripted for the evening, spilled soup over Julia's immaculate dress. Then Patricia Hockney, weepy over the return of the prodigal, spilled her wine. The Admiral, tolerant of many things, could not stand unruliness at the dinner table. As the orderly sprayed soda water over Julia and the tablecloth, the scowl on his father's face reminded Hockney of the times he had been sent to his room hungry as a boy for speaking out of turn.

Perry Cummings broke the silence. "Tell us, Bob," he said. "Have you changed your mind about becoming a reporter?"

"On the contrary," Hockney replied. "I've already started. As a matter of fact, my first big piece is coming out next month."

"I can't wait to see it," said Mrs. Hockney. "Where's it going to appear?"

"I doubt whether you've seen the magazine." Hockney inspected the pool of gravy surrounding the roast beef on his plate. "It's called *Barricades*."

"That's a funny name for a magazine." The Admiral joined the conversation. "What kind of publication is it?"

Perry Cummings came to Hockney's rescue. "It's what I believe is called a—uh—committed magazine," he said. "It sells mostly on the West Coast."

"It's a big step up from the *Berkeley Barb*." Hockney was deliberately prodding his father. He knew, from an oblique reference in a curt letter, that the Admiral had seen the piece in the *Barb* in which he described the National Guard as "storm troopers."

The Admiral ignored the allusion to the Berkeley student paper. "What's your article about?" he challenged his son.

"It's on the CIA."

"Well, *that's* an interesting departure for you," the Ad-

10

miral commented. "Did you find anything good to say about the Agency?"

"Not much," said Hockney. "*Barricades* isn't very keen on the CIA. I got the idea for my piece when an Agency recruiter approached me at Berkeley. It's mainly about how the CIA recruits kids on campus and tries to influence the world student movement."

"Were you able to gather much material?"

"Oh yes," Hockney said vaguely. "It's amazing how easily people talk, especially disillusioned ex-employees. That's part of the effect of the war."

The Admiral nodded. "That's very true," he agreed. "Vietnam has created a disciplinary problem right across the waterfront." Unlike some of his colleagues at the Pentagon, Admiral Hockney was subtle enough to grasp that once the consensus broke down in an open society like the United States, you couldn't rebuild it simply by insisting on rules that were no longer respected. But his alarm about the subject his son was exploring registered in his next remark. "I would assume," he said, "that you are naming CIA personnel and undercover agents in this *Barricades* piece."

"It wouldn't make a story otherwise."

"I think that's very dangerous, Bob." The Admiral spoke in a low voice, so that Perry Cummings, sitting at the other end of the table, had to lean forward to hear. "I hope you realize that you could be ruining a number of people's careers. You could even be making them candidates for assassination."

Hockney shrugged. "If those guys weren't prepared to take risks, they would have picked different jobs. I think we understand each other, Dad. You will defend the CIA's covert operations because you're basically in the same business. I think what the Agency is doing is wrong. I think it's part of the same system that is sending my friends to get killed in Vietnam."

Hockney's anger was partly founded in guilt. He knew that a high school football injury that had badly damaged his left knee would automatically exempt him from the draft.

The Admiral raised his hands, palms outward. Hockney knew his father well enough to understand that this was the reverse of a gesture of submission. "I won't argue with you about Vietnam tonight," his father said. "But if you're going to be a good reporter, you'll have to learn to make some distinctions. Some of my friends in the Agency are just as opposed to the Vietnam war as you are. In fact, if you ask around at the Pentagon, you'll find that many of the people there regard the CIA as a nest of liberals. I think Perry will bear this out."

Perry Cummings nodded.

"But that isn't the point either," the Admiral pursued. "We are all entitled to disagree over American policy. The point is whether we want to defend our right to disagree against outside forces that tolerate no internal dissent and wish to impose their system on others."

"I guess you're talking about the world Communist movement," Hockney interrupted, his voice edged with sarcasm.

"Your phrase, not mine," the Admiral parried. "I accept that world communism is not monolithic. But if *you* can accept—as I hope you still do—that there is an absolute distinction between a form of society like ours, where anyone is free to criticize the government, and a form of society like communism, where the government dictates everything, then can't you also accept that we have a duty to defend ourselves? Defense includes intelligence. In fact, intelligence is our front-line defense."

"You make better speeches than the President, Dad. But if you stretch your logic far enough, you'll end up justifying everything the CIA does on the grounds that the Russians or the Chinese or the North Vietnamese are doing the same. If you think American society is so wonderful, then you have a duty to ensure that it acts according to its stated values. That does *not* mean corrupting the student movement—or the media. It doesn't mean bumping off third-world leaders. And it certainly doesn't mean committing the crimes we're committing in Vietnam."

The orderly nudged the younger Hockney's elbow. "Are

you finished, sir?" Hockney waved away his barely touched plate.

Mrs. Hockney seized the chance to maneuver the conversation onto a less political plane. "I've made apple crumble, Bob," she said, "just the way you like it."

The Admiral did not return to the attack. Hockney was conscious that his father's eyes were on him throughout the rest of the meal, but he did not return his gaze. His father's reasonableness made him uneasy. The Admiral did not fit the stereotyped image that most of his friends at Berkeley had of the Pentagon brass. It was easier to argue with a stereotype.

After dinner, Hockney excused himself and wandered out, through the living room, to the porch. Julia followed him.

Outside, in the cooling air, she took his arm. The moon was almost full. Hockney looked neither at Julia nor at the moon, only into the blackness of the clump of trees across Rockwood Parkway.

"Kiss me," she invited. He was rougher, more cursory, than when he had arrived. "Do you want me?" she murmured, needing the security of his arms but surprised, even so, at her own forwardness. Julia had been a virgin until the summer before, when she had given herself to Bob Hockney one long, lazy afternoon in the sand dunes near the house her father kept at Southampton on Long Island. She had just completed her first year at Sarah Lawrence College, outside New York City; he had one year left to go at Berkeley. Until that afternoon, knowing each other from childhood, they had been like brother and sister—the more so since Hockney was an only child. Since that summer, Julia had waited for him. But she already sensed that this summer would not be like the last. He was saying, "Of course I want you," but his eyes were far away.

That did not prevent them from walking, arms entwined, around to the back of the house and making hasty love in the bushes. Her turquoise dress left trailing from a branch, Julia arched her back against the moist earth. Hockney's mind drifted back to the sun-bleached, full-bodied girl he'd slept with after the Governor bombed Sproul Plaza. When he had been with her, he had thought of Julia. Why did he always want to be somewhere else?

After, feeling guilty, he leaped up. He did not even kiss Julia. She had not yet finished buttoning her dress when he said, "There's something I have to tell you."

"I know," she acknowledged, eyeing the slight, rounded depression in the ground where she had lain.

Hockney eyed her quizzically. "I'm going away." He pulled at a twig until it snapped. "The magazine is sending me to Europe. To Paris."

"That's wonderful," she said, braving it out because it was what he wanted.

"It means we won't see each other for a while. Maybe months. When I come home, you'll be back at college anyway."

"It doesn't matter, if this is what you want."

Hockney broke another twig, frustrated by her calm acceptance. He had expected her to complain or burst into tears. Instead, he was the one who got angry. "Up there at Sarah Lawrence," he accused her, "you're out of the real world. You live among manicured lawns, ivy-covered halls, and fashionable radicalism. Well, what I learned on the West Coast is that this country is being turned upside down. At the end of the day, you can only be one of two things: the guy who does the turning or the guy who gets turned over." He had started attacking a sapling, and looked ready to break it in half.

Julia took his arm, restraining him. "You don't have to lecture me," she said gently. "Are you looking for an excuse to say good-by? Don't, Bob. I won't hold you. If you want me again, I'll still be around. Maybe."

Hockney felt smothered by sweet reason. His father's calm voice, now Julia's. It wasn't real. Beyond Rockwood Parkway there was a real war, and he was part of it.

The sapling split with a noise like an air rifle. Hockney twisted the upper part round and round until it tore free.

The next day was Saturday, and Hockney met Julia's brother Perry for a drink at Nathan's in Georgetown to talk things over. He found Perry Cummings already propped up at the bar, sipping from a tall orange drink.

"Tequila sunrise," Cummings explained. "Try one."

"I'll stick to beer. Michelob."

The trouble with Julia, Hockney remarked to her brother, was that she was as good—and predictable—as a painted saint. She didn't fight, she didn't make any demands. She just seemed to be waiting for him to get over whatever mood he was in so they could start thinking about the trousseau and the baby's room for when she graduated from Sarah Lawrence. And she seemed to accept his political views in the same way that she might have accepted him going to watch a baseball game every Saturday afternoon.

"Yep," Cummings acknowledged, looking at a leggy blonde who had just strolled into the bar in a brief tennis dress. "Girls like Julia are too good for rats like us."

"How's life at the Pentagon?"

Perry Cummings, Hockney knew, was now a junior analyst in the weapons evaluation division at the Defense Department, reporting on new techniques of mass murder.

"You know me," Cummings said with exaggerated modesty. "I always was a technology buff. Remember all those model planes I used to stick together when I was a kid? What I'm doing now isn't really all that different, except that you need a science degree and some pretty impressive security clearances."

"May I ask you something?"

"Sure."

"Doesn't it ever worry you, working at the Pentagon while we're bombing villages in Vietnam? I mean, don't you ever wake up at night sweating over the end-uses of the weaponry that you're helping to choose for Uncle Sam?"

There was a blast of hot air as a voluptuous brunette in butterfly sunglasses and a tight-fitting blouse pushed through the swinging doors into the air-conditioned saloon. Cummings stared at her in frank admiration. "This is a subtropical city," he observed to Hockney, his attention still focused on the girl. "It doesn't pay to get overexcited

15

about anything in this town in summer. Did you know that when British diplomats were assigned to Washington in the nineteenth century, they were advised to take tropical clothes?"

"No, I didn't know that." It was maddeningly hard to start an argument with a member of the Cummings family, Hockney told himself.

"As for the war," Perry Cummings went on, "it's a big mistake to imagine that the only way—or even the most effective way—to change the system is from the outside."

Cummings interrupted himself to signal the barman, leaving Hockney vaguely surprised by his elliptical remarks, which did not seem to square with the ultraconservative image his friend had cultivated since joining the Pentagon.

Cummings ordered straight tequila.

"This stuff is made from the same plant as the drug mescaline," he said to Hockney, tapping salt from a shaker onto his knuckle to take with the drink. "If you consume enough of it, you'll start to hallucinate." Cummings drained the glass in two gulps.

"Did I tell you I've got a new girlfriend?" he asked Hockney as they headed for the door. "She's terrific. She's twenty-eight, but I've always had this thing about older women. I'll introduce you sometime. She's someone you really ought to get to know. Politically, she's on your wavelength more than mine."

"Does she have a name?"

"Alexia Merchant. As in Merchant lingerie."

"I smell money." The Merchant Corporation was one of the country's leading manufacturers of women's underwear.

"It gives you that extra lift." Cummings mimicked a television commerical for the latest Merchant creation that featured a wild-looking young starlet with the unlikely name of Tessa Torrance wearing little more than her bra. The twenty-second commercial had uplifted Tessa, previously unknown, into a national sex symbol.

"Alexia's grandfather does more than hire sexpots to inflame jaded appetites," Cummings added, as they walked down M Street under a vertical sun. "Though mind you, I regard Tessa Torrance as a national institution." He stopped to peer into the window of the tobacco store, which featured a special offer on Honduran cigars, as fat and long as sticks of dynamite. "Old Vlad Merchant is the sugar daddy behind the Foundation for Progressive Reform. Alexia spends most of her working time at the Foundation."

The Foundation's widening campaigns were a popular issue at Berkeley. There was a long article about the Foundation in the current issue of *Barricades*, which described it as "the umbilical cord between the New Left and the liberal establishment." Perry and Alexia had to make an odd couple. The Foundation for Progressive Reform was a long way removed from Cummings' chosen habitat. Hockney wondered what Alexia's attraction was. Probably the Merchant family money. Or else she was a fantastic lay.

"Excuse me." Cummings opened the door of the cigar store. "I've got to work on my establishment image."

Hockney strolled on down M Street, shunning the narrow ribbon of shade beside the buildings. It struck him that Perry Cummings, who had appeared to him of late to be as predictably on the right in both his personal style and political stances as the sloganeers at Berkeley were on the left, was more complex than he allowed himself to seem.

Paris
Summer 1967

1

ASTRID RENARD pulled the sheet up to her waist, and reached for the pack of Gauloises on the bedside table.

"Michel?" she called to her husband, who had gone to the bathroom.

"What?" he shouted back.

"Let's go to the Bois."

Without answering, Michel Renard turned on the shower full blast. He stood close to the nozzle, letting the jet of water strip the sweat away from his face and chest. He turned off the hot tap and let the water pound at his back until he jumped at the cold.

As he toweled himself in front of the bathroom mirror, Renard reflected that the cold shower had not done its usual trick. He still felt limp, drained of sex and energy. Making love to Astrid was wearing him down. She was insatiable. Indifferent to his moods, regardless of the time of day or night, she clutched at him, seeking the release of the sexual act. However many times she made love, with however many partners, her compulsion was all-consuming and solitary. Sex was not something she shared. It was something she took. At the end, he felt used. Exactly, he thought, as many women must feel used by men. The Bois. So now he would be expected to perform under even more trying circumstances.

Renard stared at himself without pleasure in the bathroom mirror. Though his life belied it, he was the very image of the *bon bourgeois*. At thirty-five, with his round face, thinning brownish hair, and waistline running to fat, he did not look like an orgy goer. He looked more like the kind of man who enjoyed curling up in front of the television movie on Friday night after a couple of glasses of pastis at the corner bistro. After his battles all day at the office and his grueling workout with Astrid, there was no way he would rather have spent the rest of the evening. He had come close to walking out of his job at AMI—the Agence Mondiale d'Informations—after a shouting match with his boss, Bonpierre, over a piece of copy that Renard suspected to be a CIA plant. He had reined in his temper just in time. There was nothing Bonpierre would have liked better than for him to resign. He had hesitated to tell Astrid about the episode. She would only use it as a pretext to complain about how little money he earned.

Making sure that Astrid could not see him through the open door to the bedroom, he popped a benzedrine into his mouth. He rested his back against the washbasin, waiting for the pill to click. The effect was probably psychological. Within a few minutes, he felt his adrenaline pumping. He dabbed some aftershave under his chin and armpits and between his thighs. He chuckled to himself, remembering the friend who had observed that the definition of an optimist was a man who put aftershave between his thighs before going out for the evening. His depression had lifted a little. He sucked in his stomach and went into the bedroom to get the clothes for his other life, the life that began on Friday night.

Astrid greeted him with a theatrical moan from the bed. He ignored her. She pouted and pulled the sheet back and forth suggestively over her ample breasts as Renard struggled into a pair of tight-fitting flared jeans. He had trouble zipping them up. His burgundy-colored, tapered silk shirt was also too tight around the middle. He left the top few buttons undone to show off an Egyptian love cross on his hairy chest, wondering whether he looked faintly ridiculous.

With an elaborate sigh, Astrid slid out of bed and fumbled in the closet for her Friday night uniform. She started with her black garter belt and yellow lace panties. Emptied of desire, Renard studied his wife as a photographer might have done. Now thirty-one, she was as stunning as the day he had met her at a United Nations reception in honor of her father, the Danish chief of a scientific mission. Long blonde hair cascaded over her shoulders. Her full breasts were barely contained by the see-through bra she was straining to fasten. Her Friday nights had left only one trace. She had developed tiny pouches under her gray-green Nordic eyes. They gave her a predatory, animal look that made him uneasy.

"Don't you want a shower before we do out, *chérie?*"

Astrid shrugged. "It's a matter of taste," she said. "There are lots of men who prefer their women to smell like women instead of walking drugstores."

All the same, she splashed the new Dior perfume he had given her for her birthday over herself as if it were water.

Renard sat on the edge of the bed while Astrid pulled on a suede skirt and a tight yellow sweater.

"I had an awful day at the office," he said tentatively.

"What's happening in the world?" Her tone was bored.

"The big story of the day was the colonels' coup in Athens. But Bonpierre kept messing up my copy. He talks as if the colonels are authentic Greek nationalists who are trying to stem the Red Tide. On top of that, he insisted on putting out an item that anyone with a sense of smell would have recognized as a CIA plant. That's when I really lost my temper. I told him it would save us time if we hooked up directly to the American embassy telex."

Astrid sighed ostentatiously. She had heard the same complaints night after night. When Renard got over-emotional, she would usually remind him that there were plenty of jobs waiting in advertising or public relations. At least they would pay better than the news agency, and would leave him lots of spare time. He could use that to unburden himself of his political conscience in party work. But Renard was stubborn. Working for the news agency was to him more a vocation—even if it was constantly frustrated by Bonpierre—than a job. He was political through and through. He usually voted Communist, on the grounds that De Gaulle had become a reactionary and the other parties had sold out to the American embassy under the Fourth Republic. But he refused to narrow himself down to any formal party allegiance. He did not think of himself as a Communist, but as a man of the left whose aversion to the right and, above all, the Anglo-Saxons was characteristic of countless Frenchmen of his generation and class.

Renard's father, a railway worker under the Vichy government, had joined a Resistance network and spent his nights blowing up the lines he repaired during the day. It wasn't the Gestapo that got Renard's father in the end. It was an unexpected American bombing raid on the marshaling yards where he worked. Since then, Renard's emotions about the Fascists and the Americans had been hopelessly muddled.

He didn't like the British any better than the Americans. He had not even reached puberty when Churchill gave the order to the Royal Navy to destroy the French fleet at Mers-el-Kebir (for fear that the Vichy regime might put it at the disposal of the Nazis), but he traced a whole series of national humiliations from that event.

By contrast, Renard saw no challenge to France from the Soviet Union. Soviet power was a guarantee against any new mood of revanchism in Germany, France's historical enemy. It could also help to set limits on Anglo-Saxon aggrandizement. Stalin had frightened people, but Stalin, in Renard's view, was an aberration. Renard agreed with General de Gaulle on one thing: it was in France's interest to seek a special relationship with Russia, instead of relying exclusively on alliances dominated by the Anglo-Saxons. This view of the world set him poles apart from his boss, who subscribed to the idea that the United States was the irreplaceable sword and shield of Europe and was fighting the good fight against Communist aggression, even in the paddy fields of Indochina.

Bonpierre had even said to him that afternoon, before he had slammed the door, that if he was so distressed about AMI's editorial line, Renard should feel free to move on. Renard did not intend to give his editor that pleasure. He jabbed a Gauloise toward his mouth. It touched the outer edge of his lower lip and adhered to it.

"I'm shattered," he said as Astrid went on brushing her hair. "Why don't we forget the scene in the Bois tonight and just go out for a quiet dinner by ourselves? We could go to Sous l'Olivier. It must be months since we've done that."

Astrid was not sympathetic. "If you don't feel up to much tonight, *mon chéri*, you don't have to do anything. You told me once that just watching me turns you on. Who knows? You may even get in the mood."

She grabbed her handbag, and Renard followed her meekly out of the apartment. As they climbed into their battered green Peugeot, Astrid caught her skirt in the door. She opened it again and slammed it viciously. As she did, the door handle came off in her hand.

"When are we going to get rid of this *vieux clou*?" she complained, crossing her legs like long tailoring scissors. "Are you going to go on driving this wreck until it falls apart?"

Renard pulled out the choke and turned on the ignition. The engine spluttered and died.

"If you didn't spend so much money on clothes and on tarting yourself up," he accused his wife, "we might be able to afford a new car."

"You said you were getting a big raise. Isn't that what they promised you when we were transferred back from Hong Kong?"

"No. They promised a big title—deputy editor-in-chief— but they didn't say when I was going to get the raise. You know the news business. Big on titles, long on promises, *mais tintin pour le fric*. But who knows anyway, after today?" He stared gloomily at his hand gripping the ignition key.

The engine finally came to life.

"You bitch about not having a better car," he went on. "You don't know what I have to put up with every day. Bonpierre won't let me do my job. He tells me I need his permission even before I take a third-world minister out for a cheap lunch. How am I supposed to do my job without expenses? That bastard's had it in for me all along. And now the outright suggestion I should quit."

"Well, why don't you try to get along with him?"

"Try to get along with him?" Renard mimicked his wife, angry now. "The only way I could do that is to lie down

24

and let him trample over me. Bonpierre doesn't want to run AMI like a French news agency. He wants to run it like an American news agency. He's anti-Gaullist and anti-socialist. In fact, it wouldn't surprise me if he were working for the Americans."

Astrid yawned.

"It may be a terrible bore to you," Renard flared up, "but I have to live with this every working day. Maybe we could get rid of the problem of Bonpierre by you fucking him."

The sardonic irony of his remark was not lost on Astrid. "Why not?" she remarked casually.

They had driven out of the Marais—a former slum that had yet to become fashionable—and were driving down the colonnaded Rue de Rivoli. They swung up the Champs Elysées, clogged with middle-class couples on their way to dinner or the cinema, and then down the Avenue de la Grande Armée to the Porte Dauphine, which Renard circled before entering the fetid shadows of the Bois. By day, the Bois de Boulogne is a place for picnickers, nannies, and young mothers pushing babies along in their prams, lovers strolling hand in hand, twittering birds, and brilliantly colored ice cream carts. By night, some corners of the Bois begin to resemble the lower circles of Dante's Inferno.

"Let's go down the Allée de Longchamps," Astrid urged. *"Les travestis m'amusent tellement."*

"I suppose they are the best-looking things in the Bois," Renard wearily agreed.

They joined the long queue of cars crawling along the curb. The hybrid whores darted back and forth between the drivers, whispering their prices. A breathtaking apparition with flaming red hair, thigh-high black boots, and huge breasts spilling out of her open blouse came prancing up to Renard's car and tapped on the hood. Renard put his foot on the brake. The whore stuck her head through the window on Astrid's side.

"Trente francs la pipe, cinquante balles l'amour," she proposed in a disconcertingly husky voice. Her eyes rolled like loose billiard balls. She was high on something—probably speed on top of hormone injections.

25

"Non, merci. Pas ce soir." Renard was trying to get the engine to start.

"Voyeur," the male-female on the sidewalk shouted derisively. She hitched up her miniskirt and waved a very lifelike penis at Astrid.

"Seen enough?" Renard inquired as he shifted the car into first gear.

He accelerated fast and headed straight for the Porte Dauphine.

There is a code shared by the people who go to the Porte Dauphine on Friday night, the people who are willing to participate in an orgy with total strangers. These people look for a single car circling the great roundabout at the entrance to the Bois, flashing its headlights in a regular pattern: two shorts, one long. The signal means that the couple inside have an apartment that is large enough to accommodate up to ten or twelve couples, and are ready to play host to a *partouze*—an orgy. When the signal is spotted, other couples waiting in their own cars follow the lead vehicle round and round the Porte Dauphine, flashing their headlights in the same pattern. The silent cavalcade, almost funereal, continues until ten or a dozen cars join the convoy. It is up to the last driver in the procession to flick his red parking lights on and off to show that the party has a full house. The first couple then lead the way to the scene of the night's entertainment.

What compels these vagrants of the Porte Dauphine to give their bodies so casually? It was a question that Inspector Jaworski of the Brigade Mondaine—The Parisian vice squad—had often put to himself. Jaworski, who looked like every French detective who had ever appeared in foreign movies, was known as "Mouflon," or "Wild Sheep," by his friends in the security service—the Direction de Surveillance de la Territoire, or DST, for which he also worked. The DST had a penchant for giving its agents animal nicknames. Jaworski found his own to be singularly apposite as he roamed the wild country of the Bois. He felt a certain empathy with the outcasts of the night.

At the headquarters of the Brigade Mondaine, there is a

map that shows the Bois sectioned off like a military camp, with an area reserved for every vice. There was the Route de l'Etoile, much favored by those who had spent time in the colonies, for the lovers of black girls. There was the wondrously named Allée de la Longue Queue for the homosexuals. The entire Bois, of course, was a hunting ground for the voyeurs. This is what had enabled Mouflon to achieve his greatest coup for the DST, and an impressive increase in the size of the envelope, stuffed with banknotes, that he received each month. One summer evening he had stumbled across a junior secretary from the soviet embassy who had buried himself in the bushes in order to spy on the hurried couplings of others. The Russian voyeur was an officer of the KGB on his way to a secret meeting with one of his agents. The standard procedure for the KGB, as for other intelligence services, is for an officer en route to a clandestine "meet" to spend three or four hours circling around in order to lose anyone who may be following him. The Russian had decided to spend these few hours observing the sexual antics of the Bois. After Mouflon spotted him, the man was tracked to his meeting, and an important network of Soviet agents was exposed.

Among all the perversions of the Bois, none excited Mouflon's imagination as much as the random groupings that assembled at the Porte Dauphine on Friday night. The people came from every kind of social background, driven by—what was it? The thrill of the unexpected? A loneliness that could be exorcised only by the flesh? A fantasy of rape? The need to annihilate personal identity and emotions?

Mouflon was not a psychologist. He did not know the answers, but he found it amusing to speculate. He had a great deal of time to do so. Many of his most productive hours were spent at the Porte Dauphine, sitting in an unmarked radio car, jotting down the numbers of license plates. The numbers sometimes led to some remarkable discoveries. And the DST, like all security services, had an endless appetite for intimate details of the private lives of France's leading citizens—the sexier, the better.

That Friday night, Mouflon ignored the first car that

circled the Porte Dauphine, a Fiat 124 with a middle-aged, middle-class couple inside who looked as if they might be going to a concert. Mouflon pulled out his notebook, however, when a Bentley swung in behind them. The driver looked North African. The girl might have been a whore he had picked up in the Bois. The Renault pickup truck that joined the procession behind them was of no interest to Mouflon. He reflected that sex is the supreme leveler. All classes become horizontal.

The battered green Peugeot that came next attracted his curiosity, not least because the blonde in the front seat looked far more bedworthy than the average visitor to the Porte Dauphine. As the Peugeot circled the roundabout for the third time, Mouflon caught a glimpse of the driver. His face seemed vaguely familiar.

Mouflon radio-telephoned to headquarters to request a check on the Peugeot's license number. The answer came within minutes. License holder: Renard, Michel. Occupation: Journalist. Address: 6 bis Rue Elzevire.

Journalists lead colorful lives, Mouflon thought to himself.

2

THE OFFICE of the ISKRA bureau chief in Paris was cramped and old-fashioned. This did not bother Viktor Barisov too much. He had not spent much time there since he had taken on the job the year before. By Western standards, Barisov was a singularly unproductive reporter. His by-line had appeared on fewer than a dozen stories since his arrival in Paris. But he was most unlikely to receive a reprimand from his employers at ISKRA on that count. His ISKRA job was merely a cover. Viktor Barisov, in his mid-thirties, was a career officer of the Committee of State Security, better known as the KGB.

Barisov did happen to be paying a fleeting visit to the ISKRA office that Saturday morning when a tip was relayed from a long-standing contact in the French police that the DST had picked up something on a journalist called Michel Renard. It seemed that Renard and his wife were indulging in some adventurous sexual exploits. There was nothing unusual about that, least of all in Paris. But Barisov subscribed to the view that every lead was worth pursuing.

Barisov leafed through a directory of the Paris press corps. Renard's name definitely rang a bell. Barisov was sure that he was a top man at either Agence France Presse or the Agence Mondiale d'Informations. The directory was probably out of date. It listed Michel Renard as the Hong Kong bureau chief for AMI. Barisov picked up the phone and called AMI to ask whether Renard was still working there. "Yes," said the girl at the news desk, "he's one of our deputy editors-in-chief."

Barisov's hand lingered on the receiver after he hung up. His huntsman's instinct was aroused. He had been instructed by Moscow Center that the Agence Mondiale d'Informations was a top-priority target. Its chief editor, Jacques Bonpierre, was one of the most influential critics of De Gaulle's foreign policy in the French media, and the AMI's news coverage of the Vietnam war was more sympathetic to America's intervention than that of the French press in general. It had not taken Barisov long to discover that Bonpierre not only had an American wife but was lunching two or three times a month with the CIA station chief in Paris.

As far as Barisov knew, Bonpierre had no vices, except political ones. Bonpierre's deputy appeared to be different. Barisov consulted the press directory again. It seemed there were four men at AMI who held the imposing title of deputy editor-in-chief. What the title meant was that they took turns working an eight-hour shift. During that period, the man who was holding the fort exercised almost complete control over AMI's news operation. That meant that Michel Renard was a powerful man.

As deputy editor, Renard could create, or fabricate, the news. He could rewrite agency dispatches as they flowed

29

through the central Paris relay point. If he disapproved of a story, he could put it on the spike—in other words, kill it—subject, of course, to the authority of his boss, Bonpierre.

Barisov concluded that Renard was a man worth getting to know. How could he establish contact? It would be easy enough for Barisov, a member of the foreign press corps, to find an occasion for an innocuous first meeting with a French newsman. Beyond that, the sexual predilections of Renard and his wife offered some interesting possibilities.

Barisov was tempted to pursue them on his own initiative, although, according to the rules, he was supposed to consult his immediate boss, the KGB resident in Paris, before trying to recruit an agent. For once, he resolved to do things according to the book. He had had a violent argument with the resident, Major General Mikhail Petrovich Pronk, only the week before, over his harmless gallantry toward the wife of a Western attaché at a diplomatic reception. It might help to clear the air if he respectfully consulted Pronk on his new discovery.

The contrast between Barisov and his chief was in part the product of differences in age and breeding. Pronk belonged to the old school. He had begun his career in Soviet intelligence under the dreaded Lavrenti Beria, Stalin's secret police chief. Although Pronk had been persuaded, like his subordinates, to frequent an expensive Parisian tailor, his heart was back in Dzherzhinsky Square. He had virtually no social life outside the Soviet community, although he was supposedly a minister-counselor at the embassy. When he had a free evening, he would spend it drinking vodka and playing cards with one or two trusted cronies. He devoted an excessive amount of time to spying on his colleagues in the embassy, especially the local chief of the military intelligence service, or GRU, whom Pronk regarded as a deadly rival and who, like Barisov, had a penchant for pretty women and flashy cars. There were some KGB officers of Barisov's age who maintained that behind his stolid, bearlike exterior, Pronk was a brilliant professional who had helped to engineer the rift between De

Gaulle and the Americans. Barisov did not share this opinion.

Viktor Barisov, as his boss had balefully observed during one of their quarrels, could almost have passed for an American. He favored charcoal gray suits that might have come from Brooks Brothers. He was athletically, not heavily built, with a square jaw, straight, silver-flecked hair that flopped over his broad forehead, and ice blue eyes that turned sea green according to the light and his changing moods.

There was a shadow over his past. He had been born into the Soviet Union's new elite, the son of one of the old-guard Bolsheviks who had served as a Red Army commissar in the old-guard Bolsheviks who had served as a Red Army commissar in the civil war and had later held a succession of important party posts. But that had changed just after Viktor Barisov's eleventh birthday. His father had survived the manic purges organized by Yezhov, the morbid, fanatical dwarf who served as Stalin's secret police chief in the mid-1930s. But Barisov's father had fallen victim to Yezhov's still more notorious successor, Beria. When Beria had been summoned from Georgia to Moscow to take over the grim apparatus of the secret police, he had started hunting for a suitable residence. Unfortunately for the Barisov family, Beria's eye had lighted upon the luxurious villa that they occupied on the outskirts of the city. In order to take over the villa himself, Beria had to eliminate Barisov senior. It was not hard to find a pretext, since Stalin was neurotically suspicious of old Bolsheviks who knew that he had not played the heroic role in revolutionary history that was attributed to him in the official hagiography. Too respected to have been shot, Barisov's father was arrested and deported to a slave labor camp in Siberia. His family never saw him again. All that Viktor Barisov had been able to glean about his father's fate in later years was that his weak chest had made him an easy prey for the Siberian winter, and that he had died of pneumonia during the war.

Barisov's mother had slaved to support her children in a provincial town. Destalinization had slightly improved the family fortunes—although the villa outside Moscow was never restored to them—and had cleared the way for Viktor, as a gifted student and Komsomol organizer, to enter a promising official career. The KGB, he believed, was a very different organization from Beria's secret police. Yet he was conscious of the underlying continuity when he ran up against survivors of the Stalinist era like Pronk. He tended to identify Pronk with the order that had ruined his father's life. Pronk, in turn, had not been above mentioning what he called Barisov's "dubious family background" in some of their more heated discussions.

The support of Olga, his wife, had helped Barisov hold his ground in his conflicts with Pronk. Otherwise, his refusal to engage in the toadying that was standard practice for many of the younger KGB officers who were responsible to the KGB resident in Paris might have spelled an early end to Barisov's career. Olga's father was one of the deputy directors of the KGB's First Chief Directorate, entrusted with foreign intelligence operations. Barisov recognized that it was his father-in-law's influence, more than his own record, that had accounted for his rapid rise to a plum job in Paris in his mid-thirties. Still, he congratulated himself on the fact that he had established his mastery over an area that had become crucially important to the KGB's worldwide operations, so important that a special division, Directorate A, had been set up within Moscow Center to control it. That area was disinformation: the systematic effort to deceive Western governments and public opinion.

Whatever Pronk's view of his scheme for Michel Renard, Barisov knew the masters of Directorate A would approve.

Barisov placed a slim green file on Pronk's desk. He had taken the precaution of extracting Renard's dossier from the files the KGB maintained on the Paris press corps at the embassy. It was short, but revealing. They went out to Pronk's terrace to discuss the case. The noise of the traffic below would obscure their conversation from anyone trying to monitor it.

Barisov gave his chief a verbal summary. Michel Renard

was deputy editor of AMI. He had held foreign posts in Saigon and Hong Kong. His political sympathies were broadly leftist. He earned the equivalent of $800 a month. He was married to a Danish woman, Astrid, nee Andersen, whose father was employed by the World Intellectual Property Organization, one of the UN agencies in Geneva.

"This Danish girl is quite voracious," Barisov commented. "She was photographed nude for a girlie magazine at the age of seventeen. Her family was furious. She met Renard at a UN reception. He eventually got her pregnant, so they got married. But she had a miscarriage and is now unable to have children. Perhaps that is why she consoles herself by going to orgies with strangers."

Pronk refilled their glasses. "Where does all this lead us, Viktor Mikhailovich?"

"I can see a chance of influencing a major Western news agency. It's not without relevance that Renard's chief also happens to be one of our most hostile critics in the French media."

"You mean Bonpierre."

Barisov nodded.

"What do you want to do?"

"There are several lines of attack," Barisov explained. "We have sex. We also know that Renard can't live on his salary, given his wife's expensive tastes. We have an ideological meeting point. Renard fears and detests the Anglo-Saxons. Above all, he hates Bonpierre. In short, Comrade General, he's an easy mark."

Pronk swiveled in his chair to look out over the Paris skyline. He was not prepared to betray any enthusiasm for an idea emanating from Barisov, who in Pronk's view was cocky enough without encouragement.

"Can Renard be blackmailed?" Pronk asked, after a pause.

"Not through sex. The Renard couple have no hang-ups about that."

"So what are you suggesting?"

"We could use sex as a point of contact. We could take the Renards to a party under our control. We could intro-

33

duce them to more interesting people than they are picking up in the Bois de Boulogne. We could use Tania or Yuri to help make the approach."

Yuri, supposedly employed by the Soviet shipping company Transmar at its Paris office, was a trained lady-killer who had already turned the heads of more than one middle-aged secretary working for the French government. Tania was described as his wife, although there was no record of their marriage in the Soviet registries. Petite, slender, with high cheekbones, Tania could have passed for a ballerina.

They had both served their apprenticeship at Verkhonoye, in the desolate area outside Kazan where the KGB maintained a school for sexual operatives. Tania had lost her virginity at the academy. A girl from a good party family, she had been brought there at age seventeen to serve her country. On her second day at Verkhonoye, she was taken into a big hall and made to strip naked, together with a score of other new recruits, both male and female. That was the beginning of a carefully calculated process to make the sexual apprentices of the KGB lose all their emotional inhibitions.

On the third day, Tania's group was made to witness a variety of live sex acts in the same hall. On the fourth day, a busload of army cadets from Kazan was brought in to initiate the girls who had not slept with a man before. For the cadets, the night at Verkhonoye was a reward for good results at a nearby military college. For the girls, it was not a night of love. Tania was crudely raped on the floor of her room by a heavy Georgian peasant. The following day, back in the hall, Tania and the other female recruits were made to watch films of themselves kicking and screaming, while the instructors criticized their performance.

By the end of her three-month course at Verkhonoye, Tania was a full-fledged "swallow," trained to satisfy the most exotic sexual predilections and to display any required emotion without succumbing to it. Her partner, Yuri, had undergone similar schooling. As one of the KGB's "ravens"—the term favored for male sexual operatives—he too had practiced every mode of seduction. To complete their training, they had both been sent on to a school for spies in the suburbs of Leningrad to study foreign languages, secret codes, agent recruitment techniques, and the methods of traceless assassination. With this background, they were considered fit for Parisian society.

Despite his frequent sermons on the decadence of the West and the duty of Soviet citizens to avoid its temptations, Major General Pronk conceded that sexual entrapment—the "honey trap"—was one of the oldest and most effective ways of recruiting agents. More than one French diplomat had been lured into the bed of a KGB swallow. A French military attaché in Moscow had shot himself after learning that his wife's lover was KGB raven. There was no doubt that the Verkhonoye method worked.

"But why go to this trouble for the sake of a reporter?" the KGB resident challenged Barisov.

Barisov shrugged his shoulders. His chief was willfully ignorant of media operations, even though their primary importance had been acknowledged by the chairman of the Committee of State Security himself.

"Renard is more than a reporter," Barisov reminded the resident. "He controls the output of a major news agency. And he may provide us with the means to destroy Bonpierre. It's worth taking some trouble."

Pronk rose from his ornate desk and moved ahead of Barisov to the door, obviously anxious to get back to his game of chess.

"All right," said the resident. "Give me a written report when you have established contact with Renard."

What could be less suspicious than for one reporter to introduce himself to another over a press luncheon? The occasion that Barisov picked was a luncheon for the French foreign minister in the Maison de l'Amérique Latine on the Boulevard Saint-Germain. It was not difficult to find out that Renard was going to be there. Since there were no fixed seating arrangements, it was slightly more difficult to ensure that Barisov would have the place he wanted, seated at a table next to Renard. Barisov solved that by arriving early. A TASS colleague helped him identify the Frenchman. Then, when the reporters were summoned to take their places, Barisov was able to edge his way past an American correspondent into the seat at Renard's left.

Michel Renard was surprised to learn, over the wine and pâté de campagne, that the man from ISKRA had read and enjoyed a series of articles he had written on socialism in the third world. Barisov was engagingly frank about the naiveté of many of his countrymen in dealing with black Africans. "You French have something to teach us," the Russian said. "You are realists about Africa. Your politicians make fine speeches about their civilizing mission, but they don't make the mistake of trying to live up to them."

The conversation shifted easily to Vietnam, and Renard's curiosity grew when the Russian dropped the names of a couple of mutual acquaintances in the Vietnamese exile community in Paris. The way out of the war, they agreed, was for the Americans to open up direct relations with the National Liberation Front. The Russian expressed the view that, here again, the French had an important role to play in injecting some realism into Western policy.

They stopped talking to listen to the French foreign minister deliver a seemingly interminable speech. Barisov joined enthusiastically in the applause when the minister at last rounded off his remarks by quoting General de Gaulle's grand design to build a united Europe stretching from the Atlantic to the Urals.

Renard clapped because the speech was over. "Not much worth quoting there," he commented to his Russian neighbor. "Still, I'll have to get back to the office and hack something out."

Barisov patted his shoulder sympathetically. The Russians, it struck Renard, were even more tactile than the French. "It's a rough life working for a wire service," Barisov said.

Renard nodded indulgently, although he found it hard to draw any parallel between his job at AMI and what he imagined the Russian's job must be like. No Western reporter believed that ISKRA was just another news agency. After all, ISKRA had given a job to the notorious British double agent Kim Philby, who had been tapped to succeed as chief of Britain's Secret Intelligence Service (SIS) before his flight to Moscow, one step ahead of Britain's mole catchers. Still, Renard was amused and intrigued by Barisov's attention, all the more so because he had the immediate impression that his new acquaintance was a great deal more than another news agency hack. The thought that the Russian might just possibly be someone high up in the KGB gave Renard that pleasurable sensation that many people experience in the presence of power.

As the two men joined the crowd at the door, Barisov took Renard's arm and said casually, "It has been a real pleasure. Perhaps we could meet for lunch one of these days."

"I'd be delighted."

"May I ask if you are married?"

"As a matter of fact, I am."

"Well, why don't we make it dinner? I find that everybody is so much more relaxed at the end of the day, don't you? We could telephone."

Barisov offered his card. Renard fumbled in his wallet for one of his own AMI cards. He finally extracted a grubby, overlarge oblong card with the telephone number of one of his Vietnamese contacts scrawled in pencil on the back. Renard scribbled over the writing and printed his private number at the bottom of the card.

"Sorry. This looks a bit disreputable," the Frenchman said.

The man from ISKRA smiled politely.

Astrid Renard received the phone call the same day, before her husband came home from the news agency.

The voice was warm, full, and only slightly accented.

"Is this Madame Renard?" it said.

"Who is speaking, please?"

"I am a colleague of your husband. My name is Viktor Barisov. We agreed to meet for dinner, and I wondered whether next Thursday might suit you both. I have discovered a quite exceptional Vietnamese restaurant near the Place de l'Odéon. *La cuisine y est succulente.*"

"Oh, yes. You must mean La Hong, in the Rue Monsieur-le-Prince. My husband and I went there once and we loved it. Let me check with Michel when he gets home. I'm sure we're free on Thursday night."

They were. Renard was delighted that the Russian's taste in restaurants coincided so exactly with his own. They sat around a red-topped table while a lissome Annamite girl in a skintight *ao dai* placed an endless succession of dishes on a revolving tray in the center. The girl reminded Renard of many fleeting encounters in Vietnam in the days of Dien Bien Phu, when he was a young stringer for an American wire service. The Vietnamese girls were birdlike. They looked as if you could crush them in the palm of your hand. But Renard had learned they had steel inside. The war had done that.

He detected the same blend of surface fragility and inner hardness in the pale beauty who had come with Barisov. He was vaguely surprised that she was not Barisov's wife. The man from ISKRA had explained that his wife had gone back to Moscow on vacation. Tania was introduced simply as a "family friend."

"You look like a ballerina," Renard said to her.

She lowered her eyes modestly. "I did go to ballet school when I was a little girl," she said. "But I'm afraid I would never have made the Bolshoi."

Staring at Tania's long, perfectly formed neck, Renard directed a question at his host. "Tell me," he said to Barisov, "what is it like working here as a Soviet correspondent?"

"I am sure my life is not very different from yours," said Barisov, carelessly flicking the long ash from his cigarette —he smoked Marlboros, Renard noted—onto the floor. "We work long hours, we get little appreciation from our chiefs, and we are underpaid."

Renard wondered whether the Russian was serious. It was a fair description of life at his own news agency, but he was skeptical about whether it fitted the ambiguous Barisov. For a start, the man from ISKRA certainly did not look as if he were suffering any financial pangs. Wherever he and his lady companion had bought their immaculately tailored clothes, it was not in a GUM department store in Moscow.

"It's hard for any of us to imagine what motivates someone else," Barisov observed, almost—it struck Renard —as if he had been reading the Frenchman's thoughts. "I'm curious to know how you conceive your own role, Michel. Do you feel that it is the reporter's duty to remain a neutral observer, or do you feel that the reporter has a social responsibility to take sides on the major issues?"

"I don't believe complete objectivity is possible," Renard replied thoughtfully. "And those who claim to stand for journalistic objectivity have already taken sides while deluding themselves that they haven't."

"You mean that they have taken sides with the existing social order."

"Exactly," Renard agreed. His mind wandered back over the many situations in which he had stopped being a mere spectator and become politically and emotionally engaged —above all, he thought of Vietnam. "In Vietnam," he said aloud, "a reporter has to lose either his objectivity or his humanity."

Having said it, Renard felt uncomfortable. He wondered why he was starting to discuss journalistic ethics with a man who supposedly worked for a state-controlled news service that would print only what the party or the KGB told it to print.

"I would guess that not all your colleagues see the way you do," Barisov prodded him gently.

"You're damn right they don't."

"I don't want to encourage you to talk out of school," the Russian said with a smile, "but I am very interested in knowing how things work inside your news agency—what kind of editorial debates take place, who decides to run a particular article, that sort of thing. I have a special reason for asking."

"What's that?"

"Well, we are planning to do some restructuring at ISKRA. Any organization gets set in its ways after a certain time. We need to shift around some editorial responsibilities. I'm sure we could learn a great deal from you."

Barisov watched Renard intently, searching for any traces of psychological resistance. He found none. The Frenchman was half-conscious that the talk of reorganizing ISKRA was a flimsy pretext for drawing him out on the political in-fighting at AMI, but he was perfectly prepared to be drawn out on the topic of his pet hate, Jacques Bonpierre. On that subject, as Astrid occasionally tried to warn him, he had become obsessive.

"I wouldn't advise ISKRA to copy our editorial setup," Renard told the Russian. "The final say on almost everything rests with one man—that is, when he's not away on one of his rich friends' yachts or at some plush resort in Sardinia or the Bahamas."

"I understood that you were deputy editor. I would have imagined that your status carried great powers of decision."

"Not on the most important issues," Renard complained. "I can be sure that if I'm trying to organize the coverage of something like the colonels' coup in Greece, or a CIA scandal, I'll have Bonpierre breathing down my neck."

"Bonpierre is your editor." Affecting unfamiliarity with Bonpierre's name, Barisov waited for the Frenchman's nod before he added, "What's your opinion of him?"

"I *loathe* Bonpierre," Renard burst out, surprised at his own vehemence in talking to a stranger—and a Soviet stranger at that. "He is cocksure, he mangles copy, and when it comes to protecting the interests of his American friends, he is very, very quick with the spike."

"The what?" The Russian was puzzled by the expression.

"The spike," Renard repeated. "You know, killing stories."

"You mentioned that Bonpierre has American friends." Barisov was still feeling his way with care, not pushing the Frenchman to unburden himself faster than he chose.

"He's more American than French," Renard said contemptuously. "His wife's American. And rolling in money. They're constant guests at the American embassy."

"Do you know who he sees there? Apart from the ambassador, of course."

Renard mentioned several names of senior American

embassy officials, but not the one that Barisov was waiting for.

"Does the name Wittingham mean anything to you?" the Russian asked.

Renard thought for a moment. "No. Only in some English nursery rhyme," he said. "Who's Wittingham?"

"He's the new CIA station chief in Paris. It would be interesting to know whether your editor is in touch with him." Barisov modulated his voice to suggest that this interesting line of speculation had just occurred to him. He already knew, from the KGB's surveillance of Wittingham's movements, that the CIA station chief was meeting Jacques Bonpierre two or three times a month, if not more.

Renard leaped at the Russian's suggestion. "It wouldn't surprise me in the least to discover that Bonpierre was on intimate terms with Wittingham," he said. "In fact, I'm absolutely certain he's in close contact with the CIA. The question is, how to prove it." Renard pushed his plate aside, his appetite displaced by a different kind of hunger. His resentment and suspicion of Bonpierre had been growing day by day. That same morning, his editor had been complaining about the size of a restaurant bill that he had incurred entertaining a minister from a small African state. Now it occurred to him that if his hunch that Barisov was more than an ISKRA correspondent was right, the Russian might be able to help him nail Bonpierre. To settle that particular score, he would be willing to accept help from any quarter.

"I suppose your outfit must know quite a bit about CIA activities in Paris," Renard probed, not specifying what he meant by the word "outfit."

Barisov was delighted that the pressure was now coming from the Frenchman. He had not even needed to bait the line. But he avoided answering the question directly. Suddenly his attention was diverted by a gentle but insistent pressure against his calf. His first instinct was that Tania was passing some kind of signal—perhaps to warn him not to offer Renard too much at this early stage of the seduction. But Tania's eyes were fixed on the Frenchman's face.

Barisov realized that Astrid was staring at him from across the table, a half-smile on her lips. Enjoying the little conspiracy, the Russian slipped his hand surreptitiously under the table and caressed Astrid's foot. She had taken off her shoes.

Renard broke the lull in the conversation by reverting to the theme that excited him most. "If you should hear anything about a connection between Bonpierre and Wittingham," he began.

"Of course." The Russian cut him off, friendly but noncommittal. Astrid's toes were wriggling suggestively in the palm of his hand. He had not had to exert himself to seduce either of them.

Renard was thoughtful when they left the restaurant shortly before midnight. Holding the door open for Tania, he found himself staring into the bulbous eyes of a tropical fish in the restaurant's indoor aquarium. Could Barisov help him break Bonpierre? he asked the fish.

On the sidewalk, Astrid embraced both Barisov and Tania enthusiastically.

"Why don't you come round to our place for a nightcap?" she said to the Russians, without looking for her husband's approval.

"Not tonight, lovely lady." Barisov made his excuses. "I will have to check the office on my way home. You remember what it must have been like when Michel was running your bureau in Hong Kong."

As Tania got into the dark blue Volvo, Barisov turned back and called after the Renards, "What are you two doing on Saturday night?"

Renard and his wife looked at each other blankly.

"There's an interesting party you really should come to," Barisov explained. He looked intently at Astrid. "I think you'll find the company stimulating. And it's at a chateau. Will you come?"

"Yes," Astrid exclaimed, without waiting for her husband's reaction. She moved forward and kissed Barisov again.

They agreed to rendezvous in a bistro in Montparnasse.

3

ROBERT HOCKNEY bounded down the steps of the Air France Boeing into the warm sunshine of Orly airport. Despite the sleepless twelve-hour flight over the pole from Los Angeles, when he had been kept awake by a nonstop poker game in the next row of seats, he felt intensely alive.

Hockney's first big article for *Barricades* magazine could not have been rated a literary success. He had recounted a few cases of CIA undercover activities in the student movement in a breathless narrative reminiscent of pornographic fiction, relying heavily on Berkeley gossip and occasional advice from a beer-swilling former sergeant in Army intelligence who played guru to anyone who wanted to listen to his conspiracy theories about America's secret police. The most wounding comment that Hockney had received had come from his father on the back of a postcard: "So what?" But that had not been the reaction of other people. The *Barricades* piece had enraged the Agency and delighted the radical movement—to the extent that the magazine, with the aid of a grant from the Foundation for Progressive Reform in Washington, had commissioned Hockney to probe deeper in Europe.

There would be risks, the *Barricades* editors had warned him. As a result of his first article, his name was no doubt already on the "enemies lists" of any number of secret services. If he got too close to really sensitive operations, the editors added, there were people who would not hesitate to eliminate him.

Hockney dismissed that kind of talk as advanced paranoia. He sensed no contradiction between his belief that the Agency was involved in the assassination of third-world politicians and his feeling that he himself was invulnerable. If he had been asked about it, he would certainly never have conceded that this might have something to do with

43

the fact that he was the son of Admiral Tennant Hockney.

Paris felt like a second home. Hockney remembered the city from 1961, the year of Jack and Jackie Kennedy's triumphal visit, when life at the residence of the American naval attaché had been a heady round of cocktail parties and late night meetings, on which he, clad in pajamas and robe, had discreetly spied. He had discovered his manhood in Paris that year, in the arms of a horny maid from Languedoc whom his mother subsequently fired. Hockney was far too self-assured to accept that Paris was now about to claim his journalistic virginity too. In his own opinion he had nothing left to learn—only new conquests to make.

He had set his sights on two conquests in particular: exposing the full extent of CIA efforts to corrupt the political process in Europe, and earning himself a top job on the *New York World*. The two ambitions hung together. Hockney had been encouraged by the fact that one of the *World*'s best-known columnists had quoted a couple of paragraphs from his *Barricades* piece to support his demand that Congress impose new curbs on the CIA. If he hit real pay dirt in Paris, Hockney was convinced that the *World* would receive him with open arms, if only to avoid losing him to another paper. America was developing a taste for investigative reporting, and the competition was ferocious. If he could get ahead of the field in an area as explosive as the CIA, the big newspapers would be fighting over him.

Hockney cleared immigration, picked up his bags, and found his way to the Avis desk.

"Je suis Monsieur Hockney," he said in hesitant French. *"J'ai reservé un Renault."*

The girl understood. Hockney was relieved that his French was still functional after many years without practice.

He had difficulty steering his way in the rented car to his hotel, which was located in a tiny street off the Boulevard Saint-Germain—the Hotel des Saints-Frères, off the Rue des Saints-Frères. They gave him a box of a room, number 47, with a closet-sized bathroom and an iron-framed bed, backing onto a small courtyard. He glanced at the notice hanging inside the door. The price of the room worked out to about $10 a night, continental breakfast and service included. At those rates, he really couldn't complain. And the courtyard, when he looked out the window again, was charming. They had squeezed in four tables with checkered cloths, surrounded by luxuriant plants that straggled over the green latticework on the walls.

The telephone was going to be a problem. Very few French hotels had direct dialing, and the Hotel des Saints-Frères was no exception. Before unpacking his crumpled suits, Hockney took out his notebook and skimmed over the list of seventeen phone numbers that *Barricades* had come up with. Most of the people on the list were Americans living abroad, many of them involved in the antiwar movement. There was one Frenchman: the chief of the Agence Mondiale d'Informations, Jacques Bonpierre. Hockney decided to start with him. He reread the note he had scrawled next to Bonpierre's name on the pad: "CIA? Fought with U.S. Army. Postgrad studies at MIT. Knows Wittingham." Why not jump in at the deep end? Bonpierre was one of the biggest fish he could hope to net.

Hockney picked up the telephone and waited for the operator to answer. He went on waiting for minutes. He started banging the metal hook with rising impatience.

"Et alors, ça va pas?" the retired gendarme at reception finally growled back. "I can't do everything at once."

"I've been waiting for at least five minutes."

"Je m'en fous." The concierge's tone echoed a lifetime of insulting people. "You try being concierge, receptionist, and telephone operator all at once. Do you want a number or don't you?"

Hockney read out Bonpierre's number.

"Hang up and I'll call you back," the concierge ordered.

Hockney was halfway through unpacking his bags by the time the phone rang. He stuttered his explanations to Bonpierre's secretary, mentioning that he was working on a survey of the European media. She tried to fob him off, saying that her boss had no free time within the next two weeks. Hockney had to resort to a half-lie to get through to Bonpierre. He dropped the magic name of the *New York*

45

World, giving the impression that that was where his story was to be published. It was part true, Hockney reassured himself. If his story proved to be as dramatic as he hoped, there was little doubt that the *World* would replay it.

Bonpierre came on the line. His English was unflawed. Hockney might have been talking to someone from Boston. The mention of the *World* had apparently done the trick. Bonpierre said he could give him a few minutes before lunch the following day.

While Hockney was walking up from the Deux Magots, the bistro made famous by Simone de Beauvoir and the existentialist crowd, to the Odéon metro station, Michel Renard was slumped in his seat in the middle of the bullpen at the Agence Mondiale d'Informations. Renard was more than slightly hung over, and his temper was burning on a short fuse. By the time Antoinette, the newsroom's girl Friday, had brought him his coffee, it was cold. He rejected it in disgust and fished for another Gauloise in his pocket. The pack was empty. He screwed it up and tossed it toward the big wastebasket in the corner of the room. Renard's aim was off. He hit Courtier, a played-out reporter who was coasting downhill to retirement by putting commas into other people's copy. Courtier blinked and looked around him.

"Sorry if I woke you up," Renard snarled, as if he were the one who had been hit. He got up from his desk. "This is supposed to be a newsroom," he exploded. "Where is the news? I haven't had a bloody thing across my desk in the last twenty minutes. If someone has stopped the world, I'd at least like to read the story on our own wire."

The four rewrite men, whose tables were arranged in a semicircle in front of Renard's desk, looked up from their newspapers.

"It's a slow day," said Courtier, not trying to apologize.

"Tell it to them," Renard snapped, gesturing toward the bank of teleprinters at the end of the room pumping out long rolls of copy.

He began to walk toward the teleprinters, but stopped as he caught sight of a tall, strikingly good-looking young man who had come through the main door. The stranger strode purposefully toward Renard, as if he already knew him.

"Are you looking for someone?" Renard challenged him. A glance at the newcomer's tweed sports jacket and button-down collar was enough to tell Renard that he was American. Renard did not like Americans. Nor did he take an instant liking to men who were younger, taller, and better-looking than himself.

"*J'ai un rendezvous avec Monsieur Bonpierre*," the stranger replied. His accent set Renard's teeth on edge. But the American flashed a ready—too ready—smile.

"You say you have an appointment with the chief editor?" Renard switched into English, unaware that he sounded like a stage Frenchman in an American musical.

"I'm afraid I'm late." The American smiled again, sweeping a lock of dark hair back from his forehead. The smile was too wide, the eyes too blue—the blue of deep waters under a brilliant sun. "I'm new to Paris and I got stuck on the wrong metro line."

Renard said nothing.

"I should have changed at Réaumur-Sebastopol," the stranger explained, irrelevantly.

Renard went back to his desk and sat down. He left the American standing, unsure which way to turn.

"Who are you?" Renard demanded, affecting to be absorbed in some stale news copy.

"The name is Hockney. I'm a reporter." Hockney struck what he imagined was a tough-reporter pose, hands in his pockets.

"Who are you with?"

"I'm uh, free-lance." Hockney was unsure whether to mention *Barricades*, especially since he had dropped the name of the *World*. This was a miscalculation. Renard was convinced that all American free-lance reporters were in the pay of the CIA.

"What story are you working on?" Renard probed, wondering what this American's connection was with his editor.

"Oh, nothing special. Just comparing notes." Hockney's eyes strayed to Antoinette, who was swaying toward them,

47

laden with more cups of cold coffee. She returned Hockney's appreciative smile. Renard scowled.

"Le couloir au fond, deuxième porte à gauche." Renard reverted to French to show his displeasure.

"Come on, I'll show you the way," Antoinette offered. Renard watched her swing her hips as she walked in front of the American toward Bonpierre's office. All women are whores, he thought uncharitably.

Courtier shuffled across Renard's line of vision, a dead cigarette stub drooping from his lower lip, with a wad of incoming dispatches in one fist and a half-eaten baguette in the other. Renard glared at the mess of papers. There was the usual flood of stuff on Vietnam. A boring piece on the Wilson government's efforts to end the Rhodesian rebellion. Something on the French miners' strike. Renard added a line to the introduction. His attention began to drift back to the American who had gone in to see Bonpierre.

The next piece of copy revived his interest. It was a summary of a story published in the *New York World* on how the Congress for Cultural Freedom had been used as a CIA front. It suggested that several European editors whose publications had been funded by this body were going to resign because of the embarrassment the *World*'s revelations had caused.

Renard gave out a long, low whistle. This might just be the missing piece in the puzzle he had been trying to solve. Bonpierre had been extremely active in programs organized by the Congress for Cultural Freedom. In fact, Bonpierre had only just come back from a meeting organized by the congress in West Berlin that was supposedly concerned with freedom of the press in the developing countries.

Renard could not resist the temptation to test Bonpierre's reactions to the *World*'s story while his American friend was still in the office.

He rapped on the chief editor's door once and walked straight in.

"This is important," Renard announced, pushing the piece on the *World*'s revelations in front of his boss. "I thought you would want to see it immediately."

Bonpierre appeared unruffled. Tall and angular, with cropped gray hair, the chief editor was in shirt sleeves, the jacket of his dark blue suit draped casually over the back of his chair.

"Excuse me," Bonpierre said to Hockney. He glanced at the first sentence of the story.

"Is this all it is?" Bonpierre asked. "I know all about it. By the way, Michel, do you know Bob Hockney? He and I were just discussing it."

Renard looked from one man to the other. Bonpierre discarded the pipe he had been smoking and picked up another from the rack on his desk. Renard noticed that he spent far longer than usual stuffing in the tobacco and then tamping it. Under the smooth exterior, Bonpierre was nervous.

"Bob Hockney tells me he is writing something for *Barricades*," Bonpierre resumed as he set a match to his pipe.

Renard was startled. The reputation of *Barricades* had spread to Paris. It was a radical, muckraking publication, not the kind of magazine that was likely to employ CIA agents.

"If you know all about the CIA story," Renard addressed his editor, "could I trouble you to give me that copy back? I would like to get this on the wire straightaway."

Bonpierre blew clouds of smoke into the room as he huffed life into his pipe.

"There's no great urgency, Michel," the editor said. "I'd rather not touch this story until we can get our own report from Washington. In any case, we have a duty to follow up here in Paris. It's only fair to ask the people who have been named by the *World* to let us have their own comments. They're not exactly undistinguished people."

Hockney could feel the rising tension between Renard and his editor, who was still holding the CIA story.

"I have a hunch," Bonpierre concluded, "that if we dig deep enough, we will find that what is at the bottom of this is a shrewd exercise in character assassination."

"Well, let's find out. Maybe we could begin by interviewing you."

"I think you had better explain yourself." Bonpierre's voice did not rise, but he put down the pipe he had only just lit and began to toy with another.

Renard did not explain himself. He walked out of the office, banging the door.

He was back at his desk, trying to turn the opening paragraphs of a roundup on Vietnam into intelligible French, when he felt a slight burning sensation at the back of his neck.

Renard spun round in his swivel chair to find Hockney watching him intently.

"Got time for a drink?" said the American.

"Why not?" Renard considered the litter of papers on his desk. "But I must finish here first. Why don't you go to the bar across the street and I'll pick you up there in ten minutes? It's called Le Céleste."

Leaning on the zinc counter of the bar, flanked by taxi drivers and construction workers in blue overalls, Hockney looked absurdly American. He had to repeat his order for a glass of red wine three times before the barman consented to understand him above the babble of talk and the rattle of pinball machines. Hockney tossed his wine back eagerly, then moved to a table. The day was starting well. Bonpierre was far too smooth to give anything away in an interview, but Hockney could already smell that *Barricades* had pointed him in the right direction. The friction between Bonpierre and his deputy, the surly Michel Renard, was a bonus that Hockney had had no reason to expect.

Hockney glimpsed his own reflection in the gilt-edged mirror across the room. In the same glass, he found himself looking directly into the eyes of an office girl sitting at the other end of his long table. She flushed and whispered in her girlfriend's ear. They both turned to look at him, giggling. Hockney flicked the lock of hair back from his forehead. It was no disadvantage, in his profession, to turn women's heads without trying.

A voice from behind his shoulder ordered a pastis.

The voice came closer and said, "Admiring yourself?"

50

Hockney shifted along the banquette to make room for Renard.

"It was a great scene in Bonpierre's office," the American said. "I really enjoyed your parting shot."

"It's a scene that takes place every day." The Frenchman shrugged. He took out a Gauloise without offering the pack to Hockney.

"Can we work together?"

Renard studied the younger man speculatively.

"I don't know what you want," he said. "Bonpierre is a typical product of the Fourth Republic, when more Frenchmen than you can imagine were bought by the Americans. His reflexes are American more than French. He hates the Communists, and he hates De Gaulle, because De Gaulle took France out of NATO. He talks to the CIA. So do lots of people. You could be CIA, for all I know."

"I think you know about *Barricades*," Hockney countered. He pulled a clipping out of his pocket and handed it to Renard, who glanced at the title—"Spooking the Spooks in California"—and the cartoon illustrations of spies in trench coats and dark glasses. He passed it back.

"It's because of that piece," Hockney explained, "that *Barricades* sent me over here to do a bigger story on CIA covert action in Europe. We think your boss could be one of the key CIA agents in the French media. If you can help me prove that, I'm willing to break the story. And I promise the magazine will print it. *Barricades* didn't get its name by pulling punches."

"How old are you?"

Hockney was always embarrassed when people asked him his age. He worried that they might not think he was old enough to be taken seriously. He hesitated.

"Twenty-five?" the Frenchman guessed.

"That's about right." Hockney fudged his answer. In fact, he had just turned twenty-three.

"So what prompts an American of your age to start crusading against the CIA?"

Hockney started talking about Vietnam, and the movement. Renard cut him off after a minute or two. Hockney was using too many abstract words. He talked the way young men talked, before they have lived enough. At thirty-five, Michel Renard had lost his ear for rhetoric. But he accepted that the young American was serious.

"*Bon*," said the Frenchman. "Suppose I help you write a story on Bonpierre. What's in it for you?"

The answer, Hockney knew, could be many things: a job on the *World*, a step toward a Pulitzer price and instant celebrity, plus a kick in the balls for the CIA. But all he said was, "A good story."

"*Entendu*," the Frenchman acknowledged. "Let's drink to it."

4

IT WAS SATURDAY NIGHT, but the three lanes of the Boulevard Périphérique were still jammed bumper to bumper with French families trying to escape Paris for part of the weekend and with harried businessmen trying to force their way through the traffic to Orly airport. Viktor Barisov was dressed, as usual, in a dark suit that looked distinctly Brooks Brothers, although he had assured the Renards that the party would be very informal. Tania was dressed all in black, with a black choker at her throat and a long black cape over her shoulders. Michel Renard felt a little underdressed in his red shirt and suede jacket, but Astrid lived up to the occasion, as usual—in an expensive knitted dress she had bought that morning that must have blown a big hole in Renard's monthly salary.

The traffic ground to a halt again, and Barisov reached over Astrid's lap to extract a new pack of Marlboros from the glove compartment. His hand brushed against her exposed thigh and lingered there. Astrid moistened her lips, with slow deliberation.

In the back seat, her husband was deep in conversation with the Russian girl.

"Who are these friends of yours who are giving the party?" Renard asked Tania.

"Oh, they're a charming couple. I'm sure you must have heard of Marcel Rosse."

"Marcel Rosse?" Renard searched his memory.

"Yes. Marcel is a publisher. What's the name of his publishing house, Viktor?" Tania affected insouciance. It was best to let Barisov explain the tricky parts.

"Marcel Rosse runs Editions Demain," Barisov said over his shoulder as he edged the Volvo forward in pace with the car ahead.

"Of course," said Renard, leaning forward so he could be heard in the front seat. Editions Demain was one of France's most progressive publishing houses, specializing in books on the third world and on revolutionary theory.

"Rosse isn't French, is he?" Renard asked.

"Not by origin," Barisov replied. "He's been naturalized. His grandparents were Russian, but he was born in Algiers. He spent time in jail in Algeria when the French were still in charge because of his sympathy for the revolutionary cause."

"Can I have one of your American cigarettes?" Astrid intervened, bored at the idea of spending a whole night listening to leftist intellectuals who would never use one word when a whole book would do.

"Have you had a busy week?" Tania asked Renard.

"The usual treadmill. Oh, but I met someone quite interesting," Renard remembered. He raised his voice. "He might interest you, Viktor."

"Who is that?" said Barisov.

"An American reporter called Bob Hockney. He works for a radical West Coast magazine called *Barricades*."

"I haven't heard of it."

"The magazine's important. It's in the vanguard of the campaign against the CIA. Better still, Hockney is over here to look into the activities of our friend Bonpierre."

The man from ISKRA grunted, noncommittal.

The Volvo had cleared the worst of the traffic and was skimming along the expressway. The needle of the speedometer hovered around 120 kilometers. Peering through the windshield, Astrid was first to spot the sign that read "Fontainebleau: 10 km." Barisov swung the car off the expressway onto the side road leading to the town.

"Is it much farther?" Astrid asked him.

"We're less than five minutes away."

They rounded a bend in the road and approached a gap in the line of trees to their left. Barisov drove into it. A man examined the approaching car through a massive partly opened iron gate before pulling it fully ajar to let them pass. The Volvo crunched up a winding gravel drive for a few yards. Then Barisov braked. He sat with the engine humming, studying the rearview mirror.

"Is something wrong?" Astrid asked, suddenly uneasy.

"No, no," the Russian reassured her. "I just thought I saw some friends coming along behind us. I must have been mistaken."

Barisov lit another Marlboro and drove on, up to the front court of the house. He was sure he was not mistaken. The black Citroën had bobbed out of the traffic several times on their way from Paris. Its driver was intelligent. When they got out onto the open road and Barisov had suddenly slowed down, checking whether they were being followed, the black Citroën had overtaken them. It had dropped behind again farther on. It had followed them down the Fontainebleau road but had not gone past the entrance to the chateau. That meant the occupants of the Citroën were waiting somewhere behind them.

Outside the huge, square-built, red brick house, a dozen cars were already parked. The house was not what a Frenchman would call a chateau, Renard decided. It was more like a Gallic dacha.

A man appeared from around the side of the house. He was wearing a trench coat, despite the warm August evening, and a hat that was wider brimmed than was customary in France. Barisov walked forward to meet him and murmured something in an undertone. The man nodded and vanished back into the shadows.

The house was obviously guarded. It was a curious environment for a French publisher, Renard thought, although it was possible that their host was receiving death threats from the Fascists. Renard wondered who had loaned Rosse his foreign guards.

A white-jacketed butler took their coats at the door, and Barisov led the way into a vast drawing room, where twenty or thirty people were drinking champagne and nibbling canapés. Astrid ran her fingers over the heavy silk brocade on the walls. The room smelled like an Arab souk. Through a haze of incense from the lighted joss sticks that had been scattered around the room, Astrid caught a whiff of another, unmistakable aroma. Some of Rosse's guests were smoking marijuana. Perhaps the party was not going to be the tedious seminar she had feared.

Rosse, a sleek, silver-haired man in a blue velvet jacket, detached himself from his guests. He wore too many rings, Astrid judged at once, and far too much cologne. And he had on too many shades of blue—the blue of his bow tie and pocket handkerchief clashed with his jacket, which was expensive but stained. The effect was of insurmountable seediness.

But Astrid gave her provocative smile, eyes flashing, as the publisher gushed over her, bowing and kissing her hand. Rosse took her arm and spun her around the room. Her husband and the Russian couple followed in their train. There were far too many names and faces, all of them unfamiliar, for Astrid to take much in. The men, mostly young, were wearing everything from blue jeans to dinner jackets. One or two of them were quite good-looking.

One, in particular, had the kind of smoldering attraction that made Astrid ask Rosse to repeat his name to make sure she got it right.

"Yuri." The young man grinned.

"*Un ami sovietique*," Rosse explained, patting Yuri's shoulder.

"And what do you do with yourself?" Astrid challenged the young Russian.

"I'm in shipping," Yuri said vaguely.

Someone turned up the volume on the hi-fi. They were playing the Rolling Stones's "Satisfaction." It seemed incongruous against the backdrop of silver brocade, ornate

55

mirrors, and chandeliers. The lights were turned down a little, and Astrid saw that a few couples had started to dance at the other end of the room, beyond an enormous log fire that had been lit for effect, not warmth.

"Would you like to eat something?" inquired their host. "I can offer a modest buffet. A little caviar, perhaps? Or smoked salmon?"

"Thank you," said Astrid. "Just now, I'd rather dance." She broke into the pulsating rhythms of the music, moving her whole body.

The voice of Mick Jagger was wailing on the hi-fi.

"Oh-oh no," Yuri sang along, moving his hips a little stiffly.

"Are you sure you're Russian?" said Astrid, intrigued. Neither Viktor Barisov nor this young man in a turtleneck sweater had much in common with her previous image of stolid Slavs.

"I have a few Western vices," Yuri joked.

The publisher blew Astrid a kiss and moved back to his other guests.

Yuri put down his drink. He took Astrid's hand and led her over to the dancers. "This is a meaningful kind of cultural exchange," he commented.

Over the hi-fi, Feliciano had started to croon the words to "Light My Fire."

Yuri sang into Astrid's ear; the young Russian seemed to know every line.

"Don't they ban pop music in Russia?" she said.

"So they should. It's much too dangerous."

Astrid rested her hand at the base of Yuri's neck and pressed her breasts against his chest so he could feel their weight. She felt an answering pressure against her thigh. She pressed closer to him, rubbing her knee between his legs. Over Yuri's shoulder, she could see her husband and the other Russian, Barisov, watching them.

She broke away from her partner. "I need some more champagne," she announced.

She was intercepted by a wild-eyed young man with a beard, who offered her a joint. She puffed at it and passed it to Yuri.

"No thank you," he said. "There are some Western vices I have not yet managed to pick up."

The lights in the room were dimmed lower. The double doors at the end of the long drawing room were flung open, to reveal a bedroom suite beyond. Two couples drifted toward it. Another couple started to embrace on the rug in front of the fire. Framed by the massive marble fireplace, they appeared to be consumed by the flames that leaped up from a majestic oak log.

The man known as Mouflon to his employers in French security had abandoned his black Citroën half a mile down the road before the entrance to the chateau. It was exhausting to serve two employers—the DST as well as the police. Rather like trying to keep several women contented at the same time, which Mouflon also took pride in accomplishing.

The DST was intrigued by the connection that had been established between the journalist Renard and the Soviet spy Barisov. Mouflon's orders were simply to tail them to their evening's entertainment. The publisher Rosse was celebrated for holding exotic parties that might well be of legitimate interest to an inspector of the Parisian vice squad.

As luck would have it, Mouflon's colleague was a friendly type known within the service as Tapir, who happened to be a practiced safecracker. Mouflon had never seen the inside of Rosse's chateau, and the confusion of the noisy party that was going on inside seemed to offer perfect cover for him to take a discreet look around. With Tapir's skills to draw upon, who knew what they might turn up? Mouflon was aware that his superiors might consider an unauthorized visit to the Rosse house to be exceeding his instructions. But he had reached the conclusion many years ago that the only rule in his trade was not to get caught. If Rosse had security guards and Mouflon did get caught, he was confident that his employers would get him out without fuss. The worst he had to fear was a reprimand.

Mouflon found an easy place to scale the wall around the chateau. On the other side, crouched behind a rhododendron bush, he decided he had been right to take the risk. There were no guards in sight. The French doors to the drawing room had been opened onto the terrace, and inside, the party was in full swing. A young couple, hugging each other, wandered off into the bushes.

"Look," hissed Tapir. Mouflon followed his pointing finger to a heavy wooden door at the side of the house.

"All right, let's try it," Mouflon whispered.

Behind the door, they found a flight of stone steps, leading down to a wine cellar. Beside the racks of St. Emilion, there was a big steel door in the cellar wall.

"A strong room?" Mouflon speculatel. "Let's find out."

It took Tapir less than seven minutes to open the door by playing with the numbered buttons that controlled the lock.

Mouflon and Tapir stepped into a large vault. Against one wall, automatic weapons and plastic explosives were stacked. Tacked to the other were what looked like organizational charts. A large metal filing cabinet with a combination lock stood in the corner. It was child's play for Tapir to break it open.

Inside, they found a batch of documents with a printed letterhead. The initials STAR stood out in red at the top of each page.

"What's STAR?" Tapir whispered.

Mouflon pointed to the smaller print at the head of one of the documents.

"*Solidarité Tricontinental des Armées Révolutionnaires*," he read out.

Leafing through the papers in the filing cabinet, Mouflon saw that STAR was a coordinating directorate for European and Palestinian terrorist groups. Among the documents were plans for kidnappings and acts of sabotage. Mouflon was shocked to find material of this sort in the publisher's cellar. Rosse was a leftist, and possibly a Soviet agent. But Mouflon would never have guessed that he could be a link-man with the terrorist underground.

There was no time to digest the contents of the documents. Mouflon took out a miniature camera, made to resemble a cylindrical cigarette lighter, and started to photograph the papers that looked most incriminating.

He had barely begun when Tapir murmured, "Listen."

Mouflon paused. He heard heavy footsteps outside the door to the vault, which he had left slightly ajar.

Tapir, reaching for his gun, yelled "Police!" as a swarthy man hurled himself into the strong room. He could be Latin, Mouflon thought. He fired point-blank at Tapir, who ducked just in time.

"Police, don't shoot," Mouflon yelled, diving for cover behind the filing cabinet.

The Latin leveled his Beretta at Mouflon. But before he could fire again, a second man burst into the room and shouldered him aside.

"Idiot," the newcomer bellowed. The new man was thickset, wearing a trench coat. Mouflon guessed at once that he was Russian.

Upstairs in the house, Michel Renard was sitting, tense, on the edge of a leather armchair in the publisher's oak-paneled library. The Russian, Barisov, was relaxing in another chair, savoring his snifter of Delamain cognac. The paneling along one wall of the library had slid back, at the touch of a button, to reveal a two-way mirror concealed behind. Through the glass, Renard and Barisov could contemplate a mound of bodies, gyrating to the tribal beat of the Rolling Stones. The live people beyond the glass looked as remote to Renard as the cast of a blue movie. Including even his wife.

Mick Jagger's recorded voice carried through into the library, etching itself onto Renard's mind as he picked out Astrid, locked in the embrace of that young Russian stud—Yuri—in the middle of the orgy.

"She's very resourceful," Barisov commented.

Renard turned his head away. He felt slightly queasy. He drank some more cognac. It did not help.

Tania, crouched beside his chair, reached up and slipped her bare arms around Renard's neck. It struck him that, if Astrid had been in the library, she might have had the same ringside view of his coupling with Tania an hour before.

He broke free of Tania's clasp and walked to the library windows. Barisov, arching an eyebrow at Tania, rose to follow.

"How late do you want to stay?" Renard said to the Russian. "I think it's time we headed back to Paris." It occurred to Renard that the man from ISKRA had not even removed the jacket of his dark suit since they had arrived.

"Aren't you enjoying yourself?" Barisov tested his emotions.

"I might put that question to you, since you seem to have cast yourself in the role of spectator."

"I'm not very fond of team games," Barisov said, staring out over the garden.

Renard felt increasingly uncomfortable. Without thinking, he began to pull books from the library shelves and put them back in again, sometimes upside down.

He was glad for the interruption when the butler appeared and motioned Barisov aside.

"Excuse me for a moment." The Russian drained the remains of his cognac and left Renard alone with Tania, who had stretched her naked body full length on the carpet, still watching the scene beyond the glass. Renard could no longer identify his wife among the heap of arms and legs.

Barisov summed up the situation in the cellar at a glance. He was relieved that neither Mouflon nor Tapir had been shot. That at least would help cover the traces. Mouflon was already familiar to him—by reputation, not by the soft, jowly face. A few years before, one of Barisov's predecessors had been trapped by the DST because of his fondness for the Bois de Boulogne. From the state of Rosse's files, it was obvious that the French spies had found out too much to be permitted to leave.

"Shall I interrogate them?" demanded the Russian guard, anxious to show his prowess.

Barisov shook his head. He doubted whether there was

much more to be learned from these two Frenchmen. One thing was clear. They had to be disposed of. His superior, General Pronk, would expect to be consulted, of course. Contrary to its popular image, the KGB rarely killed at random. But Barisov had no means of communicating with his chief, since French security had Pronk's home fully covered and there was no time to arrange a meeting. At any rate, he knew Pronk was not at home and could not be immediately contacted. The initiative rested with Barisov.

He examined the lethal playthings that Rosse's friends had stored in his strong room. Among them was a seven-inch metal tube. It contained a glass ampule filled with prussic acid.

Barisov picked up the tube and motioned to the Latin guard to lead Tapir forward. He pushed the tube forward, to within an inch of Tapir's nose and pulled the trigger device. A spring inside the tube detonated a small explosive charge that crushed the glass ampule, causing the acid to spray into Tapir's face in the form of a vapor. Tapir gasped, and fell to the floor.

Taking an identical metal tube from a drawer in the filing cabinet, Barisov pressed a handkerchief to his nose and motioned for Mouflon to be led forward. Mouflon and the guards were already coughing from the fumes in the constricted vault.

"Get outside," Barisov ordered the guards. He pointed the tube at Mouflon.

"No," Mouflon screamed. He flung himself forward, grabbing for the Russian's knees. Barisov's boot struck him with full force on the chin.

Mouflon lay stretched out on the floor, apparently unconscious. Barisov knelt down, aimed the tube at his face, and fired again. He hastily left the strong room to let the prussic acid do its work. Any doctor would say that Mouflon and Tapir had died of cardiac arrest. The acid left no trace.

Barisov waited for the vapor to disperse before he returned to the vault to supervise the disposal of the bodies. With the help of the guards, he lugged the two corpses up the steps from the cellar and into his Volvo. It did not take them long to find Mouflon's Citroën, abandoned half a mile back along the road outside the chateau.

Barisov showed the guards how to prop up the two bodies in the front seat of Mouflon's car. The Russian guard, crammed in next to Mouflon, drove the Citroën, its lights switched off, the wrong way up the one-way exit road from the expressway. Barisov followed in his own car. At the top of the exit road, the guard got out of the Citroën. He pulled Mouflon's body into the driver's seat and clamped his hands to the steering wheel.

The guard returned to Barisov's Volvo. The Citroën was stationed at the very edge of the expressway. Barisov waited until he could see the headlights of several approaching cars, ripping along at 150 or 160 kilometers. Then he nudged the Volvo forward until it touched the Citroën's bumper. Barisov ticked off the seconds in his mind before he slammed on the accelerator, pushing Mouflon's car forward into the middle of the expressway. The advancing cars had no time to brake, or even to swerve aside. The first collided with the Citroën, leaped into the air above, and sailed over into the opposite lane, bursting into flames as it hit the asphalt. The driver of the second car tried to brake, with a screech of rubber, but crashed into the back of the Citroën and reeled away into a barrier at the edge of the expressway.

Barisov had already reversed at high speed back down the exit road.

When the man from ISKRA returned to the library, he found that all the lights had been switched on and the small group that was waiting for him—Astrid, Renard, Tania—was fully dressed.

"Won't you dance with me?" Astrid said to the Russian. Barisov thought Renard looked ready to hit her.

"There will be other nights," he apologized gracefully. "I think that perhaps we are all tired."

5

THE KGB RESIDENT did not appreciate initiative in his subordinates, not when it came to murder. Wet operations, he maintained, were essentially the preserve of the specialists in Department V, and required authorization from the top. It was not that Pronk himself was averse to killing. He had done his share as a subaltern in the Red Army in the fierce defense of the Black Sea port of Novorossiysk against the Nazi troops—an experience that he hoped would aid his career in the future, since another of those involved in that heroic campaign was a commissar named Leonid Brezhnev. But the rules that applied to the battlefield did not, in Pronk's view, apply to the secret war he was now waging. All methods, of course, were justified by the goal: the triumph of socialism in the international class struggle. But victory would also depend on ironclad discipline, the sort of discipline that young Viktor Barisov so signally lacked. There was no room for a James Bond in the Soviet service. Pronk had roared with laughter, like the others, when he attended a screening of the first Bond films at Moscow Center. James Bond was an absurd parody of the mercenary capitalist killer. "If the scalp hunters of SIS operated like that," his chief, Kramar, had observed, "they would all be floating in the English Channel." Yet there were times when Barisov seemed to model himself on the improbable Bond. His playboy mannerisms, his women, and his delectation for sexual entrapment—bedroom espionage—had already drawn rebukes from Pronk. Now Barisov, supposedly a specialist in deception operations, had chosen to play the part of assassin.

When Barisov checked in at the residency, he found his way to the *referentura*—the inner sanctum of the KGB station—blocked by the considerable bulk of his superior. Pronk regarded him with unfriendly brown eyes.

"Good morning, Comrade General."

63

Pronk did not acknowledge the greeting. "I want to talk to you."

Barisov followed his chief along the corridor to his office. Under the system Pronk had imposed on the residency, only he himself enjoyed the privilege of a separate office. Everyone else, including the deputy residents, had to share. This was supposedly good for security.

"You must have been out of your mind," Pronk began.

"I tried to clear it. There was no time to track you down."

"No time?" Pronk erupted. "How much time do you think we are going to have in Paris if we start killing DST agents at random?"

"Nobody's traced it to us. According to the newspapers, the deaths were the result of an automobile accident. That's what I intended them to look like."

"Do you think the DST believes what it reads in the papers? They've already increased their watch on our people." Pronk explained that he had had to organize an emergency operation to remove the incriminating material from Rosse's chateau in case of a raid by French security.

Barisov was tempted to point out that it was better to have to go to those lengths than to have the DST stumble on a direct link between Soviet intelligence and a terrorist network in Europe.

"I have sent a very adverse report to the Center on your role in all this," Pronk concluded.

"Is that all?" Barisov asked rudely.

"No, it's not all. As far as I can understand your activities, you got us involved in this mess because you were trying to recruit a French journalist and to compromise his boss, Bonpierre. Have you got any progress to report?"

"Renard is nibbling," Barisov summarized. "There's no doubt that he'll do anything to destroy Bonpierre. And he's provided us with a line on an American correspondent who could perhaps help us too." Barisov explained Renard's connection with Bob Hockney.

"Are you going to offer Renard money?"

Barisov looked pensive. "He needs money," he said. "But he would probably be insulted by too direct an approach. I think it's better, for the time being, to draw him—and his wife, of course—more closely into the kind of social round that we can control. That may give me a chance to meet the American too. If, that is, you don't object."

Pronk's look of hostility had not relaxed. "I don't want any more wild sheep run over in Paris," he said. "There is something further. I trust you can spare a few minutes to read a policy directive, Comrade Barisov? This one comes from Comrade Suslov."

Barisov creased his face into the appropriate mask of respect. Suslov was the policy overlord in the Kremlin, viewed by both the KGB and the powerful International Department of the Community Party as the ultimate font of authority, next only to Comrade Brezhnev himself. Furthermore, it was rumored among many—though known for certain to only a select few—that for years Suslov had been developing the master version of The Plan. The Plan, Barisov had gleaned from his father-in-law during a home visit to Moscow, was a blueprint for achieving Soviet domination of the West by a certain date. The deadline had been revised once or twice already. The current deadline, Barisov had been told, was 1985. His father-in-law had fallen abruptly silent when Barisov had probed for the contents of The Plan. Either his father-in-law did not know or he was too frightened to tell anyone, even a member of the family.

Pronk passed the slim document across his desk. "Read it now," he said. "You're not on the distribution list." Pronk missed no opportunity to remind his subordinates that he, not they, belonged to the inner circle.

Barisov read quickly, absorbing a whole line at a time. The Suslov directive related to the effects of America's war in Vietnam and how the Soviet Union could exploit them. It noted that the war had produced a deep rift within the United States and had lent momentum to anti-American feeling abroad. A growing body of Americans had come to accept that the war could not be won and that the best way out was through a negotiated settlement. "It is not in the Soviet interest," the directive stated, "to assist a negotiated settlement at this stage." The reason was that the consciousness of American defeat, if permitted to grow, would be bound to produce domestic upheavals and eventual paralysis. Defeated in Vietnam, the United States would refuse to contemplate military intervention abroad for many years—opening up many opportunities for the progressive forces to expand their sphere of influence. At the same time, the directive insisted, it was vital that opinion formers in the West be convinced that the Soviet Union was striving to help the Americans find an honorable way out of Vietnam. This would foster a climate of sympathy in the West for the Soviet policy of peaceful coexistence.

"Well?" Pronk grunted as Barisov reached the bottom of the last page.

"Comrade Suslov is right." Barisov usually found the appropriate words. "Vietnam can destroy the United States as the leader of the capitalist world and isolate it from its present allies. In the American psyche, the war can become an act of collective hara-kiri."

"So how can we help apply Comrade Suslov's directive?"

"The Americans will do it by themselves."

Pronk nodded. The two men agreed on one thing: it was extremely difficult for a bourgeois democracy with an unfettered press to mobilize public support for a war policy.

"All we need to do," Barisov continued, "is to help a few people—journalists, junior officials—to follow their own instincts."

Michel Renard turned up the collar of his light jacket, uselessly, against the sun shower. He ran around the corner, into the narrow, cobbled Rue des Grand-Augustins. Two blocks down the street was the window, full of tiny china frogs, of the restaurant Roger la Grenouille, where Bob Hockney had arranged to meet him. Astrid had insisted on coming too. That, on top of the choice of rendezvous, had honed Renard's suspicions to a sharp cutting edge.

He sensed that something was developing between Astrid and Hockney. Astrid had gushed all over the young American when Renard had brought him home for dinner. That

66

was nothing unusual. But an affair behind his back would be breaking the pact that held their marriage together.

The eccentric little restaurant was a favorite meeting place for lovers. Patrons were handed miniature opera glasses to read the menu, which was chalked on a blackboard at the end of a long, narrow room. Renard had sneaked in there one day with Antoinette from the office, and at the end of their meal they had been presented with two sets of china frogs, each pair mating in a different position. Had Hockney and Astrid been here together? Was that why Hockney had chosen the place?

Jealousy was such a negative emotion. Renard prided himself that he had managed to exorcise it. He felt nothing resembling jealousy when he accompanied Astrid to her Friday night orgies or to the more elegant round of parties to which Viktor Barisov had recently introduced them. Being present with her, perhaps, gave him the feeling that he had not been excluded. Certainly, he could feel disgust. Fatigue, also. But jealousy revived only at the thought that, in secret from him, Astrid might have begun an affair with the handsome young American. As he pushed open the door of the restaurant, Renard wondered what Hockney was like in bed, and regretted the night he had first brought the American home to supper.

Renard was the first to arrive. As he took off his soaked summer-weight jacket and threw it over the back of the chair, he felt the bulk of the envelope he had stuffed inside the breast pocket. He tore it open and counted the money inside. Five hundred francs. It was far too much for correcting a rough translation. Renard felt flushed and embarrassed. Should he have accepted Viktor Barisov's gift? It had seemed harmless enough when Barisov had requested that, as a personal favor, he improve the French translation from the Russian of a portion of the forthcoming memoirs of the British defector Kim Philby. Renard had been happy enough to oblige. Why not? Especially when, as it turned out, the piece contained some details of Philby's life that he was able—with Barisov's willing permission—to cannibalize for an Agence Mondiale d'Informations report. Then Barisov had insisted on paying what he described as the "standard fee" for Renard's help, claiming that he would take it as a personal affront if Renard refused. What could he say? All the same, it was too much.

He had started on a second kir by the time Hockney and Astrid arrived together, pink-cheeked, as if they had been running. He noticed that Hockney found it hard to look him in the eyes, as if he had something to hide. As Astrid giggled with him over the opera glasses, which they took turns using to peer at the menu, a good forty feet away, Renard admitted to himself that he was indeed jealous—because the relationship excluded him. He was jealous, too, because he was certain his wife would claw away from the young American that fresh-faced innocence that caused him even to blush in the presence of a cuckolded husband. Somehow, her predatory role made it that much more painful.

Hockney had a fascinating story to tell. He had spent two weeks spying on Bonpierre and had found out things that Renard himself had not known. Hockney had logged Bonpierre's meetings with the local CIA station chief, Wittingham, for lunch at the Ramponneau and cocktails at the Intercontinental. He had even taken a couple of photographs of the two men together. Hockney discovered that Bonpierre not only had an American wife but had been consorting with another American, a secretary called Nancy, who supposedly worked for the U.S. Information Agency.

"Who would have believed it?" Renard said. "Just when we had all concluded that Bonpierre was preparing himself for canonization."

Hockney had also run down all of Bonpierre's contacts with the CIA-funded Congress for Cultural Freedom—the conferences he had attended, the projects he had personally initiated, the trips he had made that were probably paid for with CIA money.

"What I need from you," Hockney concluded, "is a detailed account of what stories Bonpierre has promoted or spiked during your time at AMI, particularly the things that would have been damaging to Vietnam or the Gaullists or that might, on the other hand, have served American propaganda interests. That would give me just about enough to publish a major exposé on a specific case of how the CIA has distorted European perceptions through the corruption of the media."

"I'll do it," Renard agreed, tearing into his carré d'agneau with added relish. The day before, Bonpierre had killed an entire story that he had painstakingly rewritten and substituted a dubious piece on a Russian defector in Stockholm who claimed that a special department of the KGB had been set up to organize deception operations against the West and was masterminding the public campaign against the CIA.

Astrid hooted with laughter when the *patronne* presented her with a pair of green china frogs engaged in oral intercourse. Bob Hockney looked away into the middle distance. My friend, Renard mentally addressed him, you have a great deal to learn.

Viktor Barisov found that he actually looked forward to his talks with Renard. It was easier for them to meet alone than with the Frenchman's wife, whose provocative behavior was always a diversion—easier for Renard, perhaps, more than for Barisov. Renard was infinitely less tedious than most of the other media assets for whom Barisov was responsible. There was a world of difference, for example, between Renard and Laurie Pritchard, the veteran Australian correspondent who had faithfully echoed the party line for the past thirty years. Pritchard, married to a Hungarian woman, had broadcast anti-American propaganda from Pyongyang during the Korean war. Now he specialized in reports from behind the Vietcong lines on the Indochina war. Pritchard was highly valued by the old school in Moscow. He was, in all respects, a trusted person. Since Moscow agreed with Hanoi that there were no North Vietnamese troops in the south, that is what Pritchard wrote. Barisov had no doubt that if Moscow declared that there were no Soviet troops in Eastern Europe, Pritchard would write that too. He had to brace himself for each encounter with the self-important Australian during his frequent visits to Paris. Though the man's sole function was to be a loudspeaker for the voice of Moscow, he appeared to regard himself as some kind of world statesman.

The amazing thing was that Pritchard still had credibility with the New Left radicals, who gave him space in their magazines. Their continued acceptance of this party hack, sloppily dressed and reeking of whiskey, was the result of their inability to distinguish between an antiwar activist and an agent of Soviet disinformation.

Pritchard was both a dogmatist and a mercenary. Renard was neither. That, no doubt, was why Pronk kept nettling Barisov to establish a more tidy relationship with the Frenchman. Their meetings, Pronk complained, were leading nowhere. Nor was Pronk above hinting that Barisov's record—already blemished by the murder of Mouflon—would not be improved if, by the time he returned to Moscow, he had failed to make any important agent recruitments in Paris. Moscow Center was inclined to judge its officers in the field by the number of valued agents they had signed on, with the same deference to formal statistics that the Americans displayed with their ridiculous body counts in Vietnam.

The carping from Pronk led Barisov to do something that not only went against standard procedure. It was also clumsy. And that, he knew even as he made the gesture, was unforgivable. Renard, over too many glasses of wine, had been complaining about the stinginess of his employers and how impossible it was for him to sustain his wife's expensive tastes. It was close enough to a hint for Barisov to move in.

"I may have a solution for you," Barisov said. "You understand the restrictions we have to suffer at ISKRA as a state-controlled news service. You suffer quite a few restrictions yourself, as a result of your boss. It occurs to me that both of us have access to important news stories that, for one reason or another, neither of us is able to publish. Perhaps we could come to some sort of arrangement to share material."

"What did you have in mind?"

70

"It's just as important to know what, or who, is behind a story as to read what is in it," the man from ISKRA explained. "For instance, it would be extremely helpful for me to know something about your correspondents in various countries, and the sources they are using. That includes the socialist countries. It may be that Bonpierre is not the only person at your news agency who maintains unusual connections."

Barisov paused to assess Renard's reactions. The Frenchman picked up the bottle of Brouilly and refilled his glass. Barisov decided to take the plunge. He checked that no one in the bistro was looking in their direction. He had picked a corner behind the bar where they were virtually out of sight.

"What I am suggesting is a normal business venture. We can trade stories and background information. For example, I can give you today the full text of the new peace proposals from the NLF that we have just forwarded to Washington. That could be a major exclusive for you."

Renard looked up with heightened interest.

"But what I'm asking from you," Barisov went on, "is rather sensitive information that may take considerable effort to collect. I think that it should be paid for at the market rates."

Renard began to object.

"Please don't misunderstand me," said the man from ISKRA. "All I am suggesting is that my news agency pay you a retainer for certain background material—a quite mundane business relationship between a journalist and a media enterprise, nothing more."

"I couldn't consider it. They'd fire me if they found out. Besides—"

"You are going to say that ISKRA is owned by the Soviet government?" Barisov interrupted. "It's better than being run by the CIA." He tapped his breast pocket. "I don't want to embarrass you," he said, "but I want to offer you a small advance."

Barisov did not take out the envelope, which contained ten crisp one-hundred-dollar bills. His antennae told him it was the wrong moment to push further. In any case, Renard was already saying, "There's no need, Viktor. My opinions aren't for sale. You wouldn't help either of us by trying to bring money into our relationship. I'll go on trying to write what I believe. And we'll go on meeting because we're friends and because sometimes we can help each other. That's the best way."

Barisov brushed a fleck of ash from his polka-dot tie. "As you like," he said.

"Tell me something, Viktor. You are KGB, aren't you?"

"I am a loyal Soviet citizen." Barisov smiled.

"You wouldn't tell me if you were, would you?"

The man from ISKRA smiled again, but his eyelids dropped like a visor.

Renard hurried home from the meeting with Barisov. He had almost forgotten that they were giving a farewell party for Bob Hockney, who was going back to the beaches of California to write his piece about the underside of European journalism.

The party was not a success. Renard felt hung over and lifeless. Hockney looked miserable the whole night. Astrid caroused as usual, but it seemed mechanical, as if she were going through the motions because that was what was expected of her. Halfway through the evening, Renard found them together in the kitchen embracing in front of the icebox. Hockney was red-eyed, as if he'd been crying.

Hockney had obviously been drinking heavily. He swayed on his feet and had to steady himself against the kitchen shelves. Renard wondered how much the young American felt for Astrid. An overwhelming physical infatuation—that much was clear. He doubted whether Astrid had the capacity to reciprocate anything beyond that level of attachment.

"Just looking for a beer," Hockney said.

Renard realized how much he liked the young American. Not many of Astrid's lovers would have bothered to try to save her husband's face, even with a trivial white lie. Renard raised his hand in a parody of papal blessing and slipped back into the living room. Was Hockney in love with Astrid? The air was tense when the two of them were together. Renard imagined Hockney would be far more distressed than Renard himself if he suspected Astrid's other nocturnal adventures. Renard was aware that his wife had taken to staying out late in the afternoons—the most convenient time to meet lovers who did not have to keep office hours. He doubted Hockney was the only one.

From Renard's own point of view, it scarcely mattered whether Hockney loved Astrid or not. Hockney was going home, and Astrid was incapable of sharing conventional love with any one man. That was why it was best for Hockney himself, if he did love her, to cut the golden chains now.

Renard insisted on playing Edith Piaf on the hi-fi. His mood became more and more maudlin as the night progressed. Before all the guests had gone, he took a bottle of wine and crawled into bed by himself. He drank the wine, watching a cold half-moon through the window.

He dozed off but woke up a couple of hours later, dehydrated, with a raging thirst. He put his mouth under the cold tap in the bathroom and gulped down mouthful after mouthful of water.

It must have been the wine talking later, at daybreak, when Astrid came to bed. Afterward, he couldn't remember what he had said to her—something to do with love, and Hockney, and offers of money from Viktor Barisov. But Astrid remembered.

Barisov was delighted to receive a telephone call from Astrid Renard. He was equally delighted to agree to her suggestion that they meet for lunch.

"Let's make it Fouquet's, my dear," he proposed. "It has to be somewhere decorous and terribly proper. Otherwise I couldn't trust myself."

Barisov was elaborately complimentary about Astrid's orange cotton suit and two-day-old hairdo. "You must always have beautiful things." He leaned closer to her across the table. "Even a pearl must have its setting."

He was impressed that Astrid came straight to the point. "Michel is too proud," she declared. "He seems to think

73

that it's immoral to make money. I am more practical. I don't see any harm in being paid for doing what you want to do."

"You are very sensible about these things," Barisov said approvingly. "I admire Michel enormously, but he can sometimes behave like a holy idiot. Did he tell you that I tried to bribe him?"

She nodded.

"What nonsense. All I suggested was a normal working relationship. When you think of the spectacular fees that American writers are being paid for magazine articles, what I was proposing to pay Michel is only a trifle anyway. I really don't see why he should feel inhibited. Every news organization in the world is ready to pay for background information."

Astrid did not attempt to diet. But she did make a ritual of eating only fruit salad on Thursdays—even if the lunch was at Fouquet's. At Barisov's signal, the waiter dutifully refilled her plate. It was her fourth helping.

"I hope Michel wasn't offended," Barisov resumed. "I was hoping to make our relationship even closer, so I could indulge in the pleasure of seeing more of you both." He squeezed her hand. "Such an engaging couple," he purred.

"We've hardly gotten to know each other," Astrid agreed, rubbing her ankle against his leg under the table. "I think Michel's being very silly. And I don't intend to let him be silly."

Barisov raised a quizzical eyebrow.

"Michel may be too proud to accept your money," Astrid said, "but I'm not. That way, we could all be satisfied. I can make sure that he does exactly what you want."

Barisov let his eyes fall from her face to her generous body, considering the volatile blend of passions that this woman contained. What could he lose by taking a gamble on Astrid? She might prove, in her own way, to be as valuable as her husband.

"You are a very clever woman," he flattered her. Barisov recommended maximum discretion. A separate bank account, in her name. Perhaps in Lille. "Shall we have a little

74

champagne to celebrate? It would go so well with those delicious profiterolles."

Astrid shook her head, her mouth full, pointing at her empty plate. The waiter came with more fruit salad.

Everyone in Paris left on vacation in August. Everyone, that year, except the Renards. Bonpierre had insisted that, because they were short staffed—one of the top editors was in the hospital—Renard would have to put off his holiday until September. Renard was convinced that this was a further effort by his chief to victimize him for his dissident views. Aching for revenge, he missed no opportunity to slip into Bonpierre's office when no one was around to take a quick look at his diary and the papers on his desk—in the hope of finding further ammunition to pass on to Hockney. He had received a postcard from Hockney, with flower people in San Francisco on the front and, on the back, a curt message that the *Barricades* piece had been delayed for a while but should be running in the October issue.

At last came September, and a chance to forget Bonpierre, Barisov, and the rest of them during a couple of weeks at Marbella. Renard was astonished by the number of suitcases Astrid had managed to fill. "Your wardrobe is big enough for a theatrical company," he complained. "How on earth do you expect me to pay for all this and take a foreign holiday as well?"

"You're not paying," said Astrid smugly.

"Well, I'd love to know who else would be willing to pick up the bill for your love affairs with Dior and Balmain." As he watched her stuff a new Givenchy dressing gown into a bag, suspicion dawned. He was no more heavily in debt than usual. In fact, most of the bills had been paid.

He grabbed Astrid's arm. "What's going on?" he demanded. "Have you become a *belle de jour*? Are you turning a quick trick with a tired businessman at lunchtime? Or working for Madame Claude? Is that where the money comes from?"

"You're a bore, Michel."

"I want an answer."

"Then ask Viktor."

"Viktor Barisov? What's he got to do with this?" Oh, but he knew. Of course he knew. The realization sucked the wind out of him, and he subsided onto the bed like a burst balloon. If Astrid was taking Barisov's money, what did that make him? He thought back over the snippets of information that Barisov had pried out of him, the stories the Russian had fed him, the extra material he had mailed on to Bob Hockney. And Barisov—Renard had no doubt about it—was an officer of the KGB. Could he honestly maintain that his relationship with Barisov of the KGB was any cleaner than that of Bonpierre with Wittingham of the CIA? He had been hooked, without even being conscious of it.

Renard slammed the lid of the suitcase shut, uncaring that the hem of a Dior dress was lapping over the edge. "You've got enough of your Soviet trousseau in there to impress the Spanish waiters," he snarled at Astrid. "Let's get on the road."

He was double-locking the door when the phone rang. To hell with it, he thought. I'm on holiday. The phone went on ringing. He turned the key the other way and reentered the apartment. The call was from the office. It was Picard, another of the deputy editors at AMI.

"You'd better come over immediately," said Picard.

"Have you people forgotten that I'm on vacation? One month late at that."

"Something's happened. It's serious."

"So is my vacation. Listen, what's all this about?" He could picture the tiny Picard, nervously tugging at the loose strands of hair that hung down the side of his forehead.

"Did you read the papers?"

"I said it's my vacation. I don't read the papers when I'm not working."

"Then you'd better read them on the way over here. I'll fill you in on the rest when you arrive."

Renard hung up in disgust. If it had been Bonpierre on

76

the line, he would have refused point-blank. But Picard was all right. He got a little overwrought, but if he said it was serious, it probably was.

"Spanish manhood will have to wait for a few hours," he said to his wife by way of explanation.

He picked up the papers at the corner *tabac* before driving to the bureau. He did not have to turn the page to see what Picard was so excited about. *Barricades* magazine had released an advance summary of Bob Hockney's piece on the CIA in Europe. The most sensational disclosure was that Jacques Bonpierre, editor-in-chief of AMI, was a contract employee of the CIA. The whole story was there: photographs of Bonpierre's meetings with Wittingham, office memoranda that showed how he had slanted the news and spiked stories that were embarrassing to the Americans, details of his activities for the Congress for Cultural Freedom and other front organizations. It was even suggested that Bonpierre had used his contacts inside the French government and intelligence services to pass secret information to his American employers.

Renard threw his arms into the air and shouted "Bravo," to the amazement of the old woman in the *tabac*. Hockney had done even better than he had expected. There was no way Bonpierre would be able to wriggle out of this. He was spiked.

Renard was surprised to find a general air of gloom at the office. Even if his own hatred for Bonpierre had not been universally shared, Renard would have expected that a few of his colleagues would be happy enough to see the back of him. Antoinette was actually blubbering.

"What's the matter with you?" he said gruffly.

"Talk to Picard."

He found Picard in Bonpierre's office, fighting a losing battle with a battery of telephones. The little man motioned him to sit.

"What's the matter?" Renard repeated himself in a merciful lull between phone calls.

"It's Bonpierre," said Picard, pulling at his sparse strands of hair.

"I know. I read the papers. We've gotten rid of the bastard at last."

"Please don't talk that way about him." Picard ignored the next phone that rang. "Bonpierre is dead. He killed himself two hours ago by jumping off the second level of the Eiffel Tower. He had to climb across the wire barrier to get over the edge," he added irrelevantly.

Just the way an American tourist might have decided to do it, Renard thought to himself.

"His wife is in the hospital in a state of shock," Picard said.

Renard was silent. The Russians had a proverb, he thought: What is written with a pen cannot be cut out with an ax. That was true for Bonpierre. A few lines in the papers had finished him, permanently. Emotionally, Renard reacted to the event with the same mixture of prurience and detachment that he experienced when, satiated himself, he reverted to the role of spectator at an orgy. He wondered how Bob Hockney would feel about it. It might be hard to accept, at twenty-three, that your first big break in journalism had cost a man's life.

The Golden Gate bridge glinted as the sun, a red fireball, fused with the Pacific. Bob Hockney was not listening to the babble of voices in the back of the car as he and his colleagues from *Barricades* drove to Valhalla, Sausalito's best-known restaurant. The magazine was throwing a victory bash for its newest star, but Hockney's mind was already elsewhere. Even before publication day, his piece on the CIA in Europe had been picked up by hundreds of newspapers around the world. Scores of telegrams had deluged the *Barricades* office, most of them addressed to Hockney personally. Only a few had been hate mail. "Would you believe a Pulitzer?" read one, from a former Berkeley classmate. A Pulitzer prize was among the least of Hockney's considerations. He knew that, as a magazine reporter, he was not eligible in any case. The prize was reserved for daily and wire service journalism—which was where he wanted to be, not just for the sake of some hypothetical prize, but in order to command the mass audience that *Barricades* could never hope to capture.

Telephone calls from as far away as Stockholm, requesting interviews with Hockney, had kept *Barricades*'s three lines tied up all day. There had even been a call from the *New York World*. A certain Ed Finkel, executive assistant to the editor-in-chief himself, had called to invite him to lunch in New York at the paper's expense to discuss future projects. It dawned on Hockney that he might be on the point of fulfilling an ambition he had nurtured all through college.

The Valhalla had been designed to resemble a fin-de-siècle sporting house, which was in keeping with the colorful past of its owner, Sally Stanford, the most celebrated madam of the century. They had to wait at the bar for their table. Before he had gotten his first drink, Hockney heard his name being paged by a female voice.

He took the call in a booth lined with quilted red satin.

"Mr. Hockney," said the caller, "this is UPI in New York. Have you heard the news?"

"What news?" As he spoke, Hockney had a sudden premonition that the news would not be good.

"The Frenchman you fingered as a CIA spy," the caller began. "Lemme see now, Jacques Bonpierre. Yeah, that's the one. He killed himself today. We'd like your reaction."

Hockney was so stunned that he almost hung up. He needed time to absorb the information—if indeed it were true. In the next fraction of a second, he realized that whatever he said now would not only be quoted around the world but might make or break his chances for the next step in his career—a job on the *New York World*.

"I think you've got the wrong party," he lied. He hoped that his voice sounded steadier than his hand; he could feel the receiver trembling against his ear as he talked. "Who did you say you wanted?"

"Excuse me," said the startled voice. "I understood you were Bob Hockney."

"Hackett's the name," Hockney continued, unhesitating, gaining assurance as he developed the fiction.

79

"Aren't you with the *Barricades* group?" the UPI reporter asked.

"You really do have the wrong party. Hold on." Hockney buttonholed the nearest waiter, slipped him a ten-dollar bill, and told him to go back to the phone, double-check the caller, and then inform him that neither Bob Hockney nor anyone else from *Barricades* was in the restaurant that night.

Now, like the soldier who suddenly discovers a bleeding wound to which he was oblivious in the heat of battle, Hockney was reeling, mentally and physically. Swaying in front of the urinal in the nearby men's room, he steadied himself with one hand against the wall. He felt strangely hollow. Bonpierre dead. The French editor had obviously taken his life because of what Hockney had written. What could he tell the people who would be calling *Barricades* in the morning? That he had simply done his job as an investigative reporter? That sounded self-righteous. That spying was not a bloodless calling? That was worse than corny—it was callous. That Bonpierre's death proved that he could not face what he had done as a news executive under contract with the CIA, and that it vindicated Hockney's article? That was an accurate statement, but it did not salve Hockney's growing sense of guilt.

Hockney told himself that he was not responsible for what had happened. It was Bonpierre who had made the choices, in his life and his death. Yet the young reporter found himself thinking about the people who had depended on the French editor: his wife, his children—if he had any. Hockney realized he did not even know whether Bonpierre had kids. In fact, he knew very little about the man. It was somehow shocking, to know so little about a man and yet drive him to suicide.

Hockney felt in no mood to celebrate with the *Barricades* party. He asked the waiter to take his host aside and explain that he was feeling very sick and had gone home.

He flopped into a cab on one side as a couple slid out the other side and into the Valhalla. Cruising back across the Golden Gate bridge, he was debating whether to ask the black driver to switch off a deafening rock-and-roll station when the disk jockey, dispensing manic patter between numbers, parodied normal station identification.

"This is station WILD, broadcasting on sixty-nine kilocycles and forty-three motorcycles and one bicycle, my own," said the announcer. "And here's our latest news flash."

Hockney wondered whether the news flash was also a joke. It wasn't.

"CIA spy jumps from world-famous landmark in Paris," said the announcer. "We'll be back in a second after this flash from your favorite breakfast food."

A few seconds later, Hockney heard the *Barricades* story mentioned, then his own name. The tone was not critical.

"One more spook bites the dust," the announcer chirped. "Well, that's the way it goes. And this is WILD, bringing you the *wild* sound of the Thumpers."

The next day, *Barricades* put out a ringing endorsement of its reporter Bob Hockney, pointing out that there had been no denial from the CIA of the allegations about Bonpierre —only the ritual "no comment." When UPI finally reached him, Hockney issued a separate, personal statement, expressing sorrow over Bonpierre's death while standing behind his original story. "If we have learned anything from this," he told the wire service, "it is that reporters should stick to reporting and stay out of espionage." Apart from the thunder from two or three conservative syndicated columnists who railed against the inexperienced young reporter who—in their view—had unwittingly fallen prey to the Soviet propaganda machine, press reaction grudgingly acknowledged that *Barricades* had blazed a new trail in investigative reporting.

That night, Hockney caught the red-eye flight to New York, leaving himself more than twenty-four hours to spend with Julia before his lunch with Leonard Rourke, the editor of the *New York World*, at the University Club. When she joined him in his hotel room after driving into the city from Sarah Lawrence, Julia expressed polite congratulations over Hockney's journalistic coup. But she was visibly cool and reserved. "Anything wrong, sweetheart?" he tested her.

"We've become strangers," she said sadly. "And it doesn't help when you take me for granted. You just blow into town and expect me to drop everything, cut classes, in order to be with you. I've got a life too, you know."

Julia got out of bed. Hockney, exhausted by the overnight flight, buried his head in the pillow.

"Now you say you might be about to land a job on the *World*. Does that mean you're going to be living in New York?"

"I don't know. And I haven't got the job yet."

"What are you really getting into, Bob? I don't understand this trouble with the Frenchman who killed himself."

"There's a tragedy every day," Hockney said curtly, not wanting to talk about it. "Bonpierre happened to be accident-prone." But, listening to himself, Hockney was appalled by his own apparent callousness. He followed Julia to the window, wrapped his arms around her shoulders, and led her gently back toward the bed.

They spent most of the day in the room, watching soaps on TV in order to avoid conversation.

At the University Club the next day, Hockney found Ed Finkel, the editor's assistant, waiting for him in the lobby. Finkel was unusually effusive.

"I hope you haven't put down roots on the West Coast, Bob," Finkel said as he led Hockney through to the dining room, where Rourke had already occupied his table. "We'd like to see you working for the paper."

No major American newspaper or TV network in the late 1960s had any kind of rational hiring policy. It was done on an ad hoc basis, through an osmotic process between the top editors—some of whom had concluded, as had Rourke's assistant, that the brightest new talent was being siphoned off into the anti-establishment underground press and had to be lured back with good jobs and above-scale salaries. To their disgust, some veteran reporters found themselves being vetted and revetted by editorial bureaucrats, only to be told weeks later that there were "no vacancies for the time being," while the underage writers of the underground press who seldom let an inconvenient fact interfere with their prejudices were hired on a whim. Rourke himself was a reluctant promoter of this trend. When Finkel had delightedly brought him the advance copy of Hockney's *Barricades* piece, Rourke had initially tried to brush it aside as irrelevant muckraking.

"What's the matter, Len?" Finkel had challenged him. "Still a member of the CIA fan club?"

Rourke had started mashing his molars, as he always did when agitated. But Finkel's most telling argument had been that if the *World* failed to hire Hockney, the competition— meaning the *Times* or, worse still, the *Washington Tribune* —certainly would.

"Why do you want to work for the *World* rather than the *Times*?" Rourke asked Hockney after the waiter had taken their order.

Hockney had anticipated the question and had rehearsed his reply.

"The *World* is a reporter's paper," said Hockney. "You're not afraid to give young reporters responsibility and a large piece of turf. You're where the action is, and that's where I want to be."

Rourke was pleased, but did not show it. In Finkel's mind, Hockney was as good as hired.

Hockney looked at Finkel, who he now understood to be his ally. Tall, with black crinkly hair, Finkel had the posture of a broken sapling. Hockney was grateful for his support but didn't trust him. He sensed that Finkel might be trying to use him in some effort to undercut Rourke.

"Where would you like to be?" the editor of the *World* asked Hockney.

"Vietnam." He guessed that might be what they both wanted to hear, but it was also an honest answer. Vietnam had hung over his formative years, a heavy, oppressive pall. He wanted to see it for himself. It was also in Vietnam that a generation of young news reporters were making the big breaks into important careers.

"Why?" Rourke asked.

"The press is one of the big problems in Vietnam."

"What does that mean?"

"There are still too many reporters in love with the war. There's too much military reporting and not enough about the political sickness. If the United States is ever going to get out of Vietnam, it will take a new style of reporting. And there I think I have a contribution to make."

"Are you married?" Finkel asked.

"No," Hockney replied, surprised by the question. Finkel had a special reason for asking. The *World* was planning to expand its Saigon bureau to compete with the *Times*'s four-man staff, and Rourke and Finkel were agreed that it was best to send single men. That way, if a correspondent got killed, there were fewer heartbreaks and insurance problems.

A week later, Hockney was filling out forms in the *World*'s personnel department. Neither he nor anyone else on the paper had expected that his departure for Saigon would be quite as hurried as it turned out to be. The *World*, like most of the American press, had disregarded the scanty reports that indicated the buildup of a massive new Vietcong offensive.

When Finkel called him to convey the editor's instructions to get himself on the first plane to Saigon, Hockney knew he was not going in completely cold. His friend from Paris, Michel Renard, had been transferred to Vietnam immediately after Bonpierre's suicide. The shakeup inside his news agency had cost Renard his old job as deputy editor-in-chief. The new management considered it wise to retire or shunt aside all the senior journalists who had been involved in the Bonpierre controversy and appoint a political neutral as the new chief editor.

Renard was quite sanguine about his assignment to Saigon; it was an escape from the social hurly-burly in which Astrid had trapped them in Paris. Astrid protested bitterly about being exiled to the outer provinces, but Renard consoled her with the thought that she was bound to reign supreme among the European colony in Saigon.

Before even arranging his plane ticket, Hockney sent a cable to Renard at his bureau in Saigon.

Vietnam
1968

The nose of the C-130 dipped without warning. So they were diving toward the burning city. Bob Hockney

1

BOB HOCKNEY tightened his seat belt as the C-130 taxied along the runway of the American military airfield outside Bangkok. The loadmaster moved between the legs of the men who were crowded on board, handing out what looked to Hockney like pink chewing gum. He took his pellet and popped it into his mouth, but he found that it tasted like wax. The old grunt on the red canvas seat next to him nudged the soldier on his other side and pointed. "It's for your *ears*, asshole," someone hooted derisively. Red-faced, Hockney spat the wax into his hand, tugged it into halves, and stuck it in his ears. He had a lot to learn before he could call himself a war reporter.

His brand new blue-and-white striped seersucker suit was caked in dust and grease after the all-night wait at the air base. He was conscious that he looked absurdly out of place among his fellow passengers, who were mostly GIs in battle fatigues. There were a couple of tough-looking civilians in well-cut safari suits whom Hockney could not quite place. As the plane hauled itself off the ground, Hockney saw the point of the wax. It was the noisiest aircraft he had ever traveled on.

Two hours out of Bangkok, the C-130 shuddered through a pall of thick black smoke. The darkened interior of the plane lit up suddenly, suffused with an eerie orange glow. Twisting his neck around painfully to peer through the porthole behind his back, Hockney realized that the light was the reflection of huge fires, raging out of control in the city below. Uneasily, he recalled what the major had said in the briefing before takeoff. Tan Son Nhut, Saigon's airport, was still secure. But street battles were raging not far away, and there was a lot of sniper fire. Their plane would not be making a normal approach to the runway; it would have to drop sharply from three thousand feet.

The nose of the C-130 dipped without warning, and they were diving toward the burning city. Now Hockney could see tracer flares. A bullet whistled through the fuselage but lodged harmlessly in the bulkhead of the plane. Hockney held his breath as they made their final descent. As the plane bumped to a halt along the tarmac of Tan Son Nhut, he pulled his bag free from the pile of luggage lashed to the deck along the middle of the cabin and joined the queue of GIs, sprinkled with a few correspondents, waiting to climb down the ramp at the back of the plane. "It's after curfew," the major bellowed at them. "Everything's shut—police, immigration, everything. You newsmen can sort out the formalities with the Vietnamese press office in the morning. An Army bus is waiting to take you into town."

Hockney listened for gunfire. All he could hear was the roar of war planes taking off from what was frequently described as the world's second-busiest airport, after Chicago's O'Hare.

The clammy heat wrapped itself around Hockney, bathing his body in sweat, as it had done the day before in Bangkok. He mopped his face awkwardly with his sleeve. Gripping his bag, he started to file behind the others toward the Army bus.

"Uh." Hockney jumped as a powerful hand connected with his shoulder blade.

"What's a nice boy like you doing in a hell hole like this?" inquired a familiar French-accented voice.

"Michel!" Hockney wheeled around, with genuine relief, to face his friend from Paris. "You got my message. But—how on earth did you find out when my plane was getting in?"

"No problem for an old hand. Here, give that to me." Renard took charge of Hockney's bag. "I suppose you've heard of MACV?" That was the acronym for Military Assistance Command Vietnam, the official euphemism used to describe President Johnson's expeditionary army. "Your military command may not be very efficient at keeping the Vietcong out of Saigon," Renard continued as he led Hockney toward a cream Renault that he had somehow managed to drive onto the tarmac. "But they're a mine of useless information, like the estimated arrival time of the first batch of correspondents coming in from Bangkok."

"How did you beat the curfew?"

"You can beat any regulation here if you know the price," Renard replied, deliberately mysterious.

"I heard there's fighting all over town," said Hockney as Renard drove through the airport. "What's the story?"

"The Vietcong have been pushed back from most of the city, but they are fairly solidly dug in at Cholon. Don't worry, Bob. You'll sleep sound enough at the Caravelle. As a matter of fact, we can watch a good war movie there tonight."

"War movie? In the middle of all this?" Hockney was puzzled.

"You'll see."

Renard slowed as they approached a double line of kerosene drums, strung together with barbed wire across the road.

"*Bonsoir. Ça va?*" Renard sounded cheerful enough as he flashed his curfew pass at the Vietnamese guard. "You'll find your French useful here," he observed to Hockney as they were waved on. "It will mark you out from the other Americans."

A few hundred yards on, Renard swerved to avoid a man's body, sprawled messily across the edge of the road. Hockney looked back at the corpse as the car picked up speed again. It was the first time he had seen a dead man.

"Curfew breaker," Renard explained, matter of factly. "They shoot them on sight and dispose of the bodies in the morning."

"How does Astrid take all of this?" Hockney pictured Astrid the last time he had seen her.

"She's living in a world of her own. Wait and see."

Yes, Hockney mentally agreed. Astrid Renard was probably tougher than either of them. Images of the bedroom flashed through his mind, and he dallied for a moment with the thought of reopening the affair he had left behind in Paris a few months before. He decided it would be wiser to abstain, at least for the time being. It was not that seeing Julia again had made him inhibited; he would not accept that his feelings for one woman should deprive him of all others. It was not even that he wished to avoid complications with Renard, on whom he would be leaning very heavily for guidance in an unknown and untested environment. It was that, for the first time, he was entering the maelstrom of war, with a mission that dwarfed any personal attachment: to end the war.

The Caravelle Hotel, on the corner of Tu Do Street, was heavily shuttered against the uncertainties of the night. A sleepy Indian porter unlocked the door for them.

"I had a lot of trouble booking you in here," Renard remarked as they stepped into the lobby. "Luckily I have a friend at reception. His heart is with the Vietcong, but his pocketbook is with the American press. That makes him an authentic citizen of Saigon. There he is behind the desk. Slip him twenty dollars when you check in and you'll have a useful friend—for the next week."

The lobby was in darkness, apart from the small lamp on the reception desk. Officially, the blackout that had been ordered when the Vietcong launched the Tet offensive was still in force.

"You'd better keep your curtains closed," Renard advised as they rode in the elevator up to Hockney's room on the third floor. "Although I doubt whether the police would bother to pay a call if they saw your light on. Nearly everyone in this hotel is a reporter. It's the same with the Continental across the square. If your American colleagues had known what the Vietcong intended to do with these places, they might have looked for a room elsewhere."

"What do you mean?" asked Hockney, turning his key in the door. They entered an anonymous room with twin beds and a gray linoleum floor.

"Along with the American embassy, the Vietcong planned to occupy the Caravelle and the Continental and hold all the American correspondents hostage, pending an agreement by Washington to negotiate with them. Some guns were found inside this hotel." Renard tested the springs on one of the beds before squatting on the edge.

"The guns had been smuggled in as TV equipment by Vietcong posing as local cameramen for the American networks. Come to think of it," he added puckishly while Hockney started to hang up his suits, "locking up the American press corps for a few days would not have been such a bad idea. Your colleagues would have been exposed to a different viewpoint. At least they would have been forced to make contact with Vietnamese other than bar girls."

"Come on," Hockney protested, "they're not all that way."

Renard peeked inside Hockney's bag, searching for the duty-free whiskey. He extracted the bottle, three-quarters full, with a mock whoop of triumph. He found two tumblers in the bathroom and poured them each a generous slug.

Hockney pulled back the edge of the curtains a fraction, to look out on the two sandbagged machine gun posts in front of the National Assembly building.

"What's that?" he asked Renard.

"That's the democracy your government says it's fighting for. Mr. Thieu's rubber-stamp assembly. Well, are you ready for a war movie?"

"I'd rather have another drink."

"You can have that too."

Renard ushered him out to the elevator and up to the bar on the top floor of the hotel. As they entered, Hockney was deafened by the noise of the Muzak, which was blaring out a warped version of "I Left My Heart in San Francisco." Correspondents were fighting for space along the bar, trying to order their drinks.

"Michel, how goes it?" someone called from the end of the bar. Others heard Renard's name and shouted "Greetings" and "Bonsoir." Hockney realized that his friend must have become something of a celebrity.

An American reporter accosted him. "Michel, you're the man who knows everything that goes on in this town. What about an exclusive?" Hockney noticed the network of purple veins that stood out on the man's cheeks, through the deep suntan.

"All right." Renard smiled patronizingly. "Here's your scoop. Ho Chi Minh flies in tomorrow morning, 9:30 A.M., at Tan Son Nhut—the civilian terminal." He turned to retrieve the two vodka tonics he had ordered from the bar.

"Hey," a drunken Australian journalist thundered, "hold the story. The frog forgot to tell you Uncle Ho is arriving in a pine box."

"I think the war movie must have started," Renard said to Hockney, ignoring the Australian. "Let's get up on the roof."

Renard steered Hockney toward a winding staircase. It led up to a rooftop terrace where reporters were standing shoulder to shoulder along the railings, watching the tracers and the flash of gunfire around the tormented city. Lit up by a spotlight, with his back to the tracer flares and protected by a tin helmet, was a figure that Hockney instantly recognized. "What the hell is going on?" Walter Cronkite asked rhetorically. "I thought we were winning the war." He was getting ready to deliver an on-the-spot report to America, giving the lie to President Johnson's claims about the progress of the Vietnam war.

"Look!" someone shouted above Cronkite's voice. "There goes Spookie."

"Who's Spookie?" Hockney asked, but immediately bit his lip. The question would expose him as the new boy.

"Spookie," replied another voice in the dark, "is Puff the Magic Dragon." This left Hockney more mystified than before. Had he walked into a madhouse?

"Spookie," Renard explained, "is an old Dakota, converted into a gunship. It has three Gatling guns that fire simultaneously from where the passenger seats used to be. You can imagine how much lead the thing can pump into a crowded street."

"Old Puff can lay down one bullet per square foot in an area the size of a football field in three seconds flat." Yet another voice joined the conversation. "If you're lying down, you've had it. The only way to avoid being zapped is to lean into it. But Charlie hasn't worked that out yet."

Hockney stared incredulously at the speaker—a bullet-

93

headed, stocky figure in fresh starched combat fatigues. "Who the hell is *that*?" he whispered to Renard.

"Oh, he's from *Stars and Stripes*. A war freak, as you'd expect."

Bullet Head overheard, and was roused to further comment. "See that?" He pointed, over the city roofs, to a new explosion of light in the middle distance. "Spookie's dropping flares. If Charlie's down there, he'll be lit up like a dummy in a Fifth Avenue store window at Christmas." Hockney visualized men in black pajama suits ducking and running. "Do you know, kid," Bullet Head continued enthusiastically, "just one of those sodium flares costs Uncle Sam eighty dollars? And they drop four thousand of those flares every night. Do you know how much that works out to a week?"

"Beats me," said Hockney, unimpressed.

"That's over two million clams a week. Just to give Charlie something to read by. And that's peanuts. We're spending eighty million dollars a day to fight this war."

"Do you want me to applaud?" Hockney burst out. "For that kind of money, we could give every Vietcong cadre a split-level house, a convertible, and a college education—not to mention what we could do for the blacks back home."

Bullet Head glowered, transferring his gaze from Hockney to Renard. "You been working this kid over, Frenchie?" There was a pounding of mortar shells, and Bullet Head left to peer over the railing in the direction of the new action.

"What part of the city is that?" Hockney asked Renard, pointing toward the flares.

"Cholon, Saigon's twin city. That's where the Chinese live. It's only a mile and a half away. If you want to see the war at closer hand, I can take you over there."

"I can't wait."

2

BUT HOCKNEY'S FIRST DAY in Vietnam was spent
far from the war—it seemed to him—in and around the
street that *Newsweek* magazine had once described as
"Saigon's Fifth Avenue." The comparison was a very bad
joke, Hockney decided as he trundled back and forth along
Tu Do Street to visit, in succession, Dick Sharpe, the
World's bureau chief; the Vietnamese press office; and
Minh's, the tailor shop where he had himself measured
for a couple of safari suits, the uniform of the well-dressed
reporter about Saigon. Making his rounds, he had to fend
off the beggars and the early shift of bar girls. A war
orphan with beautiful eyes and no legs held out her hand
from a tiny cart on the sidewalk. Hockney stuffed piasters
into her palm, trying not to look. Marking him as a soft
touch, a ragged boy—eleven at most—immediately accosted him. "You want girl, mister? My sister number-one
girl." Hockney hurried on, but was intercepted by a woman
cradling a horribly burned baby. "Napalm," he thought he
heard her say as she shook her begging cup.

The heat, the stench, and the human anguish made him
feel queasy. Dodging the Hondas, he crossed the road to
the old-fashioned Continental Hotel. The bar girls twittered
like birds as he ambled along the terrace, looking for a
table. They had an unerring instinct for a new arrival in
town. Once he had settled himself into a bamboo chair,
armed with a vodka tonic, Hockney was besieged by a
whole procession of girls, some of them—he thought—
surprisingly attractive. One, in particular, was a perfect
Oriental beauty—apart from an ugly tattoo on her left
arm, no doubt the relic of some Marine Corps lover.
Hockney waved them all away. "You no like?" the girl
with the tattoo protested, in a tone that implied she
thought Hockney must be insane. "I no like," he confirmed, unyielding.

Hockney brooded over the press release on the President's latest statement that he had picked up at the *World* bureau. The President was still trying to deny that Tet was a Communist victory, quoting dubious casualty statistics indicating that the Vietcong had suffered intolerable losses. Bureau chief Sharpe received official body counts with weather-beaten cynicism. Hockney, fresh from New York, knew that nobody took them seriously over *there*. "What people say about Tet back home," he had lectured Sharpe, "is that it's proof we have lost this war. It's the beginning of the end."

"Maybe," Sharpe had replied, more cautious. "But don't be too sure. The war could go on for another decade."

But Hockney was certain it wouldn't. The American press wouldn't *let* the war go on for another ten years. He had taken to Sharpe, despite the bureau chief's reserve. Sharpe had even lent him a bush shirt and a pair of jungle boots until he sorted out his own wardrobe. But Sharpe had not been exactly brimming over with advice and suggestions about his own role in the *World*'s coverage of the war. Sharpe had merely told him to turn up at the routine briefing for correspondents at the American propaganda center, JUSPAO—and Hockney could guess at the quality of these briefings from the fact that they were referred to among the press corps as the "Five O'Clock Follies."

It struck him that his bureau chief might regard him more as a competitor than as a colleague. He had arrived in Saigon with a big reputation, although he was well aware that it rested on a single lead article in *Barricades*. All the same, Sharpe might well view him as someone who was out to grab the big scoops, overshadowing the others in the bureau. Sharpe might also see him as a threat in another sense. Hockney's instant fame had been the product of an exposé on the CIA, and Sharpe depended heavily on maintaining good contacts with American officialdom in Vietnam. In their first chat, Sharpe had already hinted that he would not welcome embarrassing disclosures on what the CIA was doing in Vietnam. But Hockney had heard that 10 percent of the Agency's operatives were now stationed there, and they would constitute an obvious target for him.

So Hockney was left with a problem. How could he get ahead of the field? What could he produce that none of the hundreds of other American correspondents who were flooding into Vietnam, notebooks at the ready, would be able to match? His mind, drifting back to the flares over Cholon that he had watched from the roof of the Caravelle, settled on a possible answer. He had imagined the Vietcong, fighting and dying under the sodium flares, as a faceless enemy. That was the way the rest of the American press corps—and therefore the American public—saw them too. But why should the enemy remain faceless? Why couldn't he himself, instead of wasting time at the Five O'Clock Follies, establish direct contact with the Vietcong and write their story?

In the midst of the Tet offensive, with thousands of people being killed, the idea could be insane. Hockney had been told only that morning of a French photographer who had been badly wounded trying to get in close to the Vietcong lines in Cholon. On the other hand, the Vietcong were still holding out in parts of the Chinese city, and this could offer a tremendous opportunity—if he had the guts and the know-how to take advantage of it.

As Hockney considered the options, a war veteran, missing a leg, hobbled along the terrace and thrust a document containing his life story under his nose. The waiter shooed him away.

As he watched the limbless Vietnamese staggering down the hotel steps, Hockney realized that if he tried to get himself across the lines in Cholon by waving a white flag, he would stand a reasonable chance of ending up in the same condition, or worse. But the lure was strong. Unless the Vietcong managed to kill the American ambassador, he was confident that no news story from Vietnam would draw bigger headlines at home than an eyewitness account of a reporter who had visited the Vietcong in action and returned to tell their side of the story. His one advantage was that he knew someone who understood infinitely more about the Vietcong than the *World*'s bureau chief or the gaggle of reporters on the roof of the Caravelle: Michel Renard.

The Five O'Clock Follies were held earlier than usual because of the curfew. The daily briefing took place in the ground-floor auditorium of the JUSPAO building, just two blocks away from the Continental. Dick Sharpe was waiting in the lobby to give Hockney a guided tour.

"Anything you want, you just ask for in this building. All the Army types you'll see around are here to serve us." As he handed Hockney his JUSPAO press credentials, Sharpe added, "By the way, congratulations. You're a major now." Hockney looked incredulous. "All correspondents hold assimilated rank," Sharpe explained. "It counts only in deciding who gets a seat on a military flight. But don't let that go to your head. There are plenty of colonels ahead of us on the lists."

Sharpe led Hockney along the corridor, giving him a rapid description of what went on behind each door. A thickset, ginger-haired officer came marching toward them.

"Here's the key guy," said Sharpe. "Meet Captain Briggs. He's the man you have to ask for a chopper."

"Yeah," said Briggs, nodding curtly at Hockney. "I'm the one who provides facilities for anyone who's interested in running down the war effort."

"Are they all like that?" Hockney asked his bureau chief as they advanced along the corridor.

"Oh, Briggs isn't a bad guy. You can see he's a Goldwater type, of course. But we get all sorts down here."

The two-hundred-seat auditorium was jammed. There were two podiums on the platform—one for the military briefer, the other for the civilian.

"This is where the Saigon analysts try to fool us that they know what's happening up the length and breadth of the country," Sharpe commented in an undertone. "If there's any resemblance between what they tell you here and what you find out for yourself in the field, it's purely coincidental."

"Hey, Dick." A reporter in the row behind tapped Sharpe's shoulder as they sat down. "Did you hear the ambassador is giving a briefing? Phoenixlike, he will rise up from the ashes of his embassy and extol America's historic victory in Vietnam."

"Yeah," said Sharpe. He looked at Hockney. "Ambassador Bunker's briefing is right after this. You'd better take plenty of notes in here. I want you to write the daily wrapup so I can take care of the ambassador. This is just routine stuff. All you have to do is make sure you spell the names right. It'll be a load off my back if I can persuade New York to kill these daily war wrapups for good. No one understands them back home."

Hockney looked distinctly unenthused. It was not the way he had planned to initiate his career as a war reporter.

An overweight major appeared on the platform and cleared his throat. A titter of laughter ran round the room. "This one's a real gem," Sharpe said to Hockney without bothering to lower his voice. "He's known around here as Credibility Gap."

"Good afternoon," the military briefer began. His pained expression provoked more snickers among the reporters. "I have nothing to add to the release." Hockney glanced at the bald body counts on the handout he had found on his seat. Some of the snickers turned into guffaws. "If you've got nothing to add to the release, how about subtracting from it, Major?" shouted one correspondent. The Major blinked.

"I can make just one addition." The briefer corrected himself. "That is to give an explanation of why you see us comparatively void of additional ground information at this time. This is because there is no more available to plug the gaps in the existing situation apart from those we've already closed in the past and-there-are-no-casualty-updates."

The briefer began to run his words together, as if he imagined they would make more sense that way.

"Did you get that?" Sharpe asked Hockney.

"I look forward to additional casualty updates in tomorrow morning's release." The briefer plowed on. "Right now, I will answer as many questions as possible, keeping in mind that there are numerous events taking place all over the area and it is impossible to keep a running account of everything that is going on at this time."

"He must have learned his syntax from General Westmoreland," Hockney murmured to Sharpe.

"It's either that or cerebral palsy."

Hockney was quick on his feet with a question. "What is the state of the fighting in Cholon?" he asked the briefer. He pronounced the name of the Chinese city like *colon*. A few reporters laughed, thinking it was a deliberate slip of the tongue to fox the Major.

"Colon?" the briefer queried. "I am sorry, sir, I'm not familiar with that location." There was more laughter from the assembled correspondents.

Hockney, embarrassed and annoyed, pursued his question. "I'm asking about a place that is only a mile or so down the road and has a population of two million Chinese."

"Oh, you mean *Cholon.*" The briefer smiled benignly on Hockney, delighted to have a rare chance to score off a reporter. "That is a fluid situation, sir. There is still some house-to-house fighting going on. But I understand the South Vietnamese expect to have the area cleared within two or three days."

Hockney realized that if he was going to visit the Vietcong positions in Cholon, he would have to get moving.

"Is it true," he asked the briefer, "that South Vietnamese fighter-bombers strafed parts of Cholon this morning?"

"I have nothing on that, sir." The briefer looked apologetic. "But right after this," he offered, determined to help, "the civilian briefer will be able to fill you in on the latest Vietcong atrocities in Cholon." This was received with an almost universal groan among the correspondents.

"You can skip the civilian briefing," Sharpe indicated to Hockney. "That's just CIA bullshit. You'd better get back to the bureau and write your war wrapup."

"But Jesus," said Hockney, feeling increasingly rebellious as he scanned the press release again. "I have fuck-all to write about."

"That, my boy, will be the daily test of your ingenuity," Sharpe said smugly. "Come on, let's go. We'll pick up a

pedicab and you can drop me off at the embassy." Most of
the other correspondents joined them in a rush to the door
as the civilian briefer began a graphic description of Vietcong executions in Cholon.

Sharpe stopped the pedicab outside the big concrete pill-
box on stone stilts that was the American embassy in Saigon. No windows showed through the masonry rocket
shield that protected the building. But the shield had been
punctured by the Vietcong's antitank rockets on the last
night in January, and the polished granite slab by the front
door that bore the seal of the United States had been
shattered.

Hockney was surprised that the damage seemed to be
only superficial. "From what I read in the papers," he said,
"I thought the embassy had been reduced to a heap of
rubble."

"That was a little exaggerated," Sharpe conceded. He
himself had filed a report suggesting the embassy had been
burned out. "Ambassador Bunker was back in his bunker
by noon the next day. But you've heard of journalistic
license."

3

THE HOUSE that Renard had found for himself
was worthy of a French rubber planter in the days of
empire, Hockney decided as he picked his way along a
bamboo arcade, enveloped by bougainvillea, to the door of
the whitewashed villa. Remembering Astrid in Paris, he
wondered whether she thought of the arcade as her tunnel
of love.

A wrinkled Vietnamese manservant who looked exactly
like Ho Chi Minh led him into an airy sitting room that
opened onto an interior courtyard. Astrid was draped over a
sofa, leafing idly through a copy of *Paris-Match*. When she
saw Hockney, she let the magazine fall to the floor and,
without moving from the sofa, stretched out her arms to

him, inviting. He leaned over her and kissed her full on the mouth.

"Mmm," she purred. "It's good to feel you. It's been far too long." Using Hockney's arm for support, she rose languorously to her feet. "I couldn't believe it when Michel said you were coming. It will be just like the old days."

Holding her waist with both hands, Hockney stepped back a pace. "My God, you're lovelier than ever," he said. It was not flattery. With her light tan, her hip-hugging raw silk skirt, and a generous cleavage showing through her casually buttoned blouse, Astrid was more compelling than he remembered. Letting his hands slide from her body, he took another pace backward, resolving to keep his distance—unless or until he could sort out the clash of emotions she had rekindled inside him.

"Where's Michel?" he asked.

"He's on his way. Sit down and have a drink. The heat must be killing you."

Hockney admitted that it was. The heat, and the smell. He had decided that the city smelled of rotting fish, mixed with the blue haze of exhaust fumes from the G.I.-imported Hondas and the Vespas that seemed to be America's main contribution to Vietnamese society—apart from hybrid, unwanted babies in back alleys and the inescapable racket of transistor radios.

"Now, let me tell you who's coming," Astrid continued after he had selected the longest drink from a tray. "We have an extra girl for you. If you look at her too much, I'll be insanely jealous. She's the prettiest girl at the Cercle Sportif, which is better than being Miss Saigon. Her name is Nguyen Canh Lan. We call her Lani. You'll like her even more because she's political. She's in with all the third-force politicians—you know, the ones who say 'a plague on both your houses.' "

"Who else is coming?"

"Well, there's Theophile Marchand. He's a doctor. You'll enjoy talking to him about his work. He specializes in social diseases—you know, the delicate ones. That means he knows *everyone*. He's been here for ages. Now he's going out with a girl from the American embassy who's young enough to be his daughter. Disgusting." She made a face of simulated disapproval and put her hand on Hockney's knee.

She made no attempt to remove her hand when Michel Renard walked into the room, so Hockney jumped to his feet to greet his friend.

"How have you enjoyed your first day?" Renard asked.

Long-faced, Hockney described the tedium of the Five O'Clock Follies. When he came to the exchange with the military briefer on Cholon, Renard snorted.

"What have you heard?" Hockney asked him.

"The South Vietnamese are pouring in their artillery. There have been more air strikes too. Fires are blazing throughout the city. But the Vietcong still aren't pulling back. With the pounding they are taking, the ones who are holding on must be real kamikazes."

Hockney could see his plan for visiting the Vietcong going up in the smoke of a howitzer shell. All the same, he seized his moment to try it out on Renard. When he had finished, Renard whistled in disbelief. "That would be one way to ensure that you'll fly home in a rubber body bag," the Frenchman commented acidly. He proceeded to explain how a Vietnamese free-lance cameraman had been captured by the Vietcong, who were on the point of shooting him when an American gunship appeared and hovered over their heads, causing them to flee for cover. "That's a bigger risk than I would take for a story," Renard concluded.

There was the noise of guests arriving in the hall. "Can we talk about it?" Hockney pleaded.

"We can always *talk*."

Over dinner, Hockney was painfully aware that he held the attention of the pretty Vietnamese girl beside him. He tried to maneuver a morsel of raw fish toward his mouth with his chopsticks. He had almost succeeded when the piece of fish fell off and plopped into his lap.

"Bob, use your fork," Astrid called from across the table. "Nobody minds."

Hockney turned to his attractive neighbor. "Tell me

honestly," he asked her, "what do the Vietnamese think of us gauche Americans?"

"I don't think you really want to know," she said impassively.

Hockney was astonished by her coolness. "But I do," he protested.

"That would make you different from most of the American reporters who come here. The answer to your question is very simple. We hate the Americans." There was not a flicker of emotion on Lani's delicate face. From what the Renards had told her about Bob Hockney, she knew that he was opposed to the war. But she had also learned that the surefire way to enlist maximum support from American liberals was to insult their country. "You need only look around to see why," she continued. "Your countrymen are incinerating our countryside and turning our women into whores and our generals into pimps because they can't grasp the difference between nationalism and communism."

The girl from the American embassy—Debbie, Astrid had called her—looked embarrassed.

"I agree with you," Hockney said to Lani. "Don't confuse the American people with the government's policy. Some of us have been fighting to stop this war on another front back home. You've read about the demonstrations. I was involved in those back at Berkeley. I'm sure that public opinion in the United States will eventually force the President to end the war."

"How many more years will that take?" Lani challenged him. "How many more people have to die?"

"I wish I knew the answer. But I think I know where it lies. It lies with the media. If we can bring home the full horror of what is happening here, it won't just be the kids on campus who are protesting."

"What do you plan to do about it?" Although Lani's manner was rude, Hockney now sensed that there was no hostility in her voice. Under the glass-topped table, he could see the tips of her tiny feet, sheathed in white sandals, poking out from beneath the hem of her simple black-and-yellow *ao dai*.

"Well," Hockney replied, "I certainly don't intend to sit around in a bar all day waiting for my next handout from the military briefers."

"That doesn't quite answer Lani's question." Dr. Marchand joined the conversation for the first time. "I think you are absolutely right on the role of the media, Mr. Hockney. I think the press coverage will determine how long the United States goes on fighting a war it cannot possibly win. But I would be very interested to know what, in specific terms, you feel could help most to change public perceptions."

The doctor had a mellifluous voice, a voice that would have been very pleasant to listen to, Hockney thought, had it not been part of an excessively unctuous bedside manner.

"It's much harder to hate an enemy with a human face than one that is just a sinister caricature," Hockney said thoughtfully. "The image of the Vietcong that has been created by the American administration is one of Communist terrorists in black pajamas, killing on the orders of Hanoi and Moscow. I think that the most important thing that could be done, journalistically, would be to get close to the Vietcong and tell the American public who they are and what they really want."

"Some Western journalists have tried to do that," the doctor observed. "Especially that Australian Laurie Pritchard."

"Yes," said Hockney. "But Pritchard doesn't really have an audience in the United States, except among the Old Left. He doesn't get printed in the *World*, for example."

"You are saying that you are in a better position than Pritchard to report on the NLF," Lani interpreted for him.

"Yes," Hockney agreed. "I'm ready to meet the NLF and report their views fairly. My only problem is getting to them."

"It's not difficult to meet the NLF," Lani said. "They're all around you." Her tone made Hockney wonder whether Lani herself was a Vietcong supporter, or perhaps part of an active cadre. The idea excited him.

"I'm talking about the real thing," Hockney explained.

"I mean the guys with guns who are shooting it out over there in Cholon."

"You should not imagine that the only people in the NLF are the ones who wear black pajamas and carry guns," the doctor said. His tone suggested he was trying to soothe a hypochondriac patient. "The NLF also means the man who drives your pedicab, the waiter who serves you in a restaurant, and sometimes the government official who speaks loudly in praise of the Thieu regime but is secretly plotting its overthrow."

"The NLF means the boy who changes your sheets at the Caravelle," Lani contributed, with the first hint of a smile. "And the bar girl who offers to share them with you."

"Okay," said Hockney. "I accept all that. I still have a problem. I'm willing to write any number of stories that will tell what the Vietcong are really like and what they are fighting for. But that could be a waste of time unless I get to where the action is. The only way I can ensure *that* is to walk right into the middle of this war and talk to the Vietcong where they are fighting and dying. As far as I can see, that means some street corner in Cholon. Now, can any of you suggest to me how I might manage to do that?" Hockney's eyes interrogated Lani, the doctor, and Renard in turn.

The doctor opened his mouth, as if about to speak. But then his glance shifted to Debbie, the girl from the American embassy, who rattled her spoon as she scooped up the last of the lychees in her bowl. The doctor frowned imperceptibly and remained silent.

"We'll all put on our thinking caps," Renard reassured Hockney. "But you should remember that it's no circus over in Cholon. Have you ever been under fire?"

"I'm prepared to take the risk." Hockney was conscious that his inexperience was showing.

"There's a first time for everything," Renard said, slightly patronizing. "Now, let's move next door for coffee."

Renard shepherded the women, and then Hockney, into the living room. But Renard himself and the doctor did not join them for another twenty minutes. Hockney guessed from their absence that there must be a special understanding between the two men. What he had no way of knowing was that the doctor was a senior member of the French Communist Party who conveyed information from his extensive network of informants in Vietnam to the Soviet embassy in Paris during his frequent visits there. Nor could he know that his friend Michel Renard, who had at first resisted Viktor Barisov's attempt to compromise him by bribing his wife, had finally reconciled himself to accepting Soviet guidance. Renard did not regard himself as a KGB agent, but the KGB regarded him as a singularly important asset—less for the information he could glean on the American military machine in Vietnam, although this was considerable, than for the avuncular influence he could bring to bear on the American press corps in Saigon. In some ways, Renard was proving to be more valuable in Vietnam than he had been as deputy editor of a Paris news agency. He agreed with Barisov and the doctor—who acted as his control agent in Saigon—that the most important theme to develop in the Western media was that the Vietcong comprised a broad coalition of opposition groups, fully independent of Hanoi and Moscow. Thus he had proved a willing collaborator in their efforts to disinform the American press. The difference was that Renard had initially believed in the image of the Vietcong he had been assigned to promote. He had been almost as innocent as Hockney. His acquaintance with Viktor Barisov and the doctor had taught him better.

In the doctor's view, Hockney's plan to visit the Vietcong in Cholon had tremendous journalistic potential but was absurdly dangerous. Clearly, Hockney would need a guide.

"I can't order you to do it," he said to Renard.

"I'll take him," Renard responded. He wondered afterward whether he was developing a death wish.

"It mustn't look like a setup," the doctor stressed. "He must be treated exactly as any outsider would be treated."

When they joined the others, Lani was asking Hockney a series of questions about his childhood and his time at Berkeley. Seeing the doctor, she rose to leave.

"May I take you home?" Hockney offered.

"Another time." She excused herself.

"I hope there will be one soon."

The doctor did not linger for coffee. "Good luck," he said to Hockney. Then he whisked Lani and Debbie, who looked more bewildered than ever, into a powder blue Citroën.

Ten minutes later, Hockney extricated himself with difficulty from Astrid's lingering embrace at the door. Renard walked with him to the end of the arcade of purple bougainvillea.

"I've been mulling over your plan," said Renard as he took Hockney's arm. "On your own, it would be suicidal. You would need to go with someone who knows Cholon well. Would you have any objection to me as your traveling companion?"

"Are you serious?"

"Of course."

"That would be tremendous."

"I will have to do some homework," Renard said matter-of-factly. "The last news was that there are still several blocks occupied by the Vietcong that the fighting has not yet reached. But the position is changing from one hour to the next."

Renard suggested that Hockney wait at his hotel for a message the following morning. "May I offer one word of sartorial advice?" the Frenchman concluded. "Don't wear anything that looks remotely military. Minh suits are not in fashion with the Vietcong."

4

HOCKNEY had chosen a blue-and-red striped shirt and jeans as the least military combination in his wardrobe. He was amazed by his friend's coolness as Renard weaved his car around burned-out wrecks and bomb craters, bluffing his way through the last roadblocks and an arrogant stare and a distant wave of an identity card.

"This is Cholon," Renard murmured, arching an eye-brow above his dark aviator glasses. Hockney became aware of an odd lull around them. He could not make out any soldiers or military vehicles ahead.

"What's happened to the war?" he asked Renard.

Then, through the windshield of the Renault, Hockney saw them first: three South Vietnamese Skyraiders, break-ing formation over the heart of the Chinese city.

"Michel! Up there!" Hockney yelled.

Renard slammed on the brakes. "Out!" he ordered. "Get out and hit the road!"

Hockney did not question the urgency in his friend's voice. Belly down in the ditch beside the road, he cocked his head to watch the first jet diving toward a target he could not see through the clouds of billowing black smoke. When it released its rockets, they left a blue-gray trail in the air. The other jets wheeled to follow the attack path of the lead plane. Until the first explosion, the scene seemed as remote to Hockney as the spectacle from the roof of the Caravelle, as remote as a war movie. The first bang made the ground vibrate under his stomach and set his teeth chattering. For a few seconds after the rocket went off, a great stillness descended over everything; he thought he had been deafened. Nosing down into the dirt, he pressed his hands over his ears. The next five explosions were only slightly muffled. When Hockney raised his head again, he saw South Vietnamese soldiers taking shelter in the door-ways of the line of buildings on the other side of the main road from Saigon. Behind, there was the rattle of machine guns and the crunch of mortars. Twenty minutes from his hotel, Hockney had found the war.

"Bob," Renard called from the ditch across the road. "I think it's safe to move now."

Hockney cautiously propped himself up on his elbows and peered under the car to see what Renard was doing. He could make out the shape of a man just beyond the front wheels.

"Michel?" he called. The shape did not speak or move.

He hauled himself out of the ditch and crawled around the car on his hands and knees. Hockney found himself staring into an empty red hole where an eye was supposed to be. Sunlight glinted on a piece of shrapnel that had pierced the dead soldier's skull. Hockney looked lower down. The man's stomach had been ripped open: his intestines had spilled over the road like white German sausages. Hockney clutched at the hood of the car for support. He had barely managed to raise himself to his feet when he started to retch.

Renard kicked him lightly on the shin. "This is no time for sentiment, *mon vieux*. We've got some walking to do. Follow me, and keep close to the walls."

With the sick still oozing over his chin, Hockney lurched along behind Renard. Haunted by the scene on the road, he failed to notice the outstretched boot of a Vietnamese soldier squatting in the doorway of a gutted store. He tripped and fell headlong on the broken sidewalk, grazing his forehead and palms. As he pulled himself together, Hockney saw the soldier tapping a finger against his helmet, and recognized the universal sign. Maybe it *was* insane to be here, he thought.

He had to jog to catch up to Renard, who was now more than half a block away. Renard was shaking the handle of a door that appeared to be locked, willing it to open. He finally gave up and beckoned Hockney to follow him round the corner to the side entrance. Hockney looked up at the sign on the garishly painted building: "Arc-en-Ciel Restaurant." The side door was not locked. It opened into a cavernous green-and-orange room. The chairs were neatly stacked on top of the tables. Apart from the shattered glass on the floor, Hockney thought that it looked like a place that might open for lunch later on. Even the bar seemed to be intact—a near-miracle in the midst of a war.

"Anyone home?" Renard shouted, then repeated the question in French. The only answer in the shadowy gloom was the crunch of footsteps shuffling over broken glass. Wordless, Hockney and Renard ducked down into a booth close to the door.

A fat, swarthy European clad only in baggy khaki shorts slouched into the middle of the room.

"It's all right," said Renard, extricating himself from the cramped booth.

"Who's there?" The man in baggy shorts approached them. "Ah, is that you, Renard? I thought you were more looters. What the hell are you doing down here? I thought they must have cooked your goose by now."

Renard embraced him. "You're one to talk, you old bastard," he said affectionately. "Why haven't they flayed your hide yet? I thought you'd had enough of this sort of thing at Dien Bien Phu."

The Corsican, Renard explained to Hockney, had set up his restaurant in Cholon after the French were defeated by the Communists at Dien Bien Phu fourteen years earlier. His years in the Foreign Legion had instilled in him a healthy respect for the soldiers of Uncle Ho. Married to a local girl, he had made his peace with everyone and was tolerated by the Vietcong as a benevolent neutral. The owner of the Arc-en-Ciel paid his dues to the Communists more regularly than his taxes to the government.

"That's right," the Corsican confirmed. "The Vietcong have a more efficient debt collection service." He ran his finger from ear to ear, across his windpipe. "This calls for a celebration!" he exclaimed, exuding good humor. Renard and the Corsican were soon huddled over a bottle of anisette and a street map of Saigon–Cholon. Hockney strained to make sense of the unfamiliar street names as the Corsican explained the latest phase of the battle for the Chinese city.

The bottle of anisette was a third empty when Renard said, "Good. That will have to be it."

"What's that?" Hockney was still lost in the maze of the street map.

"My friend says that there is a Vietcong command post only four blocks away from us," Renard explained. "The South Vietnamese haven't attacked there yet—they don't like to move until their planes have flattened a hostile area."

"What about those Skyraiders we saw?"

"No problem so far. My friend says they were wasting

III

their rockets on an area the Vietcong evacuated yesterday."

"Can we get through to the Vietcong command post?"

"We can give it a try," said Renard. "At least we know which way to walk."

"You might improve your chances with these," said the Corsican, offering them a pair of soiled white napkins: "You can return them when you come to dinner. I'm not expecting any customers today."

As he waved good-by from the door, the Corsican shouted after Renard, "Give my regards to Commissar Mau."

"Who's Commissar Mau?" Hockney asked his friend.

"Oh, he's a bit of a legend. He's one of the top Vietcong organizers in Saigon. If you believed what people say, you'd think Mau was capable of popping up in half a dozen places at once to coordinate the fighting."

It struck Hockney that Renard still seemed remarkably composed. In the restaurant, he had felt his fear return, churning at his stomach. He had wanted to take refuge in the men's room but had not been able to bring himself to ask the way, fearing that the request might show the others he was afraid. He wondered what his parents and Julia would think if they got a message that he had been killed in action in Cholon, before filing his first story from Vietnam. Perhaps the Admiral would feel proud, choosing to interpret what his son had been trying to do according to his own wishes; maybe he would even boast to his friends about how his son had been prepared to take on the Vietcong. He wished he had written to Julia before setting off on the Cholon expedition. He owed her at least a letter.

As they made their way along the narrow street, Hockney had the strange sensation of being trapped in an air bubble. The noise of the shooting was continuous, but it seemed to come from several blocks away, in every direction. The street they were in was utterly deserted.

Following a few paces behind Renard, clutching the white napkin, Hockney felt prickly heat at the back of his neck before he heard the metallic click immediately behind him. He stopped dead and slowly turned around, holding his hands high in the air. Level with his stomach was the barrel of an AK-47. The man holding the gun was a tiny Vietnamese, in black pajamas and rubber sandals, who barely came up to Hockney's lower ribs. Hockney almost burst out laughing. The Vietnamese could not have been more than thirteen or fourteen.

But Hockney felt no temptation to laugh when the boy soldier prodded his stomach with a gun. Two more Vietcong appeared, not much older than the first. They proceeded to frisk Hockney and Renard and, finding nothing, tied their hands tightly behind their backs with wire.

"*Bao chi, bao chi,*" Renard kept repeating.

"What are you saying to them?" Hockney whispered.

"I'm trying to explain we're reporters."

The Vietcong did not appear to be impressed. The first started to walk up the street, and the gentle pressure of a gun barrel between Hockney's shoulder blades left him in no doubt that he was meant to follow.

At the end of the street, the Vietcong who was in the lead turned abruptly into an abandoned store whose entire front was open to the street. He opened a trapdoor in the floor at the back of the store, and Hockney and Renard were prodded down a vertical bamboo ladder. As he descended the ladder, Hockney slipped and nearly fell. With his hands tied behind him, there was nothing he could grip for support.

"Like this," Renard urged, easing himself down with his back to the bamboo rungs so that he could clutch them with his imprisoned wrists.

The ladder took them down thirty feet or more, into the blackness of a tunnel with wooden props that had been burrowed out of the raw earth. Standing at the foot of the ladder, Hockney could see more Vietnamese in the distance, silhouetted against the shifting light of a kerosene lamp. As he stumbled closer to them along the tunnel, he could see that one of the Vietnamese was an emaciated figure in a white shirt, seated at a simple table beside the lamp. Ignoring the new arrivals, the Vietnamese laboriously finished writing a note, which he then handed to a man with a red arm band who was standing attentively at his side.

"Is this the command post?" Hockney murmured to Renard.

"Taisez-vous!" the Vietnamese at the table snapped in unblemished French.

They were left standing in the tunnel for another ten minutes before the commissar looked up from his table again, this time to issue orders in Vietnamese to the guards. The contents of their pockets—a few piasters and dollar bills, notebooks, letters—were taken from them and scattered over the table. The commissar pounced on Hockney's laminated press card from the American military command. He turned the card over, looked quizzically at Hockney, and then compared the face in the photograph with that of the prisoner in front of him. Hockney's nervousness grew. Could the Vietcong tell the difference between press accreditation and military ID? Did this commissar even care about the difference?

"It's all right. He's *bao chi*," Renard intervened.

The commissar gave a cursory glance at Renard's press card and tossed it aside.

"You may be *bao chi*," he said to the Frenchman. "But this one," he pointed at Hockney, "is an American spy."

"It's not true," Hockney stammered. "If I were a spy, do you think I would come here carrying incriminating documents? Those are just my press credentials, like all American reporters have."

"Silence!" screeched the commissar in a high nasal voice. "You will confine yourself to answering my questions."

"I came here for a reason," Hockney protested. "I came here to find you."

The commissar stood up and shouted an order in Vietnamese. The guards grabbed hold of Hockney's arms.

"You will be taken before a people's tribunal," the commissar yelled at Hockney. "You will be judged as an American spy. You will receive the people's justice."

"Michel?" Hockney appealed to his friend.

"The Frenchman stays here," the commissar ordered.

Hockney felt weak at the knees. He could guess what a people's tribunal would mean in the midst of a war. No lawyer. No defense. Summary justice. The firing squad. It can't end here, like this, he told himself.

"Michel," he implored again.

"Don't worry." Renard spoke rapidly, with no confidence in his tone. "I'll talk to the commissar. I'll tell him that you've been fighting your government's war policy. I'll make him understand."

"Silence!" screamed the commissar.

Hockney was shaking so violently that he could not get a purchase on the bamboo ladder after he had blundered back along the tunnel, his arms pinioned by the guards. They half-pulled, half-prodded him up the ladder; it was only after he had felt the naked steel of a bayonet against his calf that he began to climb backward, clutching the rungs with his hands as Renard had shown him. At the top, they pushed him through a door in the back of the store that led to a narrow alleyway behind, where the smell of rotting meat was even more pungent than it was beside the Saigon river. Hockney realized that he must be smelling decomposing human flesh.

He heard the whir of an approaching helicopter, and then glimpsed the white flash of the U.S. Air Force emblem on its fuselage. Please God, make them come back. He found himself praying involuntarily. But he heard the chopper blades dying away in the distance.

"I'm here!" he shouted, uselessly. "Down here!"

One of the guards struck him with his rifle butt. As the Vietcong shoved him along the alleyway and into a vacant lot, walled on three sides, Hockney was conscious that—for the first time—he saw Charlie as his enemy.

There was no evidence of a people's tribunal. Instead, half a dozen Vietcong, some wearing civilian clothes but all displaying the distinctive red arm band, were relaxing around the walls of the vacant lot, cradling their automatic weapons. On the far side of the lot was the explanation for the stench that had appalled Hockney when they came out of the store. Blurred by a palpitating cloud of flies was a pile of bullet-ridden corpses. Hockney observed that one was still bleeding.

As a mortar shell exploded on the other side of the far wall, Hockney considered trying to make a run for it. The South Vietnamese must be closing in. But with six Vietcong ahead of him, and two behind, how far could he hope to get?

Using the flat of his bayonet like a cattle prod, one of the guards backed Hockney up against a wall.

"There's been a terrible mistake." Hockney burst into French, trying to identify a leader among the indistinguishable Vietnamese. "I must speak to your commander." There was nothing in any of the men's faces to suggest comprehension. "Someone must speak French," Hockney insisted. "Which of you speaks French?" No one spoke. "English?"

Languidly, the Vietcong arranged themselves in a line along the opposite wall. The firing squad, Hockney realized in mounting horror. So they were not even going to give him the semblance of a trial. A trial for what? He had wanted to help these people, and they were going to shoot him. It was a crazy way for the world to end at twenty-three.

"Why don't you understand?" Hockney yelled, angered as well as terrified by the absurdity of death in Cholon. "I came to help you, not to fight you."

He was cut off by a shouted command in Vietnamese. The guards aimed their weapons at his chest.

"You could at least untie my hands," he told them, surprised at the steadiness of his voice, "and give me some paper and a pen. What kind of army refuses to let a condemned man write to his family?" This time, his voice broke.

Hockney heard the Vietcong release the safety catches of their weapons. He shut his eyes. Without thinking, he heard himself bellowing the slogans of the antiwar demonstrations at Berkeley.

"Ho, Ho, Ho Chi Minh!" The words echoed around the walls of the empty lot. He had last shouted them at a line of uniformed guardsmen in riot gear. Even in terror, he could appreciate the surrealistic quality of shouting them here, under the guns of the Vietcong.

He did not stop yelling until he was hoarse. The fatal bullets had still not come. The only sound was the chatter of automatic weapons a few blocks away. Hockney opened his eyes.

The commissar from the tunnel was watching him from the shadow of the entrance to the alleyway, arms akimbo.

"Please come with me, Mr. Hockney." The commissar's English was as fluent as his French.

Commissar Mau—Hockney recognized the name from the talk in the Arc-en-Ciel restaurant—offered neither apologies nor explanations for his ordeal. In fact, he did not even offer him company. He left Hockney alone for several hours in a faintly lit alcove scraped out of the earthen wall of the tunnel, with only a pamphlet in French, signed by the nominal chief of the Provisional Revolutionary Government of South Vietnam, for amusement. Physically and emotionally drained, Hockney dozed fitfully on a mat on the floor. During what he imagined to be the midafternoon, a guard brought him rice flavored with *nuc nam* sauce. It reeked of rotten fish. He pushed the bowl away.

His watch had been broken, but he calculated that it was at least six o'clock before Commissar Mau came for him. What looked like a party committee had been assembled in a tiny room at the end of the tunnel. There were several soldiers, in olive-drab uniforms as well as the familiar black pajamas, a girl in peasant dress with bobbed hair, and a tall Chinese wearing white undershorts and a white T-shirt.

"We don't have much time," Commissar Mau announced. "We are about to evacuate this area."

"Where is Renard?" was Hockney's first question.

"He has made his own way back," Mau said smoothly. "The more of us here, the more dangerous it is. We know Renard can be trusted. We didn't know about you. Now we are sure."

"Did you have to go through that lunatic rigmarole out there?" Hockney said. "Is that the way you treat all your well-wishers? I can tell you that you're not likely to make many friends if you give them a reception like that." Relieved that he was alive and had at last been accepted, Hockney gave vent to his fury at having been used for what now seemed like an exercise in casual sadism.

Commissar Mau shrugged. "When you know us better, you will begin to understand how little the life of an individual counts in the revolutionary struggle of a whole people. You will also understand that we don't automatically accept outsiders as friends. They have to prove themselves. But for now, we have a war to fight and you have an article to write. So ask your questions. Everyone here belongs to the district committee. They are all free to answer you."

In the dank air of the tunnel, scrawling words he could only half-read in his notebook, Hockney conducted the most unusual interview it had ever fallen to him to do. "The United States has already lost this war," Commissar Mau declared. "You may not see this clearly as yet. There is often a long gap between the time something happens and the time people come to appreciate exactly what has happened. The French lost their war with the Vietnamese people long before Dien Bien Phu. When your historians write their books, they will acknowledge that the Americans lost their war with my people during Tet."

"How can you say that when you are being driven out of every town that you captured, and when you have taken terrible casualties? Our President is claiming that more than ten thousand of your men have been killed in action." Hockney no more believed that figure than any of the other spurious body counts publicized by the administration in its efforts to prove that the war was being won. He used it in the hope of prodding Mau into providing some more revealing details.

"Numbers don't matter," Commissar Mau said wearily. "The United States will lose because it worships statistics. The whole American strategy is based on arithmetic. But mere arithmetic doesn't work over here. If it did, your war machine would have exterminated us already. You see, it doesn't matter how many men we lose. It doesn't matter whether we hold on to this part of the city for a month or a year. Our answer to the superior material force of the

United States is a superior moral force. We oppose the patriotism and revolutionary zeal of our people to the false slogans your government uses to camouflage greed and lust for power. We are winning now because your countrymen have begun to understand that they are bound to lose, and are more confused than ever about what they set out to do. The more planes and guns and troops that your government sends to Vietnam, the more bitter will be its inevitable defeat."

The others in the Vietcong bunker—even the girl with the bobbed hair, who said she was a schoolteacher—talked in similar language. Hockney soon lost the thread of who was saying what. Had they all been brainwashed, or was the communication between them really so total that they all talked like different voices reciting passages from the same text?

He probed for the human details that would help to individuate them. How could a schoolteacher fight the revolution? How did the Chinese community get along with the Vietcong?

At one point, a blast shook the bunker. The timbers of the ceiling creaked, dirt spattered over Hockney's hair, and he rolled instinctively to the floor. The Vietnamese did not move. A second blast—a bomb or artillery shell—shook the room with greater force, and the kerosene lamp plunged over the edge of the table. Commissar Mau caught it expertly and replaced it in its previous position. "Don't worry," he reassured Hockney. "The shelter is bombproof."

Late in the evening, or perhaps it was early morning— Hockney had lost all consciousness of time—they offered him beer and rice wine. Commissar Mau, he noted, drank only tea. Hockney again asked point-blank why he had been subjected to the ordeal of the mock execution.

Mau reminded Hockney that they were fighting a war and that, even at that moment, the government forces were steadily closing in on their bunker. For an American to try to cross the lines was unheard of, and there was no time for interrogation. Hockney was not satisfied with the explanation. There had been no time for interrogation, yet they had been sitting together for several hours discussing the Vietcong view of the war.

"In a battle of ideas," said Mau, "we must always allow time to explain."

None of the words allayed the storm of emotions still gusting within him. He had seen death at close hand, and had not run from it. That allowed him a measure of pride. But he was still confused by what had happened in the vacant lot, and by his reaction to it. Under the guns of the Vietcong, he had shouted the same slogan that he had heard chanted by thousands of Berkeley students, under the tear gas of the National Guard in Sproul Plaza. Had he been sure what it meant on either occasion? At one moment that morning, as he was frog-marched toward the firing squad, he had realized he was closer, in every sense, to his fellow Americans in the Air Force helicopter that had offered him a transient hope of safety than he could ever be to Commissar Mau and his people, whatever the justice of their rival causes. It was easier to identify with revolution from far away than to walk into it. Close up, Vietnam was a question not of right or wrong, but of brute survival. In the course of his day in Cholon, everything had blurred around the edges of that one preoccupation—staying alive. In what remained of the night, Hockney thought more about how to get back to the safety of the Caravelle Hotel than about making sense of the day's events.

In the end, Commissar Mau solved the problem. After Hockney had spent a restless night in the bunker, a small boy was assigned to steer him back to the outskirts of the advancing South Vietnamese positions. An American adviser was with them.

"How come you're slap bang in the middle of all them gooks, newsie?" the bald-headed adviser demanded.

"Just trying to find a little sweet-and-sour cooking," Hockney joked, relieved to hear an American voice.

"Where you from?"

"The sunshine state, California, most recently. But I was born in D.C."

"Well if I was you, I'd head right back downtown, new-sie. Otherwise, you're gonna end up as a dim sim."

It was not until he was back in the familiar surroundings of the Caravelle that Hockney was able to order his thoughts sufficiently to begin transforming his experience in Cholon into a story that the *World* would be compelled to run on page 1. He had gone where no other reporter had gone. That was a story in itself. But what about his original purpose—to present the human face of the Vietcong? The sour-faced Commissar Mau, coldly rationalizing the execution of "traitors" and suspected spies, would not pick up many votes in New York City. Hockney would need to humanize his characters a little.

No purpose would be gained, he decided, by making too much of the mock execution. There was more than enough local color for the piece in the description of the tunnel, the bombs, the rotting corpses. There was a danger that a literal, blow-by-blow account of what had happened the previous day might be used by Americans who viewed the Vietcong as inhuman Communist robots—which, despite the mock execution and the slogans, Hockney was convinced they were not. You could not judge a people at war by conventional standards. He had to find a positive twist, something that would give his story the psychological impact in the United States that he had planned. He remembered a remark Commissar Mau had let drop about the possibility of reopening peace talks. Hockney envisioned a headline: "Inside Liberated Saigon: Captured U.S. Reporter Brings Back Vietcong Peace Offer." His story might even rate a Pulitzer. Dick Sharpe would probably never forgive him if it did.

5

THE ARTICLE on the Vietcong bunker in Cholon brought Hockney his front-page banner headline in the *World*, a eulogistic telegram from his editor, Len Rourke, and, when the mails finally got through, an emotional letter from Julia, begging him not to take too many risks. Hockney's piece was quoted on the Senate floor by leading critics of the war. The most satisfying side effect, as far as he was concerned, was that his bureau chief was sufficiently intimidated by his success to pull him off routine chores like attending the Five O'Clock Follies. Hockney was turned loose to pursue his own lines of inquiry.

The friendship of the Renards opened many doors to him that were permanently closed to other Americans. It took him to the core of the Vietnamese opposition to the Thieu regime, whose corruption he was able to expose in a devastating series of articles. But the majority of his stories were about the American side of the war, since that was what the home public demanded to know about. He described the inner workings of the colossal meat grinder into which America was bundling its male children by the thousands; the scene at the military airport where the bodies of dead conscripts were loaded onto planes to be taken home; the countless scenes of nameless Americans, often high on marijuana, pursuing the meaning of the incomprehensible war in whorehouses and bars and, with smoking guns, in villages where they could not distinguish their enemies from innocent victims.

He began to generate a voluminous hate mail, in which phrases like "yellow belly" cropped up with boring frequency. "When you are ready to share the dangers they face," one letter read, "I might be ready to take account of your poisonous, yellow-bellied efforts to run down our boys in Vietnam because they've got the guts you newsmen lack." Hockney received a curt note from his father which, though couched in more elegant vocabulary, made the same basic point. The letter from the Admiral convinced him. He would accept the challenge. If he could walk through the lines to a Vietcong command post, it would take no great enterprise to visit the front with the Americans—and it would supply a neat riposte to his increasingly vociferous critics. The visit would be pointless, of course, unless he found more exciting action than the reporters-turned-war-freaks who did the same thing every day. After a little homework, he thought he had found the right situation. The journey would take him north to I Corps, where the Marines had come under intensive attack in some outlying positions.

"Fire in the hole!" the Marine sergeant screamed. Hockney did not know what it meant, but he threw himself face downward on the ground, like all the others.

Ten seconds later, a huge explosion set the ground heaving across the entire area—an area less than half the size of a football field, where the remants of a Marine Corps company were desperately holding out against the onslaught of two North Vietnamese battalions. And pro-Hanoi commentators like the Australian Laurie Pritchard continued to make out that there were no North Vietnamese troops in the south, Hockney reflected bitterly. Let Pritchard come and take his place on Hill 383. Pritchard, of course, had more pleasant things to do. Hockney had heard before leaving Saigon that Pritchard was chaperoning a party of film stars and literary types—including Tessa Torrance, the glamorous star of the new box office success *Sex Wars*—around North Vietnam. No, Pritchard wouldn't want to swap places.

When Hockney had joined the company that was clinging to Hill 383, it had still numbered more than a hundred men. Within twenty-four hours, the lethal barrage of fire from the North Vietnamese had sliced company strength down to forty-seven men. Those were the ones who were capable of pulling a trigger or crawling a few yards. The rest were dead, or nearly dead, or too badly hit to get their hands around a rifle stock. There was no water and no medical supplies, not even bandages. Ammunition was running low.

The wounded kept calling out, "Corpsman! Corpsman!" No one answered. There was no help to give them—not even the comfort of a prayer or a final absolution. The catholic padre was lying face down in a heap of dead bodies.

The experience of the past day had taught Hockney that it was possible to feel more scared than he had felt in

Cholon, as the Vietcong firing squad cocked its rifles. Anxiously, he watched the marines who were busy blasting earth and hacking a clearing in the jungle to make a helicopter pad on the side of the hill. He knew that that would be their only way out—if the choppers were able to land.

Belly down, he crawled back to the foxhole he had been ordered to dig for himself the night before. He had not taken the instruction very seriously, and as a result his shelter was shallower than the others. The only way he could conceal himself in it was by stretching out full length. Now, although his hands were raw from digging, he began to scoop out more earth.

There was a sudden thud as the Marine sergeant dumped a box of grenades at the edge of Hockney's foxhole. "Here, newsie, you'll be needing these soon."

"I'm a reporter, man."

"Tell that to the gooks. They're getting ready for one last big push, and if I were you, I'd want to greet them with something better than a press card. Just remember to release the spoon before you throw these things. Otherwise, the gooks could have time to throw them back in your face."

He looked more closely at Hockney. "Where's your helmet?"

"Uh, it's here." Hockney scrabbled at the end of his foxhole for the helmet and flak jacket, taken from a dead man, that they had given him the night before.

"Keep it on," the sergeant ordered. He chuckled when he noticed the markings. "Why bless you, father," he said. "Looks like we got our padre back."

He looked skyward as another flight of Phantoms screamed overhead, spewing out napalm and five-hundred-pound bombs down both sides of the hill. The napalm burst into great balls of fire as it hit the top of the jungle canopy.

"That napalm's no fucking good," growled the marine in the foxhole next to Hockney.

"What do you mean, no fucking good? At this rate, we'll all be fried alive."

The marine spat out the wad of tobacco he was chewing. "Naw," he said. "In this kind of jungle cover, Charlie's as

124

safe as in a cement tunnel." The jungle, which had appeared to Hockney as an unbroken mass of green vegetation rising three or four hundred feet above the ground, was actually composed of three distinct layers. Under the napalm, the top layer would be broiled, the middle layer would be warmed up, but the bottom layer would often be barely touched. The jungle absorbed most of the bomb fragments too, like a great green sponge that protected the men who were moving through the undergrowth.

The Phantoms flew on. Within seconds, it was obvious that whatever they had hit, it was not the North Vietnamese mortar batteries. Mortar shells slammed down around the shrinking perimeter of the Marines' positions. To Hockney, it was the noise, not the falling bodies, that was most terrifying.

He tried to make out what the marine in the next foxhole was yelling. "Down! Keep your head down!" Only the top of the man's helmet showed above the lip of his shelter. "Keep down," he repeated. "Then you'll only get hurt if the gooks score a direct hit. And *then* you won't feel a fucking thing."

The advice was clearly well intentioned, but Hockney was not sure he would be able to follow it. His ragged-edged foxhole seemed to be caving in; the mortar blast had dislodged the loose earth around the sides. He started to push some of the earth back. It reminded him, incongruously, of trying to pat sand castles into shape on the beach as a boy. It would have been about that time, at age ten or eleven, that he first met Julia, skipping half-naked through the foam.

His reverie was brutally interrupted by a searing pain in his right hand. Hockney screamed, certain that his fingers had been cut off. He placed his other hand tenderly over the one that was hurting, not daring to look. The fingers were still there, but they were wet and sticky. He looked down and saw that the earth around the edge of his foxhole was spiked with bits of hot metal. He had gashed himself on a piece of shrapnel. He gave up trying to repair his shelter.

The same question tormented him that had entered his

consciousness in Cholon: Would any story he could hope to take back to the bureau make it worthwhile risking his neck? The question, if anything, was more pointed than before, since he was cowering for cover on a hill that did not even have a name. The men of Bravo Company of the Third Battalion of the Fourth Marine Regiment had a legitimate excuse. They had been ordered to hold this insignificant piece of real estate. Hockney was the only man on the hill who was there of his own choice.

"Gooks! Ten o'clock!"

It took a couple of seconds for Hockney to realize that the warning was directed at him, and another couple to grasp that he was not sure exactly what it meant.

"*Where* are they?" he queried.

"Down below, to your left."

Peering through the undergrowth, Hockney could at first see only jungle and more jungle. Then he saw movement. A whole bush seemed to be inching toward him. But no, it was not a bush. It was a helmet, camouflaged with leaves and twigs. Then another helmet. Then three, four more. The North Vietnamese were crawling up the hillside on their bellies, using their elbows for leverage and gripping their weapons with both hands.

Hockney wanted to swallow, but his mouth was too dry.

"What are you waiting for?" the neighboring marine bellowed at him.

Hockney looked at the box of grenades, then back at the advancing helmets. The sergeant was right. They wouldn't pause to inspect his press accreditation. He pulled the box into his foxhole and grabbed a couple of grenades.

"Come on, newsie," the marine next to him urged. "What the fuck are you waiting for?"

Hockney could now see the face of the first North Vietnamese soldier. It reminded him of Commissar Mau. The crazy thought flitted through his mind that if he stood up and yelled *"Bao chi"* the Cholon episode might be reenacted.

He was still hesitating to throw the grenade he was

126

clutching in his uninjured left hand when a big black marine zigzagged across the clearing toward his side of the perimeter. The North Vietnamese opened fire, and the black man fell, spread-eagled, over Hockney's foxhole, blotting out the light. Another manic idea occurred to Hockney: if he lay motionless under the black man's body, the Vietnamese might leave him for dead as well. He changed his mind when he felt a warm stickiness oozing down his neck from the inert form above. With all the strength he could summon, he heaved backward and upward with his shoulders. He tilted his body, and the dead man rolled over to one side.

Now that he had exposed himself to the attackers, Hockney rose into a crouching position. He could see his targets, fifteen or twenty yards away. He stopped thinking. Mechanically, he pulled the pin from one of the grenades, let the spoon flip up, and hurled it down the hill at the man who looked like Commissar Mau. He was dimly aware that he was flanked on either side by marines who were pumping away with their M-16s. He pulled the pin from a second grenade and threw it after the first before ducking back into his foxhole to wait for the blasts.

"You got 'em, newsie." He heard his neighbor congratulate him.

"Not bad for a rookie," chorused another marine.

Hockney's hands were shaking uncontrollably as he dipped into the box for more grenades. It was the first time he had killed a man. The Admiral would be proud if he could see it. But what was he, an antiwar reporter, doing throwing grenades at the Vietnamese?

The question was evidently less important than that of whether he was going to stay alive.

"Hey, newsie, more gooks on your left!" warned his neighbor. Hockney guessed that the marine was three or four years younger than him, and wondered how many men the marine had killed in Vietnam.

"Newsie will soon be pitching in the major leagues," quipped the sergeant from somewhere farther back.

Hockney stole a quick glance over the edge of his hole.

The Vietnamese were out of the jungle and swarming over the hill. They seemed to have broken through the defense perimeter at several points. He threw two more grenades at the thickest cluster of attackers. As he hurled himself back into his hole, bullets sprayed above his head.

"Run for it, newsie," his neighbor yelled. "We can't hold. Get out and run for the other side of the perimeter. I'll cover you."

Snatching up another couple of grenades, Hockney leaped out of the foxhole and started to run, body bent almost double. There were puffs of dust on either side of his feet as the bullets bracketed him.

"I got him, newsie!" he heard the marine exclaim. "Keep right on running."

But almost in the same breath, the same voice shrieked, "Shit. I'm hit."

Hockney turned to look. The young marine was still on his feet, but he had dropped his rifle and blood was spurting from his neck. A few yards beyond him, a Vietnamese soldier was aiming his AK-47 from hip level.

Hockney dropped to the ground instinctively, pulled the pin, and threw his grenade. "Get down, soldier!" he called to his erstwhile mentor.

His grenade must have found its target, because the young marine was still alive when Hockney got to him. Miraculously, he was even talking. The bullet had gone clean through his throat and out the back of his neck, missing the windpipe and the vocal cords. It was beyond a miracle, Hockney appreciated afterward, that he had managed to get the marine's arm around his shoulder and carry him to shelter on the other side of the perimeter, under the hail of fire, without even getting nicked.

The effort would have been useless if the battalion had not managed to finish the helicopter pad. As Hockney reached the clearing, a whoop of joy went up from the handful of marines who were defending it. The first chopper was coming down, through a murderous blanket of fire.

The remaining marines started to shove the wounded in

one side of the helicopter while boxes of ammunition and cans of water were still being unloaded from the other. As Hockney helped to lift the young marine on board, the man croaked, "You're quite a guy, newsie. You're a real marine." The chopper was hovering a couple of feet above the ground, churning up a dust storm. Shielding his eyes from the whirling dirt, Hockney strained to hear what his new friend was trying to tell him. "My third Purple Heart in six months," the marine whispered hoarsely. "I guess it will be home for me now. You just remember you got yourself a friend for life in Wichita called Billy Boyce. My dad runs a real nice diner there."

Hockney's eyes watered as he watched the chopper lift off. He saw it rise above the jungle canopy. Amid the pandemonium on the ground, he could not distinguish the sound of whatever was responsible for what happened next —probably a rocket, or perhaps a heavy machine gun. In the small circle of sky above the clearing, the helicopter erupted into flame and lurched crazily off to the left, beyond Hockney's field of vision. As he waited for the sound of the crash, he broke down and wept.

They let him leave on the ninth chopper with the last casualties, ahead of the corpses. No one on board spoke until the clearing was lost beneath them in the jungle, and they were safely beyond the range of enemy fire. Then a Marine captain with a shattered elbow put his mouth next to Hockney's ear and said, "I hear you did a real fine job back there." He inspected the identity patches sewn on the breast pockets of Hockney's fatigues. "You press guys don't have to be up here." The captain sounded puzzled. "Tell me," he said, "why do you do it?"

Hockney searched for an adequate answer. "I had to find the real war," he tried to explain.

"The real war?" The captain's brow was still furrowed. "Hell, you don't have to go up to Hill 383 to find that. Who's going to remember Hill 383 anyway?"

"That's just the point." Hockney thought of the cynical Saigon press corps, breakfasting at the Givral on Tu Do Street, or heckling the floundering briefers at the Five

O'Clock Follies. "I bet," he shouted against the squall of the chopper blades, "I bet they won't even mention the fight for Hill 383 at the Five O'Clock Follies. But I'm going to make sure people know about Hill 383 at home."

6

HOCKNEY kept his promise to the wounded captain and the dead marine, with results he could not have anticipated. He received not one, but four, telegrams from New York. One was from no less a personage than Xenophon Parrish Nutting, publisher of the *World*, who told him his story was the best—and most human—piece of reporting he had ever read out of Vietnam. Another cable announced that he was going to be nominated for a Pulitzer prize. Yet another was from the American Legion, conveying congratulations for what they called "an honest portrayal of American bravery in the face of the enemy of a kind that we rarely find in the media." Hockney found, too, that when he ran into embassy people in Saigon, instead of trying to dodge conversation, they offered to buy him a beer. Some people had read him wrong, he complained to his friend Michel Renard.

"Don't worry," Renard reassured him. "We'll still let you into the house."

The Renards' next dinner party was for a few congressional staffers who had come out on a fact-finding visit with their bosses. Hockney quickly struck up a conversation with a young man in a white linen suit who was introduced as the executive aide to Senator Milligan. The Senator was emerging as one of the leading critics of the war in the Senate Foreign Relations Committee. Hockney guessed that his aide, a boyish-looking man named Rick Adams, was in his early thirties. He found they had a friend in common.

"I believe you know Perry Cummings," said Adams.

"He's my oldest friend. Do you see much of him?"

"Oh, he turns up for a few things at the Foundation—you know, the Foundation for Progressive Reform."

"But Perry's still with the Pentagon, isn't he? I didn't think they'd let him hang around the Institute too much."

Rick Adams grinned. "It's not a police state yet, you know. You'd be surprised how many junior officials in this administration see things our way and are ready to do something to stop the war." He paused to swap his empty glass for a full tumbler of whiskey and soda from the waiter's tray. "Of course, Perry's had his headaches. But that's going to change now that Johnson is stepping down."

Hockney did not believe that Johnson's decision not to run again—which had caused widespread jubilation among the press corps—was going to end the war.

"I wish I could share your optimism," said Hockney. "Johnson may be burned out by the war, but that doesn't mean his replacement is going to be any better. From what we hear, his successor's likely to be Nixon."

"Could be," Adams acknowledged. "But Nixon can't last if he makes it. Congress and the people won't let him. Any President who tries to go on fighting this war is going to be carried out of the White House on a stretcher."

"How about your senator?" Hockney asked. "Does he feel as strongly about the war as you do?"

"Aw, you know senators," said Adams. "They mostly say what their staffers write." Conscious of a possibly dangerous indiscretion, Adams pulled himself up. "Mind you, Milligan is a lot better than most. At least he goes through his speeches before he reads them out."

Senator Edward Milligan had become a household name because of his outspoken criticism of the Pentagon and the Vietnam policies of successive Washington administrations. He had suggested that the United States withdraw all troops from Vietnam and simply declare a victory. Ambitious young radicals from the Foundation for Progressive Reform clamored to join his staff, and he let several of them in. At the root of Milligan's refusal to regard communism as a threat anywhere in the world was a kind of arrogance: a conviction that the only menace to the United States was from Americans themselves, among whom he most despised the leaders of the military-industrial complex and the CIA. Tall, spare, lantern-jawed, Milligan looked more than incorruptible—he looked like a comic-strip hero.

Hockney looked over the shoulder of Senator Milligan's aide at the latest girl who had entered the room. She was the Vietnamese girl he had met at his first dinner at the Renard house—Lani. As before, she was accompanied by Renard's French doctor friend and his American girlfriend, who did something at the embassy that sounded vague enough to suggest she could be working for the CIA.

"By the way." Adams recalled his attention. "You shook some of us up with your story about those marines on that hill up north."

"What do you mean?"

"Well, you may have missed the stateside reactions. The hardhats loved that piece. The way they read it, the cavalry saved the day. You stirred up all that red-white-and-blue patriotic fervor."

"That's not what I intended."

"I'm sure it wasn't."

Hockney, remembering the helicopter in flames over the jungle clearing, was irritated by the implied rebuke. "Look," he said, "I write things the way I see them. I'm not writing senatorial speeches. What I saw on Hill 383 was a part of this war. It just so happens that it's also a pretty good argument against allowing wars to begin."

"No offense intended." Rick Adams ran his hands over his pressed-down black hair. It shone under the light of Renard's candelabra like an old Brylcreem advertisement. "You are in the presence of one of your most fervent admirers, Bob. I want you to know that. All I'm saying is you shouldn't underrate the importance of your own articles. I'd say that by cutting through the crap in the past, you've helped to swing a few votes on Capitol Hill. I can tell you that there are plenty of people, inside the administration as well as in Congress, who thought long and hard about approving increased budgets for Vietnam after reading your stories on corrupiton in Saigon. And your piece on that Vietcong leader in Cholon—what was his name?"

"Commissar Mau."

"Yeah. That piece on Commissar Mau really gave the Vietnamese revolution a human face. It's a lot easier for politicians back home to send the boys across to fight world communism than to send them to slug it out with real people with names and ideals and private lives. So you've had a big effect. And you've built up quite a following. That means you've also got a responsibility."

"What kind of responsibility?"

Adams, his glasses halfway down his ski-jump nose, glanced around the room. "See that guy over there?" He pointed to a famous columnist from the *Washington Tribune* who had flown over with the congressional party. "He has a following too—at least in the sense that people read him in three hundred papers around the states, and if he changes his line on something, the White House takes notice. But I doubt whether he's had any sleepless nights over the morality of what he writes or what our country does. It took the Tet offensive to persuade him we were wrong to get involved in Vietnam. Up to that point, he was as gung-ho as any four-star general."

"So what?" Hockney was slightly repelled by the pontifical manner of the man delivering the lecture. "Lots of people changed their minds because of Tet."

"You didn't."

"I guess not." Hockney signaled the waiter over. He caught sight of Lani, talking to a group a few yards away. He was calculating a polite way to excuse himself and join her when Milligan's aide said, "I don't want to harangue you, Bob. I'd just like to be sure we agree that, in times like these, there are some things that are worth writing and some things that are not. We *know* that American youth can show courage on the battlefield. What we have to keep hammering home is that there is no cause for them to be on that battlefield to begin with."

Remembering the boy from Wichita with a bullet hole in his throat, Hockney nodded. "Got any story ideas for me?" he said.

"A pretty good one just walked into the room," Adams replied, gesturing toward the group of people who were chatting in the courtyard beyond the sliding doors of the living room. Hockney surveyed them. There were a couple of Americans he did not know along with Renard, the French doctor, and his girlfriend from the embassy.

"Who do you mean?"

"The girl, of course. Debbie Walters. Don't you know what she does?"

"She works for the embassy."

Adams raised his hands mockingly toward heaven. "You lost your reputation as the greatest investigative reporter in town. Debbie works for Bill Crawford, the chief of the CIA's so-called pacification program. Okay?"

"Okay," said Hockney sheepishly, embarrassed that he had not quizzed Debbie earlier.

"Look me up when you get back to Washington," said Adams with a flutter of his hand. "I'll show you around."

"I'll do that."

Hockney started to walk, dutifully, toward the group in the courtyard with whom Debbie was chatting. He had hardly noticed her the first time they had met. He now observed that she was a strawberry blonde, but with the kind of homely face and dowdy figure that he tended to associate with schoolteachers and dentists' secretaries. Come to think of it, Debbie was a little old to be an unmarried secretary. Maybe that was the way the CIA liked them.

Before he had mentally phrased his opening line to Debbie, Renard, moving back inside from the courtyard, intercepted him.

"Are you enjoying yourself?" said Renard, as always the perfect host. "I think you're becoming too serious. In the face of tragedy, seriousness, not to mention sobriety"—he indicated Hockney's empty glass—"is totally unacceptable. You're even neglecting our most beautiful guest." Renard guided him over to Lani's group. "I must warn you," he added, "I don't think you're entirely in favor with Lani at present. Is that not so, Lani?" Renard raised his voice to ensure that she heard.

"One can be mistaken about people," the Vietnamese girl said, leaving the question open.

"Are you upset because of my piece on Hill 383?"

"Why should I be upset?" She looked around the room, as if trying to make up her mind which of the other groups to join. "Your article was like all the others. You wrote as if the only human beings in this war are you Americans."

Hockney was about to defend himself, but Renard interposed. "Lani has a special reason for feeling a little—er—disturbed, Bob. You couldn't possibly know."

"I'm sorry. Is there some problem?"

"There is a village called Can Lai," she said. "I don't suppose you've heard of it. It's in Long An province, just south of here along Route 4. A number of civilians were murdered there this week by a pacification team working under the orders of the CIA."

"Forty-two civilians," Renard specified. "One of them was Lani's aunt."

"That's—well—it's terrible." Hockney stumbled over his words. "I don't know what to say." She was far more beautiful than he had remembered, standing, pale and anguished, in her *ao dai* of gold on purple.

Lani stared at him. The wells of her eyes were deep, so deep that, with her back to the light, all he could see in them was an impersonal, impenetrable blackness. "If you are sorry," she challenged him, "then you can do something about it."

"Like what?"

"Like go to Can Lai and interview the survivors and write their story. If you're willing to go, I'm willing to take you."

He moved to his right so that the light shone on the side of her face. The eyes were still impenetrable. But the way the light fell on her *ao dai* showed that her body was sinuous and alive under the silk sheath. It occurred to him that she was not, after all, untouchable.

"I might just do that," he said.

Lani lived in a large apartment on the ground floor of a tenement behind Saigon's central market. As they disentangled themselves from the pedicab outside her door, it seemed entirely natural to Hockney, but in the manner of a dream, that he should be there. What was totally real was the odor of rotting fish, mingled with crushed flowers, that hung in the air.

Inside, she lit a scented candle. Her bed was a large mattress on the floor, curtained with mosquito netting that hung down from a wooden frame suspended from the ceiling. The overhead fan rotated slowly, barely stirring the still, dank air in the room.

"Tea?" Lani asked after she had switched on an old victrola that emitted the harsh twang of a traditional Vietnamese tune. "I have no alcohol."

"I've had all that I need." He looked for a place to sit. There were only some fragile lacquered chairs, and the mattress. He remained standing, watching as she made tea on an electric hotplate in the corner of the room.

"I haven't even asked you what you do," he said, to break the silence.

"I'm an interpreter. At the French embassy. It's only temporary."

"What will you do afterward?"

"After the revolution, I'll find something more relevant."

He moved behind her and gently caressed her shoulders. "If you are the revolution," he breathed, "I'd like to join."

She turned to face him. "Do you want to make love to me?" she asked solemnly. The way she said it, Hockney thought, she might just as well have been asking if he had been circumcised.

"Yes," he said, taken aback.

With the same serious expression, Lani switched off the hotplate and started to take off her clothes.

When she was completely naked, she stood in front of the mattress, her arms hanging limply by her sides.

"Well?" she said.

"You're beautiful," Hockney stammered. He began to tear off his own clothes.

"You realize," she said, as he pulled back the mosquito netting and crawled onto the mattress beside her, "that for me this could be a kind of treason."

"What do you mean?" His hands were already roving over her slim, exquisitely molded body.

136

Lani did not respond. Under his fingers, she was cold. He tried to knead warmth into her, to make her feel the same urgency that was now driving his body. Before he was sure she was ready, her deft, slender fingers pulled him deep inside her.

Passive at first, she began to move with him as he pursued a slow, sure rhythm. It was not until he had stopped moving, but was still resting inside her, that Lani said harshly, "Is it true that you killed some of my people?"

Startled, Hockney propped himself up on his arms.

"What are you talking about?"

"Didn't you fight with the Marines on Hill 383?"

Of course, he thought. She was still upset about his article.

"I didn't *fight* with them," he said. "I *reported* on the fighting."

"Oh no, Robert. You threw grenades. You even got a telegram from the Marine Corps commander congratulating you for it."

How could she know about that? Hockney demanded of himself. He had not mentioned the grenade throwing, not even to Renard. The telegram had been personal.

She answered the question before he gave voice to it. "In Vietnam," she said, "there are no secrets from the revolution."

Hours later, as he lay between sleeping and waking, with his head against her breast, lulled by the whirring of the slow fan, Lani said: "The women of Vietnam have many ways of serving the revolution. If you had been with the French when my people were fighting them, you might have found yourself in the arms of a razor girl. Then not even Dr. Marchand would have been able to help you."

"What's a razor girl?" he asked blearily.

"You'd know soon enough if you went to bed with one. They acted according to your American slogan—'Make love, not war.' They went to bed with the enemy. But not until they had stuffed a cork with a piece of razor blade embedded in it inside themselves."

"Ouch!" Hockney twitched under the sheets.

137

"I prefer you intact." It was the closest she had come to a statement of personal feeling. Sensing a subtle change in the girl, Hockney tried to take her in his arms again.

But at the same instant, without explanation, she leaped from the bed and darted like an arrow across the room. Hockney sat up and saw that she was crouched naked behind a small table. Something else had changed: she was holding a 9mm Makarov PM pistol in her hand.

Hockney froze. For an instant, he heard nothing. Then there was a crash as the door burst open. The sputtering candlelight picked out beads of moisture on the shoulders of a half-naked Vietnamese man. The stranger lurched forward and collapsed on the middle of the floor like a beached fish. He was drenched, as if he had been swimming in a canal. His navy blue shorts were stained with something darker than water. Lani turned on the overhead light and pulled down the man's shorts to expose a gaping hip wound.

Hockney knew nothing of first aid, so he confined himself to slipping a pillow under the man's head.

"Do you know him?" he whispered to Lani.

She nodded and put her finger to her lips.

The wounded man was babbling in Vietnamese. Hockney could make out only one word. It sounded like "Theophile."

"Theophile," Hockney repeated. "Isn't that Dr. Marchand?"

Lani shook her head impatiently. Hockney was sure he heard the man on the floor say "Theophile" once more.

"You'd better go," Lani said to him.

"I don't understand," said Hockney. "Hadn't we better get a doctor? Who is this man, anyway?"

"One of our couriers," she explained hastily. "Shot by the police as he was swimming a canal. He says the police were following him. You'll really have to leave, Robert."

"And leave you with this on your hands? No way." Hockney folded his arms in a show of resolution, but felt faintly ridiculous striking that posture in the nude.

"It's my job, Robert, not yours. Please go."

There was something in her voice that made him obey.

"When will I see you again?" he asked when he had put his clothes on.

"I don't know. Tomorrow, maybe the day after. We'll go to Can Lai."

Lani was dressing and bandaging the man's wound, with apparent expertise. A siren wailed somewhere outside, beyond the cathedral.

"Take care," he said.

7

CAN LAI was like any other hamlet in Vietnam: a hundred or more huts perched among flat paddy fields. The ragtag government militia took no interest in the arrival or departure of Hockney and Lani on a crowded bus, except to cadge cigarettes. Lani certainly knew the place. She led the way unerringly to several huts where Hockney heard the same story of how a team of Vietnamese special forces with American advisers had raided the hamlet before dawn and staged a mass execution. They claimed that women and children, as well as men, had been dragged into the dirt street and mowed down with machine gun fire. Yes, they said, it was true that there were Vietcong sympathizers in the hamlet. But they insisted that there were no active Vietcong cadres in the hamlet when the slaughter took place.

Hockney was revolted by the physical descriptions that Lani translated, but also puzzled. There was no physical evidence of a massacre, apart from the black patches where three huts—according to Lani—had been burned down. He tried to collect the names of the victims but realized, when he looked down the list of Lams and Quangs, that the ones he had collected were probably as common as Smith or Brown, and a lot more difficult to trace.

"I'll need more than this," he warned Lani on the way back, as he tried to find the right posture to cushion himself against the bumps. "Bus" was a polite term for the vehicle in which they were traveling. It amounted to nothing more than a six-seater crate on wheels that was towed behind a motorized tricycle. Hockney rubbed knees with a Vietnamese peasant who was carrying a ventilated box on his lap. The heads of two live ducks stuck out through the holes.

"What more do you need?" Lani demanded. "Aren't eyewitness accounts good enough for your paper?"

"It's not quite that simple. These things have to be checked and cross-checked. If there were American advisers involved, I'll have to find out their names and try to interview them. My editors just won't accept a story that a CIA pacification team was involved on the say-so of a few villagers who claim that white men visited their hamlet."

He instantly regretted his choice of words. Lani flared up instantly. "You know the CIA is bound to deny it. What you're really saying is that the word of Vietnamese isn't as good as the word of Americans."

The bus jolted violently over a pothole in the dirt road, and Hockney's knee collided with a duck's bill. The duck protested noisily. "Sorry," he said to the farmer. The man looked at him blankly. Hockney turned to Lani.

"I'll do this," he said. "I'll go to Crawford. He runs the entire CIA pacification program. It's high time I looked into what they're doing anyway." There had been rumors —to which Renard for one subscribed—that the CIA, in its efforts to prove that it could beat the Pentagon generals at winning the war, was systematically assassinating suspected Vietcong cadres. He had started to investigate the reports before, but Sharpe, the *World*'s Saigon bureau chief, had pulled rank and reserved the investigation for himself. Nothing had come out of Sharpe's inquiries— probably, Hockney had begun to suspect, because Sharpe had not bothered to make any. Hockney had noticed that, while the bureau chief viewed the American military establishment with a healthy skepticism, he seemed to have a soft spot for the Agency. "There are plenty of guys in the CIA who are more dovish on Vietnam than the press corps," he had once confided to Hockney. It was a good moment to test whether the doves were responsible for Can Lai—assuming that the massacre had actually taken place.

He was acutely aware, as they continued the trip back to town, that a veil had dropped again between him and Lani. She seemed to expect such total compliance. Yet he had discovered in her apartment that there was fire under her ice. He was determined to rekindle it. There was no way of comparing her with the other women who had mattered to him—with Julia, who was committed only to him, or with Astrid, who was committed to the impossible quest, through the abuse of her body, for something the body could not give. Lani was committed to a cause, and to a degree he had never expected to find in a woman. Her commitment was frightening, because he knew that it made most things, including him, dispensable.

They stopped at a hamlet on the outskirts of Saigon, and the peasant with the ducks got off.

"Why don't we eat duck tonight?" he said to Lani.

"I thought I might cook for you."

"We can do both," he said firmly, with a sudden inspiration. He made Lani call back the farmer, who drove a hard bargain for the sale of one of his birds and then nearly called the deal off when Lani told him that Hockney wanted the box thrown in for nothing.

The sight of Hockney with the duck on his lap provoked broad smiles from the other passengers, who chattered excitedly to each other.

"I shouldn't have done it," he confessed to Lani. "This duck is virtually an old friend. I couldn't possibly kill it."

"I'll kill it," she said.

Hockney had not expected a CIA chief in Vietnam to be so accessible. It was not in character with running an assassination program, as Bill Crawford was reputed to do. Hockney had gained a useful ally in Debbie, Crawford's secretary, after taking the precaution of buying her lunch in Saigon's most expensive French restaurant. Yet there was something odd there too. Debbie was obviously on intimate terms with Renard's friend Theophile, the expert in social diseases, and seemed unembarrassed about being seen in public with him. Was Theophile part of Crawford's network? Or was the situation more complex than Hockney, with only a beginner's insight, could grasp?

Crawford, Hockney discovered, was the reverse of a sinister figure. Of slight build and medium height, Crawford had the kind of anonymous face often found behind a bank teller's window. The CIA man's style struck Hockney as early-1950s soda fountain: he used words like "shuck" and "fink" a lot, and actually offered Hockney a choice of Coca-Cola or root beer. But there was an agile mind behind the vulgarisms, because he demolished, with a few flips of his permanently mobile wrist, the mere possibility of a Can Lai massacre in Hockney's mind.

The detail that clinched the question left Hockney confused and depressed.

"I understand you had a—uh—unusually attractive guide on your trip to Can Lai, Mr. Hockney."

"What of it?"

"Well—uh—I think you should know that Miss Lani has been telling the same story she told you to a few other guys around town."

"If the story is accurate, it should be told to everyone."

"I sure do agree with you on that," Crawford replied with apparent gravity. "Now the trouble is that *I* know the story isn't true because our people were never in Can Lai."

"That's just your word against that of the people who claim they saw it."

"You are one hundred percent correct on that. But you don't have to take my word for it."

"What's that supposed to mean?" Hockney was astonished that Crawford had not so much as batted an eyelid when Hockney suggested that he could be lying.

"Well, you can check Miss Lan's story independently. If she told you what she's been telling other people, she said her aunt got herself killed in Can Lai. Right?"

"Right."

"Well, I know for a fact that can't be so. The only family she has that are still alive are up north in Hanoi, which is where she comes from." Crawford let the information sink in. Then he said with a wave of his hand, "Can we get shucked of this business now and get to talking about some real issues?" He proceeded to tell a dumbfounded Hockney—strictly off the record, of course, no attribution to be made—about what he thought was wrong with America's conduct of the war.

Hockney chose the coward's course. He dropped the story, telling Lani that his bureau chief had spiked it. He did not ask her about her aunt. If she had no aunt in Can Lai, he preferred not to hear about it—not, at any rate, until he had gotten her out of his system. If she had lied, he could understand it, to a degree. It was her war, not his, and she meant to win by whatever methods were required. But if that included feeding lies to him, he would have to drop her. She had her commitment, but he had his own: to whatever truth could be sifted from the quagmires of the war. So he preferred not to know the truth about Can Lai.

It was not as if there was any shortage of checkable stories. Lani's friends in the opposition led him to one that gained him even more plaudits than his eyewitness account of Hill 383—though from different people. His devastating description of the "tiger cages" of Con Son island, where the opponents of the Saigon regime were incarcerated, did as much as anything in the public print to explode the myth that America was fighting for democracy in Vietnam. His eventual reward was an international press award. His immediate reward, however, was that the Saigon government, in the teeth of vigorous protests from the *World* and its friends in high places, declared that his visa had been rescinded. He was given three days to get out of the country.

Most of that time he spent with Lani. He even suggested that she leave Vietnam and come to America. It was a suggestion he had not thought through properly. It was not just that there were lose threads hanging at home—including Julia, who had gone on writing faithfully from Sarah Lawrence despite his failure to respond, apart from a Christmas card. It was that he could not imagine Lani outside her own environment; he even wondered whether she would have the same bewitchment without gunfire in the background. But he had known her inevitable answer before he asked. "This is my war," she said simply. "My place is here. You Americans—all of you—will come and go. I will remain."

She did not come to the airport. He detested the drawn-out agony of airport farewells in any city, but it could nowhere be worse than amid the teeming misery of Tan Son Nhut. It was Renard who had the last word before he cleared the immigration controls. "Don't forget us now that you're a famous name," he said. "After all, we made you."

It was unclear whether the round little Frenchman with the perennial Gauloise drooping from his lip was talking about Vietnam, or his circle of friends, or simply himself and Astrid.

Remembering Paris before Saigon, Hockney took it very personally. "I won't forget," he promised. "I'll never forget you."

Moscow

1

VIKTOR BARISOV wiped the sweat off his palms before he gathered up his hand luggage and joined the other passengers alighting from the Aeroflot plane from Paris. His recall to Moscow had been urgent and unexplained, and had come six months before he had expected his post to end. Pronk, the KGB resident in Paris, had taken malicious pleasure in informing him that he had only forty-eight hours to settle his affairs, make arrangements for handing over his agents to other controllers, and report to Moscow Center. He had let himself grow overconfident in recent months, Barisov now brooded, especially since he had received a commendation from the Center for his role in exposing the CIA agent Bonpierre. The slow cumulation of reports from Pronk complaining about his life-style and his lavish use of residency funds might have come to weigh heavily against him. Could he even be sure that his father-in-law, General Volkov, was still the powerful advocate he had been before Barisov's assignment to Paris? Life in the French capital had come close to wrecking his marriage. He had not seen his wife, Olga, for several months, though she was now five months pregnant. He doubted whether what she had said about him to her father in the meantime had been altogether favorable. At the best of times, a sudden order from Moscow Center was a cause for unease. There had been rumors that big changes were brewing, that heads would fall. In any change, there would be casualties as well as winners. Barisov had no idea which fate lay in store for him.

His spirits rose a little when he recognized the man waiting for him at the foot of the steps. It was Ivan, General Volkov's chauffeur and bodyguard, who had served his father-in-law for many years before Viktor married Olga.

Their security passes whisked them past the customs and immigration controls. In a socialist country, it is important to belong to the *nachalstvo*, the bosses, Barisov thought as they dodged past the milling crowd waiting for their baggage.

As a major general in the KGB, Barisov's father-in-law rated a Chaika, a chunky, 1950s-style car that resembled one of the old Packards. General Volkov, to Barisov's surprise, was waiting for him in the back seat. The General greeted him with a bear hug. "You've put on flesh," he said, patting Barisov's stomach.

Within minutes, they were barreling down the center lane reserved for Soviet VIPs—the lane that less privileged residents of Moscow referred to, resentfully, as "Chaika Lane." The General flipped a switch, and the glass partition behind the driver's seat rose to the ceiling.

"You must be curious to know why you're here," said Volkov.

Barisov nodded. He pulled out a cigarette, but thrust it back into his pocket, remembering that his father-in-law detested other people's smoke, especially in the confined space of a car.

"We'll go into more detail at home. The kernel of the thing is this: The Plan is being accelerated."

"The Plan?" Barisov knew exactly what his father-in-law was referring to because of his conversations with his boss, Pronk, in Paris. But he thought it wise not to let on.

Volkov shook his heavy, white-thatched head impatiently. "I've told you a little already, although I agree you are not supposed to know. The original version of The Plan was approved by the Politburo three years ago. It dictated the broad guidelines we should follow in order to bring about the strategic surrender of the West over a period of twenty years. When Suslov presented it, there were many in our leadership who considered it outrageously optimistic, the product of one or two megalomaniacs in our service and the military high command. After the political success of the Tet offensive, views have changed. We thought three years ago that it would be easier to deal with the Europeans and other American allies than with the United States itself."

The General's words were punctuated by the screech of tires as the driver raced through a red light and then swerved to avoid an oncoming car. If the KGB was in a hurry, Moscow traffic rules did not apply.

Volkov ignored the near collision. "Our assessment now is that Johnson's decision not to run again means that the ultrareactionary, Richard Nixon, will probably be elected President of the United States. Humphrey, of course, has a good chance. But if Nixon does in fact win, American opinion will be divided even more than it is already, and a new crisis of confidence may emerge among America's allies. Many Americans, including government officials, are already in a state of revolt against their political masters because of this war. This gives us a tremendous resource to play with. Remember that Lenin said that communism will be built by its enemies. That applies even to our main enemy, the United States."

Barisov's father-in-law, like many of the old guard, had the habit of quoting Lenin whenever he failed to come up with a phrase of his own.

"I think that's an accurate assessment," said Barisov. "I'm not sure I see how it relates to me."

"There have been big changes at Moscow Center. Kramar has come into his own. Have you met Kramar?"

"No."

Kramar was a legend within his own service, personally known to very few. His enemies—of whom there seemed to be many—depicted him as a mystic. It was said that he traced his ancestry back to the czarist secret police, the Okhrana, and before them to the sinister enforcers of the sixteenth century who distinguished themselves by dressing all in black, riding black horses, and carrying a severed dog's head at their saddle neck as a mark of their trade. Yet Kramar was also reputed to be personally responsible for running several important double agents—moles—in Western governments. And he was held to be a master of deception.

"Well, Kramar has certainly heard about you. He was

impressed by your operation against Bonpierre, and also by the way you ran that French correspondent in Vietnam."

Barisov looked out the car window at the onion cupolas of the Kremlin to avoid showing his pleasure at his father-in-law's words.

"Kramar may not be the most communicative man at Moscow Center," the General went on, "but he certainly understands the importance of communications in the West. He has been pressing for years for an enlarged department, with full directorate status, to handle deception operations against the West, with special stress on media work. Now that the effect of Tet on the American media has been fully analyzed, the leadership has decided to act on Kramar's recommendations. That is where you come in. I gather he's got a job for you."

The Chaika pulled up outside the family apartment in a building off Kirov Street, near the Kievskaya metro station. All six floors in the block were occupied by senior KGB officers. Moscow Center was just down the road, at 2 Dzherzhinsky Square. The General lived well, even by Western standards. He had three reception rooms, including a spacious dining room. The furniture was Swedish, the rugs were Azerbaijani, and the Formica-paneled kitchen was full of the latest American gadgets, down to the General Electric mixer.

Barisov's four-year-old son, Sacha, ran to the door to greet him. Behind Sacha loomed the formidable bulk of his mother-in-law. His wife, Olga, was waiting farther back, at the entrance to the living room, giving nothing of herself. She was wearing a shapeless dress that effectively hid her ballooning stomach and had cut her hair unflatteringly short. She looked as if she had been spending her time cooking and scrubbing. When Barisov bent his head to kiss her on the lips, she turned away, offering only her cheek.

"It's been a long time," he conceded.

His mother-in-law began to pour tea from a big silver samovar, but the General took Barisov's arm and led him away, into the study. "We need something stronger," the General said.

Barisov surveyed the serried ranks of bottles massed

along the lowest shelf of the bookcase in Volkov's sanctum and chose cognac. "I see you have some new trophies," he observed, strolling across to the glass-fronted display case into which the General had crammed his ever-expanding collection of spy gadgets and military bric-a-brac. The latest addition was a metal fragment mounted on a piece of teakwood. The brass inscription read: "U.S. F-4 shot down over Vinh, People's Republic of Vietnam, March 2, 1968."

Volkov unlocked the cabinet. "I don't think I had this last time you were here," he said, carefully removing a hypodermic syringe disguised as a ball-point pen. "Old-fashioned, but effective. The needle is so fine that the victim doesn't feel a thing. This one is old CIA stock. We took it from an agent in Poland who won't be needing it anymore." Volkov chuckled at his own stolid humor. "I'm rather fond of this one." He replaced the pen and removed a passable imitation of a Dunhill lighter. "It has a traceless, poisonous flame. The victim will be dead within three hours of thanking you for the light."

"The only trouble is that, with the way the antismoking campaign is developing in the capitalist countries, it will soon be out of date," said Barisov.

The General relocked his trophy cabinet and slid into his favorite leather wingback. Above his head hung the official portrait of Andropov, the chief of the KGB. Barisov, who had never met him, wondered whether his character matched the face in the stark studio photograph. It was a cruel, predatory face, with a hawklike nose and jug ears above the heavy jowls. Next to Andropov's face, in a frame, was the set of quotations that Kramar had insisted that every Soviet spy learn by heart. Curiously the quotations were not from Lenin, or any other Russian theorist, but from the ancient Chinese philosopher of war, Sun Tzu. The first of Sun Tzu's maxims read: "Fighting is the most primitive way of making war on your enemies."

Volkov, following his son-in-law's gaze, recited another of Sun Tzu's dictums aloud: "The supreme excellence is not to win a hundred victories in a hundred battles. The supreme excellence is to subdue the armies of your enemies without even having to fight them." The General grunted, wagging his head. "Pretty good stuff," he commented. "Pity it had to be written by a damn Chinaman."

Volkov saved the big news until Barisov had chewed his way through his mother-in-law's immoderate servings of salted herring, sturgeon, and beet salad, washed down with vodka and sweet Russian champagne—the kind they said you had to drink quickly, before the bubbles vanished from the glass in your hand.

"They're going to make you a full colonel," Volkov said proudly. "There," he exclaimed, throwing his arm around Olga, "don't you go telling me again that I don't know how to look after my daughter's husband."

"Is it true, Papushka?" Sacha, who had been allowed to stay up late as a special treat, piped up from the end of the table. "I thought colonels are old men, like grandfather."

"He'll be the youngest full colonel in the service," Volkov said. "You see," he explained to Barisov, "I made sure you got the credit for Renard's work in Saigon. It's lucky for you I was here. It's easy to get overlooked if you're out on a limb somewhere—especially if your immediate boss is our old friend Pronk. Don't worry." He patted Barisov's shoulder. "You've seen the better of Pronk now. The rest will depend on whether you hit it off with Kramar."

"The rest?"

"It could be Washington."

Olga and her mother turned to each other. A post in Washington would make or break Barisov's career—and perhaps his marriage too. It was the most challenging assignment he could hope for. It would take him into the jaws of the "main enemy," the United States.

"About Kramar," Volkov said to his son-in-law at the end of the meal.

"Yes?"

"Don't jump to any conclusions. Some people think he's mad. Genius can give that impression. You'll see what I mean tomorrow. He's capable of sitting for hours without moving his head an inch, like a plaster cast of himself. If you get him talking about the work of the Center in general, you may start thinking that Kramar believes he's the reincarnation of every secret police chief Russia has ever had. But pay attention. Kramar is the most brilliant spymaster we have had since Dzherzhinsky—maybe *including* Dzherzhinsky. Back in the thirties, he was already helping to turn English aristocrats into Soviet agents. Since the war, I would say that the West has produced only one man who can match Kramar: Nick Flower. And Flower *is* a madman."

Barisov knew Nick Flower by reputation. Like Kramar, the CIA's counterintelligence chief was a legend in his own lifetime—and a very real antagonist for Barisov to face if they sent him to Washington.

Olga was pretending to sleep when Barisov got into the double bed that had been made up for them. He lowered himself carefully onto her so as not to force his weight on her stomach. He began to caress her, running his fingers under her negligee up and down along her spine. He went on until, unwilling, she began to respond. When at last she opened her body to him, she came almost at once and afterward lay inert, waiting for him to satisfy himself. When Barisov came inside her, it was as if he were alone.

"Will it be different in Washington?" Olga asked.

"I don't know."

He lay flat on his back, trying to relax his muscles, one by one, from his feet upward. Someone had told him that this was a sure way to induce sleep. It did not work. His mind seethed with images of the Paris barricades, from the many nights he had spent observing France's near revolution to keep up his cover as the man from ISKRA. The newsreel pictures of the antiwar riots in America suggested that the scene there was very similar. Vietnam had turned the revolt of the affluent generation—the bourgeois children born into a world of security and plenty—into an international phenomenon. Barisov wondered, half-dozing, whether the leaders of the capitalist societies had taken stock of how threatening the revolt had become for them. The young radicals who were storming the walls of the capitalist citadel today would be inside it tomorrow, in shorter hair, perhaps, but with a greater capacity to change the system. The Bob Hockneys would shape the future of America. Impelled by the Vietnam trauma, they were quite capable of bringing about internal upheavals that would prevent the United States from attempting the role of a global policeman. Yes, the Bob Hockneys could achieve that by themselves. But the Viktor Barisovs could help make sure it happened.

2

KRAMAR'S OFFICE might have served the chief of the Okhrana in the time of Czar Alexander II. It was dominated by his huge, brass-studded desk. The desk lamps, Barisov noticed, had stands that resembled the Romanov eagle—a legacy of one of Kramar's antisocial predecessors? The walls of the vast room were brought closer by the deep bookcases that rose from floor to ceiling; Kramar's personal library on the spy world was said to be one of the most exhaustive in Europe. On a shelf at Kramar's left were two photographs in heavy gilt frames. One was instantly familiar to Barisov: Dzherzhinsky, the founder of the Soviet intelligence service, wearing a Lenin cap and a goatee. He peered discreetly toward the other.

"That is Nick Flower," Kramar explained, approving of the younger man's curiosity. "Success comes only to those who study the character of their adversaries. Flower has never forgiven me for Philby, the British mole." It was well known that when Philby had been stationed in Washington as British liaison with the CIA, Flower, the man of secrets, had unburdened himself, over their weekly lunches, to the unknown traitor. "I have a few scores of my own to settle with Nick Flower," Kramar reflected aloud.

Barisov's father-in-law had been right. Kramar, who appeared gaunt, almost consumptive, never moved his head. Only his hooded eyelids rose and fell as he examined the man he had picked to report to him from Washington.

"The Plan." Kramar pronounced the words like a chapter heading. "You may or may not be aware, Comrade

Colonel"—Barisov flushed with pleasure to hear himself addressed by his new rank for the first time—"that three years ago a plan was drawn up under the supervision of Comrade Suslov for the achievement of our strategic necessities within the space of two decades. What was meant by the term 'strategic necessities' was the attainment of military and political superiority over the United States. Given our economic weakness and our military inferiority at the time The Plan was drawn up, those of us involved at its inception were always well aware that we could not hope for success simply by expanding our war machine at a faster rate than our enemies."

Kramar spoke in a monotone, as if delivering an academic dissertation. "We understood," he continued, "that, as in judo, the fulfillment of our hopes would depend on exploiting the weaknesses of our opponents. In a democracy, it is very difficult to mobilize support in peacetime for high levels of defense spending, or even for efficient internal security measures, let alone for military intervention in foreign lands. So a key element in The Plan we devised three years ago was to develop our capacity to influence public opinion in the West, through disinformation fed to governments and opinion formers and, above all, through media operations. What we could not foresee then was how corrosive an effect the Vietnam war would have within American society. We counted on the disintegration of the political systems of Western Europe before that of the United States, so we concentrated many of our resources on infiltrating European institutions and on deepening suspicions of the Americans. Now we have made a new assessment. America could be crumbling faster than Europe —and that could, by itself, drive some Western European governments to make their peace with us in the fullness of time, as a kind of insurance policy. Are you with me so far?"

"I think so."

"You have served The Plan, without perhaps being aware of its full dimensions. My reason for summoning you to this office is that I have selected you to play a more important part in achieving our broader design. But let me first ask you a question. Suppose that you were assigned to influence public opinion in the United States. How would you proceed?"

Kramar's head, as before, was rigid. Only the mouth moved.

"As far as the media are concerned," Barisov began, hesitantly, "I think I mastered one important principle while dealing with Western journalists in Paris. It is that there is something that matters more to most of them than money, ideology, or even loyalty to their country. The headline comes first. I also learned that it is within the capacity of our service to offer them many headlines."

"For example?"

Barisov thought fast, knowing that he was being put through an oral examination. "The single target most important to us," he said after only a heartbeat's pause, "and also highly appealing to many Western reporters, is their own intelligence services."

"Go on."

"You may be familiar with the work of the American reporter Robert Hockney."

"Of course."

"Well, the magazine he was with before he joined the *World* and was assigned to Vietnam set a lead for the American press by exposing the undercover operations of the CIA. In the process, it forced the CIA to sever its connections with a number of front organizations."

"You are talking about the *Barricades* article. Unfortunately, that lead was never properly followed up."

"That is exactly my point, Comrade." Barisov now felt he was treading on receptive ground. "The only real follow-up has been in our own publications. But they are not taken seriously in the West. Take the case of that book we published in East Berlin, listing CIA agents around the world. The basic idea was good, and it had significant embarrassment value, especially since we made a point of identifying many people as American spies who had never worked for the CIA. The mistake was to publish it in a socialist country. The Western public will never accept information coming from such a source at face value, even if it is entirely authentic. It is better to publish the same material in radical leftist publications that appear to be hostile to the Soviet Union. Through them, we can reach the major newspapers and television networks. In fact, with the emergence of a new generation of American reporters like Robert Hockney, reporters who have already graduated from the fringe political magazines to the mainstream press, we no longer have to work up from the bottom. If we are subtle enough, we can get directly into the pages of the *New York World*."

Kramar rewarded him with a distant smile. Warming to his theme, Barisov said, "It would be even easier if we could find a CIA defector. I don't mean another Philby." At the mention of the name, Kramar turned his head for the first time and stared at the photograph of Nick Flower tacked to his bookcase. "I mean another sort of defector. Someone who might have little intelligence value but could be led to resign from the CIA, turn against his former employers, and stir up public controversy over their activities."

Barisov stopped short, uncertain whether he had been running ahead too fast. Kramar's narrow face was now a mask of complete disinterest. Was it because he regarded Barisov's idea as nonsense or because he had already thought of it—and perhaps was already applying it?

"You have dealt with the media." As Kramar spoke, Barisov noticed a metallic quality to his voice. "Another question. How would you set about influencing members of the administration in Washington?"

This time, Barisov paced himself, trying not to let his words gallop ahead of what little he was able to read of Kramar's reactions. "I would use the antiwar feeling," he began again, slowly. "I would work on the guilt complex associated not only with that but with America's record in relation to the third world as a whole. I would deal with young, idealistic Americans who hold official positions, approaching them through intermediaries like the Vietnamese or even the Cubans. People in the West have become cynical about our revolution, but not about theirs."

"All right," said Kramar. "Enough questions."

Barisov wondered if he had passed muster.

"We have established some common ground."

So he had been accepted.

3

KRAMAR changed back from examiner to lecturer. As he spoke, Barisov tried to guess his age. Sixty? Or older? Old enough, at any rate, to figure as the great survivir of Moscow Center. Successive party chairmen had fallen into disgrace—or worse—but Kramar had remained, irreplaceable. Old enough, too, to have served in Spain.

"On October 25, 1936," Kramar was saying, "the entire gold reserves of republican Spain were transferred by Soviet cargo vessels from a hiding place in the caves outside Cartagena to Odessa. I helped to organize the operation."

Barisov nodded. The story was known to every officer in the service. It had probably amounted to the greatest theft of the twentieth century.

"What few people know," Kramar continued, "is that similar operations—naturally, on a smaller scale—were carried out throughout the civil war in Spain. Many of our boats that arrived laden with arms and ammunition would return, filled with treasure and contraband. This became the source for the nonattributable funds that enabled us to execute various secret missions. It also enabled us to reward some of our foreign friends who worked under our orders in Spain. You are perhaps familiar with the name of Vladimir Merchant?"

"Yes." Merchant owned one of the biggest lingerie companies in the United States. His name was almost a household word. Barisov wondered whether there was any connection between Kramar's reminiscences about his adventures in Spain and his own future assignment.

"Merchant was known by another name then," Kramar resumed. His eyes clouded, as if he were trying to summon up an image from the past. "It was not long after we took the gold that Merchant, who had been running supplies from France, made his own killing. In advance of the Fascist columns that were striking north, he raided a warehouse that was being used to hold valuables confiscated from rebel sympathizers and smuggled the entire contents —paintings, rugs, silver, jewelry—out of the country. That was the foundation of his fortune. It gave him the capital to establish his business in the United States after the war."

"And you let him keep it?"

"He was one of us. He described himself as French in those days, but he was born in Kiev in 1899. Today, he is of course a naturalized American, but he remains one of us."

"It's a fascinating story."

"I am telling it for a reason. The Merchant Corporation, operating according to the purest capitalist principles, makes profits that run to tens of millions of dollars a year. Like other leading capitalists in America, Vlad Merchant can well afford to distribute part of his income to various worthy causes that also happen to be tax-exempt. Over the past year, for example, he has donated no less than two million dollars to a tax-exempt organization based in Washington. It is called the Foundation for Progressive Reform. Merchant's granddaughter, Alexia, is chairman of the board."

"The Foundation for Progressive Reform?" Barisov repeated the phrase. "I don't think I've ever heard of it."

"You can be forgiven for that. Not many people outside a small coterie in Washington have heard of it—yet. That will change in the course of the next few years, and *you* will help to bring about the change. The Foundation for Progressive Reform, IPR, will be at the center of your work in Washington."

Kramar explained. He recalled that in the late 1940s, Moscow Center had helped to establish another Washington foundation—the Institute of Pacific Relations—as a cover for espionage work and as a means of recruiting and coordinating Soviet sympathizers in the American administration. That foundation had collapsed after the conviction of Alger Hiss for perjury and the testimony of Soviet defectors revealed its true functions to the American public. The new foundation had been constructed on an even more ambitious scale. The aim was to use the prevailing antiwar sentiment in the United States and the widespread sympathy of young Americans for radical third-world causes to penetrate and, when possible, manipulate the key institutions in Washington: Congress, the media, and the administration itself.

"In other words," Kramar summarized, "we are recruiting under a false flag. It is imperative that it remain impossible for anyone to prove a direct organizational link between ourselves and the Foundation. Most of the people who will be drawn into the orbit of the Foundation will come because they see it as a more effective way of expressing opposition to the system of government that dragged America into Vietnam than the revolt on the streets and on the campuses. If an extreme reactionary, like Nixon, is elected, such people will come in greater and greater numbers. They already include people with access to highly classified information—information the Foundation will know how to use to maximum advantage."

"How many of the Americans involved with the Foundation are aware of our—uh—interest?"

Kramar reached out to ring a bell on the corner of the desk, as if he had not heard Barisov's question. Barisov knew that much of his power within Moscow Center stemmed from the fact that he kept the identities of his agents secret from almost all his colleagues—including the Chairman. Kramar acted in person as case officer for several of his most valuable Western agents, and it was not unusual for him to vanish from Moscow for a few days to meet one of them, under an assumed name, in a foreign capital. Kramar had been decorated for his success in running moles inside several Western intelligence services, including Britain's SIS. It was rumored in the corridors of Moscow Center that he had even recruited an American mole who was slowly working his way up the hierarchy of the CIA.

"Will you have tea?" Kramar asked.

"Thank you."

"I will make you only one present in Washington,"

Kramar said after his assistant had served the tea and withdrawn. "Most of your targets will be men closer to your age than mine, or even younger, men like this reporter, Robert Hockney. You will not need my help in dealing with them."

"You're not suggesting I approach Hockney?"

"No, no, of course not." Kramar waved away the idea impatiently. "I've read your reports. Hockney is a liberal romantic. He sees himself crusading for truth and justice. He can only be influenced indirectly." Kramar sipped his tea, still scalding hot. "There is someone else," he said. "I believe he is connected in some way with Hockney. He is employed in the Defense Department, with access to many secret files."

"Age?"

"A couple of years older than Hockney."

"How was he recruited?"

"It was almost a model case. He is bitterly opposed to the war, and started leaking some embarrassing official documents to the Foundation and to his journalistic friends. The material included some extremely revealing technical data on infrared tracking devices and electronic sensors. That information was not sent to the American newspapers. It was sent directly to us. It was made clear to our source, in the gentlest possible way, that if his superiors should ever be informed that material of this kind had reached us from him, he would be prosecuted for espionage. He was not unwilling to cooperate."

Kramar consulted his watch. "I have a meeting," he said, rising from his chair. "Comrade Suslov has convened a special conference to decide whether we should advance our deadline for defeating the NATO alliance by methods short of war by two years—and the measures that will involve. Ponomarev will be there. I know you've worked with people from his department before. You'll find they're especially active in the Washington embassy. They seem to think that relations with Congress should be left up to them." Kramar snorted. Boris Ponomarev, the chief of the International Department of the Soviet Communist Party, was an old bureaucratic rival. Ponomarev believed that subversive operations against the West should be under his direct control, with Moscow Center providing technical backup as and when required. "We are, to be sure, the sword and shield of the party." Kramar cupped his palms together in mock reverence.

"Our source in the Pentagon," said Kramar, "appears in the files as Coyote. Isn't that some kind of scavenging dog?"

New York
Summer 1969

A YEAR IN VIETNAM—"out of the world," as the GIs said—was enough to make you a foreigner in your own country. Indeed, much had happened, not the least of which the election of Richard Nixon as President, Hockney reflected as he dressed for the Merchants' party. The Merchants, of FPR fame, were throwing a big fund raiser for the Foundation. Hockney had come home in triumph after his expulsion from Saigon. "You can write your own ticket," the normally cautious editor of the *World*, Len Rourke, had assured him—although, being Rourke, he had not failed to add, "within reason, of course," to the accompaniment of much grinding of teeth. Hockney found himself lionized by talk-show producers, leading hostesses, and even the habitually sharp-tongued crowd at Elaine's. But the more exuberant his reception, the more he began to feel like a displaced person.

He looked at the clock. There was still half an hour to kill before Perry Cummings arrived to escort him to the party. He decided to spend it rediscovering the suddenly alien landscape of Greenwich Village. On his past, fleeting visits, Hockney had grown to love the village, the only part of New York where he did not feel trapped inside the grid of avenues running north-south and streets running east-west. Now it was summer, and there seemed to be a carnival on every street. Some of the girls looked like Indian squaws, complete with headbands, bead necklaces, and feathers. An Italian boy, stripped to the waist, was crooning "Never on Sunday." He was offkey but enthusiastic. His girlfriend—one of the squaws—offered Hockney a paper cup filled with red wine.

"You look like someone famous," she said to him. "Are you someone famous?"

"Just an illusion," he said, accepting the wine.

"You must be someone famous," she insisted. "Who else would come down to the Village dressed like that?"

Hockney was suddenly conscious of his black tie and dinner jacket, ridiculously incongruous amid the summery carnival of the street. He moved on, past brownstones whose steps were jammed with both black and white revelers.

A Puerto Rican girl, partly covered by flowered hot pants and a halter top, danced a samba toward Hockney and flung her arms around his neck. "Hey, pretty boy," she said. "Guess you found a better party." She tugged playfully at his black tie. "Aren't we good enough for you?"

"Sorry, honey." Hockney gently disengaged himself. "I've got to get to work. I'm a waiter uptown."

It was not really a sensible place to stroll around in a dinner jacket. Hockney meandered back to the apartment that had been loaned to him for the week by Ed Finkel, who had just been appointed national affairs editor of the *World*. Hockney, who had formed the impression that Finkel was a ruthless self-seeker, had been surprised by the gesture. "I confess I have an ulterior motive," Finkel had said, after explaining that he was going over to London for a couple of weeks. "I like prospective rivals to owe me some. I never forget to collect on debts."

Perry Cummings approved of the apartment, just off Washington Square, with its eclectic clutter of modern art and Colonial furniture. "I see the staff of the *World* appreciate the good things of life." Cummings roamed around the corridor, trying several doors until he found the one leading to the master bedroom. The bed was unmade, and Hockney's clothes were littered over the crumpled bedspread and the floor.

"So you're going to be in Washington now," Cummings observed as they walked back to the living room. "That's terrific." They had not seen each other for more than a year. Perry Cummings was better dressed than Hockney had ever seen him. He looked distinctly prosperous.

When Rourke had offered Hockney the chance to write

his own ticket, he had not hesitated. "Washington," he had said flatly. When Rourke had pointed out that the *World* already had a bureau chief, and a good man on the White House beat, he had promised to create a slot for Dick Sharpe when he got back from Saigon. Hockney had said that he wanted a special assignment—as a roving reporter with a brief to investigate the goings-on in the intelligence community. Rourke had bridled a bit at the novel suggestion, but thanks to pressure from Ed Finkel and others, he had finally given his consent.

"How about you?" Hockney asked his friend. "How are you getting on at the Pentagon?"

Cummings shrugged. "Well, it's one way of making a living. But under Nixon, it's kind of hard to work up much enthusiasm for what I'm doing."

"What do you think about the stories that Nixon's going to widen the war? Go into the North, or something like that?"

"My bet would be Cambodia," Cummings opined quietly.

Hockney looked at his friend speculatively and took the risk of the next question. "How would you feel about a U.S. attack on Cambodia?"

"Me?" Cummings shrugged again. "I'm just a government employee. There's nothing much we can do."

"You could help me," Hockney riposted.

"We'll stay in touch," said Cummings, noncommittal.

Hockney was aware that many junior government officials were in a state of moral insurrection against the Nixon White House. He guessed that his friend Cummings —possibly thanks to the influence of his radical heiress girlfriend, Alexia Merchant—might be signed up for the same team.

As they prepared to leave, Hockney studied his friend's open-necked shirt and blazer. "I think I'd better change," he said. He had assumed that a party given by the Merchant family would be ultraformal.

"Forget it," said Cummings. "You're perfect."

But out of the fifty-odd guests who assembled in Vlad Merchant's penthouse apartment on Central Park West,

Hockney could see only seven or eight men who were sporting tuxedos. Most of the others wore open-necked shirts, like Cummings. There were even a couple of blacks in paramilitary gear with berets who might have come straight from the street party he had visited in Greenwich Village.

"I don't see many heavy hitters," Hockney whispered to Cummings as they made their entrance. The gathering was supposedly being held to raise funds for a new antiwar campaign that the Foundation for Progressive Reform was sponsoring. With the help of Vlad Merchant's largesse, the Institute had rapidly taken the lead from rival lobbies in promoting liberal causes. Its radicalism made older, more established bodies look conservative by comparison.

"There aren't many entrepreneurs who are as enlightened as our host," Cummings replied, smiling at a short, corpulent man with a halo of white hair around his bald pate. "Bob, may I introduce Mr. Vlad Merchant, the Medici of the progressive cause in America?"

"Wonderful," Merchant enthused. "It's wonderful to meet a man who has done as much as you to open our eyes to what has been happening in Vietnam, Mr. Hockney."

Hockney's eyes moved from the old man to the dark, fine-boned woman who hovered behind him, diamonds flashing at her throat and ears. "My granddaughter Alexia." Merchant introduced her. Cummings kissed her on the cheek. Hockney, suddenly gallant, kissed her hand.

Cummings led him around the room. The way most of the guests responded every time Hockney's name was mentioned, he might have been a movie star.

"Sorry, the job's already taken," Cummings observed when Hockney remarked on this phenomenon. "A real-life movie star is the leading attraction tonight. Did you see Tessa Torrance in *Sex Wars*?"

"I haven't caught up with last year's movies. But I did read about Tessa's impressions of her trip to Hanoi. That was pretty gutsy stuff. There aren't many people in Hollywood who are as outspoken as that."

"Well, she had a good tutor. Did you know Vlad Merchant discovered her? Hollywood began to take notice of her only after she made those commercials for Merchant lingerie."

"Are you talking about Tessa Torrance?" belched their neighbor, one of the handful of men in the room in a dinner jacket. "She's got the best boobs in town." He had obviously been an early arrival at the party, Hockney thought. "You wait and see," the man admonished them, wagging a finger.

The furniture had been removed from the vast, high-ceilinged room overlooking the park. Waiters circulated, offering red and white wine. There was a lull in the conversation as a celebrated couple appeared through the main doors.

"Make way for the White Panthers!" shouted Herman Quinn, the best-selling novelist who was the darling of the gossip columnists, as he threaded his way through the small groups of people squatting on the floor. His pock-marked face, creased like a relief map, was flushed with alcohol. On his arm, at least a foot taller in her high-heeled boots, was Tessa Torrance, clad in jeans and a see-through shirt. Stitched on the seat of her skintight pants was a tiny patch. Hockney craned forward to make out the words on it. "Kiss my ass," he read. He tried to guess her age, but couldn't. Late twenties, or even thirties. She was ageless.

Vlad Merchant, presiding over a table at one end of the room, tapped his glass for attention. "Ladies and gentlemen," he began in a voice that seemed to Hockney surprisingly high-pitched and reedy for a man endowed with so much flesh, "we are here for a reason. The real war is not taking place in Vietnam. It is taking place here in the United States. It is the war for public opinion. With generous support from people like yourselves, we can win that war. I would now like to present a distinguished authority well known to all of you who can tell us why we must. Ladies and gentlemen, Mr. Herman Quinn."

Hockney joined in the applause.

"My problem," Quinn said to open his speech, "is that this armored car"—he pointed at his own chest—"doesn't run on California red. Come on, Vlad, break out the Irish wine."

168

There was more applause as Merchant conferred with a waiter, who promptly vanished from the room to fetch whiskey. Drunk or sober, Quinn always got a hand. He thrived on controversy. The booze, the fist fights, and the girls were part of the cult that had grown up around him, as familiar to the public as his half-dozen best-sellers and his vociferous campaign against the Vietnam war. Quinn boasted to the gossip columnists that he never wrote about anything that he had not personally experienced. He claimed in one notorious interview that he had once experienced nine orgasms with three different women in the course of a single night. Many a liberated woman had tried to put him to the test since then.

A bottle of Jameson's whiskey materialized on the buffet table in front of Quinn. The novelist poured himself a generous slug before addressing his topic.

"Nixon lied his way into the White House by promising us that he was going to end the war," Quinn declaimed, now suitably fortified. "The catch is, he didn't say when. The way I reckon it, that could give him another seven years in which to indulge his lust for blood sports. So it's incumbent on all of us—you, me, and this sexy lady standing next to me—to do anything we can to bring this President down. The need is so great that anything, and I do mean *anything*, would be justified." Whistles and clapping from the guests drowned out Quinn's voice. He took advantage of the interruption to replenish his glass.

"But I guess you didn't come along here to look at my pretty face," Quinn resumed. "Here with us tonight, fresh from the dikes and hospitals that Richard Milhous Nixon's planes have been bombing back into the stone age, is the beautiful, the irresistible, Tessa Torrance." He raised his glass to Tessa. "Ladies and gentlemen, I give you our new Joan of Arc. She has heard the right voices."

The guests who had been sprawled on the carpet struggled to their feet to greet Tessa with a standing ovation—and to get a better look at the sex idol. From where he was standing, Hockney felt that she did not quite live up to her celluloid image. Without makeup, Tessa looked pale and drawn. Her hair, clumsily bound by a headband, hung straight down on either side of her face. Her jaw struck him as rather too masculine. But her body was advertised rather than concealed by the transparent blouse and tight jeans, and it more than lived up to the centerfold that Hockney had seen in a copy of *Pillow Talk*—a photo that had become a favorite pinup for the GIs in Vietnam. He wondered whether Tessa was conscious of the extent to which she had given aid and succor to the troops. He wondered what her reaction would be if he tried to make a joke about that to break the ice with her later on. Her stern, unsmiling face offered a warning not to take it for granted that she had any sense of humor at all.

Maybe she was nervous, Hockney thought. As she spoke, she clenched and unclenched her fists continuously, her arms hanging stiffly by her sides. Something about her intensity reminded him of Lani.

Tessa was delivering a long, monotonous diary of a twelve-day visit to North Vietnam. It began with a clichéd description of the delegation of children who had heaped her with flowers and ended with a eulogy of Laurie Pritchard. The journalist, Hockney knew, had acted as her host. She talked about Pritchard as if he were some kind of guru. Hockney grew a little uneasy, remembering the role that Pritchard was known to have played in interrogating American prisoners on behalf of the Communists during the Korean war. If Tessa had looked different, Hockney realized, most of the audience—himself included—would have switched off before she got halfway through her speech.

But because she was who she was, he waited patiently until she had finished her harangue. He clapped as hard and long as anyone else in the room, then quickly pursued a waiter to have his glass refilled. He had only begun to sample his fresh glass of California red when he became aware that Quinn had taken the floor again. "We've got one more star here tonight," the novelist announced. "A star from the media. You've all read his stories from Vietnam in the *World*. I'm sorry that he's not as sexy as our last speaker—or the one before her—but he's one of the rare people who manage to tell it the way it is. Citizens, I give you Bob Hockney."

There was more applause, but Hockney did not budge from where he was standing. It crossed his mind that his editors might be less than exhilarated if they knew that the name of the paper—as well as his own—was being invoked to support an anti-Vietnam fund-raising drive. He raised his hands in front of his face, as if trying to ward off an unwanted photographer.

"You know us reporters," Hockney apologized. "We're better at tearing other people's speeches apart than at making them ourselves." He was aware that Tessa's wide blue eyes were focused on him. "Don't let me spoil a moment of beauty," he added. "I think we'll all remember tonight as the night we witnessed the transformation of a love goddess into a political crusader. Speaking for myself, I'll always be happy to share Tessa's wars—especially if they're *Sex Wars*." The joke inspired approving shouts and whistles. Hockney bowed his head theatrically toward Tessa.

Vlad Merchant pulled him aside.

"You know," he whispered, "lovely as she is, not everyone approves of Tessa's life-style. Jane Fonda insists that by being overpromiscuous, Tessa demeans her whole political posture." Hockney answered that the more celebrated movie star was only putting down a rival.

When Tessa smiled, she was a different woman, Hockney thought as he watched her walking toward him. Her whole face was illuminated, as if by a candle shining below her chin. He laid aside the piece of lemon pie he had just taken from the buffet. The words did not seem to matter. Afterward, he could not remember what she had said to him, or he to her. Her eyes never moved from his face. Almost without thinking, he found himself in the back of her chauffeur-driven limousine on the way to her suite at the Pierre Hotel. He suggested some hours later that he should leave before dawn, knowing that the staff at some hotels supplemented their wages by feeding the gossip columnists. Tessa would not hear of it.

Washington
1974-1975

1

IN THE YEARS OF WATERGATE and the antiwar uprisings in the streets of America, Nicholas Flower, the chief of the CIA's counterintelligence staff, came to feel that he was witnessing the vindication of a lifetime's distrust of open government. The pillars of authority were being shaken, and the haughty busts on top came tumbling down. Flower felt little sympathy for Nixon, but he knew that the assault on the presidency would not leave unscathed the other institutions on which national survival depended. Even to place those institutions under question —inherently undemocratic as they were—was, Flower believed, to open the way to their destruction. He was deeply skeptical of how much could be communicated to those outside the inner sanctum of the necessity for the secret recourses that were his stock-in-trade. Steeped in Florentine philosophy, Flower was convinced of the words of his admired Guicciardini: "You are only truly safe from the man you suspect when circumstances are such that he cannot harm you even if he wants to. For security founded on the will and discretion of others is false, seeing how little virtue and good is to be found in men." And Flower's distrust of his fellow men was immense. It had been so since he had made the mistake, a quarter of a century before, of taking into his confidence an Englishman named Kim Philby.

While the media and Congress battered on the gates of the presidency, the Russians went on talking détente as if the administration were intact. The Secretary of State received the Soviet ambassador in Washington once a week for a private conversation lasting hours, attended by no other American. At the price of a Nobel peace prize, the United States had concluded a treaty with Hanoi that would—Flower had predicted—enable the North Vietnamese to take Saigon within two years. He had read reports of the Secretary of State's discussions with the North Vietnamese in Paris. At one point, the North Vietnamese had told him that the elimination of President Thieu would be a condition for a deal. "Do you mean you want us to kill him?" the Secretary had demanded. "Yes," replied the North Vietnamese, "but you don't have to put it in the treaty." In the name of détente, arms limitation treaties had been signed that Flower was equally convinced the Russians had no intention of respecting. Such exchanges, in the view of the counterintelligence (CI) chief, amounted to no more than a chloroform pad, designed to anesthetize American opinion to the real and growing threat presented by Soviet strategic designs.

Nick Flower did not believe in détente. The word was French, he occasionally pointed out to the subordinates who shared his five-hour lunches at the Provençal. It had no exact translation in either English or Russian. Therefore, if used at all, it should be used in the strict meaning of one of the French dictionary definitions—to denote the release of tension that comes from pulling the trigger of a gun. "The Russians don't even use the word 'détente,' " he would conclude his argument, triumphantly. "They talk of peaceful coexistence, which their literature holds to be perfectly compatible with the pitiless waging of the international class war."

No, the Russians believed in détente no more than he did. Flower suspected that the Soviet leadership was following an altogether different plan, one so totally alien to the mood of a democratic society that, if explained to the public and the politicians, it was likely to arouse general incredulity. Flower believed that the Russians intended to reduce the United States to a condition of strategic inferiority that would enable them to dictate the policies of America's allies in Western Europe and the third world and to control the world's most important reserves of oil and mineral resources. There had been recurring references, in the debriefing of Soviet bloc defectors and in the reports of well-placed Soviet agents—which were becoming as rare as gold dust—to the existence of a plan for the attainment of Moscow's long-range objectives by the early or mid-1980s. Sometimes, the year 1982 had been reported as the final deadline. More recently, there had been mention of the year 1985. A report from an agent who had had access to the secret papers of the conference of Eastern European Communist leaders recently held in Prague said that Leonid Brezhnev had boasted that, by 1985, "we will be able to exert our will wherever we need to."

Flower had not been able to fill in all the missing pieces in what he thought of as a great jigsaw puzzle, and he was convinced that relevant knowledge was being withheld from him by some of his colleagues at Langley, with whom he was in a state of undeclared war. He relied more and more heavily on his friends in foreign intelligence services —above all the Israelis. The liaison functions of the CI staff gave Flower a legitimate pretext to cultivate special relationships with the spymasters of other countries. With the Israelis, the association went much deeper.

Trusting Flower since he had done them invaluable services at the time of the creation of the state of Israel, and sharing his suspicions that the Agency itself might have been penetrated by the KGB, the Israelis insisted on dealing only with the CI chief at Langley. In his turn, Flower had succeeded in defending his rights to handle the "Israeli account" against all challengers in the CIA headquarters. So it was not surprising that it was Gideon Sharon, head of the Mossad network in the United States, who provided Flower with his first real clue to the contents of the long-range Soviet plan whose very existence was a cause of controversy among his American colleagues.

Under a different name, Sharon was notorious among Arab leaders as the man who had led the strike team that blew up fourteen Middle East airliners at Beirut airport. A bullet crease along his upper temple had been erased by plastic surgery, but there was still a small patch of hair missing.

"We have heard from our best Moscow source that it's called Plan Azev," Sharon told Flower over breakfast at the CI chief's house in Arlington. Gideon Sharon preferred to meet over breakfast than lunch, a custom which—though very American—was regarded by Flower as faintly barbaric. A frequent insomniac, he was entirely capable of staying up all night, leafing through Machiavelli's *Discorsi* or Ezra Pound's *Cantos*.

"Azev?"

The Israeli nodded.

"I see," said Flower. "Well, I guess that tells us a lot." He had made the mental connections instantly. The first was to the most notorious double agent in the history of the Russian secret service—Azev, who had doubled as chief of the czar's secret police and leader of the revolutionary terrorist faction that assassinated his own sovereign. If the Soviets had a plan code-named Azev, it meant that it centered on penetration—the planting of double agents, or moles, in key positions in the West. The other connection was to the man who must have invented the code name. Who but Kramar, the man who thought of himself as the walking reincarnation of every Russian spymaster who had ever lived, and the man whom Flower regarded as his most dangerous adversary, would have reached into the czarist past for a name to describe a plan for Communist domination?

There was good fishing for Kramar and his people amid the troubled reflections in the Potomac. With the help of—but sometimes, in spite of—the FBI, with whom his relations were at best, intermittent, Flower had tried to keep track of the man Kramar had assigned to the KGB residency in Washington. Colonel Viktor Barisov had surfaced in Washington society as a counselor at the Soviet embassy. He appeared more frequently on the diplomatic cocktail circuit than his Russian colleagues, always unflappably charming. His movements betrayed little of the nature of his real assignment in Washington. Flower suspected that he had been sent to run one or more important moles. But their identities—if they really existed—had continued to elude him. On two occasions, Barisov had been trailed to a movie theater in Rosslyn in the midafternoon. It had seemed improbable that a senior KGB officer would spend half his day watching the matinee of *The Planet of the Apes*. But Barisov's followers had failed to identify whomever he had gone to meet.

Again, a surveillance team had followed Barisov's car to an intersection of Massachusetts Avenue and had picked up the sound of a squirt transmission—a twenty-second radio burst that might have contained twenty minutes or more of recorded conversation—as he waited for the lights to change. Presented with the report, Flower was left in no doubt that Barisov had been either issuing instructions or receiving a recorded message from one of his agents, concealed in a nearby car. But which car? At the busy intersection, it had been impossible for the surveillance team to tell.

Flower picked up his first lead after Barisov had made a routine trip back to Moscow. Flower was a great believer in the usefulness of checking flight plans—an exhausting job even with the aid of computers—since he had realized that one of the most secure ways for an intelligence officer to meet an agent is to rendezvous at a stopover in the course of two apparently unrelated journeys. En route to Moscow, Barisov had stopped over for a couple of days in Mexico City.

"What's he doing down in Mexico?" Flower had demanded of his deputy after looking at the report. He had ordered a rundown on any American citizens who happened to stop over in Mexico City at the same time.

"In Mexico?" his deputy had complained. "It will take forever. Think of all the tourists."

"Weed them out," Flower commanded. "You can start by checking on our own computers to see whether any CIA staff went through there at the same time as Barisov." Flower brooked little discussion of his orders from subordinates. Though he was endlessly paternal to those who worked for him, people sometimes complained that they were expected to cut off their balls and hang them by the door before setting foot inside his office.

This time, Flower's meticulous concern for detail was rewarded.

"I've got a name," his deputy reported.

"Is he CIA?" Flower sat quivering on the edge of his chair, wondering whether this, at last, was the big break.

"He's ex-Agency. A guy called Phil Kreps. Used to be a case officer down in Santiago. They threw him out a couple of years ago because he was drinking too much. Indiscreet, woman trouble, shooting his mouth off in bars—you know, that sort of thing."

"I remember," said Flower. "Kreps is another of those guys who's been threatening to write a book exposing the Agency. He never got a clean bill of health from this office." Flower recalled that Phil Kreps had never even been put through a polygraph test from the time the CIA accepted him. Kreps was a product of the general breakdown of security.

"What was Kreps's flight plan?" Flower asked.

"Havana–London."

"Havana? What's he been doing over there?"

"Researching his book, I guess." Flower's deputy shrugged.

"If he's in with the Cubans, why meet a KGB officer in Mexico City?" Flower mused aloud. Anyway, he thought to himself, Kreps had little intelligence value now. After his row with his station chief in Santiago, he was a burned-out case—though he could still be used, of course, to feed leftist reporters.

"There's something else," said Flower's deputy.

"Yes?"

"Someone else made a stopover in Mexico City. Got in the same day as Barisov, left the same day."

"Name?"

"Perry Cummings. He's a senior analyst at the Defense Department."

"Now that *is* interesting." Flower paused to light a cigarette. His emaciated fingers were nicotine-stained. "What kind of access does this Cummings have?"

"He's a young guy. But he's been working on weapons evaluation. I understand he's been involved in some of the latest satellite research."

"Has he shown up in our mail intercepts?"

"I don't think so. I'll check."

179

"You do that," Flower instructed. His subordinates had occasionally warned him that his mail intercept program was in technical breach of the CIA's charter. Flower had not been impressed. Technicalities, in his view, took second place to state security. "For the moment," he added, "we'll keep this between you and me." It was Flower's favorite phrase.

2

PERRY CUMMINGS listened to the Undersecretary of Defense bellow until he ran out of steam.

"We're going to stop these leaks," the Undersecretary concluded. "I won't be happy until every government employee has to take a regular polygraph test on whether he's been talking to reporters."

At the start of the conversation, Cummings had been nervous that the Undersecretary's attack was going to focus on him. Maybe he had been seen having dinner once too often with Bob Hockney or Rick Adams, Senator Milligan's aide. His fear evaporated as it became clear that what was troubling his boss were the leaks that were reaching Senator Seamus O'Reilly's office out of the Defense Department and the CIA on Soviet violations of the SALT agreements.

"Henry's *furious*." The Undersecretary struck up his chorus again. "He blames most of it on this department. We don't want FBI gumshoes clambering all over the place, so we've got to tighten the screws."

Kissinger was the most important survivor of the Nixon administration, even more powerful under Ford than he had been before.

"I couldn't agree more, sir," said Cummings. The possibility of a general security investigation set his antennae waving again. He wouldn't want anybody to inspect his apartment too closely. He debated whether he should find a pretext to leave the Pentagon early and clean up at home, just in case. It would be ironic if they managed to pin something on him because some cold-warrior along the corridor was leaking information to Senator O'Reilly, who talked as if the Russians were about to send gunboats up the Potomac.

"Well, don't just sit there," said the Undersecretary. "Have you got any ideas?"

Cummings was tempted to point out that ferreting out the sources of press leaks was not part of his brief. Instead, he said, "I can ask around, sir."

Cummings mentioned the episode to Hockney over dinner at the new steak restaurant, the Palm. Their relationship had evolved tremendously over the previous five years. Hockney flattered himself that his own influence had helped to persuade Cummings to follow the example of other brave officials who had risked their careers by leaking information that had helped expose malingering by the Nixon and Ford administrations. In spite of government efforts to punish some of those responsible for the leaks— like Daniel Ellsberg—the trickle had swelled to a flood as a result of Watergate and the controversies over Vietnam, Cambodia, and the CIA's role in the coup in Chile. Cummings had become Hockney's best source.

"I'm surprised the Undersecretary asked *you* about the leaks," said Hockney, patting the thick brown envelope that Cummings had nonchalantly left on the chair beside him when he arrived. The xerox machine, Hockney had concluded long ago, was the investigative reporter's greatest friend. Cummings had told him that the envelope contained some explosive material on the CIA's covert operations in Africa and Latin America.

"Since Nixon went," Cummings commented, "it seems as if all the survivors are shell-shocked. They start jumping into ditches at the slightest noise."

He had touched on a sore point for Hockney's colleagues on the *World*. Their main rival, the *Washington Tribune*, had consistently scooped the *World* in reporting the major developments in the Watergate affair. The *World*'s loss of face, however, had provided Hockney with his biggest break since his time in Vietnam. The *World* had latched on to his latest stories on the CIA—mostly based on leaks from Rick Adams on Senator Milligan's staff—and touted them as a journalistic breakthrough. "The competition brought down Nixon," was the way Ed Finkel, the *World*'s national affairs editor, had put it. *"We* are going to bust up the CIA and bring down Henry." The *World* wanted more embarrassing stories on the Agency—as many as Hockney could get. That was where Perry Cummings came in.

"What you need," said Cummings, "is a real live CIA guy who's ready to go public."

"Lead me to him." Hockney looked at the bowl of home fries, as big as a shopping basket, that the waiter had just laid on the table. His eyes rose above it to the caricatures of well-known people around town on the walls. He noticed that one or two politicians who had fallen into disgrace had had their faces painted over, and wondered what the average life-span of a celebrity was.

"I've got one," Cummings said as he sawed into his New York sirloin. "He's just what you need. He was stationed in Chile until 1972, when the CIA was busy destabilizing Allende. He left before the coup last year. Now he's out, and he's fed up to the teeth. He's been talking about doing a book. If you get to him now, you might be the first with the story. And the timing couldn't be better."

Hockney knew what Cummings was referring to. Rick Adams had mentioned that there was a real possibility—if the media pressure was kept up—that the Senate might vote to set up a special committee to investigate the CIA's activities worldwide. "That could break the whole thing open," Senator Milligan's aide had observed.

"As I said, lead me to him," Hockney repeated.

"He's gone to Europe. I think he may be scared that they'll put him on trial for something if he tries to tell his story over here. But it will be easy enough to put you in touch. Alex is in contact with him. He may even help the Foundation set up a new base in Europe."

"Does the man have a name?"

"Phil Kreps."

Hockney glanced up as a large party came into the

room. Most of the other guests stopped talking, with a clatter of knives and forks, as they recognized the tall, florid-faced man with the mop of white hair who towered above the other new arrivals. Several people went up to shake his hand.

Cummings started to hum "It's a Long, Long Way to Tipperary."

"Looks like he's working on his constituency," said Hockney.

"Maybe Senator Seamus O'Reilly has forgotten they can't vote for him down here," said Cummings.

Hockney found "Shame" O'Reilly's speeches excoriating the radical Afro-Arab lobby as a collection of "tinpot dictators" offensive, but he was impressed—like much of the country—by the magnetism and verbal flair of the new senator from New York.

Next to O'Reilly, Hockney recognized his executive assistant, Dick Roth. "The Mossad's man on Capitol Hill," Cummings remarked scornfully.

Roth pulled out a chair for the only woman in the party as she smiled and blew a kiss in Hockney's direction. Hockney smiled back. It had been years since he and Julia parted ways, but she still had the power to stir him deeply.

Cummings waved to her. "Hi, little sister," he called across the room. Hockney watched Julia murmur something in Roth's ear. He nodded and pulled her chair out again. Julia walked quickly toward their table.

"Hello, stranger," she said to Hockney, kissing him on both cheeks.

"Hello, Julia," he responded, stiffly formal. "What's it like working for the mad dog?"

"Now, now, politics aren't allowed after working hours."

"I'm not sure they've heard of that rule in Washington. You must have stayed too long at Sarah Lawrence," said her brother.

"You're not allowed to knock my senator," she said to Hockney, "until you've talked to him. When are you going to come and do an interview?"

"Come on, Julia, he's already been interviewed by everyone in sight."

"Well, you don't need an excuse to look in at the office. Have you ever heard of the Dirksen Building?"

"I'm starting to feel I've been here since it was built," said Hockney. It was one of the two main Senate office buildings.

"Well, don't be frightened to come over. I'm a big girl now. Bye, bye, big brother. Don't give Bob too many secret documents."

"You're a fine one to talk," Cummings protested, laughing. "That guy sitting next to you"—he pointed at Dick Roth—"has made off with more secrets than the Pentagon even knew it had."

Julia rejoined O'Reilly's party, moving across the floor with a studied swing to her hips, conscious that she looked ravishing in her all-white outfit.

"Julia's changed," Cummings observed.

"Yeah." Hockney pushed away the remains of his steak.

"Are you sorry you and she split up?"

"No. But I'm glad she's found something worthwhile to do with herself."

"You call working for Senator O'Reilly worthwhile?"

Hockney let the remark pass. He had been surprised when he first learned that Julia had gone to work on O'Reilly's campaign staff in New York, and even more surprised when, swept into Washington in triumph, the Senator appointed her to a top job on his staff. She had been profiled in some of the glossy magazines as one of the most successful women on Capitol Hill. Hockney had speculated, at the outset, that she was pushing herself in order to compete with him, to show that she was not going to be just the girl next door, the childhood sweetheart who got left behind. He had even wondered whether she had taken the job on O'Reilly's staff in order to pursue him to Washington. But, as time passed and she failed to call him, he began to realize that Julia might actually be bent on a life of her own. Hockney had called her and had even felt insulted when she had turned down a dinner date because, she said, she had another engagement. He had not even been invited over to her apartment. A second attempt had produced much the same result.

"Are you finished?" said the waiter to Hockney.

"Yeah."

"How's Tessa?" said Cummings, noticing his subdued mood.

"She's away on location. They're making some film about World War I. It sounds like the Bulgarians have rented out their entire army as extras. We're going to meet up in New York in a month or two."

"It must be pretty hard keeping up with a movie star when you're just a reporter stuck in Washington."

"*Just* a reporter?" Hockney was stung.

"There, there." Cummings placated him. "I'll take it back the day I see the spooks tumbling out of Langley like bugs from under an old log that's been kicked aside—all because of the power of your mighty pen."

3

HOCKNEY was sitting next to the *World*'s Washington bureau chief, Pete Lawry, in the press section on the day the next CIA director, Bill Crawford, arrived to testify before the Harmon Committee. Pete Lawry was the tallest man at the *World*. Everything about him was long— he stood six foot seven in his bare feet, but looked even taller because he was skinny. His long hair covered his head like a hula skirt.

Hockney was aglow. He felt personally responsible for the very existence of the Select Senate Committee on Intelligence. After all, it was his articles, based on the reminiscences of the ex-CIA operative Phil Kreps, and the leaks from his friends who were associated with the Foundation for Progressive Reform, that had generated a political uproar, making some kind of congressional investigation inevitable. Senator Harmon, who hailed from a potato state in the Northwest, was the right man to head it; he loved the glare of TV studio lights. But what guaranteed the success of the committee was not Harmon's practiced flair for public relations. It was the selection of his chief of staff, borrowed from Senator Milligan, who also sat on the select committee. "Thanks, Bob," Rick Adams had said when he called Hockney to inform him that Harmon had awarded him the job. "I owe this to you more than anyone."

As they waited for the senators to take their seats—for once, they were all there, since today's hearings were going to be televised—and for the witness to appear, Hockney asked himself how accurate Adams's comment had been. True, Hockney had worked; he had interrogated, he had harried. But his key material had come from three main sources. From Perry Cummings, who clearly had a Deep Throat inside the Agency whose identity he had never revealed to Hockney. From Rick Adams himself, who had passed on most of the CIA stuff that reached the oversight committees on Capitol Hill. And from the renegade Phil Kreps, whom Hockney had found living in a fourth floor walk up flat on the Rue des Bouchers in Brussels with his son and a Mexican dancer, surrounded by radicals whom he had already organized into a highly professional spy network of his own. Kreps was gathering material for a book that would tell not simply of past transgressions on the part of the Agency but of ongoing ones as well. Hockney had been astonished by the prowess of some of Kreps's protégés in spying on his former employers; they organized surveillance teams to trace every movement of CIA officers, rented apartments across the road from CIA residences and safe houses, bugged telephones, and used devices like directional microphones and concealed tape recorders. "Our aim," Kreps had told Hockney, "is to expose every single CIA agent in every country where the Agency operates, so that it will eventually be impossible for the CIA to practice covert action anywhere on earth." Hockney had not doubted Kreps was serious. And he had no reason to challenge Kreps's bona fides. The CIA renegade had handed him a front-page exclusive on a platter, involving the Agency's efforts to overthrow the elected president of Chile.

Last but not least, there had been Bill Crawford, the man for whom the reporters in the committee room had been waiting. Hockney flattered himself that he enjoyed a special relationship with the new CIA director, whom he

186

had first met when Crawford was running the CIA pacification program in Vietnam. The antiwar demonstrators slapped Crawford's picture on their placards and called him a murderer. But, as in Saigon, Hockney had found that the man in no way corresponded to the image. Over several lunches in his private dining room at Langley, Crawford had laid himself bare to the Agency's most celebrated media assailant. "You have to understand that the Agency is not composed of paramilitary rightists," he had insisted to Hockney. "I have always thought of myself as a liberal. Or, in European terms, a socialist. I joined the Agency in a fit of postwar idealism from which I have never managed to recover." Listening to Crawford over many hours, Hockney became more and more inclined to believe him. Crawford was devastatingly frank about the misdemeanors of his colleagues. He swore blind to Hockney that he was determined to unearth all the abuses of the past and give those responsible their pink slips. He volunteered information on past scandals that Hockney had not even known about.

"Crawford is unbelievable," Hockney muttered to Pete Lawry, sitting next to him in the committee room. "The way he talks to me, you'd think he had swapped his cloak and dagger for a cassock."

"Steady on," said the *World*'s bureau chief, in the English accent he affected, "I'm a Catholic too. Well, a lapsed Catholic anyway."

"So's Senator O'Reilly," Hockney whispered in response. "The point is that when this guy Crawford talks to reporters or congressmen, he seems to think he's in the confessional."

"I don't know why you should complain. I hear you're building up for another Pulitzer prize."

They stopped chatting as Crawford made his entrance. It struck Hockney that the new CIA director was entirely gray—gray suit, dark gray tie, gray hair, a colorless complexion, and glasses with the type of transparent frames that looked grayish under the lights the TV crews had set up in the committee room. If it was true that the perfect spy was someone who would find it hard to catch the attention of a waiter, Hockney reflected, Bill Crawford would certainly make the grade. He looked like a faded xerox copy of himself.

Crawford sat down awkwardly in the middle of the committee table. There was a slight commotion behind him.

"I don't believe it!" Lawry exclaimed.

"What's happening?"

"Crawford's brought some kind of James Bond gun with him. Look—it's there in front of him, on the table."

As Hockney craned forward to look, one of the photographers jumped up, camera at the ready. "Bill." Hockney could hear the CIA counsel calling urgently to Crawford. "Bill, the gun. The gun!" Crawford looked baffled. The CIA counsel ran around the table, scooped up the gun, and set it down again in front of Senator Harmon.

"What kind of gun is that?" Lawry whispered to Hockney.

"Don't know. Could be some sort of laser pistol."

The upshot was that it was Senator Harmon, not Director Crawford, who was immortalized in the world media holding the laser pistol on high for all to see. As the story of how the laser pistol had come to be manufactured unfolded in the course of Crawford's testimony, it struck Hockney that the whole incident summed up beautifully the character of the man appointed by a weakened President to direct the CIA. The laser pistol, according to Crawford, had been specially produced as part of a scheme to assassinate the Libyan dictator after CIA agents learned that he was planning to visit Paris in an effort to buy the equipment and technology to manufacture nuclear weapons in his own country. The plot had aborted, and the laser pistol had been consigned to a vault by one of Crawford's predecessors at Langley. Crawford had learned about it because, immediately after his appointment, he had ordered his staff to draw up a list of *all* operations—past, present, or proposed—that would be embarrassing for the Agency if exposed by someone like Bob Hockney.

"Naturally," Crawford concluded his testimony on this point, "when I learned that we were still in possession of murder weapons of this kind, I passed on the information to your select committee, in the person of the chief of staff, Mr. Adams." Crawford, it transpired, had been instantly receptive to Rick Adams's suggestion that the laser gun be produced to lend visual interest to Day One of the televised hearings.

"You know Crawford," Lawry remarked to Hockney as they walked away from the committee room at the end of the day's hearings. "I can't figure him out. Any one of his predecessors would have been ready to lie through the teeth rather than divulge information that this guy just hands out without anyone even needing to ask. What kind of game is he playing?"

"It's shell shock," said Hockney.

"What?"

"Put it this way," said Hockney. "He's seen that *any* official in this town—from the Commander-in-Chief down —is out of a job if he gets on the wrong side of the media and Congress. Maybe in that order." He reflected for a second. "He intends to stay in his job longer than his predecessor." The previous CIA director had lasted only a few months, during which he handed out hundreds of pink slips. "So the game Crawford is playing is a very old one. It's called Cover My Ass."

How else could Hockney explain the fact that, not long after Crawford testified—or rather, confessed—to the Harmon Committee, he presented Hockney with information that he would never have thought to ask about, a scoop that dwarfed Crawford's revelations about the Vietcong in Cholon and the CIA in Chile? This came about because Hockney had ridden up once again in the CIA director's private elevator at Langley to check out a story that had been mentioned by Perry Cummings: something about how the Agency had enlisted the help of a multinational corporation in an effort to steal a shipwrecked Russian submarine from the ocean bottom.

"Forget it," Crawford said, flapping his hand.

"Do you mean you're denying the story?"

"I'm not denying it, and I'm not confirming it either. I mean I've got a better story for you."

Crawford explained, and before he was halfway through, Hockney had forgotten all about the tale of the salvaged Soviet submarine. Quoting verbatim from the ultrasecret briefing on CIA abuses that he had had compiled for his personal use, Crawford related how the chief of his counter-intelligence staff had been conducting a massive and illegal program of mail intercepts.

"All American citizens who have been corresponding with people in Eastern Europe have had their letters steamed open by Nick Flower's men," Crawford summed up in a moralizing tone. "It is—uh—excessive. And it's unauthorized. The trouble with Flower is he thinks he's a law unto himself. He has even opened letters from Moscow addressed to Senator Harmon."

"That's heavy," Hockney agreed.

"Flower is a relic of the past." Crawford passed judgment, flipping his hands upward so that the palms faced Hockney. "It's high time we cleaned house over here. I've never been able to figure out what those CI characters think they're doing anyway. They spend all their time sniffing after nonexistent moles. They just slow down the *real* work of the Agency, which I'm not ashamed to talk about in front of Congress or anyone else."

"I must say, you're amazingly frank for a director of central intelligence."

"I believe in open government," Crawford said with what Hockney felt to be exaggerated fervor. "These types like Nick Flower are throwbacks to the age of the Borgias."

4

ALL HEADS turned as Hockney and Tessa Torrance walked into Elaine's, New York's most celebrated intellectual night spot, the day after he had delivered the first of his sledgehammer blows against Nick Flower and the CIA's illegal mail intercept program in the pages of the *World*. Hockney liked Elaine's, for all the rough-and-tumble—which sometimes ended in a fist fight between someone like the hot-tempered, hard-drinking novelist Quinn and anyone whose face happened to offend him. And then, it was one of the few places in town where Hockney was likely to get as much recognition as his movie star companion. He had virtually given up wearing suits, in favor of suede jackets and turtlenecks. Tessa was clad in a black sheath, her hair dyed black too, in preparation for her next film, in which she was to play the mistress of the guerrilla martyr Ché Guevara.

Quinn was presiding over his usual table to the right of the door within spitting distance of the bar.

"Hey, Bob!" he yelled. "Great piece in the *World* this morning. That'll blast some more spooks out of their holes in the ground."

"I hope so."

"The only problem is I don't think Henry's reading you. Looks like he wants to start another Vietnam in Angola."

There had been rumors of a big CIA covert operation to support the anti-Communist blacks in Angola now that the Portuguese were pulling out.

"Oh, I think we've got that one covered, Herman," he called back cheerfully to Quinn. "Stay tuned for the next installment." Hockney's confidence stemmed from something he had heard from Alexia Merchant at the Foundation. It seemed there was a second Phil Kreps inside the Agency, a young case officer who had lost his illusions during the Vietnam war. He had been appointed to the special task force that the CIA had set up to coordinate covert operations in Portuguese Africa. "He's ready to feed us," Alexia had explained to Hockney, referring to the Foundation's CIA source simply as "Fred." Hockney had been promised he would be the first in the press to have access to "Fred's" material.

"Can you imagine it?" he asked Tessa rhetorically, after explaining Fred's contact with the Foundation. "We'll have our own spy right there inside the Agency. We can make it impossible for CIA agents to move an inch in Africa. Everything they try to do will be passed on to the Foundation, or to me, or to Rick Adams at the Harmon Committee."

"What do you suppose motivates someone like Fred?"

Tessa asked, dreamily acknowledging smiles and shouted greetings from all around them.

"Could be an idealist," said Hockney. "Probably went into the Agency thinking he was going to save the world and then got fed up with all the crap he had to take from his bosses."

"How come he's in touch with the Foundation?"

"Oh, they've set up a contact group. Phil Kreps—you know, that ex-CIA guy who's over in Amsterdam—has been suggesting a few names at Langley. I guess Perry Cummings has been a big help too."

"Isn't someone like Fred worried that if he gets found out he's going to get his pink slip?"

"The Foundation's taken care of that," Hockney replied. "In fact, what they're doing is pretty clever. They're offering a financial safety net for government employees who start blowing the whistle and get caught. In other words, if Fred is found out, he'll be looked after. Alexia would probably give him some kind of consultancy over at the Foundation, like Phil Kreps." Kreps, the first CIA renegade to go public, was on some kind of Foundation retainer in Europe. Hockney chuckled. "With this kind of setup," he observed, "I suppose the *real* spies—the Soviets and so on—are finding it pretty tough to beat the American media to the news."

Hockney surveyed the neighboring tables. The territorial imperative was enforced with a vengeance at Elaine's. He reflected that just as in the wilds animals will defecate to warn off potential intruders from the territory they have staked out for themselves, so at Elaine's the babble of voices must warn off outsiders who did not belong to the tribe. He noticed that Quinn was in fine form, threatening to beat up a magazine writer who did not share his enthusiasm for solar energy as a replacement for nuclear power.

"You realize we'd have to cover an area the size of Texas with mirrors in order to have enough solar energy to fry our eggs all over the country," the magazine writer was unwisely insisting to Quinn. "Even then, we'd have to eat them raw if the sun clouded over."

Quinn grabbed the writer's tie and pulled it like a noose.

"I want something with garlic," Hockney said to Tessa as he perused the menu.

"I thought we were going to spend the night together," she protested.

"That's the point," said Hockney. "Garlic inflames the mucous membrane. You'll have to eat garlic too. I hear that crocodile kidneys do the trick just as well, but I doubt whether they serve them at Elaine's."

5

VIKTOR BARISOV, in his office on an upper floor of the Soviet embassy, was contemplating how he could explain in his report to Kramar the reasons why Nick Flower was almost certain to be purged from the CIA in terms that would not excite general incredulity at Moscow Center. Kramar understood the gullibility of Western public opinion better than any of the old guard. But would even Kramar be able to credit the fact that his supreme adversary—a man who was in some ways his own mirror image—could be destroyed because the American public thought it was scandalous for a secret service to read other people's correspondence? No, Kramar would interpret it all as a deep-laid plot. There was that element too. Crawford versus Flower: the contest between two incompatible personalities and philosophies of intelligence work. The outcome, in any event, was plain. With the victory of Crawford and the destruction of the Agency's counterintelligence capacities, the scope of Soviet deception and penetration would be vastly increased. The safety of Kramar's moles, slowly burrowing their way upward toward the important strata of American public life, would be reassured—and, with it, the eventual success of Plan Azev.

The special phone on Barisov's desk that connected him to the Washington residency of the GRU, the Soviet military intelligence service, started to purr.

"Yes?"

The GRU resident was agitated. Barisov had never liked the man. As in other Soviet residencies around the world, the KGB and the GRU lived side by side in a state of undeclared war, competing for agents and intelligence. KGB officers tended to view the GRU as a collection of vodka-swilling dunderheads, while the GRU men disliked and feared their KGB rivals because they spent a considerable proportion of their time spying on their fellow Russians. Within the Soviet mission in Washington, the picture was complicated still further by the existence of what was, in effect, a third and parallel intelligence network: the local delegates of the International Department of the Soviet Communist Party, who especially concerned themselves with cultivating congressmen and congressional staffers. Barisov had trouble with their chief as well, since he occasionally tried to make out that, as the representative of the Communist Party, he should be treated as the top dog. However, Barisov tried to steer clear of the bureaucratic infighting that was the daily routine in Soviet missions abroad. He had even been prepared to share the production of the KGB's top agent in the Pentagon—code-named Coyote—with his GRU colleague on an informal basis.

Coyote seemed to be the cause of the GRU chief's agitation.

"They've found out something," the GRU resident gabbled. "There'll be an investigation. They're bound to interrogate him."

"Slow down," said Barisov.

The GRU man explained that he had learned from a low-level source of his own inside the Pentagon that the CIA had found proof that a senior analyst in the weapons evaluation section had been mailing secret material to the KGB in the guise of gifts for a charity in East Berlin. He assumed that the suspected official was Coyote.

"It must have been Flower," said Barisov. "That damn mail intercept program." He himself had devised the mailing system, in order to minimize direct contacts with his agents in the United States. He had been thrifty in using dead drops, since one that he considered especially subtle —a container disguised as the top of a fencepost, with an explosive device that ignited if someone handled it the wrong way—had been discovered and successfully opened by FBI agents in Bethesda. Still, there was nothing in the mailing shots that would identify Coyote definitively. Coyote was skilled; nothing in the microfilm and microdots he had been sending could point conclusively to the source of the leak. Furthermore, Barisov considered rapidly, his existence had been revealed by the very illegal methods that had now made Flower and the CIA a subject for public outcry.

"I think it can be contained," he told the GRU chief.

6

HOCKNEY was about to hang up when someone at last picked up the receiver. The voice at the other end was like the hiss of escaping gas.

"Mr. Flower?"

"Uh." The voice was noncommittal.

"Mr. Flower, this is Robert Hockney, of the *World*. We're doing a follow-up on that mail intercept story. I suppose you saw it."

"Uh. Crawford gave you my number, I bet."

"Mr. Flower, unlike some reporters, I don't need the director of the CIA to give me my information." Hockney responded fast, but he was nettled. He had, of course, gotten Flower's number from Crawford.

"Mr. Hockney." Flower's voice came back, fainter this time. "You don't happen to recall the German name for the great tit, by any chance?"

"What?" Hockney gasped. Was the old spook trying to insult him? Then he remembered: Flower was an amateur ornithologist, one of the country's recognized authorities on birdsong. He was said to spend hours in the countryside, his ear cocked to catch the fine distinction between the low "oor-roo-coooo" of a rock dove and the harsh, rhythmic "ghru-groo-groo" of the wood pigeon. Not a bad hobby for a man whose trade was to listen and wait.

Then, to Hockney's surprise, Flower said curtly, "You will meet me at the Army and Navy Club at twelve-thirty tomorrow. On the dot."

Hockney sat stretching his fingers in the yellow waiting room by the Farragut Street entrance of the Army and Navy Club. He pulled a few notes out of his pocket that he had scribbled on the back of an airline ticket, then put them back. He would play this one by ear. But he was surprised to find himself tense, unable to sit still. Maybe he had been wrong to accept this assignment. As Crawford had said, Nick Flower was finished. A bio piece would just be twisting the knife in the wound. But you didn't claw your way to the top of the *New York World* by thinking *that* way. Hockney thought of Bruce Raw, the prizewinning photographer who had shifted the bodies around before taking pictures of a massacre scene outside Saigon because he thought they didn't look horrific enough the way they had fallen. Maybe Hockney's task today was to shift the bodies.

Was that Flower? Hockney started to rise from the couch as a distinguished, pin-striped figure brushed past the doorway. There was no photograph of Flower in the *World*'s morgue. No, the man moved sedately toward the elevator.

Suddenly a tall, stooped figure in a rumpled charcoal gray herringbone suit was at the threshold, and Hockney needed no introduction. He thrust his hand out. "I'm delighted to meet you, Mr. Flower." Hockney almost recoiled from the cold, limp hand that responded, the nervous flicker across the lips on the old, sick face, which looked as if it had been smeared with flour or fine white ash.

Hockney followed Flower to the elevator. In three-quarter profile, the man looked even more like a praying mantis. They rode in silence up to the sixth floor. Hockney opened his mouth to speak several times, but was silenced by the way that Flower resolutely refused to meet his eyes.

In the babble of the dining room, Flower's silence was still infectious. Waitresses bustled back and forth between the diners, who were mostly high-ranking retired officials from the armed forces and the CIA. He ordered one martini, then another. Hockney asked for a glass of white wine. Flower pored endlessly over the menu before settling on the veal marsala. Hockney asked for a hamburger. Flower had started on his third martini, his eyes still pinned to the menu, before Hockney tried to start the conversation. Flower stubbed his cigarette into the ashtray, gesturing toward the large black waitress who was bearing down on their table.

"Let's deal with the important things first, Mr. Hockney."

"Thank you for agreeing to see me," Hockney ventured at last.

Flower looked as if he had just broken a tooth. "The food is getting worse here all the time," he said. "I guess it's the Christmas spirit."

"Now that it's all out in the open." Hockney tried again to start the conversation.

"Would you like some red wine?" Flower asked, ignoring Hockney's remark. "I don't exactly know what goes with hamburger. They do keep a passable Chateau Margaux."

"Thanks. I'll stick to white."

Hockney made a mental note: The spymaster hits the bottle. Must get those three martinis into the piece.

Now Flower had ordered the Chateau Margaux.

"Is that half a bottle, Mr. Flower?" the wine steward inquired, cocking an eyebrow at the glass of white wine Hockney had barely touched.

"Did I say half a bottle?" Flower snapped. For the first time something had stirred him into life.

"As I was saying." Hockney tried again. "Now that it's all out in the open—"

"Would I sound ignorant if I asked you what's out in the open?"

"The fact that the gentlemen of the CIA have been opening other gentlemen's mail."

"What more can I tell you about it? I thought Crawford had dictated the whole story to you."

"What makes you think that?"

"The fact that I got my pink slip today."

"The fact that you got *what*?" Hockney was startled to learn that his story had felled the man of secrets so quickly.

"The fact that you, young man, were used to cut out the guts of this country's intelligence service."

"Crawford was not my source." Hockney instantly regretted the lie. "Not my *only* source." He corrected himself. Obviously Flower knew about his link with Crawford and about Crawford's motivation for leaking information: to destroy a bureaucratic enemy and to curry favor with the liberal establishment. But Hockney had the uneasy feeling that he was in the presence of a mind reader who would *always* know when he was lying.

Flower looked him in the eye for a few seconds, then went back to drawing lines on the tablecloth with his fork. "Perhaps your meetings with Crawford on Monday and Friday of last week were merely social calls. And I suppose it was just a coincidence that Crawford phoned me on Friday at 6:00 P.M., a few minutes after you left his office, to tell me I was through."

Hockney flushed. "I'm not here to be interviewed by you."

"Well, young man, as of today I'm just a retired government employee and there's no reason why I should consent to be interviewed by you."

Flower inhaled his Margaux. "I never trust a man without a palate."

"It's a pity you have no stomach for exposure. Don't you feel accountable to the American people?"

Flower said nothing, and went on saying nothing. The silence seemed interminable.

Hockney couldn't take it any longer. He blurted out, "Don't you realize that you could be indicted on criminal charges?"

"So could some of your editors."

"That's a cheap shot, Mr. Flower."

Flower called the waiter and complained that the veal had not been sliced thin enough. "You can take my plate away." He noticed that Hockney had barely touched his hamburger. "Anything wrong?"

"I'm not hungry," said Hockney.

Flower called for an Armagnac, and coffee. Hockney asked only for coffee.

"If we can go off the record, Mr. Hockney, I might be able to explain a few facts of life to you."

"We have a rule on the paper—"

"That's the first time I've heard of rules in your profession."

"My editors have specifically instructed me to get your comments on the record."

"Did you get Crawford's comments on the record?" Flower paused for effect. Hockney was flustered. "Anyway," Flower pursued, "do you always do what your editors tell you? Do you do what they tell you twenty-four hours a day?"

"Unlike spies, most serious reporters play by the rules." Hockney, listening to himself, was embarrassed by his own pomposity. He felt he was botching the interview.

"I wouldn't wish to embarrass you, but would you feel the same way about your editors if they were helping the CIA?"

"Of all the complaints that people at the Agency have made about the *World* these past few years, I don't remember hearing that one."

"But I am right in thinking, am I not, that you would be shocked to discover that one of your colleagues was working for the Agency?"

"Of course I'd be shocked." Hockney took the bait.

"I suspect you would be even more shocked by such a discovery than if I were able to supply you with evidence that one of your colleagues had been compromised by the KGB."

"Now we're playing games," said Hockney, trying to regain control of the conversation.

"Be patient with me, Mr. Hockney. I'm just trying to understand the subtle psychology of someone like yourself, who is outraged more by the activities of his own government than by those of our self-avowed enemies. I grew up in Idaho, at a time when serving your country was not held to be unpatriotic."

"You people have made patriotism unpatriotic."

A look of infinite sadness spread across Flower's face. He lit up another Dunhill, placed it on the ashtray almost immediately, and cradled his snifter in frail parchment fingers. My God, the hands, Hockney thought. They're like the hands of a Buchenwald survivor. He pushed the thought away. It did not fit the image.

"Against my better judgment, Mr. Hockney, I will tell you one thing on the record. In the course of what you described in print as my illegal mail intercepts I came across the case of an engaging young idealist. He would be about your age. For all I know, he could even be a friend of yours. It's rather a touching story. This young man had a social conscience. He liked to send packages to orphans in other countries. You know the sort of thing—packages of candy, chewing gum, small toys. All these orphans just happened to be in Eastern Europe."

Flower took a long drag on his cigarette, holding it the Russian way, between thumb and index finger. "If I may say so, your generation is full of noble words about ending world poverty, but there are very few people who would cut their gas consumption to do so. That's why I found it so impressive that this young man should give so much of his spare time to philanthropy. He came from a good family. Excellent education. Andover. Harvard. His father was an assistant secretary at both State and Defense under LBJ."

Hockney sensed a trap. "I'm sure you're a fund of stories," he interjected. "I'm all in favor of charity. But could we get back to the main point?"

"I've never chewed gum myself. Have you?"

"Yeah." Hockney felt like a fool for answering at all.

"Well, this story could have been created for you. I got a message from our station in Berlin that this young philanthropist was sending an unusual number of packages from New York and Washington to an address that we had under surveillance—for reasons I do not need to explain—in West Berlin. These packages were being hand-carried through Checkpoint Charlie into the eastern sector. I made the decision over here to have our friend followed to the post office so we could take a look at what he was sending the orphans. And what do you think we found, Mr. Hockney?"

"Search me," Hockney said impatiently. "Secret messages on candy wrappers, I suppose."

Nick Flower was unaccustomed to other people stepping on his lines. The thought flitted through his mind that the reason Hockney had foreshadowed his next remark could be that the reporter was more than just a stooge for the director of the CIA. It was possible that Hockney himself was part of the ring that Flower was about to describe. But Flower gave that a low probability rating. From what he had observed already, Hockney had too little control of his emotional reactions to be an operative.

"Are you familiar with the Pentagon report on Soviet espionage activities around our Strategic Air Command bases?" Flower resumed.

"I've heard of it," Hockney grunted dismissively.

"Did you know that a document of that length could fit on the back of a chewing gum wrapper?"

"Don't tell me that's what you found. Microdots inside a wrapper."

"It was just good luck really. One of my people just happened to hold the wrapper up at an odd angle under an ultraviolet light and saw a strange shadow. After we brought the FBI in we found we had acquired a whole library. Dozens of secret documents—from State, the Pentagon, and the Arms Control Agency—were being mailed to candy freaks in East Berlin."

Hockney thought he understood what Flower was doing. By weaving him uncheckable stories that were worthy of spy fiction, Flower was trying to divert him from the real issue—the illegality of the mail intercept program, which had violated the CIA's own charter.

"Okay, I'll buy the chewing gum story," said Hockney. "It'll make a good read. But what I want to know is why the Agency unwrapped the orphans' candy. The law says that's a job for the FBI."

"The FBI would never have known what was concealed in those candy wrappers if I hadn't been running an intercept operation," Flower said quietly.

"I don't see that that's any excuse for breaking the law. You could have brought in FBI agents at the very beginning and had them ask for a court order."

"Do you know how many people are involved in getting a federal court order?"

Hockney drummed the table irritably.

Flower went on. "Our young philanthropist friend was working at the Pentagon until a few days ago. He had a top security clearance from the FBI. The bureau knew nothing about his interest in orphans. We discovered that. And then we went to his boss and told him about it. Our friend wasn't told why he was fired and he didn't ask. The last thing I heard about him was that he was going to set up shop at the Foundation for Progressive Reform."

Hockney leaned forward, his elbow on the table and his hand across his mouth. The mention of the Foundation set several bells ringing at once. Some of his best news sources, and one of his closest friends, were working for the Foundation. He was now desperate to hear the finale of Flower's story, but tried to maintain the expression of bored disinterest that he had affected during the earlier part.

To become a master angler requires extraordinary finesse and, above all, the capacity to wait. Flower had acquired this during his weekend respites at his fishing shack up by the St. Lawrence River. Watching Hockney, he felt the sudden tug on the line. Slowly, he began to reel it in.

"Perhaps I will have a drink after all," said Hockney.

"But of course."

Hockney ordered a stinger. Flower called for another Armagnac.

As he considered what Flower had said, it hit him that the spy chief could be talking about only one man: Perry Cummings. Anger welled up in him at the thought that Flower, the master of deceit, could be trying to frame his friend. But it was overcome immediately by a strange numbness. The strength seemed to have sapped from his body. His legs were hollow. A prickly heat—like a thousand tiny needles—jabbed at his chest and shoulders. Although Hockney was not yet able to admit it to himself, the reason for his disorientation was that he sensed that what Flower was saying might be true.

To Hockney, Flower's voice now sounded as far away as that of a man in another room. "The Harmon Committee," Flower was stressing. "While he held down his Pentagon job, our young friend was feeding the committee a bagful of dirty tricks to use in its investigation of the CIA. More than that, he was the guy who was flooding the media with leaks on the same subject."

Hockney now had no doubt that Flower was talking about Cummings. He was only mildly relieved that Flower had not mentioned that he himself had been the prime beneficiary of the leaks from the Harmon Committee. His mind wandered over all the different ways in which he and Cummings had helped each other over the years, all the secrets they had shared. Scenes from the past, though familiar, now seemed oddly disjointed, like the objects thrown together in a surrealist painting.

Hockney gulped his stinger.

"By the way," said Flower, "the man's name is Perry Cummings."

The mention of the name released the anger that had been contained by the complex of other emotions Flower's narrative had stirred inside Hockney.

"I don't believe it," Hockney erupted. Realizing that he at least half-believed it, Hockney became angry with himself as well and raised his voice. "You're lying," he almost shouted.

Flower played with a crumb on the tablecloth.

"I've known Perry Cummings all my life," Hockney began again, his voice lower, but unsteady. "I know that he would never work for a foreign government. If you found any microdots, you must have planted them. If what you say about Cummings is true, why isn't he under arrest?"

"In the present climate, the administration has decided it

can't afford to create any leftist martyrs. Cummings is under FBI investigation, but I doubt whether anything will come of it."

"Come on," Hockney exploded, "if you people are capable of plotting assassinations of foreign presidents, it's really no big deal for you to frame someone who doesn't share your right-wing paranoia."

"I gather you don't want to use the story," Flower said mildly. "Since you don't like what I tell you on the record, are you now prepared to go off the record?"

Hockney fought the urge to storm out. This broken, emaciated old man, drawing the smoke from an endless chain of cigarettes down to the bottom of his scarred lungs, was more dangerous than he had imagined. He could still wreck people's lives.

"I'm prepared to listen," was all Hockney said.

"We'll be more comfortable downstairs," said Flower, pushing his chair away.

Hockney and Flower rode down in the elevator in silence. Flower led the way to a corner of a smoking room on the ground floor and sat down next to a TV set.

Flower ordered coffee and cigars and another Armagnac. Hockney made a subliminal step toward Flower by ordering Armagnac too.

"So what are the other smears you want to try out on me?" said Hockney.

"Perhaps we could make a start with your editor, Leonard Rourke."

"I know he had illusions about Stalin before the war but he certainly never spied for the Russians."

"No, not for the Russians. But he did work for us."

Hockney sucked in his breath. Was no one clean? Were all his friends compromised somehow or other with some intelligence service?

"You man that Rourke worked for the Agency?" he said.

"I mean he was under contract to the CIA before he joined the *World*, while he was working in Europe for a news agency."

"This belongs in the same league as your allegations about Perry Cummings," Hockney protested. "Look at the stories Len Rourke has instigated. Why, it was Len who backed me to the hilt when your stooges on our board were trying to block my investigations into the Agency's dirty tricks. It was Rourke who splashed my story on that CIA defector's accusations about the Agency's political payoffs in Europe and Latin America all across the front page."

"You mean Phil Kreps," Flower clarified. "Now why do you suppose Len Rourke did all the things you say?"

"Because he believed it, for Chrissake." Hockney was clinging desperately to the hope that not all his friends were whores. "People in your trade," he attacked Flower, "don't have any beliefs and so they invent conspiracies because they can't understand true convictions."

"Let me explain it in words of one syllable." The angler reeled in a little faster. "Your editor, inspired by patriotic motives, without any remuneration from the Agency, performed some important services for his country. Then that CIA renegade Kreps told someone on the staff of the *World* that Rourke had been a contract employee of the Agency. Rourke had the choice of either reading about himself in *Barricades* magazine or of laundering his beliefs. This meant complying with suggestions on what should be published—or suppressed—in the *World*. In short, Rourke is not a free agent when it comes to making editorial decisions. There are people who have a blackmail hold over him because he once helped the Agency."

"That's sheer, unadulterated bullshit. You don't know the paper. I do. No way this could have happened."

"I'm sure that the story about the alleged CIA links of King Ahmed of Saudi Arabia is fresh in your memory, since it appeared under your by-line. You can't have forgotten how that story originated. Len Rourke suggested that you write it up and you know very well who gave him the idea—your good friend Perry Cummings."

"You've been bugging our phones."

"Off the record, you're damn right."

"You really want to go out of public life with a bang. Wait till they see that one in the paper tomorrow."

Flower waved the threat away as casually as he might have brushed a fly from his nose.

"I will deny anything you quote from this part of our conversation," he said, "and let me remind you what I am telling you is entirely off the record. But since you so obviously feel under pressure to keep up your reputation as an ace investigative reporter, I am prepared to give you a few leads."

"You mean misleads."

Flower ignored him. "I mean I can offer you a story that is bigger than Watergate. You'll need real balls to follow this one up and I really don't know whether you've got them, but I'm willing to take a chance."

Hockney crossed and uncrossed his legs. "Try me."

"Let's start with Phil Kreps, your favorite source on the CIA. Why don't you check out how he spent his time on his five visits to Havana and his seventeen visits to the Cuban embassy in Paris? We had them all bugged."

"How the hell could I ever check out a thing like that?"

"Most of Kreps's conversations with Cuban DGI agents are on file at Langley, unless, of course, one of your friends has put them through the shredder. The same goes for many of his exchanges with European terrorist leaders, from the Baader-Meinhof gang and other groups, and for his meetings with KGB officers in several Western capitals. Unfortunately, we do not have a transcript of what was said in Santiago between him and the KGB case officer who recruited him during his two visits to Moscow. But anyway I think there's enough there for you to chew on. Why don't you ask your friend Director Crawford to help you with your research now that I've pointed you in the right direction—"

"All right," Hockney interrupted him. "You've made serious allegations about Perry Cummings and Phil Kreps. Both of them were prime sources for the Harmon Committee. Are you also telling me the committee was systematically duped by the KGB?" Hockney knew the answer already. He was playing for time in order to absorb the enormity of what Flower was telling him.

"In my business," said Flower, "you are trained to use words with precision. I am not sure that duped is the right word for what happened to the Harmon Committee. I say that because one of the things we learned through our mail intercepts was that Senator Harmon himself maintained a regular correspondence with three identified KGB officers in Moscow. Of course they didn't use Dzherzhinsky Square as their address. He wrote them at various pseudo-academic institutes."

"For the sake of argument," Hockney rejoined, "let's suppose for a moment that your version of all this is true. If that's so, why didn't your people testify before the Harmon Committee?"

"That's a very good question," said Flower, pleased that the fish had leaped out of the water, wriggling on the line. "As a matter of fact, when my principal deputy was subpoenaed to appear before the committee he had the courtesy to let them know that the Senator's correspondence was one of the subjects he wished to bring up. Strangely enough, his appearance was canceled two days later. He was advised that the committee had no time on its schedule to fit him in. But Senator Harmon's chief of staff, Rick Adams, told my deputy that he and a few other committee staffers would be willing to debrief him in private. How does that grab you?"

"Where's the men's room?" asked Hockney.

After using the urinal, Hockney spent an excessively long time washing his hands and rubbing them gently under the electric drier. Flower had made a series of wholly unsubstantiated assertions. There was no reason for Hockney to accept his word on anything—especially when his own colleagues, including the director of the CIA, said Flower was a sick mind. Crawford had told Hockney that Flower had been wildly wrong on many occasions, arguing, for example, that the Sino-Soviet split was a hoax many years after it had taken place. Yet Hockney had also heard that the Europeans and, above all, the Israelis regarded Flower as little short of a genius. If Flower had made up everything he had said over lunch, he would have to be insane, and Hockney had seen no signs of insanity. On the contrary, Flower had remained the master of the conversation.

From the end of the smoking room, it looked to Hockney as if Flower had fallen asleep in his chair. His eyelids fluttered almost imperceptibly as Hockney approached. Like a great crocodile dozing on the river bank, Hockney thought, he never loses consciousness of what's going on around him.

Flower's eyelids flicked open. To Hockney's astonishment, he asked, "Did you hear whether the St. Lawrence is frozen over yet?"

"No—uh—I didn't hear about it," said Hockney.

Confident of his catch, the angler extended his net. "Maybe you have some more questions," said Flower.

"The Foundation for Progressive Reform seems to play a pretty big part in your fantasies. Why don't you tell me about it?"

"I hope you're not pressed for time. Would you like the two- or three-volume version?" Flower went on. "The Foundation is a classic Communist-front operation, closely modeled on what the Soviets sought to achieve through the Institute of Pacific Relations in the 1940s. That was a key Soviet espionage ring. But there's no doubt in my mind that the Foundation is the most brilliantly successful operation of its kind that the Soviets have ever mounted in this country."

Hockney put up a last-ditch defense. "With all due respect," he said, "I think I know more about the Institute than you. I know most of the people over there. They are men and women with a clear vision of our future, not of the past, where you seem to live. And I'm not going to believe otherwise just because someone has been poking around their garbage cans."

"I prefer to read people's correspondence before they throw it away." A smile darted, lizardlike, across Flower's thin lips. "You don't seem to realize that the Institute has been a vehicle used by American citizens in the service of Soviet intelligence to penetrate our political institutions and our media. You could do worse than spend some time

208

looking into the history of the Merchant family. Why don't you go and ask your friend Crawford what Vlad Merchant, the founder and chief financier of the Foundation, was doing in Spain before the war?"

"What evidence do you have of Soviet funding?"

"I thought you were an investigative reporter. But you've missed the whole point. The Russians don't have to hand money out at the back door of the embassy when they have tax exempt foundations controlled by Marxist sympathizers in this country who can raise the money from guilt-ridden liberal millionaires and little old ladies who in other circumstances might leave their inheritances to a cats' home or a gigolo. Why don't you ask Alexia Merchant about it?"

Hockney's mind was racing. "I don't believe even five percent of what you're telling me. But if even five percent is true, then what you're asking me is to retrace my own steps over the past eight years and investigate the sources who have given me my biggest scoops. Many of them are also among my closest friends. That's like asking me to screw my own mother. What makes you think I could begin to do that?"

"For you, it shouldn't be too much of a strain."

Washington-New York
1975-1976

1

HOCKNEY thought hard before calling Perry Cummings at home. It was not until after eleven, and after several more drinks, that Hockney decided he would not be able to sleep on what Flower had told him. It would have been easy to dismiss what Flower had said as the product of a twisted, conspiratorial mind. But he was basically convinced by the detail of Flower's accusations against Perry—the microdots, the orphans, the chewing gum wrappers.

Hockney dialed half the number and then hung up. He had made up his mind to tell Perry the whole story. But if it were indeed true? By telling Perry, he would simply alert him. He would never find out. The doubt would still be there.

Either Flower was a liar or Perry was an agent. There was one way of finding out. The week before, Hockney had invested $1,500 in a slim oblong black-and-silver box that he had read about in an Eastern Airlines magazine while flying the shuttle to New York. It was a Hagoth voice-stress analyzer, described in the ad as "a device that identifies truthfulness as soon as it is spoken . . . the gol'-darndest piece of high-technology artillery you have ever seen." He fitted the box to the telephone. He hadn't used it before, but the salesman claimed that the eight red and eight green lights on the front of the box would give an instant indication of whether the speaker was experiencing stress or was telling the truth. He had planned to use it in telephone interviews with people like Flower. It seemed a pretty smart gimmick; Hockney hadn't heard of any other reporter using a voice-stress analyzer. It would be poetic justice for the media to now use CIA technology to expose the CIA. It was unfortunate that the first subject for Hockney's home polygraph should be Julia's brother, Perry. He wondered what Julia's reaction would be if she knew what he was about to do.

Perry Cummings sounded out of breath when he finally answered the phone.

"I hope I haven't caught you in the middle of—uh—anything exciting," Hockney apologized.

"As a matter of fact, you did, you shit."

"I'll hang up and call you back in half an hour."

"No, I've lost it now," Perry said, irritated. "What do you want?"

Hockney chuckled to himself as he saw all eight red lights flashing. Clearly, Perry still had a hard-on.

"That'll be the day. Who's with you? Anyone I know?"

"No, new number," Perry growled. The red lights lit up again.

"Give Alex my best."

"She's not here." All eight red lights came on instantly. So Alexia Merchant was in bed with him, and the machine was working like a dream. Once jealous wives heard about this little box, philandering husbands would be put out of business.

"I had lunch with Nick Flower today," Hockney said hesitantly, feeling his way.

"I hope you had a good food taster," Cummings quipped. "Are you sure that Flower didn't slip you some of that stuff they tried to use on Castro? After the way you fixed his wagon, that's the only reason I can see why he would want to have lunch with you."

"Actually, there was another reason. He talked about you. At some length."

There was silence at the end of the line. Then Cummings said, "I've never met Flower. What did he say?"

"He said you were sacked from the Pentagon. Is that true?"

Another pause. "Yes, Bob. It is true. It hasn't been officially announced. But it happened last week."

"What was the reason?" Hockney asked.

"Security grounds, so they said. But you know how they define security these days. A security risk is someone who asks the right questions."

"But that's terrible," Hockney exclaimed. "What will you do?"

"I think I've landed on my feet," said Cummings. "Touch wood. I'm going to work for the Foundation. As co-director. Alexia's been terribly generous."

"Perry, if there's anything I can do, you know you can count on me."

"I'm going to be okay, Bob. But tell me, what else did Nick Flower have to say?"

"He said you took an unusual interest in orphans in West Berlin." Hockney immediately wished he had not recalled the fact.

The other end of the line seemed to have gone dead. "Perry," Hockney said, alarmed, "are you still there?"

"Flower must think helping orphans is a treasonable activity."

"So you were helping orphans in Berlin?" Hockney queried, eager to believe. "Just tell me yes or no."

"You're starting to sound like a polygraph test."

Hockney bit back a wry smile. "Yes or no."

"Well, yeah. I suffer from something called a social conscience. You've always been more eloquent on that score than me. I suppose Flower told you those orphans were Communist agents."

"Something along those lines." The lights on the Hagoth showed continuous stress. Hockney was fully aware of it without the visual confirmation. "As a matter of fact, Flower claims that you transmitted classified documents to East Berlin, using the orphans as a cover. Is that so?"

"Come on, Bob, stop giving me this bullshit. If Flower wants to come out and say that in public, I'll answer him with a ten-million-dollar libel suit."

"He said that if I quoted him, he'd deny it."

"Well, there you are. Character assassination." Hockney could hear Alexia's voice in the background. "Excuse me a minute," said Cummings.

Hockney had given up smoking six weeks before, but he found himself reaching for the weed. Cradling the phone against his shoulder, he lit a cigarette. He realized he had better lay off. It would be too stupid to lose a good friend —not to mention Alexia and his other sources at the Foundation—because of a whisper from a spymaster who'd just been sacked in disgrace.

So when Cummings returned to the phone, Hockney said, "For Chrissake, don't get the idea that I believe any of this horse manure. I just thought it was my duty to tell you what Flower is saying about you."

"It's okay, Bob. No offense. I'd like to hear more. But preferably not on the telephone."

"You never transmitted documents to the Soviets, did you?"

"No." All eight red lights were flashing.

"And you've never heard of microdots inside chewing gum wrappers?"

"Did Flower really tell you that?"

"I agree he's nuts. But tell me, Perry, did you ever use microdots in your work at the Defense Department?"

"No, you jerk. I wouldn't know a microdot if I saw one. Any more questions, Mr. Grand Inquisitor, or can I get back to bed?" The red lights on the Hagoth had all lit up again when Perry said "no."

"I'm real sorry to have put you off your stroke with something as trivial as Flower's convoluted fantasies. By the way, I did tell him I thought I knew you as well as anyone, and there was just no way you would get involved with any intelligence service, ours or theirs."

"Pax, Bob. But next time you see Flower, tell him to stick to bird-watching or he'll wind up in the cuckoo's nest."

"Perry," Hockney said, guilt-stricken again over his amateurish inquisition, "is it true the FBI is investigating you?"

"I'm not going to lose any sleep over that," said Cummings. "And tomorrow morning, thanks to Alexia, I'm moving into an office at the Foundation."

Hockney hung up and unhooked the black-and-silver box. He looked through the window of his bachelor apartment on 19th Street toward the gray hulk of the Watergate complex, and back to the box. Was there really much difference between him and the Watergate plumbers? But he was less worried about the ethics of using a voice-stress analyzer on his friend than about its reliability. Even the most sophisticated polygraphs, operated by experts, were not considered foolproof. These things could register stress and emotion, but truth was more elusive. But it was instinct, not just the flashing red lights, that had told him Perry Cummings was scared.

He thought about the gap in the conversation. Had Cummings gone to pacify Alexia, or to consult her? Flower had talked about Alexia Merchant and her family as well. She was a strange, hungry woman, outwardly prim but insatiable in bed, a Jewess who hated Israel, the granddaughter of a millionaire who gave his money to Communist causes. If Perry was suspect, was Alexia in it too?

The thought of Alexia and Perry in bed together brought home to him how much he missed Tessa. She was away shooting a film in southern Spain. It was now 6:00 A.M. in Marbella. Hockney thought of her sprawled on a bed, satiated after screwing most of the night with some stunt man. It was stupid, he knew, to torture himself with these images. Yet he found himself picturing with revulsion Tessa in bed with Phil Kreps. Hockney had read in a gossip column that Tessa had spent a weekend with Kreps in Paris. He found it hard to believe that Tessa could feel any physical attraction for the stunted, scrawny, carrot-haired Kreps. But he knew her well enough to guess what the attraction could be. Tessa was drawn, like an iron filing to a magnet, to political outlaws—Black Panthers, Weathermen, Vietcong, revolutionaries of all description, the zanier the better. Hockney respected Kreps's courage in rebelling against his former employers and valued him as the source for many of his recent scoops. But he found the CIA defector vulgar and self-seeking and, worst of all, an unworthy but successful rival in the bedroom. It occurred to Hockney that Flower had pointed the finger at Kreps too. Perry, Kreps, and Alexia Merchant. It was all dangerously close to him, so close that he couldn't stand back and see the whole picture, if there was a picture at all.

Hockney could not sleep. Tired of writhing between the damp sheets, he finally knocked himself out with a sleeping pill.

2

HOCKNEY waited after ringing the doorbell of the big, four-story house on R Street, just off Wisconsin Avenue. He knew he was being screened on closed-circuit television. It was a standing joke that security at the Foundation for Progressive Reform was tighter than at the Pentagon, especially since they had started receiving death threats from right-wing fanatics and the Zionist Defense League. The contents of the wastebaskets had been put into the shredder every night since they had found out that the FBI was rummaging through the garbage. The ivy-covered red brick mansion had once belonged to Vlad Merchant, who had donated it to the Foundation. This was the least of his contributions. The Merchant Foundation provided an annual grant of $1 million to the Foundation, whose charter was to "explore ways to correct the injustices of the democratic system."

Inside, Hockney passed the armed guard, smiled at Mabel the receptionist, and walked straight through to Perry Cumming's new office. On the way down the corridor, he ran into an Iranian research fellow—a former member of the Tudeh party who had spent time in the Shah's jails—who was preparing a report on Moslem-Marxist dialogue.

"You interrupted a pretty good fuck last night," Perry said, by way of greeting.

"I've always been noted for my timing."

Cummings put his feet on the desk. Hockney was surprised that he seemed as relaxed as ever.

"Seriously, Bob," he said when Hockney had settled in. "I want to thank you for last night. You've cleared up a big question mark that was in my mind. They didn't tell me why I was fired from the Pentagon. Now I know I was framed. I've been thinking it over, and I've decided to take

217

it up with the ACLU. With what you've supplied, and with the Freedom of Information Act, we can really crucify Flower and his friends."

"That's a great idea. But for Chrissake, keep my name out of it." Hockney watched the other man closely. Was this a huge bluff? He simply couldn't tell.

"You seem pretty comfortable here," Hockney remarked, surveying the surprisingly spacious office, which seemed more appropriate for a corporate executive than for the number-two person at the Foundation for Progressive Reform. "Have you got enough to keep yourself occupied?"

"You'll never guess where I'm spending the weekend," Cummings replied. "Ever heard of exotic Flats, Mississippi?"

"Can't say that I have."

"You're not alone. The town's so small, the local hooker's still a virgin."

"What are you going to do down there? Go fishing?"

"That's exactly what I'm going to do. And it could be big fish. Maybe the biggest." There was a smirk all over Perry's face. "Flats, Mississippi, is the hometown of one Billy Connor. Don't tell me you haven't heard of him?"

"You mean that hick congressman, one of the quiet types on the Harmon Committee? Yeah, he makes even worse jokes about his hometown than you do. He told me once that Flats is so small that when you plug in your electric razor, one of the two lights on Main Street dims. That's how corny he is."

"Now, Bob, show a little respect. You're talking about a man who may be President one day."

"You don't take that stuff seriously, do you? My paper ran the story on Bill Connor running for the Democratic nomination in the second section, page thirty-two. One paragraph. That's what he rates."

"Just remember your paper also had Dewey beating Truman. Some of us think Billy Connor has got a winning combination. We don't kid ourselves that Billy will win this time. The nomination will probably go to an establishment figure, or even to some better-placed outsider like Jimmy

Carter. His people have done a lot more preparation than we have. But Billy is putting his hat in the ring, and people are going to be more and more conscious of him. He's got a lot on his side. He's got religion, he comes from outside the Eastern establishment, and he's also very amenable to our ideas. Most people can't work out where he stands on anything, and that's a big electoral plus. You'd be surprised how many heavy hitters are going down to Flats, Mississippi, this weekend."

Hockney was surprised, and as he left Perry's office he brooded on this new dimension his friend's activities had acquired overnight. On his way to the stairs, he paused by the door to Alexia's office, which was slightly ajar. He was wondering whether to barge in and say hello when he heard Alexia's secretary say, "Alex, your call to Phil Kreps in Brussels on four."

Hockney walked straight into the secretary's room. Luckily, he got on well with her.

"I guess Alex is tied up with a call." He grinned, gesturing toward her door. He plunked himself down in a chair with his back to Alexia's wall, listening to her long-distance call while he bantered with the secretary. He was staggered by what he heard. It sounded as if Alexia was offering Kreps a job. FPR was setting up a subsidiary in Amsterdam, to be called the Third World Exchange. Half the money would come from the Merchant Foundation, the other half from the Belgian Ministry of Overseas Development. Alexia was inviting Kreps to become its director, with seed money of $1 million to buy a building and a running budget of $500,000 a year. From the way the conversation was going, it was clear that they had been kicking the idea around for months.

"What's that?" Hockney said, startled. He had switched off from the secretary's idle chatter about some movie she had just seen.

"Well, you saw it, didn't you?"

"Saw what?"

"That Robert Redford film."

"Oh. Sure. I loved it." Hockney's mind was racing

through what Flower had told him about Kreps—the contacts with Cuban and Soviet spies, the linkup with European terrorist groups. Was any of it true? Whether it was or not, Kreps seemed a strange choice to run a European offshoot of a liberal think tank.

"Bob," the secretary was saying, "Alex is off the line. You can go through if you want. She's got a few people in there, but I'm sure it's okay."

Hockney strolled into Alexia's office. She was standing with two men. Hockney recognized one of them—Rick Adams. The other was a swarthy Latin in a dark blue suit with a loud tie.

"Bob, what are you doing here?" Alexia seemed surprised to see him, and glanced—nervously, Hockney thought—at the others.

"Just thought I'd give a kiss to my favorite girl as I was passing." Hockney embraced her, shook hands with Rick Adams, and introduced himself to the other man.

"Hi," he said, putting out his hand. "Bob Hockney, *New York World*."

"Juan Pereda."

Hockney looked at Alexia, but it was Rick Adams who explained. "Juan's with the Cuban mission to the United Nations in New York."

"I didn't realize they let you travel this far," said Hockney, curious. He remembered that Communist diplomats at the UN were not supposed to travel outside New York.

"No one pays much attention to that anymore."

Hockney had the glimmerings of an idea. He decided to follow Flower's advice and bounce what he had learned off Bill Crawford, the director of the CIA. Was it possible that there was some sort of overall plan, directed from abroad, to expose the CIA and its secrets—a plan in which Hockney himself might unwittingly have played a part? To Hockney, it still seemed a ridiculous suggestion. But so many questions had been raised in the last twenty-four hours that he needed to find some answers.

Crawford suggested that he drop by his home in Georgetown for a drink before dinner that night. Crawford didn't seem to have any answers. He responded to each name that Hockney mentioned with a flick of his hand, alternately up or down. It seemed to be only loosely connected to his wrist, and was held at shoulder height.

Rick Adams? The hand flopped down. "Oh, he's okay," Crawford said.

Perry Cummings? The hand flapped up. "Not my bag."

Senator Harmon? The hand dropped again. "Ask him yourself. You know him better than me."

What about Phil Kreps? The hand remained motionless in midair. Crawford stared at Hockney for a while from behind his rimless glasses. "Now that's something else," the CIA director finally said, his anger showing. "Bad news all around. Alcoholic. Messed up his family. Money trouble. Now he's shucking his colleagues all around the world. You know what that means? Blowing the cover of CIA men means putting their lives at risk. I would call him a traitor."

"So what you're saying is Phil Kreps is an agent."

"No, I didn't say that." Crawford took a sip of his old-fashioned. "We have no evidence that he's working for the Soviets."

"What about the Cubans?"

"Sure, he's got a lot of friends down there. Seems to be in love with Castro. But why come and ask me? You know Kreps better than most people. Go and look him up in Europe if you're interested."

"You mean the Agency isn't interested?"

"We're not in the business of helping reporters do their reporting." There was a thin smile on Crawford's lips. It was on the tip of Hockney's tongue to ask Crawford about something else that Flower had mentioned—the possibility of a high-level Soviet mole in the administration. But he suppressed his question. He was on unfamiliar territory with Crawford now. But he was sure that, whether the CIA director knew anything or not, all he would get out of him was the hand flapping up or down.

"By the way," said Crawford, as he walked Hockney down the steps into the street, "I never thanked you for that article on Flower's operations. It was a very honest piece of reporting. As you know, I think the Agency only stands to gain from openness. We have to get rid of this clandestine mentality."

The Western Union operator woke Hockney before 6:00 A.M. It was a telegram from Tessa. She was flying in to New York the following day on TWA and hoped he could meet her. "Now more than ever," Tessa signed off.

Hockney hauled himself out of bed, got dressed, and walked across the street to pick up his copy of the *Washington Tribune* at the Watergate, where he usually had breakfast. As he waited in line for the hostess to seat him, he glanced at the headlines. "CIA Plants in White House, Other Government Departments" read the six-column banner on the day's big story. It was by-lined Larry Foster, Hockney's main competitor on the *Trib*. The story was mostly bubbles. It made a big deal out of the fact that CIA liaison men were stationed in other government departments. What angered Hockney was that Foster claimed this was one of the items on the CIA's list of "family jewels," implying that he had had access to the document. Then he noticed the word "exclusive" underlined above the headline. That came as a personal insult; when it came to exposing the CIA, he had felt that he owned the copyright.

He sat down to a plate of egg and country sausage and a glass of milk. He pushed the *Trib* episode out of his mind and thought about Tessa. He hadn't seen her for weeks. He was desperate to be with her again. He was still in love with her. But he had never been quite sure of what she felt. Anxiety gnawed at him. Film stars always had affairs on location. He'd been over this again and again in his mind. Everyone knew it. After all, there wasn't much else to do at night. That brought his mind circling back to Phil Kreps. He realized he was jealous. But did he really need to be? Tessa had had lots of affairs on both sides of the Atlantic. But he was the one she cabled. He was the one she came back to. He would make the trip to New York, to meet her plane.

"Check, honey?" The middle-aged waitress scooped up his plate and started mopping the table under it. Hockney noticed the long line of hung-over businessmen and bureaucrats waiting to be fed.

"Yeah," he grunted, searching for change in his pocket. Kreps. The thought wouldn't go away. Kreps and Perry Cummings. Fine friends. One screwing his girl, the other screwing him with the paper. Maybe Flower was wrong. Maybe what he saw as a grand conspiracy was nothing more than the fact that everyone was out to screw everyone else. But Hockney had to make sure.

He decided to walk to the bureau. As he strolled along Pennsylvania Avenue, up toward the White House, he made up his mind to see his editor, Rourke, after a day or two with Tessa in New York. He'd have no problem getting his bureau chief's okay for a few days off. Hockney had been putting in twelve-hour days, weekends included. But he was now thinking of asking Rourke for more than that: two or three months, detached from all regular duties, with a budget that would allow him to investigate the questions that wouldn't go away, wherever in the world that took him. Rourke would listen to him. Then Hockney remembered Flower's warning about Rourke's past affiliations with the CIA and the way this had been used to blackmail him. Could Hockney trust anyone?

The shuttle from Washington landed at LaGuardia, and Hockney took a taxi to Kennedy, which hosted international flights. He arrived just in time to meet Tessa's plane. Hockney avoided kissing her as she emerged from customs, in case there were photographers. He made up for it in the back of the studio limousine as they drove to her regular suite at the Pierre Hotel. They ate lunch in bed.

3

TESSA had changed over the years he had known her, Hockney reflected later as he watched her slip into a Valentino dress. Especially since her appearance on the

223

Broadway stage. Tessa had always maintained that no one would take her seriously as an actress until she had made it in the theater. Now jeans were out. She spent twice as long as usual in front of the mirror, getting ready to go to Regine's. Eye shadow, lip gloss, fake eyelashes—they weren't her old style. Was she dressing up for him or just the crowd at Regine's, or—suspicions pricked him—for someone else? He knew that no man who had enjoyed the favors of a national sex symbol—if only intermittently over five years—had a right to conventional jealousy. Their relationship had evolved in an on-off pattern. In between assignments, when they could manage it, they would rendezvous and try to overcome the fatigue that went with their punishing work schedules in a bout of lovemaking.

Heads turned as Tessa made her entrance into the fashionable nightclub on Park Avenue. Regine, who owned similar discotheques in Paris, Monte Carlo, and Rio and was building new ones in half a dozen cities, called it her New York emporium. Regine had flown off to Rio, and Tessa and Hockney were greeted by her statuesque sister, who said to the headwaiter, *"L'une, s'il vous plaît."* Hockney was embarrassed that they were being given the best table, since he spotted some very well-known faces around the room. At one table, there was Barbara Walters, with the President's chief economic adviser, Alan Greenspan. At another, there was Gianni Agnelli and his wife, Marella, with Bob Silvers, the editor of the *New York Review of Books.*

"Hey," said Tessa, "there's old macho himself. Let's say hello." They veered across the room to greet Norman Mailer, who was presiding over a noisy table.

When they sat down, Hockney said to Tessa, "What I love about discos is that you have to shriek subtleties across the table." He was slightly annoyed by Tessa's banter with all the people who seemed to know her well but had never heard of him.

A glance at the menu reminded him that there was no way of getting out for less than a hundred dollars. Tessa ate only one of the house specialties—foie gras salad—and two helpings of fraises du bois with masses of whipped cream.

"What's the point of skipping the main course," Hockney asked, "if you're going to double up on the cream?"

"You watch your ass and I'll watch mine."

They talked little over dinner, and Hockney was annoyed by the constant interruptions as people wandered over to say hello to Tessa. Before ordering coffee, he took her onto the dance floor. The disc jockey was playing a song called "Nowhere to Run," and Tessa started gyrating. Hockney lamely imitated her movements. He felt awkward and self-conscious—he had never learned to move his pelvis properly.

When the jockey switched to a slower number by the Bee Gees, Hockney took Tessa in his arms. She pushed him back and went on dancing by herself.

Back at the table with a large cognac in front of him, Hockney heard himself asking the question he had resolved not to bring up.

"Did you see Phil Kreps while you were over in Europe?"

Her attention was distracted by someone who had come up to the table. Hockney thought he recognized him as a movie producer. Tessa didn't bother to introduce the man.

"Sorry, Bob," she said when the producer walked off. "What were you saying?"

"I was asking about Phil Kreps."

"Oh, Phil. He came down to see me in Spain. He was on his way to Havana."

"Is he in good shape?" Hockney knew that if Kreps had gone to Marbella, it wasn't just to have a Tio Pepe before catching the next plane. Tessa and Kreps must have spent a few days together.

Hockney's chest tightened. Instead of answering him, Tessa was staring vacantly around the room. Despite his agitation, Hockney was too civilized to ask the unforgivable question of whether she had been to bed with Kreps.

Hockney found the answer to his unspoken question in the vehemence with which Tessa finally spoke.

225

"I'll tell you one thing about Phil Kreps," she said. "He's out there in the front line. You've done a hell of a lot with your articles, but Phil is risking his life every day for the cause. He needs all the support we can give him."

"Come off it, Tessa."

She gulped her wine. When her next sentences came out, her voice had become fixed in a dreary but hectoring monotone, as it always did when she attempted to make political speeches. Hockney was reminded of the night they had first met, at the Foundation's fund-raising dinner in New York. It was strange how Tessa lost all her acting skill—and her human charm—when she began to talk politics. Another personality took over. The symptoms had become accentuated since she had been moving in Phil Kreps's circles, and Hockney guessed that the CIA's "ideological defector" had been influencing her in more contexts than the bedroom.

"Look around this place." Tessa's volume had steadily increased until she was almost shouting. "Everyone here is sick. You've got to be sick to be sitting here while most of the world is starving."

Tessa the fanatical preacher was unrecognizable as the woman Hockney had come to love. Her political ideas were no more sophisticated than those of the campus radicals at Berkeley in the 1960s: she wielded slogans, not arguments. But, flushed with anger and wine, she was still beautiful. Letting her phrases wash over him as he sat in silence, Hockney thought about the phases through which their relationship had passed. He had first been drawn to her by the instant gloss of celebrity, feleing irradiated with her own fame by being in her presence. The attraction was characteristic of a social environment in which people brushed against each other only at the hard, shiny surface.

But Hockney's own reactions had matured, and he searched for the woman concealed by the contending roles. For months after they had come together, he had experienced that intensity of perception that comes with love, the feeling that things are illuminated by a sharper, purer light. Now, after several years of alternately enjoying and missing her, Hockney wished he could release Tessa from the prisons she had built for herself both as screen goddess and as radical cult figure. She had persuaded herself that it was sinful to make a fortune by flaunting her body in the movies. But, unable either to give up the movies or to live on less than her present income, Tessa tried to salve her conscience by lending her support—and sometimes her body—to every radical guru who came along. The latest was Kreps.

Tessa had always had a light head, and she had already drunk four or five glasses of wine.

"Do you know what's wrong with you?" she challenged Hockney.

"You tell me."

"When I first met you, you wanted to change things. You wanted to end the war and beat the CIA. Now you're different."

"The times are different, Tessa."

"You've become part of the consensus."

"The war's over, honey." Hockney gently taunted her.

The gibe set her off. "You've turned into a fucking limousine liberal," she accused him.

"I've never had a limo as big as yours," Hockney countered.

"I don't take any free rides." She defended herself furiously. "I give a lot of what I earn to groups that are trying to blow up this rotten system. I'm helping Phil Kreps."

"That must be a big comfort to Phil," Hockney observed sardonically.

"You establishment liberals piss me off."

Tessa was beginning to sound like she was talking to someone she didn't know. Hockney was frightened by the way Tessa's individuality could be swamped by the latest political credo she had picked up.

"You're very sexy tonight," he said to her, trying to cut off the speechifying.

She ignored the remark and returned to the attack. "I don't know why you've become so complacent. You used to care about injustice. How many press awards did it take to make you stop caring?"

"I don't know what we're arguing about. What started this conversation anyway?"

"It's high time we had it," said Tessa. "Phil Kreps told me you wouldn't follow up on some leads he gave you."

It was true. Kreps had offered Hockney a story about how the CIA was supposedly helping West German security stamp on underground leftist movements. Since his talk with Nick Flower, Hockney was glad he had not followed up the story. At the time, he had wondered whether his motive for rebuffing Kreps had really been what he said—that he wasn't interested in helping the cause of West German terrorists—or whether there had been an element of jealousy involved.

"All right," Hockney conceded. "So I didn't use Kreps's stories. There are lots of stories, and the *World* only has so many column inches."

"That particular story would have helped to show that the CIA is still in business despite all the congressional investigations. I thought that was your big theme."

"Look, Tessa," Hockney said, his patience beginning to snap, "I distrust Phil's motives. Now can we just let it rest?"

"No, we can't let it rest." After another glass of wine, Tessa was no longer in command of herself. "You've got no right to sit on your ass sniping at Phil. He does more to change things than a dozen Bob Hockneys."

Hockney was goaded by her uncritical admiration for Kreps, whom she depicted as a heroic figure. Whatever motivated Kreps, he was in no way unique. Ever since Philip Agee and Victor Marchetti had started the trend, there had been no shortage of ex-CIA officers, of all political persuasions, trying to get their reminiscences into print.

"Kreps must be quite a lay if he's got you brainwashed with all this crap."

Tessa stood up, her breasts heaving. "You jealous bastard," she spat. "It wasn't good enough that I wanted to be with you tonight. It wasn't good enough that we spent most of the day in bed together, when I was beat from the flight. Did I ask you who you slept with last week, or the week

228

before? It's none of my business. What I do is none of yours. But you can't keep your nose out of it, can you?"

Hockney got up from the table, protesting. Conversation had stopped at neighboring tables.

"Keep your voice down," Hockney pleaded, "you're not on location for *Who's Afraid of Virginia Woolf?*"

Tessa's voice rose several decibels more. "You really want to know? Okay, I'll tell you. Phil Kreps is no big deal in bed. But he's got more balls than you have."

"Well, it's just as well your acting ability extends to the bedroom."

Crimson-faced, Tessa sucked in her lips. Then she grabbed the edge of the table, lifted it, and pushed it at Hockney. The table keeled over to one side, and plates and glasses crashed to the floor. Waiters came running. Some of the other diners looked around for cameras, imagining that Tessa must be filming a scene for her new movie.

There was scattered applause from the glitterati for the performance.

4

HOCKNEY woke up with a blinding headache. He tried to focus on his watch. It was almost 11:00. He would be late for his appointment with his editor, Len Rourke. After the scene at Regine's, he had been up half the night with a whiskey bottle. He staggered to the telephone and called Rourke's secretary.

"Tell the boss I just got into New York," he lied. "The shuttle was late. I'll be there in twenty minutes."

As he rode uptown in a cab, Hockney tried to recall exactly what had passed between him and Tessa in the discotheque. The more he remembered, the clearer it became to him that what had happened was irretrievable. He wasn't going to share Tessa with Phil Kreps and nameless others. He decided not to phone her, not even after he was handed a message from Tessa at the office, saying it was urgent that he return her call.

When Hockney got to the paper, people were already milling around in Rourke's outer office on the nineteenth floor, waiting for the 11:30 editorial conference. Exchanging a few pleasantries, Hockney hurried in through Rourke's open door. The others followed. There was obviously no chance for a private chat.

Hockney found Rourke engaged in an animated argument with the national affairs editor, Ed Finkel.

"Look, Ed," Rourke was saying, mashing his molars, "I'm as determined on this as I was on the My Lai massacre. I agreed with you guys on that. We had it on the front page for weeks. Now we've got a much bigger massacre story out of Cambodia. How can we possibly justify ourselves if we bury it on an inside page? Are you trying to tell me there's one rule for American atrocities and another rule for Communist atrocities?"

"You missed the point, Len," Finkel fired back. "This is not a story out of Cambodia. It's a story out of Washington. It came to us from unnamed U.S. government sources, right? So I ran a little check. And guess what I found? The source was Henry the K. And he was quoting, off the record, from CIA radio intercepts. Henry's been predicting massacres for months, and my view is that this is self-serving bullshit!"

"I can believe a lot of things about Henry," said Rourke, "but I can't believe that he would fake CIA radio intercepts as precise as these." The chattering of Rourke's teeth made him sound as if he were chewing pistachio nuts, without removing the shells.

"Henry doesn't have to fake anything," Finkel said, with undisguised contempt. "The CIA does it for him. He probably doesn't even know."

Rourke caught sight of Hockney and appealed to him. "What do you think, Bob? You've done some pretty good massacre stories in your time. What about this one? Should we run it big?"

Hockney glanced from Rourke's mobile jawbone to the lean, sardonic face of Ed Finkel, whose eyes seemed to be saying, "Don't cross me." Taking either side could be deadly. Since he was about to ask Rourke for a big favor, he decided to duck the question.

"I don't know enough about it," he said sheepishly.

"Well," Finkel continued, "I think we should bounce this story back to the Washington bureau and get them to do some digging into how the CIA cooks up these massacres. They've probably got a printing plant that does nothing but forgeries. And Len," he added, in an ominous tone, "you wouldn't want anyone to say that the CIA was planting stuff on us, would you?"

Rourke's molars began to sound like Woody Woodpecker going through a tree trunk. Hockney's mind flashed back to Flower's claims about Rourke's past connection with the CIA and the fact that some of the editors appeared to have found out about it and were using it to manipulate him.

"Okay." Rourke gave in wearily. "Tell the Washington bureau we can't run the story unless they are actually shown the radio intercepts."

He turned to Hockney. "I've got to start the meeting, Bob. Is it something urgent, or can it wait?"

"I'll need more than a couple of minutes."

"Okay. Come back after lunch."

Having lost his point on Cambodia, Rourke vented his spleen on a cityside reporter who had just started working for the paper and had managed to get six out of nine facts wrong in a story.

"A new goddamn record," Rourke thundered.

Hockney slipped out halfway through the meeting. As he left, he heard the new reporter asking, innocently, "What kind of nuts is Mr. Rourke chewing?"

"*Yours*," Finkel sneered.

By 3:00 P.M., Hockney had made his deal with Rourke. The conversation with his editor was characteristically smooth and friendly. Hockney told Rourke that he thought he could deliver another Pulitzer prize winner. The research would be long and grueling, but would probably also result in a book.

"Sounds great, Bob," said Rourke. "Tell me all about it."

At first, Hockney was evasive about the nature of his project. "It's on my main theme," he said vaguely.

"You mean the CIA?"

"Not just the CIA. I was thinking of tackling its competition as well."

"You mean the FBI?"

"I mean the Soviets," Hockney clarified. "But I'd like your word that whatever I tell you about this stays between us."

Rourke thought the remark was impertinent. But his reaction changed when Hockney proceeded to explain the cause of his concern for secrecy.

"I'm worried about Ed Finkel," Hockney explained. "I don't think he's going to like this project very much. So I'd like to keep the details between you and me and use a cover story for the time being."

Rourke was not displeased by the thought that he might be sponsoring a project that would upset Finkel. Hockney had gambled on that fact. He went on to summarize for his editor the main thread of his inquiry—the extent to which Soviet agents were able to influence decision making inside the Western alliance.

Rourke tried to let out a long whistle, but the only noise was of air escaping. "This isn't your usual line of work, Bob," he observed. "And it's not the sort of thing that would get much approval at one of my editorial conferences."

"I think it's about time that we started looking at all sides of the intelligence problem."

"Did you stumble across anything in particular?" Rourke guessed that something unusual must have happened to bring about Hockney's change of heart.

"I think so," said Hockney. "But I need a lot of time to check it out. I need you to trust me, Len." Hockney was sensitive to the need not to scare his editor, especially in the light of what Nick Flower had told him about Rourke's past connections with the CIA and the way that had given Finkel and others a blackmail hold over him. If Flower was right, Rourke was not a totally free agent. Hockney knew that if Flower's other allegations checked out, the only hope of publishing them in the *World* would be by gathering such a damning body of evidence that Rourke would be emboldened to act again as editor, rather than as a weak chairman of the board. He sensed that, in the absence of such evidence, Rourke would prefer not to hear too many details about a potentially explosive investigation.

Then came the difficult question. "How long is this going to take you, Bob?"

"A year."

"*A year!*" Rourke exploded.

"I'm afraid so."

"Well, it'll have to be at half-salary."

Hockney knew he could not demand much in the way of expenses unless he offered some clue to the real nature of the project. So he talked a little about Phil Kreps, to whom many of the trails seemed to lead. Hockney wondered how much the growing importance that Kreps had assumed in his mind was due to rivalry over Tessa, and how much to the role the ex-CIA man appeared to have assumed—with the Third World Exchange in Brussels as his base—in coordinating the campaign against American national security.

Rourke cut him off before he finished detailing Kreps's alleged contacts with the Cubans.

"I'll bite," said the editor. "Your cover story is that you're going to do a book that will be published by our new book division."

Ed Finkel was coming into the editor's outer office as Hockney left.

"Did you see the AP ticker, Bob?" Finkel asked. It seemed that the CIA director had just put out a statement. "Get this," said Finkel, reading from a strip of wire copy. "Crawford says that, in a democracy, we should try to keep as few secrets as possible. Congratulations, Bob. You haven't only been assisting the CIA director in the fulfillment of his democratic duties. You've got him converted."

233

Brussels

HOCKNEY had visited Brussels only once before, when he had traveled—at the insistence of Perry Cummings and Alex Merchant—to meet Kreps and record some of his revelations about life in the CIA station in Santiago, where he had served before falling out with his colleagues. European governments had become a little nervous about Kreps, fearing that his anti-CIA campaign might be widened into an attack on their own secret services. The Germans and the French had refused to let the former CIA man cross their frontiers. But the tolerant Belgian not only allowed him to remain; they even permitted the Foundation for Progressive Reform to establish a satellite organization in Brussels called the Third World Exchange. Hockney could still remember the overheard phone conversation when he'd learned Phil Kreps had been appointed its founder-director.

It seemed to Hockney that discovering Kreps's real motives was an essential part of his project, since Kreps had supplied him with one of his biggest scoops on the CIA. The knowledge that Kreps had also had an affair with Tessa—however transient—gave Hockney a personal reason for reexamining Kreps's activities. He was convinced that Kreps was partly, if not largely, to blame for Tessa's drift toward the wildest reaches of the radical left. If Tessa had remained even marginally rational about the causes she espoused, their breakup might have been avoidable.

Hockney had last seen Tessa in a small beach house at Malibu, south of Los Angeles. He had resolved not to see her after the theatrical squabble at Regine's, but his resolve soon wilted. By the sound of wind and surf, in the act of love, they lost themselves again in each other's bodies. But the gaps between were filled with pointless rows, during which Tessa delivered disjointed and often hysterical tirades about the need for revolutionary violence to cleanse the world. Hockney was not surprised to learn that even radical students had been repelled by one of her appearances at his alma mater, when she heaped praise on the most militant of the Palestinian terrorist groups. After that, the Zionist Actors' Guild had issued a recommendation to its members not to collaborate with Tessa Torrance on any of her movies.

It was not hard for Hockney and Tessa to go their separate ways, since their work had always demanded that they spend much of their time in different places. Hockney had avoided making the last parting definitive. They had said good-by, not that they would never see each other again—although he wondered whether they would. For Tessa, the first destination this time had been Baghdad. Hockney had been surprised to read in his own paper that she was making a propaganda film for the Palestinians in which she played the mistress of the notorious terrorist chief Wadi Jalloud. She returned to the states to face angry demonstrations mounted by the Zionist Defense League, and a blowup with her New York agent, who warned her that she might never be allowed to make another film in Hollywood. Unheeding, she flew off again, this time to Rome, appearing to star in a new movie being made by the well-known radical Italian producer Padovani.

So Hockney had returned to Europe, alone, to retrace the steps he had taken in his advance toward journalistic fame. He had assigned himself a quixotic mission: to dig up the roots of his own success. It would have been much easier to let them lie buried. But since his lunch with Nick Flower in the Army and Navy Club, he had known he would derive no pleasure from seeing his name in print in the *World* until he found the answers to all the questions the old spymaster had raised.

Hockney called Phil Kreps at the Third World Exchange as soon as he settled into his room at the Brussels Sheraton. He had momentary misgivings as he dialed the number. Kreps must have heard through the grapevine that Hockney, a loyal supporter of the Foundation for Progressive Reform in the past, had been acting out of character. Kreps was probably on the line to Cummings and Alex Merchant every day. But whatever the former CIA man might have heard, it was not echoed in the way he spoke to Hockney on the phone. He greeted Hockney as a long-lost friend.

"We've got a film showing early this evening," Kreps announced. "Let's meet at the theater and we can talk over dinner later on."

Hockney had trouble finding the little cinema on the Rue de Malignes. The film had already begun by the time he entered, so he slid unobtrusively into a seat in the back row. He could see Kreps's shaggy head four or five rows in front of him.

On the screen, Chilean fighter-bombers were strafing the presidential palace in Santiago on the day of the military coup against Allende. The image faded, and the title of the film appeared: "Filmmaking in the Service of the Revolution." Underneath, in small red letters, was the name of the movie's sponsor, the Cuban Institute of the Cinematographic Arts and Industries. Hockney asked himself why it was that leftist bodies always chose such long-winded titles for themselves.

There were more shots of revolutionary and counter-revolutionary blood and guts, then the screen was taken over for the rest of the showing by three Cuban film producers who argued interminably among themselves on the dos and don'ts of socialist cinema. According to one of the Cubam filmmakers, fast cars, lush starlets, and stories of sex and crime were no longer acceptable. The purpose of the cinema was not to entertain, but to instruct. Hockney yawned.

The lights came on, and he could see that there were no more than two dozen people in the audience.

"You couldn't call it a box office success," he remarked to Phil Kreps.

"Little by little," Kreps replied. "Let me introduce you to our cosponsor."

Hockney shook hands with a fleshy Belgian from the Ministry of Overseas Development. Big, with a red, bulbous nose and a sagging jaw, he was wearing a green sports jacket that clashed with his blue shirt, and had his arm clamped around the voluptuous wife of the Cuban cultural attaché. The Belgian did not conform to Hockney's image of a top European civil servant.

"You mean you're able to work with the Belgian government?" he asked Kreps when the Belgian had moved on, wholly absorbed in his Cuban companion.

"Sure," said Kreps. "You sound surprised. There are officials in the Belgian administration who are to the left of, say, Alexia Merchant. And ever since Chile, European socialists have been progressively radicalized. Chile reminded them that the enemy is on the right."

Hockney had chosen the Comme Chez Soi, one of the plushest restaurants in Brussels, for their dinner. Kreps looked out of place in his baggy corduroy suit, and Hockney realized he should have picked somewhere less plutocratic. There was unspoken tension between the two men at the start of the meal, and they minimized conversation by spending an exaggerated amount of time poring over menus and consulting waiters. Hockney searched for the right note to introduce the theme that worried him. He started by being overly effusive in his praise for Kreps's continuing campaign to expose CIA agents around the world. As he heard himself speak, he thought the words rang hollow. But Kreps seemed to be responding like a dog that was being tickled behind the ears.

"You have written the definitive book on the Agency with the benefit of an insider's knowledge," Hockney was saying. "No one can match that. I'd like to do something related, but different, something like the book Woodward and Bernstein did on the hurdles they had to get over in order to expose Watergate. I'd like to write the story of what I had to contend with in trying to throw some light on the dark side of the Agency."

"It's all dark." Kreps relaxed into the red banquette. "We won't solve that problem until we put the Agency out of business."

There was a ghost of a smile on Kreps's face. By the end of the evening, Hockney even felt confident enough to mention Tessa. Kreps said he had run into her recently and had helped to set up a new features deal for her. Hockney did not inquire what the words "run into" meant. It was better not to think about it.

Next morning, Hockney was comfortably installed in a spare office at the Third World Exchange. It was on the Rue de L'Université, a block from the Bois de la Cambre. Kreps had been willing enough to put the resources of his outfit at Hockney's disposal, and Hockney was impressed to find that its facilities matched those of the mother institute in Washington. The Third World Exchange had its own telex, a small printing press in the basement, a computerized data bank that was being fed new information daily, and remarkably extensive files. The archivists took a keen interest in biographical material, and it was not confined to intelligence agents. There were personal files on politicians, corporation executives, journalists, and even church leaders—classified as "hostile" or "friendly."

"Your files are better than our morgue at the *World*,"

Hockney remarked to Kreps. "How did you manage to get everything together so fast?"

"Oh, my years with the Company taught me something," Kreps replied. "And we've had some help from our Belgian friends, especially Hendrik, the guy you met last night." It struck Hockney as ironic that the Third World Exchange was able to maintain a private intelligence collection on this scale when many Western security services had been ordered to shred their files on radicals and Communists.

Kreps showed Hockney a batch of recent press clippings, all of which, he claimed, had been generated by his efforts. Most of them, from newspapers all across Europe, dealt with the names and activities of alleged CIA agents. There was a batch on the neo-Nazi revival in West Germany, including some scream headlines about the Nazi past of prominent anti-Soviet politicians. There were a few pieces on corruption in the Persian Gulf states, and some more on the Israelis' supposed use of torture against Palestinian opposition elements.

He picked out a folder labeled "Disinvestment," which contained press reports of how radicals had systematically infiltrated the annual shareholders' meetings of some big Western companies in order to demand that all business involved with South Africa be cut off.

A loose clipping from a rightist British tabloid caught Hockney's eye. It was a Red-baiting article that attacked several Labor Party politicians, including a former minister, as Communist agents of influence. The selection of names did not make sense to Hockney, since it included MPs who had supported America's efforts in the Vietnam war. He also detected an anti-Semitic undertone to the piece, since most of the Labor Party figures named were strong supporters of Israel.

"What's this doing in your scrapbook, Phil?" Hockney probed. "Red-baiting in the *Daily Post* is not exactly your style."

Kreps grinned as if he were privy to some secret. "It doesn't hurt to confuse the opposition. This kind of stuff discourages Red-baiting."

Hockney remembered something that Nick Flower had

let drop during their final conversation—this had been over lunch at Duke Zeibert's—before he left Washington. "The key to a successful disinformation operation," Flower had pronounced, "is to start with a kernel, or *kanva*, as Kramar would say, of truth. Around that, you weave your fabric of falsehood. If you want to discredit true information, for example, the best way to do it is to circulate reports that are superficially similar, but can easily be shown to be false." According to Flower's logic, Hockney realized, it would make sense for someone who wanted to protect Soviet "sleepers" inside Britain's Labor Party to point the finger of suspicion at people who had no connection with the Communists—thereby discrediting any effort to establish who the real traitors were.

He glanced at the by-line on the story from the *Daily Post*. "Who is this Malcolm Mackenzie?" he asked casually.

"Oh, he's okay," Kreps replied vaguely.

"Does he write regularly for the *Post*?"

"Sure. He's the home editor."

"And you say he's a friend of yours?"

Kreps cleared his throat. "Malcolm keeps a low profile." He obviously did not want to be questioned further on the subject.

"Mind if I take a closer look?" Hockney gestured at the pile of folders on Kreps's desk.

"Be my guest."

There was a thick country file on Britain. Hockney leafed through it. Most of the articles were from obscure leftist publications with names like *The Spark*. The file contained a couple of issues of a magazine called *The Digger*. On the cover of one of them was a photo of Tessa at a pro-Palestinian rally in Baghdad. But the main story inside was about the computer system used by the British security service. It contained a mass of technical detail.

"This looks pretty good, Phil," Hockney said, holding up the copy of the magazine.

"Yeah. She looks like a real Pasionaria in the picture."

Hockney ignored the reference to Tessa. "Does a magazine like this make any impact in Britain?" he asked. "I've never heard of it before."

"Well, how many people had heard of *Barricades* magazine before you put it on the map, Bob? And *Barricades* gave you a foothold in the mainstream press, so you could join the *World* and carry on the good fight where you could be more effective. The same thing is happening now with *The Digger* in Britain. You'd be surprised how many of the stories it floats are picked up in the dailies, and how many kids who start out by writing an occasional piece for *The Digger* end up as staff writers on a mainstream paper like the *Sentinel* or even the *Daily Post*."

Kreps's secretary stuck her head around the door. "There's a call from Paris, Phil," she said. "Marcel Rosse is waiting on the line."

The name rang a bell with Hockney. Marcel Rosse. A leftist French publisher, Hockney remembered, possibly linked to the so-called STAR underground, information about which was just beginning to emerge. And a past friend of Michel Renard. It would be worth asking Renard about Rosse when he returned to Paris, especially since there appeared to be some connection between Rosse and the Foundation.

Hockney could not glean much from Kreps's end of the telephone conversation. Kreps confined himself to grunting yes or no to whatever Rosse was asking at the other end. The exchange ended cryptically. "A new STAR is born," Kreps said.

"What's your next project?" Hockney asked when Kreps had hung up.

"I'm going to spend some time in Rome," Kreps replied. "I'm going to expose every goddamn CIA agent in Italy."

And that wasn't all, Hockney thought. Rome. That was where Kreps had been with Tessa before. He had a premonition that Rome would bring Tessa and Kreps together again.

Hockney spent his afternoon in the library of the Third World Exchange. The archivist was feeding the latest data on the top one hundred West German industrial firms into the computer. Hockney sneaked a glimpse over the man's shoulder at the first names on the list: Veba, Siemens, Daimler, Volkswagen, Hoechst. The data seemed to range from annual profit figures to a detailed biography of the newly appointed personnel director of the Mannesman Company.

Some of the material the archivist was transferring to the computer came from inside a big steel filing cabinet with a combination lock. When the archivist slipped out to the men's room, leaving the door of the cabinet ajar, Hockney seized on his opportunity.

He pulled out a clutch of manila folders at random. They were all personal files. The names meant little or nothing to Hockney. He skimmed a couple. A photograph of a heavyset German businessman with brambly eyebrows caught his attention. The name, Franz-Josef Faber, was vaguely familiar. Hockney studied his dossier. It seemed that Faber was chief executive of a big German corporation that made machine tools. His company employed almost 70,000 people. The file noted that Faber's personal wealth was estimated at more than $4 million. He had a wife and two daughters. In addition, according to the file, he maintained a mistress in Munich who worked as a secretary at the CSU party headquarters.

The most interesting section of the Faber dossier related to his life between 1934, when he joined the Hitler Youth, and 1945, when he completed his service as a lieutenant in a Panzer division on the Russian front.

The layout of the dossier reminded Hockney of CIA and FBI documents that had been released to him under the Freedom of Information Act. The identity and relative reliability of sources was indicated by numbers and letters throughout the file. At the back of the file were sketch maps of the routes that Faber's chauffeur normally followed from his home to his office, with notes on the usual time of departure and arrival. There was even a physical description of Faber's chauffeur-bodyguard.

Hockney heard footsteps approaching along the corridor. He barely managed to stuff the folders back into the steel cabinet—conscious that they were now out of order—before the archivist reentered the room.

Now why, he asked himself, would the Third World Exchange be assembling such fantastically detailed information on the private life of a German businessman?

Rome

SIGISMUND VON KLOPP, the man the Italians called Il Tedesco, had a full week.

On Monday night, he helped his Italian friends settle a local score. Il Tedesco would normally have disdained involvement in something as trivial as an act of reprisal for a Fascist attack on a Marxist bookstore. But among those injured was a member of the group he had been assigned to work with in Rome, the underground organization that called itself—with an arrogant disregard for radical chic—the Movimento Stalin. Taking part in a revenge attack, Il Tedesco calculated, would demonstrate his personal commitment to the Movimento Stalin and help overcome any remaining distrust that the Italians in the group might feel toward a German interloper.

Corrado, the psychology student who was steering the beige Fiat in and out of the narrow side streets around the Pantheon under a half-moon, called himself an international Communist. But Il Tedesco guessed that Corrado was also the sort of Italian who would never be quite sure about Germans. He wondered what Corrado would think of him if he ever learned that his real name was Sigismund von Klopp. The name Klopp was legendary in Germany. It was synonymous with ships and shipyards, the foundation of the family fortune. It also figured high on the list of the business interests that financed Hitler's rise to power.

Corrado spotted the bar they were looking for and stopped the car twenty yards beyond the door. Il Tedesco ordered him to wait with the engine running.

He patted the Tokarev 7.62 tucked in the left-hand pocket of his raincoat, and sauntered casually back to the bar. There was only a brief lull when the German entered.

Il Tedesco ordered Campari, to give himself time to

survey the clientele at the tables crammed into a narrow oblong at the back of the café. From the photographs he had tried to memorize that afternoon, he was able to recognize several faces. He was fairly sure that the black-haired, angular young man lounging at one of the tables was a former paratroop lieutenant who was now active in a Fascist organization that had bombed the bookstore.

Unhurriedly, Il Tedesco paid for his drink and wandered back toward the door. It was only after he had stepped out into the street that he reached deep into the right-hand pocket of his raincoat and pulled out a Molotov cocktail, camouflaged as a bottle of Frascati. Holding the bottle in front of him, he whipped out a Zippo lighter with his left hand. As the flame met the wick in the neck of the bottle, Il Tedesco flung back the door of the bar and hurled the firebomb inside. The men around the bar seemed to be frozen, as in a photograph.

As the German ran to the car, the café exploded into liquid fire, illuminating the whole street. Corrado rammed the Fiat into second gear before he had even shut his door. Looking back through the rear window, the German saw a man rolling along the middle of the street, trying to smother the flames that engulfed his body. A human torch.

Within minutes, Il Tedesco and his driver were lost in the traffic along the Corso Vittorio Emanuele. They switched cars near the Spanish Steps, and the German carefully disposed of his raincoat, dark brown wig, and glasses.

Il Tedesco was blond when he sallied out the following evening to attend an opulent dinner party hosted by a well-known Italian film producer. On such occasions, the German used his real name, which was an unfailing entrance card to the salons of the wealthy and famous throughout Europe. That evening, the conversation veered from the producer's latest movie—which sounded like a cross between a porno flick and *Battleship Potemkin*—to holidays in Sardinia and who-was-seen-sleeping-with-whom. The heir to a spaghetti factory (who was celebrating his father's death, which had at last allowed him to advertise the fact that he was gay) invited Klopp to join him for a few days on his boat at Porto Rotondo.

Bored beyond endurance by the whole scene, Klopp was contemplating spending the rest of the night with an empty-headed model from New York who sported gold tassels on her skintight black boots when he noticed an improbable couple arriving late. Klopp picked out the carroty hair and ferretlike features of Phil Kreps from across the room. It was not Kreps's ill-fitting brown sports coat and check pants that made him look utterly incongruous; he would have looked equally out of place in a tuxedo. Phil Kreps was the type who could lose himself in an instant in a crowd but would forever stand apart among the glitterati. What made his presence the more surprising was his stunning companion.

"Isn't that an American movie star?" Klopp checked with the model. "What's her name again?"

"Tessa Torrance," said the model in an accent that was pure Brooklyn. The model pouted, angry that she no longer occupied center stage for this rich, leonine young German.

The German's eyes met Tessa's across the room and held for a moment before she tossed her head and turned away. Klopp made no sign of recognition toward Phil Kreps. Although most of the people at the producer's party affected radical views, their commitment went no deeper than their makeup. The German thought it would be incautious to display intimacy with the American who had set out to destroy his former employers in the CIA. Even if Phil Kreps was beginning to acquire some measure of social respectability, it would strike some people as odd that a German playboy from an ultraconservative family who was best known for his fast cars and fast women should have struck up a special relationship with a CIA defector.

Klopp waited for the producer to make the introductions.

"Siggy," the producer said, when he had squired Tessa and Kreps halfway around the room. Klopp moved closer to them, looking at Tessa. This time, she met his stare for a long time, openly challenging him.

"Tessa," the producer went on, "I want you to meet Sigismund von Klopp. Siggy to us. His only redeeming quality apart from his outrageous good looks is that he is outrageously rich."

"Hello." Tessa was studiously cool, taking an instant dislike to the German with the comic pseudo-aristocratic name who looked far too much like a fashion plate in a glossy magazine.

Phil Kreps, who knew better, was equally distant. "Hi," he said briefly, without waiting for the producer to include his name in the introductions.

"Phil is a dangerous man," the producer commented.

"So am I," the German quipped, still giving his attention to Tessa. "Is Miss Torrance doing a movie for you?" he asked their host.

"Not unless you can use a little tender persuasion," the producer replied.

"I'm rehearsing for a Broadway production," Tessa cut in.

"That's rather a change from *Sex Wars*, isn't it?" said Klopp.

"I'm tired of just being a body that men gawk at," Tessa said severely. "The Hollywood producers think they've got me typecast. I want to go on stage to show them I can act."

The German's eyebrow arched imperceptibly as he looked from Tessa, resplendent in a gold lamé dress, to Phil Kreps. The ex-CIA man said nothing.

"Acting must be a very taxing profession," the German commented, to break the silence.

"It's less boring on the stage," said Tessa. "You have to master a whole role, not just cope with a line at a time. And you're up in front of a live audience, night after night, facing the judgment of all those people."

"If I may say so, you seem like a woman who would have no difficulty learning any number of different roles."

Tessa did not even attempt a smile in acknowledgment of the artificial compliment.

"How about you, Mr. von Klopp?" she tested him. "How many roles can you play?"

"I'm afraid I have no acting skills at all."

"You mean you're happy to spend night after night among people like this?" Tessa gestured around the room. "People who talk like radical militants but spend their time living it up on daddy's money, progressives who save on their taxes by registering their million-dollar yachts in Panama?"

Phil Kreps's face contorted like that of a professional prude who had stumbled into a live sex show.

"You're very intense, aren't you?" the German said calmly. "I didn't know that all this social conscience stuff had found its way to Hollywood. How about you, Mr. Kreps?" He diverted the subject. "What are you up to these days? Still the scourge of the CIA?"

"I'm certainly not making my former employers very happy." This, from Kreps, was a considerable understatement. Since the appearance of his new book, *America's Secret Police,* he had continued to publish the names of alleged CIA officers and agents around the world. The Agency had been obliged to transfer scores of agents in an effort to keep up their cover. An American consul in Germany had been gunned down on the doorstep of his house after he had been named in a publication associated with Kreps.

"I'm surprised to find you in Rome," the German lied. He knew Kreps had been in town several weeks. The only surprise was finding the ex-CIA man with a sex goddess in tow. "Are you extending your campaign to Italy?"

"Maybe," said Kreps. "This country's system of government is maintained only by the alliance that the CIA set up with the Vatican and the Mafia after the war. That recipe for preserving Italy from communism was Nick Flower's greatest creation before he started spying on his fellow spooks and got canned for it."

"Nick Flower?" the German queried, maintaining his guise of bored innocence.

"The Agency's former counterintelligence chief," Kreps elaborated. "He was primarily responsible for marrying the godfathers and the men of God."

The heir to the spaghetti factory had sidled up to Tessa

and was engaged in complimenting her on her dress and coiffure with exaggerated charm.

"I read in the papers," Tessa said, crowbarring his inanities aside, "that there was another bombing by this terrorist group last night. What's it called? The Stalin Movement?"

"Movimento Stalin," the German corrected her. The pasta heir minced away.

"What kind of name is that for a revolutionary group?" Tessa demanded. "Sounds like a leftover from the Comintern."

"They're mixed-up students who imagine that they are the authentic Communists and therefore don't have to use pretty-sounding words. They despise the Italian Communist Party for being too soft. Since the party denounces Stalin and has rejected phrases like proletarian internationalism, these kids think it's smart to use Stalin's name and all the old Comintern jargon. They represent the phase beyond radical chic. You might call it Stalinist chic." The German, conscious that he was relaying too much information for a supposed top-drawer tourist in Rome, took care to insinuate bemused contempt into his tone.

"Are they something like the Weathermen?" Tessa asked. Since she had starred in a movie about Ché Guevara's exploits in Bolivia, Tessa had been fascinated by the guerrilla left. Her social world was full of talkers; she was drawn to the brute simplicity of those who tried to act, gun in hand. She had even attended the trial of some Black Panthers in New York and signed a petition denouncing the system of justice that had put them in jail. That gesture had passed virtually without comment in Hollywood; not so her flirtation with the Palestinians.

"There's no comparison between the Movimento Stalin and the Weathermen," the German was saying, with sudden intensity. "The Italian underground isn't a bunch of preschool crazies. They know what they're doing. And they are part of an international movement."

"STAR," Phil Kreps contributed, enigmatically.

Klopp glanced over Tessa's head to see who was within hearing before repeating the word. "STAR," he confirmed.

Tessa considered the handsome, broad-shouldered German with quickened interest. His physical presence was commanding, even to a woman who had had a procession of attractive men dancing attendance on her for years. There was even a fleeting resemblance between Klopp and Bob Hockney, if she could imagine Bob as harder and broader, with the heavy hands of a lumberjack and a killer's potential in the slightly hooded eyelids and the wide, fleshy lower lip. She now realized there was another dimension to this carefree German playboy.

"You use the word STAR," she probed. "You mean like in Red Star Army—the Japanese organization?"

"More than that," said the German, pausing to let a waiter weave his way past with a tray.

Klopp put his arm around Tessa to draw her close to him, so that his lips were almost touching her ear. "STAR is the head of the body," he explained. "Organizations like the Movimento Stalin and the Japanese group are merely the fingers and toes."

"Siggy." The producer's voice boomed from behind Tessa's shoulder. "I don't want to break anything up, but there's someone here that Tessa absolutely must meet. He might break down her inhibitions about starring in my next movie." The German released Tessa's arm and Phil Kreps moved aside to reveal the husky form of Sandro Saccucci, who had become celebrated overnight as the star of a film about the Mafia.

While Tessa engaged in the mandatory flirtation with the Italian actor, the German chatted discreetly but intently with Phil Kreps in a corner. A wonderful idea had occurred to Klopp. Imagine the effect that the public involvement of a celebrated movie star in a terrorist operation would have on the world media. It would beat anything since the kidnapping of the OPEC ministers in Vienna as a media event. Klopp thought he recognized Tessa's type. She was bored, exhausted by the Hollywood set, probably on the rebound (who wasn't?) from some torrid affair, drawn to the exotic and the violent as only well-heeled Americans without experience of real danger or suffering could be. The German sensed an opportunity. He had no intention of discussing his vaguely formulated plan with

Tessa Torrance; it would have to take her by surprise once she had been persuaded to take a small step along the way, in ignorance of the intended destination. It would not do to discuss the idea with Phil Kreps either. Kreps knew a certain amount about STAR and the German's connections with it, but the American was hardly likely to lend his support to a scheme involving a woman that he was visibly (but perhaps unsuccessfully) courting. However, Kreps's help would be needed to prepare the ground.

"I'm infatuated by Tessa," the German told Kreps, using the kind of language that serves equally well to convey or conceal a truth.

"So is most of the United States."

"What's she doing here? Is she going to be here long?"

"Just a break before her debut on Broadway. She's spending a couple of weeks in Europe."

"And you?"

"Oh, we just happened to overlap." Kreps explained that he had come to Rome from his base in Belgium in order to publicize a cover story in a radical magazine on CIA covert action in Italy, including bribes to well-known politicians and editors. It was an obvious fiction; the article had come out the week before, and caused quite a flurry at the time. Kreps was clearly hanging on in order to spend time with Tessa.

"When are you going back to Brussels?" the German asked with brutal directness.

"I don't know." Kreps looked toward Tessa, who was trying to stay clear of the Italian movie star's roving hands. "In a couple of days, I guess."

"We must rendezvous before then. Don't forget to bring your lovely companion. By the way, where is she staying?"

"At the Hassler." Kreps looked as if he wanted to bite out his tongue for saying it.

"Fine." The German bowed to Tessa. *"Arrivederci."*

Strains of Chopin echoed through the formal drawing room beyond the lobby of the Hotel Hassler when the Baron Sigismund von Klopp arrived to escort Tessa Torrance to dinner two nights later. Tessa had not been swayed by the yellow roses he had sent to her suite, although it gratified her that he had sent only one dozen, and not six or seven dozen—as her more tedious and demonstrative admirers in America had been known to do. She had agreed to meet the handsome German again because she was more than usually restless, bored by Phil Kreps's monologues about the CIA, and irritated by a letter from Bob Hockney that was more reproachful than apologetic. She wanted to get to the bottom of Klopp's mysterious allusion to an organization called STAR.

They sat facing each other in massive, old-fashioned armchairs: the German somber and correct in a navy suit and a gray silk tie, Tessa ostentatiously casual in a lurid red-and-orange kaftan and sandals.

"You look like a banker," she challenged him, pronouncing the word as if there were no lower form of life.

"It's the best way to dress if you don't want to be stopped by doormen or customs officials." Slowly, to the incongruous accompaniment of the chamber music, he began to explain. As a student at Heidelberg University, he had been haunted by his family name and what it stood for among those who remembered Hitler. He had gravitated toward the Marxist student organizations and had been selected by one of his professors to attend a seminar in Paris in support of third-world liberation movements. At the seminar, organized by the prominent French publisher Marcel Rosse, he came into contact with Palestinians and exiled revolutionaries from Africa and Latin America. He also heard about the existence of a secret organization called STAR, which coordinated the operations of different international guerrilla groups. Thanks to Marcel Rosse, he was able to meet people connected with STAR.

The German gauged Tessa's reactions to his patchy account of his early life closely before deciding to tell her the next part of the story. Although his frankness cut across all the security rules instilled in him by the men who had prepared him for STAR, he could see that what would capture Tessa was the lure of the romantic guerrilla—and he enjoyed being able to play her like a musical instrument as he told his tale.

"Did you join STAR?" she asked.

Through STAR, he explained, he arranged to spend a month of his university vacation in Beirut, where he met Palestinian guerrilla leaders, and in a camp in Iraq, where he received an intensive training course in small arms and sabotage techniques under Cuban instructors.

The German elaborated on the hardships of life in the desert training camp, which had been rather less grueling than he made it out to be. For one thing, since the leaders of the Palestinian host group were not Moslems, they imposed no restrictions on drinking or womanizing around the camp—to Klopp's initial disgust, since in his imagining a guerrilla base should be run with the same austerity as an order of soldier-monks. Watching Tessa's rapt expression, Klopp threw in a fictional account of his supposed blooding in a guerrilla raid across the Lebanese border against an Israeli military position. It was a measure of Tessa's innocence, the German noted, that she heard this out wide-eyed. It was well known that the Palestinian terrorist groups were extremely reluctant to attack Israeli army posts, preferring to take on schoolchildren or unarmed civilians. The only casualties that Klopp had witnessed at first hand during his month in the Middle East were a couple of overenthusiastic Dutch girls who blew themselves up trying to lay a land mine.

"And when you got back?" Tessa was asking. "What happened then?"

"It came as a shock to me at first," the German said. "My instructions were to carry on as before—to go on living my life as the son and heir of Manfred von Klopp as if nothing had happened. You can imagine that those were not exactly the orders I was expecting to receive." But of course, the controllers of STAR were right. As his father's emissary, Klopp had a pretext to travel almost anywhere in the world. Later, as he began to enjoy the life that his father's money opened up for him, he found that his weekend visits to the exclusive resorts of the Mediterranean—from Monte Carlo to Porto Rotondo—offered the perfect opportunity to select candidates for terrorist kidnapping. It amused Klopp to imagine his affluent neighbors—tycoons, profligate princes, movie stars, even the occasional paperback writer—trussed like hens in a six-by-six "people's prison."

Klopp did not attempt to explain that to Tessa. Nor did he answer her with complete frankness when she started asking him why he remained committed to STAR's strategy of armed revolution and where it would all lead. He offered her hand-me-down phrases about the oppression of the third world, the failure of conventional politics, the need to compel the authorities to become more and more repressive so that the people would finally rise up. Tessa nodded, not contradicting, apparently content with what she heard.

The German knew there were people who killed for abstractions, because he had seen them, men and women in their late teens and early twenties, trooping into the Iraqi camp from the universities of northern Europe. But Klopp was spurred by more visceral factors. One of them was the sheer pleasure of betrayal, of wearing the mask of devoted son, trusted colleague, or intimate friend with people whose world he was helping to shatter and whose lives he would not hesitate to take, at a moment's notice, if that became necessary. There was that purer, colder pleasure too: the joy of killing. The satisfaction that Klopp had experienced after his first murder and after each subsequent one was so intense that it had led him to ask himself whether he was becoming a psychopath. The reason he thought he was still sane was that he was able to admit to himself that his joy in the act of killing was deeper than that in the moment of sexual orgasm. But perhaps this degree of clarity was the mark of the truly insane.

All things considered, however, it was something else that bound the German inextricably to STAR. Once you had been admitted to the organization, the organization never willingly let you go, and it was a dangerous business to ignore the directives that were occasionally dispatched by the faceless men behind Marcel Rosse and his Palestinian associates.

But STAR did not forbid individual initiative. Indeed, a secret army can prosper only through the enterprise of its cell leaders in acting independently and through the quickness of their reflexes in taking advantage of a new situation. It was in that spirit that the German moved in on Tessa.

Interrupting his life story, he gestured around the magnificent salon. "Splendid," he commented. "But you should see more of Rome. Tonight, I want you to dine with me al fresco. I know a little place in the Piazza Navona."

"I'm not all that hungry," Tessa demurred. In fact, she felt slightly feverish. She noticed the mesh of blond hairs on the back of the German's powerful hands.

"The night air will change that," said Klopp decisively.

Later, a little drunk, it was Tessa's turn to impart confidences about her personal life. She became maudlin on the subject of Bob Hockney and sexual mores in general.

"Jane Fonda once told me," she announced, "that if I wanted to be effective as a radical, I'd have to stop running around. She said if radicals want to be taken seriously, they have to *act* serious. I don't know if that's supposed to mean I'm promiscuous. Otherwise I'm certainly serious. Do *you* think I'm promiscuous?"

"I really couldn't say," said Klopp, clearheaded despite the quantities of Chianti and grappa they had downed.

They stopped the taxi on the corner of the Via Veneto and walked the last several blocks back to the Hassler. As they neared the door, it was Tessa who put her arms around the German's waist. She stood before him in the moonlight, head tilted back expectantly.

"You're very exciting," she said. It was not Klopp she was talking to, but the mythic figure she had constructed from the details of his life that he had let fall.

To Tessa's surprise and mild annoyance, the German did not clasp her in the lingering embrace that she had cued. Instead, he kissed her perfunctorily and led her on into the lobby of the Hassler, under the constraining eye of the concierge.

"I have a proposition," he said softly.

"I'm relieved to hear it," said Tessa. "So do I." She started to giggle a little at the idea of a national sex symbol propositioning a German terrorist in the lobby of a five-star hotel, and nearly slipped on the polished floor.

"My proposition is that, instead of waking up all the other guests, we should go to Hamburg together."

"To Hamburg?" Tessa yawned from the alcohol. "What on earth would we do in Hamburg?"

"We would stay in my house. You'll like it. It's in Blankenese, in the woods beside the Elbe, outside the city itself. You'll be surprised by how much there is to do there."

"I don't know, Siggy." Tessa struggled to get her thoughts together. "I've got to start rehearsals for my play."

"Come on," he said, in a tone which suggested that there was no question of his not getting his way. "You have lots of time left."

"What about Phil?" She suddenly felt a twinge of remorse for Kreps, who had been packed off to deliver a speech to a student group about the CIA's involvement in the antiterrorist campaign in Italy.

"I'll take care of Phil Kreps." The German used that same tone, stronger now than before.

He had no doubt Tessa would come.

Paris

1

HOCKNEY was not much of a letter writer. This was not unusual among people who produced words for a living. He did have his off-periods, when the effort of writing to absent friends was a way of salving his conscience about not writing enough for the general public. But Hockney's annual correspondence was normally confined to Christmas cards, expense statements, and communications with the IRS. In the interstices of his new research, however, he began to write to Tessa every week or so. That was a signal, in part, that the new phase was an off-period; his by-line was no longer appearing in the *World*, and he was far from ready to start entrusting his suspicions about Cummings and the others to paper in anything more than the scrappiest notebook form.

But the letters to Tessa were also a dialogue with himself. In reasoning against her emotional radical stance, he was also sloughing off what remained of the early convictions that had driven him into journalism. He was not surprised that Tessa failed to reply to the first few letters. But as the weeks turned to months, he became irritated, and then angry, about her failure to acknowledge the bulky envelopes he was sending from successive European capitals. He wondered whether she even opened them.

He sent the letters care of Tessa's agent in New York, Hobe Wallerstein, since he knew she was constantly on the move between different resorts and movie locations. It was not until the night before he flew to Paris, with the aim of looking up the Renards and of checking out an important lead Nick Flower had given him, that he decided to call Hobe Wallerstein to find out what had happened to Tessa. Wallerstein was notorious for his gruff manner and his short temper. But even taking that into account, what the agent growled over the transatlantic line was enough to transform Hockney's anger into alarm. No, Wallerstein did not know where Tessa was. The agent also said that he didn't care if he never heard from her again. She had walked out on her first Broadway production without so much as a word of explanation. Wallerstein said that he wouldn't blame the producers if they decided to sue. They had had to replace their star with an unknown stand-in at the last moment.

Could Tessa be having a breakdown? Whatever her vices, she was not the kind of star who threw down a script in the middle of rehearsals.

Hockney knew only one person he could ask: Phil Kreps. He called Kreps in Brussels. Yes, Kreps had seen Tessa. In Rome. According to Kreps, she had decided to take an extended vacation. No, Kreps did not know where she was.

Hockney hung up in disgust. He felt sure that Kreps knew more but wasn't telling. But what right did he have to probe?

"*Bonjour, chef.*" Hockney greeted the concierge at the Hotel des Saints-Frères after driving in from Charles de Gaulle. "Remember me?"

Almost a decade had passed since he was last in Paris. But the concierge at the hotel was still the same weather-beaten ex-gendarme he remembered from his last visit, when his path had crossed that of Michel and Astrid Renard.

Through the fog of the years, the concierge scrutinized Hockney's face. At first, he seemed to draw a blank. Unwilling to concede defeat, he squinted more closely. "*Ah, oui,*" he said at last. "You're the American reporter. *L'en merdeur du téléphone.*"

Having demonstrated that his memory was unimpaired, the concierge proceeded to pick his nose with elaborate disinterest.

"You're a true *physionomiste,*" Hockney conceded. "I asked for my usual room, number forty-seven."

Scratching his buttocks through his baggy pants with one hand, the old man leafed through a tattered folder with the other. He found Hockney's name, only to inform him that room 47 was already booked. Hockney settled the question by handing the concierge his passport with a fifty-franc bill sticking out, as if through an oversight. He got room 47, on the ground floor. Sunlight glinted on the tiny latticed courtyard outside his windows. The creepers had grown thicker over the years, but were carefully pruned. The wooden chairs and tables he remembered had been replaced by yellow plastic versions.

But the hotel's telephone service had not changed. It took five minutes to place a call to Renard's new office at the conservative magazine *La Lame*. From what Hockney had been able to pick up, it sounded as if his old friend had changed his colors—unless his job as deputy editor of *La Lame* was only a cover. Perhaps Michel's heart had never really been in the work that Flower had hinted he had carried out for the Russians. Perhaps Astrid had been the driving force.

Hockney was finally connected to Renard's secretary, only to be informed that he was in Germany for the rest of the week.

"I wonder if you could give me the number of Madame Renard," he said. "I'm an old friend."

"Excuse me, monsieur," the girl said. "They're no longer together. I mean, they're divorced. I don't have Madame Renard's number." She paused. "But I believe that she is running a restaurant."

"Do you know the name of the restaurant?"

"I think it's called La Sauterelle. It's just outside Paris," the secretary said. "The Grasshopper."

Hockney got the address from directory inquiries. The restaurant was outside Paris, just off the expressway to Chartres.

Hockney did not unpack. He walked briskly down the Boulevard Saint-Germain to the Hertz rent-a-car agency. An hour later, he had pulled up outside La Sauterelle. The place looked more like a private house than a restaurant. The sign on the gate was illegible unless you drove right up to it. When Hockney got out of the car, he found that the main door to the restaurant appeared to be locked, even though it was lunchtime and there were obviously some customers. At the back of the house, he discovered three Citroëns and four Mercedeses parked in front of some old stables.

He peeked through a ground-floor window, into the kitchen. He caught his breath as he recognized Astrid, rapping out instructions to a solemn headwaiter in white tie and tails. Astrid had squeezed herself into a tight black velvet dress, with a cameoed choker at her throat. She looked extravagantly sensual, even more so than he remembered.

He tested the back door. It also seemed to be locked. The restaurant, clearly, was not striving to offer hospitality to the hungry passerby. The clientele must be very select indeed. Hockney rang the bell.

A white-jacketed man who looked more like a bouncer than a waiter opened the door a few inches, snarled *"C'est privé,"* and slammed the door shut again, nearly catching Hockney's fingers in the crack.

Hockney went back to the kitchen window and rapped on it with his knuckles. Astrid walked toward it.

"It's me, Bob," he called.

She frowned before she smiled. What did La Sauterelle have to conceal? he wondered.

"How did you find me?" she asked after the bouncer had let him in.

"I heard you'd got divorced," Hockney said. "So I thought I'd try my luck."

Hockney studied her face and figure closely, to see how nine years had changed her. She had aged hardly at all. The lines of her face were so taut that he wondered for a moment whether she had had a face lift. She was still good to look at, still eminently desirable. His curiosity and suspicion were tempered by a revived interest in Astrid as a lusty woman. Although he had avoided renewing the old affair when they had encountered each other in Vietnam, he realized he was already keyed up to try it again now. But his mood was not exactly that of a lovers' reunion—more like the excitement of stumbling into a plush whorehouse, which was where he supposed he was.

Astrid hustled him past the bar and restaurant and up a flight of stairs. He had time for only a passing glimpse of a blaze of red velvet, crystal, and chandeliers. The clientele seemed to consist exclusively of well-fed men in dark suits lunching with women who were young enough to be their daughters.

"Can't I buy you lunch?" he said to Astrid as she led him by the hand up the stairs.

"Today, *chéri*, lunch is on the house."

Astrid's private quarters consisted of a split-level living-room-cum-bedroom. The reception area contained a fur-covered sofa and two large television screens built into the wall. Raised a few steps above it was a vast four-poster bed that dominated the apartment. The white wall-to-wall carpet set off the Mirós on the walls. Astrid flicked a switch, and the room vibrated to the haunting strains of Jacques Brel's song about black skies over the North Sea.

Patting the sofa beside her as a signal to Hockney to sit down, Astrid pressed a buzzer and spoke into the intercom. "Dom Perignon and caviar," she ordered. Hockney thought that her voice was huskier, more deliberately seductive.

"How did you get into the restaurant business?" he asked when the unfriendly bouncer had deposited their lunch.

"It got so boring with Michel. He's really a bourgeois at heart. So I decided to strike out on my own. I've never been trained to do anything for a living, so I thought I'd concentrate on the things I enjoy most—food and drink and love."

"What is this? A kind of *maison de rendezvous?*"

"Call it what you like," she said. "We're very exclusive. You don't get in here unless we know you. So you see how lucky you are."

"You don't need to tell me." He ran his fingers softly over her knee. She took his hand and led it further up her thigh.

"Is this your own place?" he asked her.

266

"I have a partner," she said, popping a tiny triangle of toast, loaded precariously high with caviar, into Hockney's mouth. "It's half mine." She unfastened two of the buttons on Hockney's shirt and slipped her hand underneath, caressing his chest.

"Why don't we move to your favorite battlefield?" he suggested. He had already half unzipped her velvet dress.

"Why not?" She walked toward the bed, letting the dress fall from her body as she moved.

"Is this where you live?" Hockney asked as she pulled back the curtains from the four-poster and flung herself onto the bed.

"Yes. I live on the premises because we stay open all night. We find that some of our clients don't feel like driving back into Paris after a five-course meal."

"In that case," said Hockney, unsnapping her bra, "I think I might stay overnight."

"I don't remember that you were *that* good," she taunted him, arching her back so that her nipples were pointing provocatively at his face.

"Wait and see."

Astrid moved like a rattlesnake in bed. But when it was over, she was suddenly cold. Folding her arms under her breasts, concealing the stretch marks above where they had sagged, she said, "I've got work to do. And you've got to get back to Paris."

She vanished into the bathroom. Hockney, pulling his shirt over his shoulders, wandered down into the reception area, picking the rest of his clothes off the white rug. The two television screens, side by side on the wall, struck him as odd now that he looked at them for a second time. One did not look like a normal TV set at all, but more like a closed-circuit monitor. The dial around the single knob was marked with figures, running from 25 to 31.

While hitching up his trousers, Hockney switched on the set. As it warmed up, he found himself watching a black-and-white porno film. A cropped blonde in a kinky leather outfit with holes cut out for her breasts was trying to arouse a grossly fat naked man. As far as Hockney could tell her efforts were less than successful. Then the woman picked up a riding crop and started to thrash her companion. His loose flesh shook in an obscene way. Slowly, his limp organ became semi-erect.

This, too, must be part of the entertainment offered by La Sauterelle, Hockney thought: blue movies to excite the very special clientele. Yet there was something strangely familiar about the room where the filmed antics were taking place. The layout was almost identical to that of the room in which he was standing. Then, as Hockney stared at the spectacle, the man who had eagerly submitted to the riding crop turned his head. Hockney recognized the squashed nose, ramlike forehead, and puffy jowls of Heinz Hinkel, a well-known leader of the German Socialist Party. Then Hockney understood that he could not be watching Hinkel in a blue movie. The scene was being enacted inside La Sauterelle.

Hockney heard the bidet in the bathroom running and calculated that he would have a couple of minutes more before Astrid emerged. Quickly, he twisted the knob on the monitor to number 28. He saw a woman with prominent buttocks riding a man whose face he could not make out.

There was silence in the bathroom. Hockney switched off the set. The image on the screen died agonizingly slowly, shrinking to a minuscule point of light. Hockney collapsed onto the sofa, pulling on his socks as he watched the light fading away. It was still there, though barely visible, when Astrid came out of the bathroom. She looked from Hockney to the screen, then back again. But all she said was, "How long has it been?"

"Since what?" he asked, playing dumb because he was relieved. She seemed not to have noticed anything amiss.

"Since we were last in bed together."

"It seems like yesterday."

"You've improved," she said thoughtfully, as if she were awarding points. She zipped up her dress.

"I'm surprised you can remember. It's not as if you lack male company," he said without jealousy, his mind on the problem he had come to investigate.

There was a buzz from the intercom. Astrid pushed a

button and the voice said: *"Madame, Monsieur Rosse est là."*

"Don't run away just yet," Astrid said to him. "Wait here for a few minutes. I won't be long."

As Astrid hurried downstairs, Hockney lingered in the doorway. A maid walked past, carrying a pile of fresh towels. A door opened down the corridor, and Heinz Hinkel, pink-faced, puffed his way toward the stairs. Hockney wondered whether the efforts of the German politician's playmate had eventually been rewarded.

"I assume your Monsieur Rosse is the publisher," he remarked to Astrid when she returned.

"Do you know him?" Astrid seemed surprised.

"Just the name." Hockney reflected that Rosse's name had come up again twice in the space of a few days. It was a coincidence that could be worth exploring.

2

HOCKNEY hardly touched the brakes on his rented car as he sped back along the expressway to Paris. But just before he reached the Saint-Cloud bridge, while pulling out to overtake a long line of cars that were jammed in behind a slow-moving minibus, he was forced to slam on the brakes to avoid colliding with a sports car that darted out in front of him without signaling. He noticed that the brake pedal was not working properly. He had to pump it several times before the brakes took hold, and only narrowly avoided plowing into the back of the sports car.

After the bridge, Hockney swung off to the left to follow the route through the Bois de Boulogne back into central Paris. As he cruised along the road beside the Longchamps racetrack, with the river Seine to his left, Hockney puzzled over the scenes he had witnessed on the closed-circuit monitor in Astrid's room. Who could guess what Heinz Hinkel might confide to a whore about world politics, in between strokes of the riding crop? Astrid, of course, must *know*. What was televised was also, presumably, being recorded

269

for sound. The tapes and the still photographs they could extract from the video would be worth a great deal on the blackmail market. And even more to the Russians—assuming they were Astrid's partners in the restaurant venture.

Speeding along the Avenue de Longchamps, Hockney swerved across the middle line to avoid a car that halted suddenly, yards from the curb, opposite a gaggle of prostitutes who were lolling on a bench. But Hockney misjudged the speed of the oncoming car. He realized too late that there was no way he could pass the stationary vehicle without colliding, head on, with the car that was approaching him. He pushed the brake pedal to the floor, willing the car to stop. Nothing happened. The brakes had failed.

The crash seemed unavoidable. It was merely a question of whether Hockney was going to hit the parked car or the one that was driving straight at him. Instinctively, he ducked his head and closed his eyes.

There was no collision. With only an inch to spare, the oncoming car jumped the curb onto the dirt track beside the road. Hockney barreled on down the Avenue de Longchamps, unable to stop his car. He traveled almost the entire length of the avenue, shifting gears up and down and working the hand brake, before the car finally stuttered to a halt.

Hockney left it beside the road and thumbed a ride for the short distance to the Porte Maillot, where he called the car rental agency to report the incident. Giving vent to his anger and relief, he recited all the French swear words he could recall. "Are you trying to get your customers killed?" he yelled at the girl on the other end of the line.

"If you check your odometer," her unruffled voice replied, "you will find that your vehicle has done less than ten thousand kilometers. It was checked over thoroughly the day before you rented it. Everything was in perfect order then."

"Don't bother to send me a bill." Hockney was aware that, in France, you can never hope to win an argument unless you happen to be French.

3

THE CONCIERGE was still excavating his nostrils when Hockney got back to the Hotel des Saints-Frères.

"Monsieur, there is a message for you. The man wouldn't leave his name." The concierge stared at Hockney accusingly, as if he had discovered an unregistered woman sneaking out of his room in the early hours of the morning. He handed Hockney a scrap of paper with a telephone number.

"Shall I get the number for you now?" the concierge volunteered. Hockney was startled. Since when had the old man offered to do anything to speed up the telephone service?

"Never mind, thank you. I have to go out now. I'll call later on."

Hockney walked around the corner to the Brasserie Lip, speculating on who might call him without leaving a name. It could conceivably be Phil Kreps or someone connected with the Foundation. All of them were paranoid about security. But there was an outside chance that it was someone else. At his last meeting with Nick Flower in Washington, Hockney had asked for advice on people who might be able to help him in Europe. The former spymaster mentioned that he still had some close friends in British intelligence who shared some of their mutual concerns. Hockney had told Flower where he would be staying. Was it possible that Flower's British friends had decided to establish contact?

Hockney made the call from the phone in the basement of the Brasserie Lip. "This is Robert Hockney," he announced to the woman who answered. "I was told to call this number."

"Un petit instant, s'il vous plaît." The woman's French was all but swamped by her British accent.

A man's voice came on. "Mr. Hockney? My name is Campbell. I think we have some friends in common who are interested in—gardening. Any chance of seeing you tonight?" Campbell's accent was pure Oxbridge. Hockney guessed that the man on the other end of the line was the Paris station chief of SIS, the British intelligence service.

"How about dinner?" Hockney proposed.

"That's a bit tricky. Got a lot on. I was thinking of a bit later, say around midnight. Have you been to the Crazy Horse?"

This could not be very serious, Hockney told himself. The Crazy Horse Saloon had the most celebrated nudes in Western Europe. It was also a place where it was a considerable feat to hear yourself think—let alone hear what anyone else was saying—above the deafening music, accompanied by breasts and buttocks bouncing a few feet away from your nose.

"Whatever you suggest," said Hockney.

"That's fine. Shall we say midnight?"

Hockney decided, without asking, that he would make the reservations. Madame Pipi, who combined the functions of lavatory attendant and telephone operator, looked up the number of the Crazy Horse for him. He chuckled as he read the slip of paper she gave him: BAL-6969.

Back in his hotel room, propped up against the headboard of his bed, Hockney scribbled notes in his private, indecipherable shorthand. The phone interrupted him.

"Encore un appel," the concierge complained.

It was the car rental agency.

"About your car," said a woman's voice. It sounded like the same unflappable girl who had been on the receiving end of his abuse earlier on. Or did they all talk that way? "We found that the brake cable had been severed," she went on. "Do you have any theories about that? I'm afraid we've had to inform the police."

"Severed? How do you mean?"

"The cable was cut most of the way through, probably with a pair of pliers. Whoever did it assumed—correctly— that the rest of the cable would snap after you had pushed the pedal a few times."

Hockney had lots of time to think about who might have had a motive to kill him—and an opportunity to tamper with the car—before the police inspector turned up, unannounced, just after 10:30 P.M. If the brake cable had been cut, that could only have been done at Astrid's place. He remembered the tiny spot of light on the closed-circuit monitor in her room. If Astrid had concluded he was spying on her, she might have tried to take precautions about being unmasked. But would Astrid be capable of trying to murder him, straight after making love? No, he thought, surely not. Yet Rosse had been at La Sauterelle too. If Astrid had told Rosse, it would be a different matter. Rosse, from what he had gleaned, was entirely capable of issuing instructions to kill. Whether his suspicions were right or not, they could hardly be discussed with a French police inspector.

The inspector, young, sharp, tieless, studied him skeptically as he rattled on about how he had been taking a casual drive through the Bois de Boulogne when the accident occurred. The inspector was not easily satisfied, especially since he knew that Hockney was a world-renowned journalist whose articles had led to the suicide of the head of a Paris-based news agency. He made Hockney recite his entire itinerary since he had rented the car—where he had driven, what stops he had made, where he had eaten lunch. Resolved not to mention Astrid's restaurant, Hockney nearly tripped over the last question nonetheless. He had a sudden blackout on the names of Paris restaurants, and had to say he had skipped lunch. It was not a complete lie. Champagne and caviar did not really qualify as lunch.

"You're a journalist, Monsieur Hockney?" The inspector delivered his question as if it were a formal indictment.

"Yes."

"What are you writing about now?"

"I'm doing a thriller. But it's mostly sex. That's what sells. What better place than Paris to research the subject?"

The inspector was not amused. "I think you are running away from something," he said solemnly.

"Only from girls."

When the questioning was finished, it was almost time to set off for the Crazy Horse. Hockney walked out with the inspector.

"Bonsoir, monsieur," the concierge said to the policeman, untypically unctuous. After the inspector had passed his desk, he wagged an accusing finger at Hockney, as if to say, "I knew you were no good."

4

HOCKNEY arrived at the Crazy Horse before Campbell. He did not like his table, where he was jammed kneecap to kneecap with a raucous party of Japanese tourists. So he tipped the headwaiter and was ushered to a quieter table at the side, farther away from the chorus line that was gyrating under strobe lights.

"We are proud to introduce Greta Megaton," announced a voice from the loudspeaker. "The nuclear blast from Munich." Greta flounced onto the stage, kicking her heels high into the air. She was dressed only in ropes of pearls. She tore them off, one by one, and the fake pearls went rolling across the stage and onto the nearest tables, to be scooped up by giggling Japanese. Totally naked, Greta began to do a split. As her legs spread, a miniature mushroom cloud rose from the floor.

"They should call her Hiroshima Mon Amour, especially with this audience." Hockney turned to identify the sardonic voice. He found that a dapper figure in a double-breasted suit with wide pinstripes had slid, unnoticed, onto the seat beside him. With his tie askew, ruffled hair, and a yellow silk handkerchief exploding from his breast pocket, the stranger had a vaguely bohemian aristocratic air.

"Chris Campbell," the Englishman introduced himself. "Welcome to Paris." After ordering the mandatory bottle of champagne, he asked, "Tell me, Robert—if I may call you that—how do you fit into Nick Flower's life-style?"

Hockney glanced uneasily at the neighboring tables.

"The best way to be inconspicuous is in a noisy crowd,"

said Campbell, following his glance. "No one could be as interested in us as in what is going on up there." An imposing black beauty from Martinique who had been introduced as Hot Licks was wiggling her behind at the audience.

Campbell leaned closer to Hockney, who began, uncertainly, to explain his new investigation and what had led up to it. Trying to sum it all up, Hockney said into the Englishman's ear: "A Black Panther once claimed that you are either part of the problem or part of the solution. I may have gotten the two mixed up."

Campbell quaffed his champagne in silence. The Englishman had never believed in instant conversions. Baptism in cold water, in Campbell's view, did not make a practicing Christian. You had to keep watch to see who turned up for church on Sundays.

"What can you tell me about Marcel Rosse?" Hockney was asking above the din of the music.

"Now that's an interesting name," said Campbell. "Why are you interested?"

"I think Rosse tried to have me killed this afternoon."

Campbell inclined his head closer still to catch every word of Hockney's account of the day's crowded events. "I must say you seem to be on the right track," he commented when Hockney had finished. "Even if that has its—er—drawbacks. It took my firm quite a long time to establish beyond doubt that Rosse's real employers were in Moscow. I must confess it helped to concentrate our minds when his cousin, who used to work for my firm, was exposed as a traitor."

Campbell swiveled to examine the stage. A conjurer-clown bedecked with joke medals was completing a series of tricks. For his finale, he took a deck of cards in one hand, stretched his arms wide, and catapulted one card after another into his free hand until he had gone through the whole deck. To a round of thunderous applause, the clown bounced off stage trailing the deck behind him like a paper streamer, showing the audience that the cards were connected by almost invisible threads.

Campbell joined enthusiastically in the clapping. "All

successful tricks," he observed, "depend on traceless connections."

Campbell signaled the waiter to bring more champagne. "By the way," he said. "After seeing the irresistible Astrid, are you planning to reestablish contact with your old friend Michel Renard?"

"He's out of town."

"I gather he'll probably be back this weekend."

"Do you know Michel?" Hockney asked.

"Only by reputation. I think you'll find he's changed considerably since you last saw him."

"In what way?"

"He's more independent. He makes his own judgments. I think it helps that he's no longer dominated by Astrid. She could steal the balls away from any man. It was because of her that he made his worst mistakes. Fortunately, nothing in life is irreparable."

On stage, a man coated in gold paint and a woman covered in silver paint were performing a ballet depicting varied sexual positions.

"Does that appeal to you?" Campbell challenged Hockney.

"I don't go in for spectator sports."

Campbell turned back to face Hockney. "What I was beginning to say," he resumed, "is that Renard is ready to lay himself bare to someone he can trust completely. That person could well be you."

"Do you have any advice?"

"You're on a very tricky wicket. You should be forewarned that the Renard you knew here and in Vietnam was not a free agent. He was under control. His former control was an extremely important man on the other side."

"You mean a Russian."

"Precisely." Campbell stubbed out a Gauloise. The ashtray, Hockney noticed, was overflowing. "I don't know how serious you are in this mission you've assigned yourself," the Englishman went on. "But if you will allow me to assume for one moment that you are serious, there are a few things you might do to help."

276

"Hold on," Hockney snapped. "If you're thinking of things that would help your organization, just remember I'm not in business to do any intelligence service any favors."

Campbell suppressed a sigh. It could be very trying to deal with a certain type of American. He sipped his champagne while the emcee announced the next act—the Juicy Banana from Managua.

It was Hockney who reopened the conversation. "I apologize," he said. "I guess I've spent so many years acting on the assumption that I was surrounded by people in the CIA who wanted to manipulate the media that I haven't yet managed to break the mold. *I'm* the one who needs help right now. If I can help you in return, let's talk about it."

Campbell looked at Hockney speculatively. "We'll have to play things by ear," he said. "First of all, you'll need to know everything there is to know about Viktor Barisov."

"Nick Flower told me a few things about Barisov last time I saw him."

"Did he tell you that Barisov is having his problems back at Moscow Center?"

Hockney shook his head.

"It will be worth looking into," Campbell predicted. "Barisov has been the high-flier in his service. Now there are indications that he's about to come a cropper. I wouldn't be surprised if he turned up in some fairly minor post in Europe. Perhaps Geneva. The opposition has been having a lot of headaches in Geneva."

"What has all this got to do with my project?"

"I would have thought the answer was obvious," said Campbell reproachfully. "Barisov was the man behind Michel Renard for a number of years—which also made him, at least indirectly, the man behind some of your stories. If Barisov gets egg on his face and ends up in a routine assignment in Europe, that could supply you with your chance to get the story from him firsthand."

"I'll keep in touch," said Hockney. The deeper he dug, the more he came to feel that, as a journalist, he had a lot to atone for. Perhaps the casual Englishman with that yellow handkerchief was the man who could help him do that.

5

RENARD negotiated his way through the crowded Brasserie Lip toward the table where Hockney was waiting for him, stopping en route to shake hands with some of the politicians and diplomats who were regular lunchtime visitors. Hockney did not recognize Renard until he had almost reached his seat. His friend looked at least ten years older than he really was. His hair was gone—except for a few grey strands around a bald pate—and he had let his body collapse into a sagging paunch. He looked as if he had not seen the sun for years.

They had not been in touch since Saigon, apart from an occasional postcard. Hockney had learned that his old friend had been called home after the Communist takeover in South Vietnam, but he had not kept track of his journalistic career.

"Michel, you haven't changed a bit," Hockney said.

"You still don't know how to lie," Renard reprimanded him. "You're the one who doesn't look a day older."

"My problem," Renard explained over a pastis, "is I now spend twelve hours a day hunched over a desk. I spend all my time trying to appease the unions, trying to figure out the new computer technology, and trying to cope with brash young kids who think they know better than I do how to perform my job."

They spent a long, boozy, philosophic lunch reminiscing about Vietnam. Hockney waited until the plates had been cleared away before popping the question that had been on the tip of his tongue since Renard appeared.

"Tell me, Michel, were you a free agent in sixty-eight, back in Saigon?"

"Freedom is a relative concept," Renard said pensively.

"Michel, let's not fuck around philosophizing." Hockney's tone was gentler than his language. "Why don't you tell me what kind of relationship you had with Viktor Barisov in those days?"

The answers did not come at once. Renard did not deny his friendship with Barisov, but began by claiming that they had had an entirely healthy relationship, exchanging perceptions of various international issues.

Hockney found this less than convincing. "How can you have an entirely healthy relationship with a Soviet journalist who you suspected was KGB?" he demanded. It was not until Hockney dropped a hint that he knew a little of Astrid's links—and where the money for La Sauterelle had come from—that Renard began to open up.

Sweating slightly, Renard said, "This is very dangerous, Bob. I haven't seen Viktor Barisov for five years, maybe more. But I live in fear of a phone call. If my relationship with him ever became known to my corporation, I'd be completely washed up."

Before their meeting, Hockney had tried to calculate his own reactions to this confrontation with a man who had helped to shape his life by duping him systematically a decade before—in Paris, in Saigon—under the guise of a kindly benefactor. Because of Renard, Hockney now understood, much of his early journalistic success had been built on a lie, a succession of lies. Renard had been a dealer in falsehoods—not total but partial falsehoods, since, again, an effective lie must contain a kernel of truth. Hockney's thoughts flashed for a moment back to Nick Flower and his theories on the subject. The information that Renard had given Hockney on his former editor, Jacques Bonpierre, was essentially true; Bonpierre's suicide proved that. But Renard's motives for supplying it were another part of the truth, which Hockney had neglected at the time. In Vietnam, Renard had worked harder to deceive him. With hindsight, Hockney was now convinced that some of his most terrifying experiences—like the mock execution in Cholon—had been elaborately staged.

He had expected to become very angry when he guided their discussions toward this theme, just as he had become angry brooding about it before the meeting. Hockney was surprised to find himself entirely calm, able to discuss the events of his own life as if they had happened to someone else. And he felt a kind of pity for a friend who lived in fear of the dark.

"When did you break with the Russians?" he asked Renard.

"After Astrid left me," Renard said. "She was what tied me. But for her . . ." The Frenchman's voice trailed off into the emptiness of might-have-beens.

"And they let you go? Just like that?"

"They lost interest when I got out of journalism." Renard said it too quickly to be convincing. Hockney wondered whether French security, or Chris Campbell's friends, could have had a hand in Renard's apparent change of allegiance. Having trusted Renard completely—and thus been completely deceived—Hockney was now reluctant to accept anything from him at face value.

"Was every story you gave me in the old days a Soviet plant?" he asked the Frenchman.

"No." Renard looked behind Hockney, as if trying to locate someone in the restaurant.

"But some of your stories were plants."

"Yes."

"Did you stage-manage my capture by the Vietcong in Cholon?"

"Yes and no. I mean, I couldn't know exactly how everything would turn out. I'm sorry." Renard kneaded the crumbs that had been left on his side of the tablecloth into a ball. "My hands were tied."

"Tell me about Barisov," Hockney demanded. "What's he like? What makes him tick?"

"When I first met him, I might have offered you the old cliché—wine, women, and song. Even when I came to know him better, he gave me the feeling that he preferred Western decadence to Soviet discipline. But you can't be sure with a KGB man. They're professionals, after all. Still, I don't think it's ideology that propels a man like Barisov. He loves the *game*. He likes raising the stakes, bidding high."

"Is he vulnerable? What would touch him?"

"He is proud," Renard said, brooding on the question. "He would not easily recover if someone in higher authority slapped him down. He would not forgive someone who made him out to be a fool or an incompetent."

"What else?"

"What's the point of this, Bob? Are you trying to get Viktor Barisov to defect?"

"I'm just trying to understand the forces that have controlled a number of things that I thought were important at the time."

"And if you succeed in understanding, what are you going to do about it?"

"I'm going to write about it. That's what I do, Michel. I write."

Renard called for the bill and insisted on paying it. It was, as he pointed out, *his* territory.

"A word of warning, Bob," the Frenchman said. "Don't play with fire. I can understand what motivates you. I don't like what happened, and I can't make amends for it—not to you, at any rate. But don't take on too much. The people you want to expose can destroy you by lifting their little fingers. Is that really worth risking? What do you think you can achieve?"

"Wait till you read it."

Hamburg

1

TESSA woke late, with a headache and a sour taste in her mouth. When she forced herself to throw back the covers, she began to shiver violently and felt a stabbing pain across her back, below the shoulder blades, as if she had caught a chill. She hurried, slightly bent, to the dresser and swallowed several pills from the unidentified bottle that was standing on it. She pulled on a coarse turtleneck sweater and jeans and lit a cigarette before advancing to the window to draw back the curtains. The sunlight hurt her eyes, even though it was filtered through the thick pine forest outside the bedroom window.

Far off, she could hear the horn of a passing ship—the sound of a world of freedom and movement as remote from her static confines as the image of the puffing steam engine, forever unattainable behind a blank, impenetrable wall, in the paintings of de Chirico.

It was fall, outside Hamburg, in the family mansion of Sigismund von Klopp, and Tessa was a prisoner—less because of the bars across her window than because of the bars that her captors had placed across her mind. To try to remember her life before Blankenese, to think about the reactions of her friends and producers to her disappearance, was like trying to put herself inside the head of another person. Reality was the interval of time between the dosages of what Siggy called her "medicine," and the moments of soaring relief that it gave her. She had no past, no identity except the one they gave her. She was no longer Tessa Torrance. She was Ulrike. There had been another Ulrike, a martyr. She no longer belonged to Hollywood producers and Broadway impresarios. She belonged to STAR.

There was breakfast debris on the huge table in the heavy-beamed dining room. Tessa took only coffee. Since she had been receiving her "medicine," even the thought of food nauseated her. She had not eaten a full meal for days. How many days she was unsure. It was impossible to keep track of time.

The man they called Kurt came into the room wearing a chauffeur's uniform.

Tessa looked at him with naked, animal expectancy.

"It's not time yet," said Kurt, unfastening the top button of his high-collared, Prussian-style jacket. He had thin, colorless lips and looked permanently in need of a shave. Kurt inspected his watch. "Why don't you make yourself useful? You can feed the prisoner."

There was another stranger in the house who was more of a prisoner than Tessa. If she had been led to the door and set free, she would have needed someone to take her by the hand in order to leave the grounds. The prisoner in the cellar had not yet reached that stage. He had been in the house for days, not months.

Tessa's empty stomach churned when Kurt returned from the kitchen with an enamel plate filled with what might have been chopped horsemeat.

"Afterward?" she said to him as she reluctantly took the plate.

"Afterward," Kurt assured her. He raised the flap of his breast pocket so she could see the plunger of the hypodermic syringe inside.

"Do I have to do this?" The unsavory contents of the plate brought back, with a rush, what she had undergone in the cellar months—or was it only weeks—before.

"Don't you want your fix?" The sneer on Kurt's thin lips was part of the recent memory Tessa did not want to revive.

Tessa had accepted Klopp's invitation to Blankenese, anticipating a leisurely few days of lovemaking with a man who exercised a distinct biological attraction but whose real appeal lay in the promise of the dangerous, secret world that he could introduce to her. She had given little serious thought to what initiation into STAR would entail; she imagined little more than furtive plotting and the display of captured trophies in a German hunting lodge, something in keeping with the kind of revolutionary tourism she had indulged in before—with Black Panthers and Palestinians—a brief flirtation with danger, followed by a safe return to the cushioned existence that money and fame had built for her. She had expected something she could boast about to armchair radicals in New York.

The first evening at the Klopp mansion had fully conformed to her expectations. The house was vast and full of servants. The dinner was elaborate, the wines extravagantly rare. After, Klopp had showed off his private armory. The cold steel of the gun barrels, after the wine, made her read a sexual innuendo into the German's meandering dissertation on the revolutionary cause. Klopp met no resistance when he suggested a nightcap in her bedroom. The framboise seemed perfect for the occasion. Tessa ran her fingers through the German's blond hair as the fire crackled in the grate opposite her overlarge four-poster. But if he touched her, she did not remember it.

She returned to consciousness in dramatically different surroundings, lying on a thin piece of matting on a stone floor. She knew her senses had to be deranged, because—despite the flagstone floor beneath her—she was not in a room, but in a tent. At least, the walls that were close to her on either side felt like canvas. She could not see, because a blindfold had been knotted tightly around her head, encasing her eyes. She could not tear off the blindfold, because her wrists had been bound with what felt like wire behind her back.

At first, Tessa thought she was in the midst of a nightmare. When the pain in her wrists and the cramp from lying trussed up on the stone floor persuaded her that she was fully awake, she began to think that Klopp must be playing some kind of sadistic game. She found it difficult to think rationally about her situation because of her splitting headache. She was either badly hung over or drugged. Either way, she could not have known that Klopp and his mentors in the STAR organization had agreed that the quickest and surest way to secure the total involvement of untrained outsiders was to break down their individual identities to the point where they were ready to be remolded entirely, receptive to any order or role the movement chose to assign. Sensory deprivation was only one element in this theft of identity, designed to transform Tessa Torrance into Ulrike.

For what seemed like a day or more, she was left entirely alone, without food or drink or even sanitary necessities. When at last she heard the pad of crepe soles over the stone floor, she begged to be given water, and to be taken to the lavatory. But the footsteps went away. She was revolted by the stench of her own urine in the tent by the time an anonymous person brought her a bowl of gruel, some water, and a bucket. The visitor did not untie her hands. She had to roll over onto her side to eat and drink, like a wounded animal.

Later, she heard the clatter of heavy boots. Someone raised the flap of the tent and pressed his bulk against her. Tessa screamed as he tore at her clothing, and tried to push the man back with her knees. But she was too weak to resist. The only sound the man made was his rasping breath. She was sure the man was not Klopp. His broken nails scratched her breasts, her stomach. Klopp's hands, though strong, were beautifully kept.

Not long after the rape—or maybe it was longer than she thought, since she was drifting between consciousness and unconsciousness—two people came together to the tent. They untied her hands. The pain of the blood returning to her wrists was rapidly overcome by the sharper pain of a needle inserted awkwardly into a vein in the hollow of her left elbow. When they finally removed the blindfold, she no longer cared. She could see Klopp, but his face and voice were somewhere far below her.

There were other people with Klopp, she noticed with dreamlike detachment. Kurt, the chauffeur, was leering. In her vision, his hands swelled to several times their natural size, and she could see the coarse, broken nails. In front of Kurt, next to Klopp, was another man she had never seen before, dressed in a white coat. He was wearing thick-lensed glasses that dwarfed his face and magnified his eyes. He might have been a doctor, but he looked too young and there was nothing reassuring about his manner. He frightened her more than the others, but she felt suspended between floor and ceiling, incapable of speech or movement, monitoring her reactions to the men in the cellar instead of experiencing them.

"Tessa is dead," someone said in the dream.

"Ulrike," said the same voice. It must have been Klopp's. "You are Ulrike."

Ulrike. Her lips tried to form the alien syllables.

Klopp was not overly worried about the commotion that Tessa's disappearance had caused in the United States. He forged her signature on letters to her agent and her Broadway producer, saying that she had decided that the theater was too much of a challenge for her just now and that she wanted to stay on for a few months in Europe to reconsider the whole pattern of her life. Phil Kreps would bear out the story if anyone thought to ask him. Still, Kreps had been anxious, not just for reasons of sexual jealousy, when he was told that Tessa was going to Hamburg. "Promise me she won't come to any harm," Kreps had implored the German. Klopp was not concerned about the reactions of the ex-CIA man to what he now had in store for Tessa. Kreps was in too deep to cause trouble.

It was the copious files maintained by Kreps's staff at the Third World Exchange that enabled the German to select the candidate for one of the most ambitious abductions that the STAR network had attempted in Europe. At their last secret conference in Cyprus, the associates of STAR—men and women coming from Hamburg and Beirut, Moscow and Dublin, Tripoli and Havana—had spent long hours in the villa of a prominent Greek Cypriot politician debating the next innovations in the international terrorist campaign. Many technological possibilities had been explored, including nuclear terrorism, the systematic sabotage of computer centers, and an attempt to hijack a supertanker and hold it for ransom.

The German was skeptical about many of these suggestions. From a European perspective, he had told the other members of STAR, the most effective technique was still the oldest and simplest: to sow fear within the establishment by the elimination or abduction of key individuals. This in turn might serve to panic Western governments into resorting to excessive repression and thus stir up sympathy for the radical cause. He recalled Lenin's phrase: "The purpose of terror is to terrify."

The question that remained was how, at a time when terrorist kidnappings were starting to be regarded as routine, STAR could increase the psychological threat to the establishment. Since his return from the Cyprus meeting, Klopp thought he had found an answer. It was a bizarre scheme, and he had no intention of seeking approval for it from any of the shadowy men who ranked above him in the organization. If the plan failed, the consequences would be on his head. If it worked, it would sow terror within the Western business hierarchy—and bring unprecedented sums flowing into STAR's coffers as protection money. All that was needed was the right victim: a powerful and wealthy man whose past history could be exploited to deprive him of public sympathy, regardless of how ruthlessly he was dealt with. The files of the Third World Exchange helped the German find the ideal candidate.

The gap in the elaborate security screen that the German industrialist Franz-Josef Faber had constructed around himself was not uncommon: he dispensed with all but one of his bodyguards on the weekends he spent with his mistress, the occupant of a fifth-floor apartment in Munich. Faber regularly scheduled business meetings in Munich for Friday, so he could escape his wife for the weekend without complicated explanations. Faber's private life made him accessible to STAR; but that was not his attraction for Klopp. Nor was it the fact that he represented the most reactionary faction among West Germany's business and political establishment. What made Faber the perfect kidnap victim was that his past record as a Nazi would be seen by many to justify even the most extreme measures against him.

The kidnapping was planned with meticulous care. One member of Klopp's cell visited the apartment of Faber's mistress disguised as a delivery boy. Possible escape routes were reconnoitered. Through the family firm, Klopp was able to discover the date of the next meeting of the employers' association in Munich, which Faber was almost certain to attend. The following Saturday, before breakfast, when Faber was asleep in his mistress's bed, Klopp led the assault in person. As expected, he found a drowsy bodyguard in the entrance hall. Without hesitation, Klopp shot him at close range, using a silencer. The industrialist was a heavy sleeper. They actually had to shake him awake after chloroforming his mistress. Klopp ordered Kurt to take a photograph of Faber in bed with his girlfriend, naked, to send to the newspapers. Then they drove back to Hamburg, with Faber tied up in the trunk of the black Mercedes. It all happened so fast that police roadblocks were not set up until Faber was already safely deposited in the cellar of the house at Blankenese.

Klopp enjoyed the next step: delivering a sensational story to the press that was certain to dwarf any other front-page news. Kurt took more photographs. They showed the industrialist tied to a chair in front of a placard that depicted a huge red star and a fist clutching a Kalashnikov rifle. Looming over Faber, clad in a black leather jacket with her hair cropped under a matching beret, was Tessa. Klopp took considerable pains to arrange Tessa's pose, since he regarded this picture as the *pièce de résistance*. He made her rest one booted heel on the arm of Faber's chair and lean as closely as possible to the prisoner, so that the barrel of the FN rifle she was cradling pressed into his chest. Tessa responded to his instructions as mutely and obediently as a doll.

Two days later, after the German had drafted and redrafted his ransom demand—and the accompanying, unheard-of threat of what would follow if those to whom it was addressed refused to comply—copies were delivered, by roundabout means, to the news agencies. The photograph of Tessa with Faber exploded on the front pages of the world press. For the Germans (if not for the Americans) the shock of the visual evidence that a famous movie star had joined the terrorist underground was muted by the horror conveyed in the clipped prose of Klopp's communiqué. The ransom demands were absurdly inflated. In return for Faber's release, his company would be required to pay $10 million to STAR and an equivalent sum for the welfare of the refugees in the Palestinian camps. The West German government was also required to release twenty specified political prisoners. More unusually, twelve designated German businessmen and politicians who had held official posts under the Nazi regime, including Faber himself, were to be removed from their jobs and subjected to a war crimes tribunal.

Outrageous kidnap demands were not unusual, and these would have received little press attention but for the warning that Klopp inserted at the end of the communiqué. Failure to comply with the demands would mean that STAR would subject Faber to surgery to remove the frontal lobes of his brain. It would also mean that each of the other eleven Germans on STAR's list of "war criminals" would be targeted for abduction and a similar surgical operation. The effect of a lobotomy, Klopp thoughtfully explained in his communiqué, was to turn a person into a statistic. For this reason, he concluded, it was an appropriate form of social retribution for "those responsible for the form of capitalism that has treated people as a heap of statistics."

Klopp had gotten the idea from watching an American movie, *One Flew Over the Cuckoo's Nest*. When death became insufficiently terrifying, he had explained to his cell, it became necessary to find a sanction more terrifying than death.

The German had given the authorities and Faber's company a week to respond to his demands. As the days passed, the reactions from the media and the public met with his entire satisfaction. The newspapers carried long picture-profiles of Tessa Torrance, and psychologists bobbed up on television to debate the reasons she had aligned herself with the STAR organization. They were divided over whether she was acting under duress; there was much speculation about her public sympathy for the Black Panthers and the Palestinian cause.

As the shock of the initial headlines faded, a few reporters started digging into Faber's past and the Nazi antecedents of others on STAR's list of twelve supposed war criminals. It did not take long for some embarrassing details to begin trickling out.

Shortly after, two of the businessmen on the list decided to depart for extended vacations outside Germany. A Bavarian politician, also on the list, made himself, by contrast, the spokesman for the "no negotiations" school of thought, insisting that any dealings with the terrorists would only encourage them to repeat their crime. The government refused to consider the release of prisoners and declared a partial state of emergency. Faber's company announced it was willing to meet part of the ransom demand.

The response from the company provoked a brief debate within Klopp's cell. Kurt was in favor of taking the money, whatever they did with the industrialist afterward. Klopp insisted that money was not the object; the group had to show it was in earnest. He seemed to welcome the necessity of carrying out the threat in the letter.

"Ulrike" had now been admitted to the group's counsels. She sat, a silent witness, glazed eyes registering no comprehension of what was being discussed, even when the others switched their conversation to English to include her.

When the deadline expired and the cell decided, over Kurt's objections, to go ahead with the lobotomy, she felt no twinge of compassion or horror for the trapped man in the cell. She stopped the medical student with the enormous glasses as he gathered up his instruments to carry out the operation in the gameroom of the mansion, but it was not to voice a protest.

"Is it time yet?" she asked, her face a study in desperation.

The young man who had introduced her to heroin looked without sympathy at the chalk-white features and pockmarked arms of the gaunt woman who had once been beautiful.

"Later." He dismissed her.

It was only then that Tessa began to sob without control.

Tessa could not distinguish whether what followed was a real event or merely part of her drug-laden internal nightmare. Klopp took her hand and led her into a room that was dominated by a huge billiard table. It had been covered with sheets. The medical student, masked and wearing surgical gloves, was arranging scalpels and syringes on top of a cabinet beside the table. Kurt appeared in the doorway, prodding the blindfolded man from the cellar forward into the room. Even when they ripped the blindfold away, exposing Faber's eyes to the harsh glare of the naked bulb over the billiard table, the industrialist uttered no sound.

The medical student slipped a syringe into Faber's arm. Tessa's hand moved involuntarily to the tortured veins of her left arm, and she began to tremble again. The student lifted Faber's eyelid, peering underneath, preparing to do something inconceivably awful with an instrument resembling an ice pick, probing into the sockets of the prisoner's eyes. She turned from the grisly scene, feeling nauseous. Even a simple glaucoma test—a puff of air into the eyeball —had been enough to make her gag in the past. She could not face what they were doing to Faber.

Images of the next hours flashed through Tessa's consciousness like slides run too fast through a projector. She was dimly aware that something had gone wrong in the gameroom after she left. When she drifted back, urgently in need of her next fix, the sheets had gone from the billiard table, exposing a small patch of red in the middle of the green baize. Klopp was standing with a billiard cue, chalking it as if about to play. Instead, he drove the cue into the felt, leaving a ragged hole where the bloodstain had been.

Then there were voices in anger, telephone calls, the drab bulk of Faber's body as Klopp and Kurt carried it out to the garden.

Someone was shaking her. "Come on," Klopp said. "We've got to leave."

"Is it time?" she asked dully.

Something had gone wrong. The industrialist was dead, killed by a nervous slip of the student's unpracticed hand. In addition, the house was no longer safe. Klopp had been warned that his own secretary in the Hamburg office had become suspicious about his erratic comings and goings and might be prepared to talk to the police.

"We have to split up," Klopp said.

Kurt, the student, and the others in the house sped off into the night. Tessa was with Klopp in the black Mercedes, shivering despite the blanket he had wrapped around her. She was disguised in a cheap reddish wig but was almost unrecognizable anyway because of the flesh she had lost and the pallor of her skin. The German was driving toward the harbor. He ditched the car in the shadow of a warehouse and tugged Tessa behind him along a wooden jetty to where a small motor launch was moored.

"Where—where are we going?" Tessa stammered.

Klopp's only response was to point toward the freighters anchored out in the harbor. Tessa did not know that he was pointing toward one in particular: the *Leipzig*, an East German merchant vessel that was suspected by the Hamburg port authorities of smuggling arms to STAR's associates in Cyprus and Ireland.

But had she been able to focus, she could have picked out the letters of the *Leipzig*'s name on the stern of the freighter a quarter of an hour after Klopp had gotten his engine started. She was aware only that Klopp was trying to drive the launch harder, to avoid contact with another, more powerful boat that was looming up on their starboard side. There was shouting in German through a megaphone, which Klopp ignored. After more shouting, a searchlight flashed on, hurting Tessa's eyes. She raised her arms over her face to protect them.

The one word that detached itself from the incomprehensible flow was *"Polizei!"*—repeated over and over. Klopp was not behaving with his normal self-control. Instead of trying to bluff his way through the harbor police, he continued to race toward the *Leipzig*. And his Tokarev pistol was clearly visible in the waistband of his trousers.

There was a shuddering collision as the police launch

rammed into the side of Klopp's boat, which tipped over as if about to capsize. The impact sent Tessa careening over the deck; only the low railing prevented her from hurtling into the water.

Klopp's pistol spurted fire. There was an answering burst from an automatic weapon.

"Jump," Tessa heard the German call. "Swim out to the *Leipzig!*"

There was a splash as Klopp threw himself overboard. The water around him was raked with machine gun fire from the police launch. Tessa let herself slide under the railing into the water on the far side of Klopp's boat, invisible to the men on board the police launch. The police continued to fire at Klopp's flailing arms until they vanished from sight.

Tessa had always been a strong swimmer, but her months in captivity had left her with little strength in her body, and a mind inadequate to the task of deciding where she was headed or why. She blacked out halfway across the harbor and regained consciousness to find that she had floated to shore at a deserted ferryboat landing.

The crisp fall breeze cut through her as she struggled along the pier and up a broad flight of stone steps to reach street level. Her thin, sodden blouse, glued to her breasts, offered no protection. She found herself in a district of seedy bars with names like OK and Oklahoma. The word *Reeperbahn* floated out of her dulled memory. Drunken sailors lurched out of a bar where the jukebox was blaring the hit tunes of a decade before and called out to her. She had surfaced in the lowest quarter of Hamburg's red-light district. She sensed the need to hurry up the badly lit street toward the brighter lights at the other end.

The sailors, who looked Asian, were walking behind her. She quickened her step until she was half running, half stumbling up the narrow street. She heard thudding footsteps behind her, advancing on her.

At the top of the street was a police station. As she rounded the corner, a policeman came out and stood in the doorway, smoking. The sailors' footsteps died away. Her head spun as she tried to focus on the wide road ahead. Dazzled by neon and headlights, she caught a fleeting glimpse of hamburger joints, blue movie shows, strip clubs, and men loitering in little knots on the sidewalk. She was scared; it reminded her of Eighth Avenue in New York.

The policeman was watching her closely, inspecting her drenched hair and clothing. She turned to him, intending to ask for help, but the words died in her throat. On the wall of the police station, she saw a picture of herself that must have come from a movie still, and her name—the name she had used before she became Ulrike—in big letters. It was not an advertisement for a Tessa Torrance movie. It was a poster for wanted terrorists.

She must have stared at the old photograph for a long time. The policeman turned to follow her gaze. He looked at her again, then back at the photograph, comparing.

"Fräulein?" he said, wondering.

Tessa stood frozen for a long moment. Then she was running again, without thought of direction, running so blindly that she collided with a heavyset man in a seaman's cap who swore at her loudly and profusely, running till she came to an alleyway suffused with an orange glow and a sign that she was beyond reading that blazed out the words "Eros Center."

She lurched past two brick partitions and found herself inside a walled-in amphitheater. On display against the pillars and around the walls, arranged in an obscure hierarchy, were fifty or sixty girls in varied stages of undress. Men circled them like moths.

This was one of Hamburg's celebrated open-space brothels. Tessa turned to go back the way she had come, but now a policeman barred the entrance. Her heart thumping, she darted behind a pillar and propped herself up against the masonry. Conscious that she was under observation from hostile eyes, she turned to find that her neighbor was a peroxide blonde with stupendous breasts that were fully exposed under her fishnet blouse.

"Raus," the whore hissed. Clearly she took Tessa for out-of-town competition.

Tessa could now make out another entrance to the enclosure, through glass doors that led into the lobby of something resembling an apartment block—probably the place where the girls took their customers. She began running toward it, but her legs no longer obeyed her. She tripped and fell, grazing her knee badly on the rough concrete floor, and lost contact with the world again.

Tessa did not hear the conversation between the two policemen who carried her limp body out of Eros Center.

"It can't be her," one of them objected.

"I tell you we've found her," the policeman who had first spotted Tessa on the corner of the Reeperbahn insisted. "This is Tessa Torrance."

The other was not convinced. "Didn't you see her in *Sex Wars*?" he objected. "This is not the same woman."

2

NO ONE CALLED HOCKNEY with the news. He had to stumble across it the morning after his reunion with Michel Renard, when he paused at the news kiosk on the corner of the Boulevard Saint-Germain. The same photograph was featured on the front page of every paper that the old woman who ran the kiosk had pegged to bits of cord across a canvas screen, like washing on a line. "Movie Star Leads Terrorist Kidnap" read the headline in one of the most sensationalist of them. Hockney scooped up nine or ten different newspapers, forgetting the change from his fifty-franc note until the news vendor called him back.

His instinct cried out that whatever subeditor had written that headline was wrong. Tessa could flirt with violence, but she could never practice it herself. Closer inspection of the photograph confirmed him in this belief. The woman in the picture was not the willful, defiantly independent Tessa he knew. The eyes were dead. If she was not a prisoner herself, Tessa was no longer in command of her actions.

It took half an hour before he was calm enough to study

the details of the news reports. He recognized the name of the kidnapped industrialist. Where could he have heard it? His knowledge of German business was next to zero. Then it came to him: there had been a file on Franz-Josef Faber in the archives of Phil Kreps's foundation in Brussels. Several of the papers carried background pieces on Faber's early life. On page 2 of the English-language paper, the *International Record*, was an item headed "Kidnapped German Industrialist Had Nazi Past." The piece contained a detailed account of Faber's activities in the Hitler Youth and the German army. It suggested that Faber had continued to be a moving force in extreme right-wing circles after 1945.

The resemblance between the article and what Hockney remembered of the dossier Kreps's people had compiled was almost uncanny. Wherever the *Record* had gotten its material, it was unlikely to have emanated from the public relations director of Faber's corporation. Yet the paper had the whole story the morning after the kidnap.

He now had a double reason for calling Phil Kreps. But Kreps could not be reached at his office all day, and his secretary denied knowledge of where he was. Hockney was sure she had been ordered to block certain calls. He called the Bonn bureau of the *New York World*. He was put through immediately to Dick Sharpe, his former boss in Saigon.

"Did you know that there's an alert out for you?" Sharpe asked. The interference on the line was so great he sounded as if he were talking underwater. "Len Rourke's been trying to track you down everywhere."

"I'm on leave," said Hockney, unapologetic.

"Well, Rourke seems to think you're still on the staff of the *World*, and he wants a backgrounder on Tessa Torrance from you pronto."

"No way, Dick. That's a personal matter." Before Sharpe could object, he pressed his question. "Are there any leads on where Tessa might be?"

"Take your pick. My guess would be Hamburg."

"Hamburg? I thought the kidnap was in Munich."

"Yes, but STAR's German headquarters is supposed to be in Hamburg."

"Has the paper got anyone up there?"

"A local stringer. Timmermann. German-Jewish-American. We don't use him much. But he knows the local security people."

"Thanks."

"Hold on. Where can we reach you?"

Hockney broke the connection.

It was not until after midnight that Hockney got through to Kreps at his home in Brussels.

"I hold you accountable, Phil," were his first words.

Cutting through Kreps's disclaimers, Hockney said, "I have only two questions. Number one: Where did she go after you saw her in Rome?"

There was a long pause at the end of the line.

"Was it Hamburg?" Hockney pursued.

When Kreps still failed to reply, he said, "Okay, I take it that silence is a positive response. Question number two: Who did she meet in Rome?"

"I'm not Tessa's keeper," Kreps objected.

"If you were, you'd have a helluva lot to answer for. And don't think that absolves you from what you have to answer for already. Are you going to answer me?"

"Oh, the usual set—movie stars, producers, playboys. You know the kind."

"And you know another kind as well. Don't hold out on me, Phil. Her life is at stake."

"Look, you're the investigative reporter. You find out."

It took Hockney a long time. Too long. He flew to Rome, trying to trace back through the contacts Tessa might have made several months before. It took three days to run down the radical producer who played host at the party she had attended with Kreps. The producer was less than ready to talk. If anything, Hockney thought he detected a lurking sympathy for STAR. To judge by the producer's movies, he was a gourmet of sadomasochism—the last person to be shocked by the threat of a terrorist lobotomy. He ducked questions about who had attended his party.

Hockney finally demanded point-blank, "Was there any-one from Germany? Hamburg, for example?"

The producer's shrug was the giveaway. "I play host to the world," he said. "But of course, my guests must be *suitable*."

"Like what? Actors? Playboys? Bankers?"

The producer shrugged again. Hockney tried desperately to conjure up a mental image of what went on in Hamburg.

"Shipowners?" he threw out, arbitrarily.

The producer rose from his heavily padded armchair. "I don't think I can help you," he said.

But his reaction was too fast. Hockney was on to something.

It was Timmermann, the paunchy, slack-jawed *World* stringer in Hamburg, who enabled Hockney to put the information to some use. Timmermann explained that Germany was full of poor little rich boys—and girls—who exercised their resentment against the system that had freed them from the necessity to work by helping the ter-rorist underground. A notorious case involved the heir to a steel fortune who had blown up one of his father's fac-tories, but had postponed the operation for a couple of days in order to enjoy a weekend at the Georges V Hotel in Paris with his girlfriend. A shipping heir? Why not? They could attempt to find out. Timmermann had all the right connections.

It may have been because the name Klopp was too ob-vious—and too respectable—that it took more than two days for it to arrive at the head of their list. The heir to the fortune was a well-known socialite, so there was nothing inherently surprising in the fact that he could not be con-tacted at his office. But Hockney decided to check in per-son. Sigismund von Klopp's secretary was chatty, single, and the wrong side of forty. She was instantly receptive to the proposition of lunch with a handsome, younger Ameri-can, even though he worked for a newspaper. Over lunch, she talked freely about her boss, who regularly vanished without explanation, it seemed. She had, in fact, begun to feel suspicious.

"Has he been to Rome?" Hockney queried.

"Oh, Siggy spent two months in Rome this year," she replied, affecting a familiarity that Hockney was sure she did not actually share with Klopp.

It took the promise of dinner the following night to extract Klopp's home address and telephone number from her. Before that, Hockney knew, the terrorists' deadline on Faber would have expired.

He discussed the possible courses of action with Timmermann. Hockney favored checking out the Blankenese house in person. Timmermann advised against it.

"If you're right," the stringer warned, "anything could happen."

"Then what do you suggest?"

Timmermann scowled. "I can take it to a friend in Security."

"But what can you tell him? We haven't got anything to go on except the hunch that Klopp met Tessa in Rome."

"These people know the lay of the land," Timmermann assured him. "They can make some discreet inquiries."

Hockney had been mistaken. It was incredible stupidity, he realized afterward, to imagine that the authorities would rush in on a man named Klopp—a family name that was, after all, above suspicion. It was no less stupid to imagine that a move against a member of the Klopp family could be planned without a leak to the father, if not the son. Poring over the news accounts of Klopp's death at the hands of the police, Hockney tried to console himself with the thought that though Faber had perished, Tessa, in a manner of speaking, had survived. It was small consolation. Hockney realized he had in the end done little to help the woman he had thought he loved.

After Tessa's capture, Hockney met no resistance from the local security men when he asked to see her. On the contrary, they thought his presence might help to relax her. She had been through a lot, they warned him. He should not be surprised if she failed, at first, to recognize him.

At the maximum security jail in Hamburg, Hockney felt he was walking the inner circumference of a metal drum.

Every sound he made, as he hastened behind the security guard along an endless, clinically white corridor, was boomed back at him. His shoes clanged against the steel floor. The scrape of metal as his wristwatch brushed accidentally against a wall told him that, too, was steel. Every angle of his approach to the cells was covered by closed-circuit television. The jail had been designed to avoid repetition of a previous, widely publicized escape by Baader-Meinhof terrorists.

The passage ended at last in a blind steel wall. Suspended from the curved, tubular ceiling by adjustable metal rods was a small television set. Hockney assumed it was another closed-circuit monitor. When the guard swung back the door of the cell to reveal a panel of bulletproof glass behind, Hockney understood that the set must be intended for the occasional entertainment of the prisoner inside.

It was unlikely, however, to provide any light relief for Tessa Torrance.

Nothing the security men had said had prepared him emotionally for the apparition inside the cell. He had seen junkies before, in subways and alleyways at all hours of night and day—some of the worst cases of all in the Piccadilly Circus underground station in London. He had even seen a woman of indeterminate age who had killed herself by taking the golden bullet—a heroin overdose—carried away on a stretcher. But none of those encounters had had any personal meaning. They were things that did not touch him.

But the whimpering, dribbling form on the bed, curled up in a tight, fetuslike ball, was something different. She was part of his life.

The guard closed the panel of bulletproof glass and stood behind it in the corridor, keeping watch. This offered minimal privacy.

"Tessa." The way he pronounced the word, it was almost a question. There was no response. As he drew closer to the bed, he could see that Tessa's entire body was shaking and that she had several fingers stuffed in her mouth, like a baby.

They had said she was now on methadone. But she had been mainlining so intensively that it could take months to break the heroin addiction—if it could be done at all. What worried the police doctors more was that she had been so weakened by her ordeal and the lack of food that even the most common medical complaint might prove fatal. She had contracted severe bronchitis after her night in the harbor, and they feared it could turn into pneumonia despite the antibiotics and the vitamins they were pumping into her.

Though Hockney stayed with her until a doctor came, thirty or forty minutes later, Tessa gave no sign of recognition. The sounds she made were not intelligible. They did not resemble human speech.

When the doctor lifted her eyelids, all Hockney could see were the white orbs. The pupils seemed to have disappeared.

He visited the cell three more times. On his second visit, he found Tessa crouched in a corner, propped up against a wall. Her eyes were open, but the pupils were fixed, staring into midspace. When he passed a hand back and forth in front of her face, she did not blink or shift her gaze.

On the next visit, she looked more frail, more absent from the world than when he had first come to the cell. The doctor said her weight had dropped to eighty pounds. She had said a few words in the interval between his visits. She had mentioned his name several times. Also that of Kreps. Better not forget Kreps, Hockney told himself. One way or another, Phil Kreps was going to answer for this.

On his last visit, they did not let him see Tessa. They had moved her into an intensive care unit.

"She's slipping fast," the doctor said apologetically.

"What's the matter?" he demanded. "Pneumonia?"

The doctor spread his hands helplessly. "*Everything* is wrong with her," he said. Compassion prevented him from telling Hockney that Tessa had even contracted VD. "Now she's got hepatitis, and it could kill her. The trouble is, she's got no resistance, and she seems to have no will to fight back."

"She's *got* to fight back. Let me see her."

"Later." The doctor patted his arm. "Give us a little longer."

But when the doctor returned, sooner than expected, to the bench where Hockney waited under a harsh fluorescent lamp, it was to tell him there was no reason to go on waiting. Tessa had died without recovering consciousness.

"I don't think she even knew her name," the doctor concluded.

"It's going to be remembered," Hockney said fiercely. "I'll see to that."

Tessa's body was flown back to the West Coast for cremation, and the ashes were scattered out at sea over the Pacific. That was the only feature of her funeral rites that Hockney found even vaguely appropriate.

A kind of memorial pop festival was organized on a hillside for thousands of grieving fans. People like Quinn, the novelist, turned up to deliver orations about how Tessa Torrance had been sacrificed on the altar of the system she had struggled to overthrow. The editor of *Barricades* even suggested that she might have been murdered in jail by the German police. The people at the festival sang folksongs of the Vietnam era. Their myths were intact. Hamburg had not touched them.

Hockney did not attend the commemoration. He kept his silence when those of all persuasions—including the editors of the *World*—asked for his views on Tessa's life and death. He believed that what had cost Tessa her mind, and ultimately her life, was bigger than the playboy-guerrilla Sigismund von Klopp, bigger than his accessory Phil Kreps, bigger even than STAR. As a journalist, Hockney knew only one way to deal with it: exposure. It was a method that had worked against other targets, even the CIA. It could work this time too—provided he was sufficiently armed.

New York

1

DURING HIS LAST WEEKS in Europe, Hockney took care to put himself out of contact with everyone—except for his key sources, among whom Chris Campbell had clearly emerged as number one. Hockney knew that the *World* would want the inside story of Tessa's role in the STAR underground from him. He was not ready to write it. When he was, he would do it on his own terms and in his own time.

He owed it to the past not to use their love as a titillating ingredient in a sensationalist news story. He asked himself whether his reluctance to leap into print meant that he was ceasing to be a journalist. He put the same question to his friend Campbell. "It simply means that you are becoming a good journalist," Campbell had reassured him. "It means there are values and loyalties that you care about more than a quick headline." In any case when the time came to write Tessa's story, it would have to be the whole story—which meant proving his hunches about the involvement of Phil Kreps and his outfit in Brussels, and of the more shadowy Soviet-controlled network around Marcel Rosse in Paris. Tessa had not been an initiator; she had been a victim. Hockney fully intended to take revenge on her behalf against those who—for a scarifying few months—had stolen her soul and, ultimately, her life.

After he returned to New York from Hamburg, Hockney still moved with discretion. He intended to use every minute of his hard-won year's absence from the *World* for his own purposes. He did not have to confront his editor, Len Rourke, until the last day of the last month. It was certainly not in his interest to keep anyone on the *World* briefed on his activities before then. What the *World* knew, Hockney was fully aware, would also be common knowledge in the circle around the Foundation for Progressive Reform—which meant Perry Cummings. He had read somewhere that Perry was moving up fast in the world. He was not only co-director of the Foundation; he was one of the leading members of the transition team that had been set up by the President-elect to advise on foreign affairs priorities.

There was no doubt now in Hockney's mind that Nick Flower's allegations against Perry Cummings had been accurate. That meant only one thing. However close they had been since childhood, Cummings would not scruple to use any methods available to him or his Soviet friends to put a stop to Hockney's project—if Cummings happened to find out what it was.

Hockney could no longer stay with his old friends in New York, most of whom belonged to the same milieu of radical chic that he had inhabited until he had been drawn to question his whole conception of the reporter's role. The safest thing to do, he decided, was to shut himself up in a hotel until he had finished his writing. He found a suitable place on Eighth Avenue, sandwiched between a sex shop and a cheap café. It was not exactly the best address in town—which was an excellent reason for choosing it. The attraction was anonymity. The hotel clerk, after some haggling, supplied Hockney with an electric typewriter and a rickety table that he installed in front of his windows, overlooking the gasoline fumes of the street and a drab wall across the way.

Locked in his room, Hockney wrote in a fever. He tapped out 5,000 words a day for four days. Then he pushed what he had written aside and began all over again. The first draft had helped to resolve in his mind what he needed to say and what he was obliged to leave out—because of lack of evidence or the risk of a million-dollar libel suit, or because, even now, there were connections he had not been able to work out. He wrote about Tessa's death. He wrote about the STAR underground, about Phil Kreps and the Foundation for Progressive Reform, about the shadowy figure of Viktor Barisov—shadowy despite a brief period of visibility as a Soviet diplomat stationed in Washington—and about the apparatus of Soviet deception that Chris Campbell had painted for him in graphic detail. He even wrote about Perry Cummings, who was quoted in a wire service report as having claimed that the United States would establish diplomatic relations with both Hanoi and Havana in the first year of the new presidency.

But his years in journalism told Hockney that what he was trying to say was much too big for a series of articles, perhaps even for a book. In the original version, it was also too hot for the *World* to handle. He could visualize the curled lip of Ed Finkel as he set out to shoot Hockney's series down in flames as a specimen of new-look McCarthyism. Hockney told himself that he needed to lower his sights and take more selective aim.

He gathered up his manuscripts in a big folder and stepped out through the tawdry lobby of the hotel to get some air. There was no fresh air to be had in the smog of the early evening traffic, so he wandered up to a Chock Full O' Nuts coffee shop a few blocks north of the hotel to get some coffee. Looking through his drafts, Hockney realized that what he needed to lend the whole story authenticity was the firsthand confession of someone who had been deeply involved. He had Renard, but he could hardly name his French friend without destroying the new career that he had built for himself. Why do that, after all the personal tragedies that Renard had suffered? His friend had made amends, in any case. No, Hockney needed someone else: a defector. He thought back to Campbell's comments on Viktor Barisov, the Soviet master of deception. Was Barisov the man he was seeking? It was barely conceivable that the Russian would give anything away in a conversation with an American reporter, and almost inconceivable that a colonel in the KGB could be induced to cross sides to the West. Yet he had formed the distinct impression from Campbell—and also, to a lesser extent, from Renard—that Barisov was a high-flier whose ambitions had been brutally frustrated. Wasn't that the most familiar reason for a man to betray his own side?

The more he thought about it, nibbling at a wholewheat doughnut, the more it seemed to Hockney that, without Barisov, his series would be like *Hamlet* without the Prince. In almost every direction in which his researches had led him, he had found the shadowy form of Barisov grinning at him. It was Barisov who had corrupted Renard. It was Barisov, again, who had teleguided Renard's activities in Vietnam—and therefore, presumably, planted some of the stories Hockney had been induced to write. Behind the Foundation for Progressive Reform, which had provided so much material for Hockney's anti-CIA crusade in Washington, were Barisov and his masters in the Moscow Center. Barisov's shadow fell over Perry Cummings, Alexia Merchant, and Phil Kreps—the shadow of the puppeteer.

"Geneva," Hockney said aloud.

"Pardon me?" said the waitress.

"Oh. Just tell me how much I owe you, please." Geneva, Hockney repeated mentally. If he was to drive his researches to a conclusion, it was there that he would have to do it—with Barisov, in Barisov's new station. How long would it take? Months? Or years? Or was the task simply beyond his resources?

Whatever the answer, it belonged to the next stage in Hockney's life. He could not save the world in six months, he consoled himself. His immediate task was to produce a series that the *World* could publish. He hurried back to the hotel and banged out another draft. This time, he condensed his ideas and picked an obvious peg: the Foundation for Progressive Reform. He sketched out the Foundation's curious connections, extending right back to Vlad Merchant's profiteering as a gun runner for the Soviets in the Spanish civil war—those connections, that is, that he could document from several sources. Reading over his final draft, he concluded that it was a lot weaker than the first. But he felt confident it was at least strong enough to run the gauntlet of the editorial conferences at the *World*.

2

HOCKNEY dialed Len Rourke's direct number at the paper.

"I was just about to tell accounting to take you off the payroll," Rourke complained humorously. "Where the hell have you been?"

"Hauling in the biggest catch of my professional life."

"Well, it had better be big enough to justify all those four-star hotel bills I've been initialing over the past six months."

"Can you stand another Watergate?"

"I can stand anything as long as the *World* has it ahead of the *Tribune*." Any mention of Watergate reopened the old wound. "When are you coming around?"

"Right away, if that suits you."

"The first edition goes to bed in three hours. But don't count on getting into it."

Rourke was cradling one phone while talking into another when Hockney walked into his office. Hockney sat down to wait. It sounded as if Rourke was talking to Pete Lawry, the Washington bureau chief.

"Hold on, Pete," Rourke shouted into the receiver. "Do you mean to tell me we've had no less than six goddamn reporters down in Plains, Georgia, and they haven't found a single wart on our new President's pristine backside? You seem to be telling me that the new occupant of the White House is a Southern politician who doesn't curse or drink and whose favorite dish is apple pie à la mode with a glass of milk on the side. Sounds like he didn't even play hooky from school. That right? Well, I don't believe it."

As Rourke listened to Lawry's comments, he started mashing his molars. "Okay, okay," Rourke groaned into the telephone. "So our sainted Jimmy Carter isn't another fella with bell-bottom cheeks." Hockney guessed he was referring to Richard Nixon. "We've got to dig deeper, Pete," Rourke continued. "For instance, we still don't know who's likely to be Carter's new White House chief of staff."

Lawry said something on the other end of the line, and Rourke snorted. "Come again?" the *World*'s editor exclaimed in disbelief. "Hamilton Jordan? What kind of name's that? What's he been doing for a living? *What?*"

Rourke put his hand over the receiver again, and flicked

on the squawk box so that Hockney could have the full benefit of the conversation.

"He used to work as a mosquito exterminator."

"Listen," Rourke said to Lawry, "Jimmy Carter is starting to worry me. He's like a throwaway plastic bottle. You can pour anything into it you want. And the newspapers, this one included, have been filling up that bottle with pap, pabulum, and puffery. Unless we start finding some warts on that sinless body, people will start saying we must be on Jimmy Carter's payroll."

Rourke hung up, his teeth still grinding—as they always did when he was excited—and smoothed his thin, graying hair over his bony skull. Rourke did not carry a single ounce of spare flesh. Hockney had always marveled over the fact, since Rourke consumed gargantuan meals and drank enough to put most of his colleagues under the table.

"Len," Hockney ventured. "I can't show you any warts on Jimmy Carter. But I think I have evidence of a tumor. Malignant, I believe."

"I'm all ears," said Rourke.

"Read this." Hockney passed him the manuscript.

Rourke was on the fourth page when his secretary walked in.

"Later, please," the editor said. "And please put my favorite sign up." Hockney had seen the sign on Rourke's door often enough. "Editor thinking," it read.

Rourke leafed through the manuscript, skimming the pages faster and faster and ignoring the calls that came through on his direct line. When he got to the end, he removed his half-moon reading glasses and scratched his nose. Nick Flower, the master spy, had warned Hockney that a man who scratched his nose before saying something was about to lie.

"Great yarn," said Rourke. But the pause was too long before he added, "If I read you right, you believe that there are people very close to the new President whose allegiance is not to the United States."

Hockney looked his editor straight in the eye. He didn't speak. He waited for Rourke's next comment.

"I guess you realize, Bob, that this isn't the sort of thing we can rush into print. We'll have to talk it over with the other editors, and get a considered, collective opinion. The Washington bureau will have to be brought in for cross-checking with its own intelligence sources."

"I thought you were the boss, Len," Hockney said mildly.

Rourke sighed. "When I started in this business, editors were pretty much like generals. When they gave an order, everyone moved. It's not like that anymore. I'm your chairman, not your general. You know as well as I do that your series is dynamite. It could help blow Jimmy Carter out of the water before he's even inaugurated. It's just not something I could take on without consulting a lot of other people, starting with Ed Finkel."

"What's your personal opinion, Len?"

Rourke's teeth began to sound like a horse cantering on cobblestones. "You want my honest opinion? I think you're on to something, Bob. As a matter of fact, this could be the biggest story you've done."

Hockney did not mask his pleasure.

"But don't get overexcited," Rourke warned him. "You know the way things work here. There's no way I could run your story in its present form. With a lot of editing, maybe. The whole thing has to be toned down."

"You should have seen the original version."

"Bob, I do understand. I know you're emotionally involved."

Hockney was about to say, "What happened to Tessa had nothing to do with it," when he realized that Rourke hadn't actually mentioned her name.

"I can see from your story what's happened to you," Rourke went on. "You've got religion, Bob. You're a convert. The trouble with converts is they preach louder. They think everyone else should see the vision they saw on the road to Tarsus."

"I think you mean the road to Damascus, Len," Hockney corrected him. "But what I want to know is whether you're going to go to battle for my story. Or are you just going to go along with the consensus?"

It was Rourke's turn to get angry. "Don't give me that consensus shit," he snapped. "You were part of the ruling consensus on this paper. Hell, you helped to create it. Just because you've changed, don't imagine the paper has."

"Are you suggesting that I've become a conservative while the paper remains liberal?" Hockney inquired tartly.

"Something like that," Rourke conceded, embarrassed.

"I haven't changed all that much," Hockney countered. "Sure I've grown up a bit. I needed to. But I'm still trying to be an honest reporter. *That* hasn't changed. And I've discovered the real world, a world you once knew too. Just because a new generation of history revisionists and Marxist economists—and the new school of journalism they've spawned—tell you that we were responsible for the cold war and for fucking up the world, doesn't mean it's true. Even if the ruling consensus thinks it is. The consensus may not know it, but it's out of sync with what's happening."

When Rourke was embarrassed he looked at his own shoes. When he wasn't embarrassed he looked at your shoes. Now, swiveling his executive chair around ninety degrees to face Hockney on the couch, Rourke looked past his shoes at the floor as if he could read signs on the rug that no one else could see.

Rourke did not respond. Hockney wondered whether he had gone too far. He tried to bring the conversation back to investigative reporting.

"When you originally gave me the time off I needed for this assignment, I didn't try to conceal the area to be covered, or uncovered. I have spent a year digging into places embarrassing to the establishment. Is that what you're objecting to?"

Stung, Rourke sat bolt upright and fired back, "That's ridiculous, Bob, and you know it."

"Then what is it?"

"I guess what I'm saying is that your series appears to be ideologically motivated."

"You mean we should be neutral between the CIA and the KGB?"

"And what's wrong with that?" Rourke demanded.

To Hockney, watching him, Rourke looked frail and tired, almost a broken man. Perhaps Nick Flower had been right about Rourke too: that his career had been dominated by the skeleton he could not afford to let out of the closet—his long-past association with the CIA. When Hockney had exposed the CIA connections of Bonpierre in Paris, the man had jumped off the Eiffel Tower. Could he blame the editor of the *World* for wanting to save his career, at the cost of doing what Finkel and his other enemies on the paper told him to do? Hockney had observed the way Ed Finkel used hidden persuaders on Rourke. He could not expect his editor to ride into the valley of death on his account.

"It's okay, Len," Hockney said gently. "I don't expect you to lay your job on the line for me."

"I'll do my best," Rourke promised. "I'll bounce your series off a few people. The lawyers will also need to look at it. Then we'll have a story conference to decide how to handle it."

Hockney left Rourke's office with the sinking feeling that the editor's prescription meant euthanasia. It was obviously easier for a reporter on the *World* to take on the CIA than to take on the KGB.

3

THE ATMOSPHERE at the story conference two days later was icy. Colleagues who had not seen Hockney for six months or more appeared to snub him or greeted him only with a perfunctory "Hi, there." Pete Lawry had flown up specially from Washington for the meeting. Hockney noticed that despite the change in fashion,

Lawry's hair was even longer than the last time he had seen him. Ed Finkel, seated in the leather armchair in Rourke's office, did not even bother to look up from the copy he was reading when Hockney said hello.

Rourke kicked off the discussion. "I guess you've all had a chance to read through Bob's articles," he began. "I think he's done one hell of a reporting job. All the same, his copy obviously needs editing and checking, especially at the Washington end. What do you think, Pete?"

A vain, languorous figure, with his legs stretched out full length and his ankles crossed, Lawry spoke in his impression of an Oxbridge accent. "I don't buy this stuff on Perry Cummings and the Foundation. Perry's been an invaluable source for a number of us, Bob included. I'd call him a liberal rather than a radical, and I just don't believe in any Soviet links. The Foundation is not some Soviet front. When you think of the caliber of the people who support it—Senator Harmon, Senator Milligan, several dozen congressmen—the whole idea that the organization is a concoction of some department of the KGB becomes laughable."

"I don't think Bob went that far in his story," Rourke observed meekly.

"He went further," Ed Finkel cut in acidly. "I must say, you shock me, Bob. I understood Perry Cummings was a good friend of yours. What's this stuff you've put in about Perry sending secret material to Moscow on chewing gum wrappers? Haven't you heard he's on the new President's transition team?"

"That's what makes the story so important," said Hockney softly.

"I feel I don't know you anymore," said Finkel, addressing the entire room. "You're not only prepared to do in an old friend, Bob. You've even forgotten our basic rules on sourcing. You don't say who gave you this fairy tale about chewing gum wrappers. In fact, about the only sources you specify in your piece are unnamed European intelligence sources. It just doesn't wash, Bob. Here you are accusing a friend of the next administration of espionage, and you don't quote a single identified witness against him."

"All right," said Hockney. "Why don't you get Pete Lawry to do an on-the-record interview with Cummings? I assume he'll deny everything, but you could run a Washington story side by side with my piece, carrying the denial. We've done that in the past. In fact, we did that with some of my pieces on the CIA. And I don't remember that you ever quibbled about nebulous sourcing in my pieces exposing the CIA, Ed."

"I thought I understood what you were trying to do in those days," Finkel replied. "Now you baffle me. Perry Cummings was your friend, after all. Why didn't *you* ask him about what you are proposing we print in the *World*? I'll tell you why." Finkel closed in for the kill. "You knew Perry would deny everything, and you weren't prepared to include a denial in your own story."

"That's where you're wrong," said Hockney, conscious that he had lost some important ground. "I did talk to Perry about it."

"Are you saying he admitted the chewing gum story?" Finkel sneered.

"No, of course not. He denied it. But I have proof that he was lying."

Ignoring the last part of Hockney's statement, Finkel exclaimed in mock disbelief, "You mean to tell me that Perry Cummings gave you a denial and you refused to print it? You should have taken a longer vacation, Bob. You need it."

Rourke cleared his throat. He had been doodling on his memo pad, waiting for the conflict in the room to resolve itself. He tore off the top sheet of the pad, to avoid letting the others see that he had reverted to his favorite doodle in times of stress—the mustachioed face of a German officer in a pumpernickel helmet. Once he had gotten rid of the incriminating paper, Rourke came to Hockney's aid. "I'd like to hear from Bob," he said, "about what he means when he says he has proof that Cummings was lying."

"I interviewed Perry by phone," Hockney said. He was about to mention the voice-stress analyzer but realized that this would make him sound like a real fool. Instead, Hock-

316

ney began to describe his conversations with Nick Flower, the former counterintelligence chief.

"Sick think," Finkel sneered. "I seem to remember that you had Nick Flower's number once. I'm amazed that you would swallow anything he told you now."

The national affairs editor levered himself out of his leather armchair. "Sorry, Len," he said to Rourke, "I've got some serious work to attend to. You know where you can put this story. On the spike."

Finkel strutted out of the office. Hockney's facial muscles twitched nervously, and the color drained from his cheeks. He found he had difficulty holding his fingers steady as he reached toward the ashtray to stub out a cigarette.

Peter Lawry retracted his long legs, raised himself to his feet, and stretched out his arms in an ostentatious yawn. "We don't want to get off on the wrong footing with the Carter administration," he announced to Rourke. "I agree with Bob on one thing. It does look as though Cummings's background would justify some serious reporting. But it's no excuse for wild conspiracy theories that none of us would want to see published in this paper."

Lawry and the others made their apologies and left the office.

Alone with Hockney, the editor said, "Believe me, Bob, most of the conspiracy theories in this room are on my side of the desk. But that doesn't mean we should serve them up to our readers for breakfast."

"So what do you want to do with the story?"

Rourke scratched his nose. "I'll have to think about it."

"You mean spike it."

Rourke returned to doodling German helmets on his memo pad.

"I'm going to fight this, Len," Hockney threatened.

Rourke raised his watery eyes over the half-moon glasses. "Fight *me*?" he asked plaintively.

"No, not you. The spike."

317

4

XENOPHON PARRISH NUTTING, publisher of the *World*, was a man of shy, nocturnal habits. His timidity about meeting strangers was believed to have stemmed, in part, from the ridiculous first name with which his parents had endowed him. It had caused him torment at school, and he had tried to conceal it in later life by contracting it into the syllable Zen—which had led to speculation in some uninformed quarters about his religious convictions.

Xenophon Parrish Nutting never went to parties, rarely attended business lunches, and appeared only infrequently at his suite above the offices of the *World*, which could be approached only through a separate entrance and a private elevator. He preferred to spend most of his time in his triplex above Fifth Avenue, where his privacy was defended by three Alsatian dogs, his taciturn butler, and his morose, aging sister. For an editor of the *World* to gain access to the owner was like being admitted to a private audience with the Pope.

A first encounter with Nutting was a daunting experience. After shaking hands with a visitor, he would break off physical contact at once and rush away to the bathroom to wash. He wore surgical rubber gloves to leaf through his own newspaper. His morbid obsession with germs and his life as a recluse inspired the staff to refer to him, mockingly, as "Howard Hughes."

Hockney knew that the best time to make an approach was just after midnight, when he had been told that the publisher was to be found, unfailingly, in his study, ripping up the first morning editions of his newspaper. Nutting was in the habit of tearing out any story that especially pleased or annoyed him. He would then scribble ratings, ranging from zero to ten, on the mutilated articles with a red grease pencil. Why the owner wanted all these ragged clippings remained a mystery, since he just squirreled them away into his own arcane filing system and rarely sent a memo to Rourke. Good, bad, or indifferent, the owner's ratings appeared to make no difference in the way the *World* worked. Xenophon Parrish Nutting left editing to his editors and had never fired anyone from the paper. He did not like to dirty his hands.

Hockney arrived at the owner's apartment block shortly after midnight. He had to wait while the doorman conversed with someone in the Nutting triplex on the house phone. Hockney knew he was likely to be turned away; Rourke was the only member of the *World*'s staff who managed to see the owner more than once every five years. But equally, Hockney knew he had nothing to lose, and he was quite convinced that he would have been refused an appointment had he telephoned in advance to ask for one.

"The gentleman says he works for Mr. Nutting's paper," the doorman was saying. "A Mr. Hockney. He says it's an emergency."

There was a long pause. Then, to Hockney's surprise, the doorman put down the phone and ushered him into the elevator.

The operator set him down on the eleventh floor, at the entrance to the apartment that occupied the top three stories of the building. A white-gloved English butler showed Hockney into a book-lined study where a log fire was blazing under a portrait of the publisher's great-grandfather, Darius Shipley Nutting, the founder of the *World*. The whole apartment echoed to Gregorian chants, being played at full volume on the hi-fi. The music made Hockney feel he was about to be admitted to an unfamiliar religious rite.

The publisher was ensconced behind a huge mahogany desk. From across the study, it looked as if he were making paper gliders. As Hockney approached a few paces, he saw that Nutting was busy ripping the front page of the second edition of the *World* into seven or eight pieces.

When the publisher still did not look up after what seemed an interminable length of time, Hockney coughed politely. "I'm sorry to disturb you at this time of night, sir," he said. "But I hope you'll agree that what I want to discuss is important enough to merit your personal attention."

Hockney placed the typescript of his series on the edge of the owner's desk. "This represents a year of intensive research, Mr. Nutting. It points to the influence of Soviet agents in Washington. And it's just been spiked."

"You embarrass me." When Nutting spoke, he was almost inaudible. He did not meet Hockney's eyes, or offer his hand in greeting. "The editor deals with matters of this kind. I do not particularly appreciate it when employees of my paper seek to go above his head."

"I think you know, Mr. Nutting," Hockney protested, "that I have *never* had any trouble in the past getting my stories into the paper."

"So what is your problem on this occasion?" The publisher inclined his head to suck at a dark-colored drink through a bent glass straw.

It took Hockney a full ten minutes to outline his problem. "I think you could sum up my difficulty by saying that the editors of the *World* consider it impermissible to expose the exposers," he concluded.

"What's that supposed to mean?"

Hockney felt instantly deflated. If the publisher still needed to ask such a question, Hockney had not managed to communicate anything. He resolved to make one more attempt to explain. "What it means, sir," he replied, "is that there is entrenched opposition within your paper to investigating the biggest news story there is. I am convinced that a Soviet-inspired campaign is now under way to deceive, penetrate, and manipulate our government. A precondition for the success of this campaign is that the media should be gagged and blindfolded when it comes to reporting it. This may already have been achieved through a much longer-term campaign to influence the Western media, in which I myself—and your newspaper, sir—may have been unwitting victims. In fact, I know we were."

"Baloney," snapped the publisher. "You must be overworked. Why don't you go across to the bar over there and fix yourself a drink?"

Hockney examined the bottles on the shelf while Nutting picked up one of the battery of pastel-shaded telephones on his desk. He noticed a quart bottle of *crème de cacao*. That must be the dark substance that looked like an element in a chemical experiment as Nutting ingested it through his bent glass straw. Hockney settled for a small puddle of Rémy Martin at the bottom of a large brandy snifter.

The publisher was on the phone to Rourke for about five minutes. Most of the time, he listened to what his editor was saying on the other end of the line. "That sounds like a great idea, Len," the publisher finally said, cutting off the conversation.

He said to Hockney, after hanging up, "Len suggests, and I agree with him, that you take an extended vacation at company expense. You can use my house down at Lyford Cay, if you want."

"What about my story?" Hockney demanded.

"If it's as big as you think it is, it will hold for a while. I think you'll have a healthier perspective when you've had a break and Jimmy Carter has had a chance to show his paces in the White House."

"The story has to run *now*." The publisher darted a look at Hockney, surprised by the vehemence in his voice. Hockney rose to his feet, trembling slightly. "If you won't run my story in your paper," he continued, "I'm going to make sure that it runs somewhere else."

"Remember the terms of your contract."

"Don't worry about the contract," Hockney said. "I'm quitting."

"Let your conscience be your guide. Good night, Bob."

The publisher did not rise or shake hands. He returned to ripping up the second edition.

Hockney's letter of resignation was on Rourke's desk the next morning. He called in at accounting later the same day to pick up the money that was owed to him—fourteen weeks' salary. He was entitled to two weeks' pay for every year he had worked on the paper. The grand total came to $10,729.23. Hockney knew he would not get very far on that. He was going to need help.

Washington
The Near Future...

1

THE YEARS OF THE CARTER ADMINISTRATION were lean ones for Hockney. He spent them in the journalistic wilderness, ostracized by many of his colleagues, finding it almost impossible to claw his way back to the kind of position he had formerly enjoyed on the *World*. Most of his work was free-lance; he picked up a few retainers from foreign publications, mostly of a conservative hue, but found it difficult to support himself on the proceeds. Reluctantly, he had to turn to his father for financial help. The Admiral proved more than generous.

In his early thirties, Hockney looked older, his hair streaked with gray. His face was leaner, the jawline more pronounced. He dressed carelessly but conservatively in sports coats, wearing his clothes until they began to fall apart.

He had remained a bachelor. His relations with girls were superficially shadowed by the other women he had known—especially Tessa, the last sight of whom in the prison clinic in Hamburg was firmly etched in his memory. He would let an affair drift on for a month or two, but break it off without so much as a good-by if the girl became too serious. In his black moods, he would sometimes drift into the singles bars, seeking release in the kind of sexual sparring that did not require drawn-out preliminaries.

He moved in a narrow social circle, shunned by his former liberal friends, uncomfortable with the conservative admirers of his new line in investigative reporting. He foraged around the fringes of Washington politics, paying a monthly visit to Nick Flower's house out in Arlington, where they would play poker late into the night, Hockney waiting for the former counterintelligence chief to dredge up another nugget of information from the dark, bottomless shaft of his memory. One night, Flower remarked that one of Hockney's former colleagues on the *World* was writing a book that claimed to expose Flower as the Soviet mole in the CIA. Hockney stared at the old spymaster, unsure whether to laugh. Flower chuckled dryly. "When a society is unable to deal with treason," Flower commented, "it avenges itself on those who maintain that treason exists. You'd better watch out. It could happen to you."

Hockney's first big break came in the second half of Carter's term in office, shortly before the collapse of the Shah's regime in Iran, when he broke the story of covert Soviet, Libyan, and Palestinian involvement in the revolution that swept the fanatical Ayatollah Khomeini into power. At the time the piece ran in the *Reader's Companion*, official White House spokesmen refused to confirm or deny the accuracy of his revelations, which were mainly based on his surviving European intelligence contacts. It was only after the revolution had triumphed, and it was too late for such disclosures to influence the course of events, that a CIA report to the President was leaked out, confirming the bulk of Hockney's allegations.

The appearance of Hockney's article in *Reader's Companion* triggered off a savage smear campaign. The radical gossip sheet made out that he had been on the Shah's payroll. The campaign continued and intensified when Hockney published a follow-up article on the covert involvement of Castro's agents in the successful revolution in Nicaragua and its spreading political upheavals throughout the Caribbean.

Although these clashes imposed severe nervous strain on Hockney, they also hardened his resolve to attack the main theme that had led to his rift with the *World*. His sense of urgency increased when, as a result of Jimmy Carter's slumping popularity and his failure to hold the black vote after the resignation of Andrew Young, his controversial UN ambassador, another Southern Democrat of more radical persuasions, Billy Connor, sharing the ticket with Senator Milligan, captured the party's presidential nomination. Perry Cummings resigned from his job in the Carter administration to work on Billy Connor's campaign team.

Many of the other key aides on Connor's staff—outside the hard core of fellow Mississippians—were alumni of the Foundation for Progressive Reform.

It was not until after Connor's election victory that Hockney felt sufficiently confident to publish a *Reader's Companion* article that detailed the radical backgrounds of several key members of the incoming Administration, including his old friend Perry Cummings. After that piece appeared, he learned that name-calling and the editor's spike were not the only risks that accompanied his chosen line of inquiry.

Hockney had lived in a succession of cheap hotels, from San Salvador to Salt Lake City, researching his stories. Back in New York for a few days, he watched a late-night horror movie in his West Side hotel room before turning in. He had barely pulled the blankets over himself when the phone rang. He picked up the receiver.

"Hello."

There was no voice on the other end of the line. Listening closely, Hockney thought he could hear breathing.

"Hello," he repeated firmly, now fully awake.

After a few moments more, the connection was broken. Hockney looked at the luminous hands of the cheap alarm clock on the bedside table. It was nearly 3:00 A.M.

He turned on the TV set again and dozed off to the accompaniment of a Thompson submachine gun firing continuously in the soundtrack of an old James Cagney movie.

The phone rang again at 4:00 A.M.

"Who is this?" Hockney demanded. But the line went dead.

The phone rang again at 4:30, then at 5:00. Hockney decided to leave the receiver off the hook if it rang again. But at 5:30, he heard a man's voice on the line. The accent was definitely foreign, but difficult to place.

"Leave your old friends alone," said the voice.

"Who *is* this?"

"A well-wisher. You're making too much trouble, Mr.

Hockney. We can make trouble for you too. Trouble of a terminal nature."

"Is this some kind of threat?" Hockney asked, his heart beating faster. But the man hung up.

Hockney sat up in bed, wondering what to do about the call. It was still dark outside. The first thing he needed to do was to catch up on some sleep.

When the phone rang again, he had fallen into a deep, dreamless slumber. The phone rang several times before he emerged from it. He blinked at the TV screen, where a couple of announcers were joking their way through the breakfast program.

"Go to hell," Hockney growled into the receiver.

"You must be psychic," said a woman's voice. "How did you know it was me?"

Startled, Hockney propped himself up against the pillows. "I'm sorry," he said. Then he realized who was calling. "It can't be—Julia?" He had called her once or twice to ask questions about Perry, but had not invited her out. He knew she was living with a congressional staffer, and did not want to interfere.

"Do you always greet early morning callers that way?" Julia asked.

"It wasn't that." Hockney explained about the threatening calls.

"Actually, that could be related to what I need to talk to you about," Julia said when he had finished. "Bob, you ought to know you're walking on broken glass. You're in real danger."

"I don't understand."

"Listen. I've heard that the Foundation is buzzing with angry talk about you."

"Do you think that's news?"

"Bob, you've got to take this seriously. Alexia and my brother are convinced that you're out to destroy them. I know Perry. He'd do anything, really *anything*, to protect himself."

"Well, he needn't worry too much." He told Julia how his articles on the Foundation had been spiked.

327

"There's more, Bob," she warned him. "Some of the crazies believe you're a dangerous man. That you've got to be stopped."

"I can't believe I'm listening to this. Hold on a minute." Hockney got out of bed and pulled back the curtains. The scene outside, under the rain, looked like an old sepia picture, drained of color. A wino was huddled under the scant protection of a doorway across the street, wrapped up in newspapers and clutching a bottle.

"I think my blood sugar must be very low this morning," he said to Julia, turning away from the gloomy scene beyond his window. "I can't seem to take much in. Tell me, how do you know all these things? How did you track me down here in the first place?"

Hockney knew Julia had good sources through her work for the hawkish Senator O'Reilly, but he doubted they could be *that* good.

"Please believe me, Bob. I'll explain when you come to Washington."

"I wasn't planning to go to Washington just yet." In fact, he had been thinking of returning to Europe and trying to sell another story on the Connor administration over there.

"Please come," Julia was saying. "There are people here you need to meet."

"Like who?"

"Dick Roth, to begin with."

Dick Roth. Hockney brooded on the name. Senator O'Reilly's top aide and the closest man on Capitol Hill to the Israelis. If Roth was the one who had asked Julia to relay a warning to him, it could mean the Israelis were on to something. It could also explain how Julia had found out the name of the seedy hotel where he had gone into hiding. Dick Roth. A warning from that quarter was not to be taken lightly.

"Okay," he said. "I'll get on the shuttle this morning. On one condition."

"What's that?"

"That you have dinner with me tonight."

"Oh, Bob," Julia said.

"What's the problem? Have you got a date with Bill? You can cancel it."

"Bill and I have broken up," she said quietly. There was a tremor in her voice. "It's just that—it's been so long. Are you sure you want to?"

"Right now, I can't think of anything in the world I want more."

Hockney had said it spontaneously, without thinking. She must have changed completely from the child-woman he had made love to on the beach at Southampton. She would be confident, assured, sexually experienced, outgoing—and also, Hockney had been told, one of the finely honed intellects grinding away behind the Irish-American senator's root-and-branch attack on the "appeasement mentality" in the United States. Life on Capitol Hill had not turned Julia into a harpy, but she had become a very formidable woman. Thinking of her, Hockney succumbed to a complex of emotions he had not experienced in relation to Julia before: respect, curiosity, admiration—above all, the sense of challenge. Those feelings were new. But as he visualized her, with her hair floating free and her supple, mobile body, he knew an old feeling had returned as well. He wanted her.

2

SHAME O'REILLY'S OFFICE was on the ground floor of the Dirksen Building. Hockney arrived lugging a bulky briefcase. The guard at the entrance on Constitution Avenue did not bother to check it. In fact, the guard did not even look up from his newspaper as Hockney walked through. Hockney's investigation of the terrorist underground in Europe had made him security conscious. He had forgotten how lax controls had always been on Capitol Hill—although he had profited from that laxness in his reporting work in the past. Today, he might have been a Cuban smuggling in concealed weapons or a Soviet agent sneaking out with a load of stolen documents, for all that anyone seemed to care. No wonder the Hill was the easiest place in the world to lay hands on classified material. Hockney himself had exploited his charm often enough over the years to bluff copies of confidential documents from secretaries on a pretext along the lines of "Senator So-and-So wants a copy of such-and-such a report."

On the shuttle from New York, Hockney had chanced across an interview with Senator O'Reilly that had just appeared in *Playboy*. He had leveled a scathing attack on the past activities of the Senate Intelligence Committee, formally created after the Harmon Committee wound up its hearings on CIA abuses.

After the lethal disclosures on intelligence operations that had surfaced as a result of the much-publicized hearings, both houses of Congress had resolved to establish new, permanent committees to oversee the work of the intelligence agencies. The past rapport, founded on mutual trust, that had existed between Congress and the CIA had been replaced by an adversary relationship. Under the ambitious former Senator Milligan, the Senate Intelligence Committee had continued the harassment of the CIA initiated by Senator Harmon. O'Reilly's judgment on one of the committee's latest reports—which contained hundreds of pages on the activities of Western secret services, but not a single reference to the KGB—took the form of a quotation from the immortal words of Pogo: "We have found the enemy, and he is us."

O'Reilly had clearly lost none of the talent for delivering verbal machete chops that had cost him his job as an American ambassador before he took to congressional politics. O'Reilly began his public life as a liberal and a keen supporter of domestic reform programs. His views had hardened during his stint as American ambassador to the United Nations organization in Geneva. After the United Nations voted to condemn Zionism as racism, O'Reilly had declared at a press lunch that the United States was "in danger of being pushed around by a gang of miniature Dr. Goebbels in the third world who are constantly lauded in our media as progressives. I would prefer to call them retromingent reactionaries." After some of the United Nations delegates with whom O'Reilly had tangled looked up the word "retromingent" and discovered that it meant "backward urinating," several black African states recalled their ambassadors from Washington. It cost the State Department months of diplomacy—and the American taxpayer millions of dollars in increased aid expenditure—to patch up relations. The incident also cost O'Reilly his job, although he had the satisfaction of learning from a nationwide opinion poll that 79 percent of the American people agreed with his approach.

O'Reilly was a new phenomenon in American politics, and it struck Hockney, as he threaded his way through the press of secretaries leaving for lunch, that the irrepressible senator could prove to be a powerful antidote to the crowd that was about to take charge of Washington under the aegis of Billy Connor.

Julia and Dick Roth occupied adjoining cubicles at the end of a big, bustling office. Hockney zigzagged toward them through a maze of desks where young staffers in shirtsleeves, ties loosened, were pounding away on their typewriters with a ferocity that suggested they had been ordered to reproduce the collected works of Shakespeare by the following day.

Julia greeted him with a brief but tender embrace.

"I've been wanting to bring you two together for years," she said, introducing Dick Roth, who pumped Hockney's hand warmly. Like Hockney, he seemed to be in his early thirties. Stocky, curly-haired, olive-skinned, casually dressed in a lumberjack's checked shirt, Roth looked more like an Israeli sabra than an American Jew.

"I'm glad we found you," said Roth.

Hockney glanced from one to the other. "Okay. What's the program?" he asked.

331

"I make it time for lunch," said Julia. "There's a pizza parlor just up the road if that's all right with you."

"Sure," said Hockney.

"This afternoon," Roth contributed, "you have an appointment with the Senator."

"With O'Reilly? Great. But I didn't know it was on the schedule."

"The Senator is anxious to talk with you about some of the investigations you have been doing. I guess you know he's going to be the new chairman of the Intelligence Committee now that Ed Milligan has moved on to higher things." Senator Milligan, who had used the Intelligence Committee as a springboard for national television appearances, had been the choice of the East Coast liberals as Billy Connor's running mate—the ideological successor to McCarthy, McGovern, and Mondale. Now he was the new Vice President of the United States.

"With O'Reilly chairing the committee, we'd better look out for fireworks," Hockney commented.

"Right on." Roth and Julia started to laugh. Hockney joined in.

A fourth person was waiting for them at the table in the crowded basement of the pizza parlor.

"I'm Gideon Sharon." He introduced himself to Hockney. "I hope you don't mind the noise. There are two schools of thought about the best way to have a discreet chat in a public place. Some believe in choosing a corner in a quiet restaurant, nicely placed out of earshot of the next tables. I have always preferred a crowd scene."

Sharon, Hockney quickly learned, was the chief of the Israeli secret service—the Mossad—in the United States. His choice of rendezvous reminded Hockney of his night with Chris Campbell at the Crazy Horse Saloon in Paris. The decor in the pizza parlor was less opulent, but the noise level was about the same.

Sharon's message was succinct. Hockney's name had figured on a terrorist hit list ever since the episode in Hamburg. He should not consider himself automatically secure even in Washington because, with the demolition of the FBI and police intelligence departments, the United States, in the Israeli's view, was wide open to terrorist attacks. Hockney objected that it was highly implausible that any serious political faction would want to kill a journalist, because of the public uproar that would cause.

"Don't be too sure," Sharon warned him. "You have two groups to fear. There are the crazies, like the cell that recruited—or kidnapped—Tessa Torrance, and there are the people who pull the strings. You have managed to anger both."

After the chilled beer and the thick, Chicago-style pizzas had been served, Hockney tested Gideon Sharon's reactions to the theories he had developed in his series for the *World*. He was on the right track, the Israeli assured him. If anything, he did not go far enough.

"Wait and see what will happen under the Connor administration. If people like your friend Perry Cummings have their way . . ." The Israeli paused and looked at Julia. "I hope this won't offend you," he said.

"It's all right," she said. "Perry and I stopped being close years ago."

"What I was about to say," Sharon resumed, "was that the people from the Foundation for Progressive Reform who will try to guide the national security policy of the new administration are not only likely to hand over whatever secrets your country has left. They're also likely to hand over some chunks of real estate that no one in the West can afford to lose."

"Meaning?"

"Saudi Arabia. Southern Africa. Those will do for starters. If the Europeans see their sources of fuel and raw materials falling into hostile hands, it won't be long before they start pulling out of NATO and making private deals with the Soviets."

Hockney was dangerous to those who wished to see this come about, Sharon explained, because he had started digging into a story no one else wanted to touch. "Write a book," he urged Hockney, mentioning that there were a

333

number of sympathetic publishers in New York. He also mentioned a Jewish monthly that might carry a revised version of the series. Dick Roth nodded approval of the suggestion.

"In the meantime," Sharon concluded, "watch your back. If you need help, you can reach me through this number." He passed Hockney a piece of paper. "And watch out for the Agency," he added. "It's not what it was in Nick Flower's day."

As Julia and Dick Roth escorted him to O'Reilly's private office after lunch, the Senator's aide advised Hockney: "Give it to him straight. You'll find that you and the Senator have a lot in common."

O'Reilly's handshake was firm and long, and his blue eyes were friendly beneath the tumble of snow-white hair. Hockney felt an instant empathy.

"Important things first, Bob," said the Senator. "What can I give you to drink?"

Hockney accepted a beer from a small icebox behind the Senator's desk. O'Reilly drank bourbon on the rocks.

"We can help each other," the Senator began. "You know a lot about the Foundation and its links with Billy Connor's Mississippi Mafia. And *I* am determined to stop that crowd from driving the United States deeper into the mud than the last administration managed to do. The question is, what can we do about it?"

"We can expose what's going on," Hockney ventured.

"Right. But your old paper, the *World*, isn't going to help us there. It didn't even report my speech to the Committee of Concerned Americans last week." Julia had mentioned the speech to Hockney. O'Reilly had claimed that the United States had conceded strategic parity to the Soviet Union under the SALT I accords and strategic superiority under SALT II, and was now in the process of handing the Russians control of outer space because of decisions to put off the manufacture and deployment of American antisatellite weapons.

O'Reilly had made further predictions. He had suggested

that Soviet advances in satellite technology, combined with the theft by a Russian agent of top-secret blueprints in the Pentagon—the plans for the ultrasophisticated KH-19 satellite—had brought nearer the day when Moscow would be able to "blind" the early-warning surveillance systems of the United States. This way Moscow would be able to use and apply nuclear blackmail against Washington while the Administration had not the faintest idea whether Russia's missiles were about to be launched. O'Reilly had referred to the threat of a Soveit nuclear strike under these conditions as "Armageddon without war," suggesting that America's greatest vulnerability lay in middle and outer space.

"The *World* didn't run your speech," Hockney agreed. "It didn't run my pieces on the Foundation either."

"The other East Coast papers aren't much better," O'Reilly went on. "What we have to do if we want to wake the public up is to drop a bombshell that the media won't be able to ignore."

"You're the one with a platform," Hockney observed. "I think most of the country has been waiting for someone with the right credentials to blow the whistle. No one else from the Republican camp can command much of a hearing. So it seems to me it's going to be pretty much up to you."

"Have another beer." O'Reilly poured himself another slug of bourbon simultaneously. "If I can get enough ammunition," he went on, "nobody can stop me from firing it. With Harmon and Milligan off the committee, there's no one left who's prepared to stand up to me."

"What about Frank Mahee?" Hockney knew that the freshman senator from California had participated in a Foundation seminar on government whistle blowing and had even attended a conference of the World Peace Council, the leading Soviet front organization, in Washington.

"Mahee will surrender if I am well enough armed," O'Reilly said thoughtfully. "It's one thing for these liberals to attack the CIA or the FBI. It's altogether different for them to have to come out into the open and defend the KGB. Not even Frank Mahee would want to do that. What

335

I intend to do is to organize a series of public hearings that expose the facts on Soviet penetration of our institutions. What advice can you give me?"

Hockney studied the bubbles in his glass of beer. "No one can argue with a defector," he said, voicing aloud what had gone through his mind as he labored over his articles in the New York hotel room. "Whatever you or I or the Western world's combined intelligence services might say, it will only have one percent of the drama—and ten percent of the credibility—of the firsthand testimony of a man who has spent his life on the other side."

"You mean we should try to convert someone inside the Foundation?"

"I was thinking of a *Soviet* defector, someone who has been running deception and penetration operations against the United States."

As O'Reilly poured himself another measure of bourbon, Hockney remembered a snide remark that Ed Finkel had made about him during a story conference at the *World* after the Senator had been elected. "It's the spirit that moves O'Reilly," Finkel had said. "Eighty-proof spirit."

"Easier said than done," O'Reilly commented on Hockney's proposal. "There are people who say we haven't had an important Soviet intelligence defector to this country in a long while—maybe because we're starting to look as if we're on the losing side, or maybe because we're penetrated. Nick Flower talks as if he thinks even the CIA is penetrated. You know Nick Flower, don't you?"

Hockney nodded.

"So where do we find your defector?"

Hockney took the risk. He had to tell someone, so he might as well start with Senator O'Reilly. "Viktor Barisov," he began, "could just be our man. He has been demoted, he is in disgrace, he is completely disappointed." When Hockney had finished describing what he knew of Barisov and why he might be approachable, the Senator rubbed his heavy chin.

"And Barisov was here in Washington," the Senator veri-

fied. "I guess the FBI must have quite a hefty file on him."
He brooded for a moment. "If what you suggest can really
be done," he resumed, "it would be perfect. I think you're
right to try it with the help of the Europeans—and the
Israelis, if they're prepared to participate. But there are two
men here I think we should talk to, provided, of course,
that you agree. One is Nick Flower." Hockney showed
instant approval. "The other"—the Senator paused—"is
Milorad Yankovich, who is going to be President Connor's
national security adviser."

O'Reilly waved away the objections he anticipated from
Hockney. "I know, I know—Yank is soft. He's not another
Brzezinski, let alone another Kissinger. But he does hate
the Soviets. That's one good reason for this country to
have central European national security advisers: they
know all about the Russians. And I firmly predict that
within a few months of Billy Connor's inauguration,
enough disasters will have piled up for Yankovich to become a very worried man indeed—to the point where he
might even welcome the role that this committee would
then be able to play."

"I know," said Hockney, "he was my political science
professor at Berkeley. He was one of those Kennedy liberals who turned out to be more hawkish than anyone else
on Vietnam."

Hockney left O'Reilly's office uncertain whether the two
of them had not embarked on a fantasy. Was it remotely
possible that he, a journalist without a paper, could help
bring about the defection of a top KGB officer so that an
American senator could open the eyes of the American
public to the Soviet game plan? No, he told himself, it was
not possible—not even remotely. Things just do not happen that way in the real world. Still, he was ready to give it
a try.

Hockney lay naked under the bedspread on Julia's narrow
bed, inhaling a cigarette.

"Was it good?" she asked for the second time.

"You know how good it was." He kissed her, and let his mouth slide back to her neck, her breasts. It had never been so good. Julia *was* different, practiced, but wholly giving.

"I'm glad I'm here," he said.

"Why don't you stay?" Julia murmured. Then she looked frightened that she had said it.

"I think this time we're going to stay together," said Hockney. "But there is something I have to do."

During her years in Washington, Julia, now thirty-one, had become a sophisticated political operative who knew her way around Capitol Hill and Embassy Row better than most senators. Unlike Hockney, she had never succumbed to the easy lure of radical chic. Her deep commitment to congressional politics was anchored in an instinctive faith in the superiority of the American way of life over all ideologies—something she had never discussed with Hockney because she feared the phrases she might use to communicate her feelings would sound trite.

Since Julia had been working for O'Reilly, she had access to a wealth of classified material that had given her a radically different picture of the world scene from what she could glean by reading the newspapers or watching television. Her friend and fellow staffer, Dick Roth, had given her a crash course on the tactics and strategic objectives of the Soviet Union that had persuaded her that Shame O'Reilly was right to pursue what had been virtually a one-man crusade for the moral and physical rearming of the United States against its foremost adversary.

She saw that Hockney had been weathered over the years since their first coming together, and that it suited him. She felt that the course of their lives had been like two converging arcs. They had drifted wide apart during Hockney's radical phase and his intense involvement with Tessa, but now they seemed to be matching up again, like a metal bracelet that had sprung open and was at last about to be snapped shut.

"What?" Julia said.

"I have to go to Geneva."

338

"Why?"

"I have an assignation with someone I have to get out of my system."

"A woman?"

"A Russian."

Geneva

JUST AFTER 11:00 P.M., Bob Hockney rang the bell at the door of the Griffins nightclub in Geneva.

A small trapdoor opened at eye level. Hockney peered through it, into the face of a fading middle-aged blonde.

"Are you a member?" she asked.

"I was told to ask for Mr. Turki."

The woman pressed the buzzer that opened the door.

Hockney descended a flight of red-carpeted steps and was greeted by the deafening sound of one of the current hit tunes, "I Lost My Heart to a Starship Trooper," blaring from the disco.

Hockney had been astonished that a Soviet intelligence officer would suggest a nightclub as a meeting place. But that was exactly what Colonel Viktor Barisov had proposed at the end of a long and very liquid lunch at Hotel du Lac in Nyon three days before. Hockney was beginning to wonder what proportion of their time spies spent in discotheques. Maybe even more than foreign correspondents.

The headwaiter showed him to Mr. Turki's table. Turki described himself as an attaché at the Libyan mission to the UN. He seemed to have plenty of money to throw around.

Three women, all heavily made up, were seated with Barisov and Turki, bouncing up and down to the beat of the music. Two champagne buckets were on the table. While Hockney tried to exchange pleasantries with Barisov above the din, two of the women got up and started dancing by themselves.

Hockney soon stopped trying to communicate with Barisov, a handsome, graying man with a prominent widow's peak whom he judged to be about fifty. The noise was deafening, and the Russian, though charming, had clearly been drinking heavily. In between swallows of champagne, Barisov was downing brandies. He was letting the woman next to him—whose bosom seemed about to pop out of her low-cut black dress—caress the inside of his thighs, apparently oblivious to the fact that he was in a public place. Hockney guessed that the scene must have been staged to put him at his ease. Senior Soviet intelligence officers, he told himself, were unlikely to behave like Arab playboys unless they had a purpose.

One of the women dragged Hockney onto the dance floor as the music switched to a tune honoring the latest American dance craze, "The Freak." Hockney tried to ape the girl's movements as she bent her knees, spread her legs wide, and swayed her pelvis suggestively. He was not managing very well when he caught sight of the Russian across the dance floor. To Hockney's astonishment, Barisov had crouched down, his thigh between his partner's legs, his nose only a few feet from the floor. The girl was crouched beneath him. The Russian and his partner then proceeded to straighten their legs and lean backward. To Hockney, their dancing technique resembled fornication without penetration. Neighboring dancers giggled and applauded.

Barisov's behavior was becoming even more implausible. No Soviet citizen—not even a Cossack—danced like that. If Barisov was trying to win Hockney's confidence, perhaps in the hope of compromising him by making him feel sufficiently at ease to spend the night with one of the whores, the Russian was going to excessive lengths. Maybe the most obvious explanation was also the true one: the Russian was drunk, and was letting his hair down. But if that were the case, how long would Barisov survive in a town that was crawling with Soviet agents who would undoubtedly report his nocturnal habits to his superiors?

Hockney woke up with a splitting headache and a dim memory of Barisov disappearing with the busty woman in the black dress.

Barisov woke up in his apartment in the modern complex on the Chemin de la Tourelle with something worse than a headache. His wife shook him awake not long after dawn.

"Pronk was trying to trace you about 3:00 A.M.," she told him as he gulped scalding black coffee. "There's more trouble at the UN." Since the Swiss security service had discovered that the KGB was using the cover of the United Nations agencies in Geneva to steal Swiss defense secrets, it had become less tolerant about the goings-on in the inflated Soviet spy community.

"Who are they going to expel this time?" Barisov groaned.

"I think it's Yuri." Yuri was a KGB officer who supposedly worked for the International Labor Organization. "But it's not just that," she went on. "Pronk sounded furious with you. He expects you at his office at seven."

Barisov dressed hastily and stole a quick nip of brandy from the bar in the living room, making sure Olga wasn't looking. He did not consider himself an alcoholic, although his drink consumption was well above what Western doctors would have regarded as the danger level. But heavy drinking was characteristic of members of the KGB, as of many other intelligence services. Nonetheless, Barisov was well aware that his intake had increased sharply since his posting to Geneva, even more so since the arrival of Pronk as the new KGB resident.

The transfer to Geneva had been a serious demotion for Barisov. There was no doubt about that. What had made it worse was that he could not understand what he had done to deserve it. Kramar had told him he thought Barisov's work in orchestrating deception operations against the West from Moscow Center and from the Washington residency had been brilliant. There was a string of exclusive stories in the American press, indirectly inspired by Barisov, to prove it. He had extended the agent network he had inherited in the United States, paving the way for the next phase in Plan Azev: the penetration of the American administration by Soviet agents of influence and "trusted persons."

Barisov could only conclude that his relative disgrace

had been the product of the whispering campaign that Pronk and a Stalinist faction inside Moscow Center had promoted against him ever since his posting in Paris, and that the patronage of Kramar and his father-in-law had not been enough to protect his interests. There were signs of a shift of power inside the Kremlin toward the most hawkish elements. Although there was no fundamental disagreement within the Soviet leadership about the ultimate strategic objective—world hegemony—there were important differences over tactics and operating style. In the eyes of old-style hardliners like Pronk, Barisov was far too Westernized to be fully trusted.

Perhaps Pronk's suspicions were not altogether unfounded. Barisov had become extremely attached to the finer things in life, such as he had found in the West. Although he enjoyed equal privileges at home, as a member of the Soviet Union's gilded elite—with access to luxuries denied to the proletarian masses—he felt restricted in Moscow, as if he were wearing a collar that was two sizes too small. It had even occurred to him that this sense of constriction might be due to the absence of freedom, a thought that was worse than heretical in the mind of an officer of the Soviet secret police.

Then Pronk had arrived in Geneva hot on Barisov's heels. Pronk's assignment was to clean up the mess caused by the defection to the British of a young military intelligence officer named Vladimir Rezun. In Pronk's view, defections were possible only when indiscipline ruled. His recipe for the Geneva residency was to tighten all the screws. Even Barisov had been ordered to report all his movements outside his apartment and the embassy compound. And Pronk had actually gone so far as to suggest that Barisov move out of the complex on the Chemin de la Tourelle and live with other members of the Soviet mission behind a guarded wall. Rezun, Pronk had not forgotten, was able to make an easy getaway from Geneva because he had been living outside the compound. To Barisov, Pronk's suggestion amounted to an insult, which he contemptuously dismissed. He wondered afterward whether Pronk considered him a potential defector.

As he prepared to leave his apartment for the mission, the thought crossed Barisov's mind again. What made a defector? He might, to a suspicious security man, present some of the characteristics. Barisov regarded himself as a Russian patriot, but he had lost any vestige of belief in the Communist ideology. He preferred living in the West to living in the Soviet Union. What maintained his loyalty, in real terms, was his senior and effective role in the most powerful secret service in the world. Yet his status within the KGB was now under attack. What had happened to his father reminded him how suddenly a man who fell into disfavor within the ranks of the Soviet elite could vanish altogether.

Of course, Barisov's father had been sent to Siberia by Stalin's secret police chief. Things might work differently in Moscow today, but Pronk was, in every respect, a product of Stalinism, and Barisov was sure that his chief would not hesitate to use the techniques of Beria. Faced with a possible choice between disgrace at Pronk's instigation and escape to the West, Barisov was no longer sure that his emotional loyalty to Mother Russia would keep him from following the example of Vladimir Rezun.

The entrance to the Soviet mission in Geneva—known to some of the local residents as La Villa and to Western diplomats as The Bunker—was almost invisible, in a recess off the Rue de la Paix, across the street from the UN compound. At the end of a twenty-yard drive was a guard-house and a weighted gate. Barisov was well known to the guards, but they still went through the rituals of checking his identity card and of phoning Pronk to verify that he was expected.

Pronk was fuming.

"I have a report on your behavior at some seedy night-club called the Griffins last night."

"It's not seedy," Barisov objected, fully aware that he would only inflame Pronk's temper. "It's quite an elegant discotheque."

"This report has already been sent to me by Moscow Center," Pronk went on with a warning glare. "While you were at the Griffins, we had a security problem on our hands. You are supposed to be within reach at all times. Furthermore, the report I received says that you attempted to rape a woman on the dance floor. What do you have to say for yourself?"

"Did the report tell you who I was with?"

"Yes. Our friend Turki, the Libyan, and an unidentified American. Who was he?"

"He is one of my prime targets," Barisov explained. "An American reporter with considerable influence. Through go-betweens, I used him to have important material published in the Western press in the past. I was about to report him to Moscow Center through you as a subject for agent recruitment."

"That does not explain your sexual antics in a nightclub where you were observed by one of our sources and could have been observed by anyone else. Even if you were no more than you are supposed to be—the deputy chief of UN public information in Geneva—your actions would besmirch the image of the Soviet government. Given your real position, you should be fully aware that these pornographic exhibitions are rendering you, and this residency, vulnerable to our professional opponents. You may have forgotten Paris, but I haven't."

"I know we continue to disagree on this, Comrade General," Barisov countered, "but I still think that my Paris experiment showed the value of what you call pornographic exhibitions in recruiting agents."

Pronk screwed a cigarette into a tortoiseshell holder. "Comrade Colonel," the KGB resident said, "I will be recommending to Moscow Center that you be recalled for disciplinary action. I think you have spent too long in the West. You seem to have forgotten what it is to be a Soviet officer."

Bob Hockney ordered a Swiss beer as he waited for his Soviet contact to arrive for lunch in the delegates' lounge of the Palais des Nations. It was a clear day, with a perfect view of Mont Blanc through the plate-glass windows, and of hundreds of brightly colored spinnakers on the lake.

Hockney was glad he had come to Geneva. It hadn't been a waste of time. He felt he was getting to know Barisov, and the incident at the Griffins had convinced him that the Russian was becoming disenchanted with his present employers. Hockney was also gathering material for a report on KGB activities within the United Nations setup in what was sometimes described as the smallest big city in the world. There was no shortage of dirt.

Hockney watched a Russian who worked for the UN's Human Rights Division make his way to a table by the window in the company of a Czech colleague. Chris Campbell had told Hockney that the man was a KGB officer whose real brief was to suppress incoming evidence of Soviet human rights violations and to send details of Russian citizens who lodged protests with the UN back to Moscow for what was politely termed "administrative action." At another table, Hockney spotted the tall, immaculately tailored director-general of the UN operation in Geneva, a Piedmontese Italian who rarely quarreled with Soviet wishes. He was lunching with the newly appointed Russian personnel director—another KGB officer who was said to be sending all the files on applicants for UN employment back to Moscow to provide a base for spotting new agents.

Barisov arrived late, looking extremely depressed. He ordered a double scotch on the rocks.

"Still suffering from last night?" Hockney asked.

"In more ways than one," Barisov replied, gloomily contemplating the menu.

"What's the trouble?" Hockney probed.

"Bosses," said the Russian. "They're the same all over the world."

Hockney wondered whether he dared press a further question. He decided not to be too hasty.

"If I can ever be of any help," Hockney volunteered, "please let me know."

It was an odd thing for a Western correspondent to say to a KGB officer, and Barisov caught the undertone.

"How could you help me?" the Russian challenged.

"If you ever feel in need of a vacation," Hockney said

vaguely, "I'd be more than happy to help with the arrangements."

Barisov looked quickly around the delegates' lounge. No one seemed to be taking an interest in their conversation.

The waitress came up and they both ordered the plat du jour.

When she had gone, Barisov leaned over the table, apparently trying to light a cigarette.

"CIA?" the Russian breathed. He cupped his hand over his mouth to prevent any lip-readers in the room from deciphering his words.

Hockney shook his head, smiling. "No. But I have friends. Especially British friends."

"You know the British resident here?"

Hockney shook his head again. "No. In Paris. It would be easy enough for him to come over."

Barisov said nothing. The waitress returned with the blanquette de veau. Before starting to eat, Hockney excused himself and left for the men's room. He found a pay phone and called Chris Campbell's number in Paris.

"I'm no expert, Chris," Hockney said. "But my sixth sense tells me that our mutual friend here is fed up and has an emergency on his hands—the kind of emergency that requires your personal touch."

Chris Campbell caught the next flight to Geneva.

Viktor Barisov shook Olga awake. It was 4:30 A.M., but he was already dressed. So were the children.

"What time is it?" she asked sleepily.

"Don't talk now. Just get dressed. And please hurry."

"What's happening? Are we going somewhere?"

"Orders. It's urgent." Barisov knew that his wife would accept that unquestioningly. After all, she was the daughter of a KGB officer as well as an officer's wife. He didn't like to keep the truth from her, but there was no time for explanations. Anyway, it was by no means certain that she would agree to leave if she knew where they were really going.

He put the children, still groggy with sleep, into the back seat of the Volvo. He had brought only his briefcase. Fully awake now, Olga could see he was nervous from the way he fumbled with the ignition.

"Viktor, I want to know where we're going," she insisted.

"Later." The engine finally came to life.

"Does Pronk know?"

"How do you think I got the orders?" It was not technically a lie. Just an evasion.

Unknown to Barisov, Pronk was about to be informed. The apartment of the KGB resident in Geneva was in a block across the street from the modern complex on the Chemin de la Tourelle—a penthouse whose terrace overlooked the parking lot. Madame Pronk had been unable to sleep. Mikhail's snores had been even louder than usual. Taking the chill night air on the terrace, she was surprised to see people moving about under the streetlights in the car park below. She was even more surprised when she recognized the entire Barisov family climbing into their navy blue Volvo.

Mikhail Pronk didn't like to be woken early. He was like an enraged bear by the time he got through to the chief of security at the Soviet mission, Yuri Getman. Pronk's orders were rapid and precise. The car at the mission with four armed men on round-the-clock call was to be sent to cover the most obvious escape route under the main runway of Cointrin airport and over the French border to Ferney-Voltaire—and to check on the airport itself. The Soviet mission had two other security squad cars on five-minute alert. Pronk ordered Getman to send one to cover the escape route over the Mont Blanc bridge at the eastern end of Lake Geneva to the French border post of Annemasse. He told Getman to take the third car himself and go to the lakeside village of Nyon. He had a special reason for thinking that Barisov might be headed in that direction. Barisov had turned in a report three days earlier on a conversation he had had with a French correspondent at the Leman Restaurant in Nyon. At the time, the choice of venue hadn't struck Pronk as unusual; KGB officers were routinely instructed to take Western contacts to out-of-the-way places. But now it struck him that Nyon, only fifteen minutes away from Geneva on the expressway to Lausanne, offered two more escape routes that Barisov might have gone to explore. There was a paddle steamer from the port of Nyon across the lake to Evian in France, and there were plenty of small boats along the lakefront that Barisov could take. Alternatively, Barisov could fork left off the expressway instead of turning right for Nyon and drive up the road through the Jura mountains over the Col de la Givrine to the French border at La Cure.

"Call all available personnel at home," Pronk concluded. "Get them to the mission immediately. I'll be there within ten minutes."

As Pronk hung up, he realized that Getman would hardly fail to mention in his report that Pronk had violated all security regulations by using his home telephone, which was certainly monitored by the Swiss, to convey sensitive orders. Pronk was now in a state of shock. He had acted like a sleepwalker, assuming that the only reason Colonel Barisov and his family could have left without luggage before 5:00 A.M. without informing him was that Barisov was defecting. If it was a defection, it would be the most devastating blow that Soviet intelligence had ever suffered. Barisov held more secrets in his head than any previous KGB defector to the West. If he got away, Pronk might be the one spending the rest of his career in a labor camp east of the Urals.

Out on the expressway, Barisov pushed his Volvo to the limit. With the accelerator on the floor, the speedometer read 170 kilometers. He knew that the highway patrols would not be out so early. The only other traffic was coming the other way, southbound from Lausanne. He ignored the compulsory stop sign at the end of the exit ramp and sung left to follow the directions to St. Cergues and Paris.

"Are we going to France?" Olga demanded.

"I have orders to drive to Paris."

"But Father, what about school?" thirteen-year-old Dimi queried from the back. "I'm in the rugby game today."

"Shut up, Dimi," said his older brother, Sacha. "Father knows what he's doing."

Barisov drove through vineyards and flat wheatfields

until the road started to climb and twist through pine forests into the Jura mountains. He didn't lift his foot from the accelerator as the car swerved round a series of hairpin turns. Olga and the boys were hurled violently from side to side as the tires screeched as if they were about to come off their rims.

"Father," Sacha called from the back. "Dimi's sick. He's throwing up."

Barisov handed back his handkerchief without slowing down.

Olga clutched his arm. "Viktor, you've got to stop. The boy's sick."

Barisov made out a sign in faded blue letters beside the road. It read "SOS: 1 km." There was a picture of a telephone receiver over the letter O. Barisov assumed it was a telephone for stranded motorists. "I'll stop at the phone," he grunted.

While Dimi was sick at the edge of the woods, Barisov examined the SOS phone inside a red box on a pole. There was no dial. He couldn't use it to call the American contact number that he had been told would be manned twenty-four hours a day. It was probably just a direct line to a police station.

"Who are you trying to call?" Olga challenged, as Barisov started the motor again.

"It's to make sure the border is clear."

The car skidded on up the mountain road to the ski resort of St. Cergues, where Barisov vanished into a hotel to make his call. The American voice told him he had driven too far. He should double back to Nyon and wait at the pizzeria opposite the railroad station. It opened early. There would probably be a man waiting. They estimated it would take them fifteen minutes to get there from Geneva, and twenty minutes for Barisov to make it back from St. Cergues.

"Can't you meet me here?" Barisov gave the American the name of the hotel.

"No," the voice came back. "It's out of range. You'll have to meet us halfway."

As Barisov slalomed back down the road toward Nyon, hardly braking at the turns, Dimi was moaning and Olga, who had changed places with Sacha, was on the verge of mutiny.

"Are you out of your mind?" she protested.

"There's trouble with the Swiss," he lied, hoping to avoid a showdown before he got the family across the border.

By the time Barisov had reached a motel called Le Pressoir near the turnoff from the expressway, Yuri Getman had already checked the departure times of the ferry from Nyon at the jetty. He found that nothing left before 9:30. The KGB security chief scanned the lake for small boats with his binoculars. He could see nothing. His next move was to drive along the lakefront to the Leman, the restaurant where Barisov had had lunch, to see whether any of the boats in the marina were missing.

Barisov spotted the Pizzeria de la Gare, opposite the station in Nyon, and parked around the corner. After a quick glance around the almost empty restaurant, he led his family into the back room behind the bar. He ordered coffee and rolls. Olga hadn't noticed the man with his hands on the bar who lifted his thumbs in an almost imperceptible sign of recognition as they entered. When the coffee was served, Barisov went to the men's room. The other man followed.

When Barisov came back, he looked at his watch. It was 6:32. "We have ten minutes," he said to Olga.

"Ten minutes for what?"

"Ten minutes before the train leaves."

"What train? What about the car?"

"That's been taken care of."

While one of the two CIA men who had been assigned to handle this phase of the Barisov defection watched the road in front of the station from his parked car, the other took the car keys that Barisov had handed over and drove his Volvo down to a small parking lot near the wharf.

Barisov heard the train before he saw it. Coming up the middle of the right-hand lane in the road, its hooter sounded like a foghorn. Dimi, miraculously recovered, went to the door to look. "It's a toy train," he called. "It's not a real train at all."

The narrow-gauge track ran through the middle of Nyon; the final stop was right outside the pizzeria. On the side of the red single-carriage train, the name of the mountain line was painted in gold letters: "Nyon—St. Cergues—Morez." Instead of turning the train around, the driver got out of the control cabin at one end and walked down to the cabin at the other. The train was less than seven feet wide.

At that time of morning, there were only a few people waiting under the trees beside the track to take the train to one of the half-dozen stops it made on its hour-long journey through the pine forests to the French border at La Cure, just beyond St. Cergues. The station for the mainline trains was directly opposite. But the first train for Paris didn't leave until 7:38, almost an hour later, and that was too risky because there was a fifteen-minute delay between trains at Lausanne before crossing the border.

Barisov made his family wait inside the pizzeria until the trainman, puffing away at a corncob pipe, looked ready to leave. As he pretended to linger, Barisov stared at a collector's item on the wall of the pizzeria—an old British poster for Howe's Cycles that showed an absurd figure in plus-fours riding a motorized tricycle. Barisov wondered gloomily whether the train would travel much faster.

Through the window, he saw the American in a parked car raise his thumb. He shepherded Olga and the boys into the tiny six-by-six first-class compartment of the train. There were only four people in the other compartments, two of them hikers with their rucksacks and climbing boots. Barisov walked through the train to check the minuscule toilet and the two-foot-wide corridor where mailbags were stacked. He also noted that the blinds in his compartment could be pulled down to cover the whole window.

The advertisement on the wall read "*Avez-vous votre billet de Loterie Romande?*" I hope the Americans have bought me the winning ticket, Barisov said to himself.

As the train began to climb toward St. Cergues, Olga

relaxed a little. Apart from the early hour, it could almost have been a family excursion.

The American in the Citroën with reinforced bumpers picked up his colleague, who had walked back from the wharf. They set off at once along the mountain road to St. Cergues and La Cure. The road ran more or less parallel to the miniature railway. Their orders were to set up a blocking operation in case Pronk's men decided to hunt in that direction. One of the agents picked up the Motorola walkie-talkie. From its stand between the bucket seats, it could be recharged automatically. The station chief told the agent in code that the hostiles were crawling all over Geneva looking for the runaway, and that Claw himself was searching his area. The CIA men knew that Claw was Yuri Getman, chief of KGB security, a veteran killer who had been assigned to tighten discipline within the Soviet community after Vladimir Rezun's defection.

Finding no clues at the Leman, Getman ordered his driver to head back along the Route du Lac through Nyon. As the big black Mercedes sped past the ferry landing, Getman exclaimed between his teeth, "I don't believe it."

There, in the parking lot, was Barisov's navy blue Volvo. Getman instantly recognized the CD license plate ending in 01, the designation for some United Nations officials. Pronk's hunch had been amazingly accurate.

But the car hadn't been there twenty minutes before. Where had Barisov gone? Getman swept the lake with his binoculars. He paused to focus on two sailboats. No sign of Barisov, and the boats were too small to hide on. No ferry. Could Barisov be hiding in a house along the lakefront in Nyon? If that was the case, why didn't he hide his car?

The car had to be a decoy to make Barisov's pursuers think he had already escaped across the lake. Getman looked up at the Jura mountains. It was so obvious. Barisov was trying to escape that way.

The receiver became wet in Getman's hand as he told Pronk on the radio telephone that his hunch had been right, but that Getman had been able to find only the car, not the man. Getman knew that his head was really on the block. Barisov might already have barreled up the mountain road and over the border. Or he could have taken the Paris train from Nyon station. While Getman and his men rushed to check out the station, Pronk ordered all available units to converge in the area of St. Cergues and the French border. The radio messages were picked up by both the CIA and the Swiss.

One of Getman's men jumped out of the Mercedes to check the Paris schedule on the wall of the station. "Nothing until 7:28," he said. Getman looked at his watch. It was only 6:54. Could Barisov be hiding somewhere, waiting for the train?

Getman noticed the Pizzeria de la Gare opposite the station, and decided to take a look inside. He strode briskly across the road and was nearing the other side when he was almost deafened by a foghorn. He hadn't heard or noticed the tiny electric train until it was nearly on top of him. He was struck by the disparity between the noise and the minute size of the train. Could Barisov have made his escape on his model railway? No, it was too ridiculous.

Still, when Getman asked inside the pizzeria whether anyone had seen a family with two teenage children, he was told they had gone up the mountain on the first train. It left at 6:42.

"How long does it take to get to La Cure?" he asked the patron.

"About an hour."

That meant the train would get to the border at 7:42. He consulted his watch again. It was now 6:58. That gave them exactly 44 minutes to get there.

"How long does it take to get there by road?" Getman was agitated, speaking bad French at machine-gun speed.

The *patron* casually wiped the white marble counter. "Oh, it's an easy thirty-minute drive," he replied unconcernedly. "If you're in a real hurry, maybe twenty-five. No traffic, maybe twenty. *Et pour vous, qu'est-ce que je vous sert? Un p'tit café?*"

But Getman was already running to the car.

Getman's chauffeur drove like Niki Lauda up the road

356

to St. Cergues, taking the hairpin turns at 80 kilometers. Through a break in the trees, Getman suddenly caught sight of the train.

"Faster," he ordered the driver.

They screeched round another bend and nearly crashed into the back of a slow-moving caravan with GB license plates. The Mercedes skidded as the driver slammed on his brakes to avoid a collision. Getman's chauffeur flashed the lights and clamped his hand on the horn, but the British driver ambled along at a steady 25 kilometers, unflappable, through three more turns. Once the Mercedes tried to overtake the trailer on an S-shaped bend, but was forced back by a truck rolling downhill. Getman calculated that they lost three or four minutes before the road straightened, just as they approached St. Cergues, and the Mercedes was able to accelerate past.

Ignoring the speed limits, the driver careened through the town. Getman's spirits lifted when he saw that at some points the railroad track was running right alongside the road. But there was no sign of the train.

Beyond St. Cergues, they passed the crest of the Jura mountains. The road leveled off at 1,200 meters before gently sloping down to La Cure, 6 kilometers away. As the Mercedes sped into open country, Getman spotted the red carriage, moving at a third their speed, beside the road. It was only a few hundred meters away. They were closing in fast.

"Get ahead of it," Getman ordered his driver. "We've got to get onto the tracks and wave it down. Stop when we're five hundred meters ahead."

Through the rearview mirror in his Citroën, one of the CIA agents saw the black Mercedes coming up fast. He couldn't read the number on the license plate, but the flash of blue on white told him it was diplomatic. He saw the driver of the car behind pulling out to overtake him, and swerved into the middle of the road to force him back. Now he could make out the two last digits on the plate— 73. The Mercedes belonged to the Soviet mission.

The Mercedes hooted and pulled out again. Again, the American blocked it.

Getman was now sure that the Citroën with ordinary Geneva license plates was part of Barisov's escape plot. Getman barked at his driver to feign a pass to the left. "When they try to cut us off again, hit the accelerator to the floor and cut through on the right."

The American's reflexes were too fast for the Russian. He swung back to the right in time, and there was a crash of metal as the right bumper of the Citroën slammed against the fender of the Mercedes.

From the window of the train, Viktor Barisov watched the two big cars fighting for the road, crossing back and forth. He pulled down the blind in his first-class minicompartment.

"I don't want the sun to bother you," he said to Olga, who had sat in silence, nervous and unhappy, through most of the journey. Fortunately, she was sitting on the other side of the carriage and hadn't seen the action on the road. The two boys were dozing.

Facing the rear of the train, Barisov peeked through the blind. He could see sparks as the two cars collided again. The track veered away from the road. To his horror, Barisov saw the black Mercedes break through on the right, the gravel flying as it hurtled along the shoulder of the road. The track forked behind some chalets, and the cars were out of sight.

Getman checked his watch against the clock on the dashboard of the Mercedes. The train would arrive at La Cure in six minutes, if it was on schedule. Knowing the Swiss, it could even be a minute or two ahead of schedule. That gave him just six minutes to get 500 meters ahead of the train, stop, jump out, get to the track, flag the train down, and give the trainman time to brake.

But by the time Getman saw the train again, it was almost at the border, too late to intercept. The Mercedes was slightly ahead of it, but the Swiss border post was looming up fast. There was no way of stopping Barisov before La Cure.

When the track came out of the woods again, the first car that Barisov saw was the Citroën, racing along just behind the train, about to pass it. He released the blind, thinking that the American had somehow managed to get rid of the Russians. Then he peered forward out of the window and saw the black Mercedes ahead. He jerked the blind down again, sweating profusely.

"What's the matter with you, Viktor?" said Olga. "You look sick. When is all this going to end?"

"In about five minutes."

"I'm thirsty, Papa," Dimi complained, rubbing his eyes.

"Me too," said his older brother.

"You'll just have to wait a bit longer."

Getman knew that the French would not let him through. He needed a visa to get into France. He didn't have one, and he was one of the least likely Soviet citizens in Geneva to be granted one. But he hadn't expected problems with the Swiss border control on the way out. Normally the Swiss weren't interested in people on the way out—only on the way in.

But the Russian car was forced to stop at an emergency roadblock that the Swiss had erected. The police refused to let it cross into the 60 meter strip of no-man's-land between the Swiss roadblock and the French border post down the road. Getman got out of the car and tried to argue with the police. To his immediate right, still on the Swiss side but jutting out into no-man's-land, was a garage. Beyond it was a vacant lot bordering on the railroad track. Beside the line, midway between the Swiss and the French controls, was an old gabled stationhouse that doubled as a post office. Getman watched helplessly as the train pulled up beside it.

Getman saw Barisov, his wife, and two sons descend from the carriage. A well-tailored man in a Prince-of-Wales check with thinning hair appeared around the corner of the stationhouse. Barisov and his family followed him beyond the far side of the building, so that Getman lost sight of them for a moment.

Barisov didn't attempt to disguise the relief he felt as he greeted Chris Campbell.

"Well done, Viktor," Campbell said. "We're nearly there."

As they stumbled over the pebbles behind Campbell, Olga whispered urgently to Barisov, "Viktor, who is this man? Is he American? Is he British?"

Without answering, he gently pushed her forward. "Stop, Viktor," she said. He didn't stop, so she walked backward in front of him, still talking. "Viktor, I must know what you're doing. Are you defecting? I'm not saying I won't come with you. I just need to know first. I have my father to think of."

"You'll see him very soon," Barisov said soothingly. Anything to get her to take those last few steps.

Getman, leaning on the police barrier, could see that Barisov and his wife were having an argument. He couldn't hear what they were saying, but he could see they were playing out some strange charade, Barisov's wife walking in front of him backward toward the French post. The man who had met them was already standing with the French police. Getman thought he recognized him. He was British. So the British were in this too.

Still arguing with his wife, Barisov was less than a dozen paces from the French roadblock. Getman couldn't let it happen. Barisov the traitor would be an incalculable asset to the West. Getman fingered the butt of the poison dart gun in his shoulder holster. It was his favorite weapon. It killed silently by delayed action. The victim felt nothing more than a sharp prick, like an insect bite he might rub away with his hand. The only disadvantage to the gun was its range. Even Getman's improved model was reliably accurate only within a range of 25 meters. Barisov was already 45 or 50 meters away.

But Getman eyed the farthest gas pump in the garage. It was possibly only 30 or 35 meters from the French post. If Getman could sneak up behind it quickly there was a gambler's chance of getting close enough to hit Barisov before the French police whisked him away. The three other Russians had gotten out of the car and were standing along the barrier. Getman murmured to his driver, "Distract the police."

Then Getman darted behind the car, between two gas pumps. When he reached the farthest pump, he whipped out his dart pistol. Using the pump to screen himself from the Swiss police, he drew a bead on Barisov.

The Americans, in their Citroën, had stopped 10 meters behind the Mercedes with their engine still running, taking in the whole scene. The driver watched Getman dart into the garage, and responded instinctively by accelerating the car forward. By the time they reached the entrance to the gas station, the Citroën was in second gear.

The driver could see Getman half-crouched between two rows of pumps, aiming a gun. He slammed the accelerator down, and drove straight toward the Russian. The car wheels crunched over a thin piece of rubber hose that triggered a bell to call the gas station attendant. Getman, startled by the noise as he squeezed the trigger, lost his aim. The dart landed harmlessly in the wall of the Bureau des Douanes Françaises, just above the head of a French policeman. Getman jumped to avoid the Citroën. The American didn't even try to brake. As the wheels rolled over the Russian, there was a dull thud.

Barisov and Olga, now shielded by French police, had heard the scream but couldn't see what the commotion on the Swiss side was all about.

The three other Russians, who had been shouting abuse at Barisov across the barrier in order to distract police attention from Getman, now had their revolvers drawn. They were pointing them at four uniformed Swiss policemen, who were pointing their own weapons back. A moment passed. Wordlessly, the Russians lowered their guns. It was Swiss territory.

The American had turned the Citroën around in the vacant lot and now drove back through the gas station, avoiding Getman's inert body. A Swiss Sûreté inspector in plainclothes gently waved him to a stop. The Swiss police had already pried the gun loose from Getman's hand.

"Qu'est-ce qui se passe, monsieur?"

"Un accident."

"Yes, we all saw it," said the inspector. He looked at the three Russians. They said nothing. *"D'accord. C'était un accident."*

Washington

1

FROM WHERE HE SAT, the national security adviser could not see the President's face above the soles of his tennis shoes, propped up on the big desk in the Oval Office. Ever since the Carter administration, tennis and casual dress had been regarded as essential to maintaining a youthful and populist image of the presidency. Milorad Yankovich, the latest in a succession of Central European security advisers, sat stiffly in his somber, double-breasted suit. In the semicircle in front of Billy Connor's desk, Yankovich—known as Yank to his friends and as "the only Yank in the White House" in the media—was flanked by the President's press secretary, Sam Cody, and his crony from Flats, Timmy Hicks, who was hunched down in his chair, legs spread out, cradling the can of Schlitz that seemed to be grafted to his hand. Yankovich was trying to give the President a last-minute briefing on foreign policy points that might come up in the morning's press conference, but Timmy Hicks kept interrupting with irrelevant reminiscences about the weekend he had just spent in the desert with Libya's latest strongman, a twenty-six-year-old manic-depressive named Lieutenant Muhammad Lufti. Muhammad and a group of young officers had set fire to his predecessor's tent while he was sleeping, and then played poker to decide which one would take over.

"Guess what went wrong," Timmy drawled. "Muhammad told me he made one mistake. He damn-well forgot to get the number of the last president's secret bank account in Switzerland."

Yankovich, who had heard the story several times before, groaned inwardly. He was convinced that the Mississippi Mafia tormented him deliberately. Every morning, as he came down the corridor to give the President his 8:00 A.M. briefing, Jonah Cobb, Connor's chief of staff—known to the media as the White House Chief of Chaos—would be lying in wait. "Look out, the Yanks are coming!" Cobb's greeting never varied. This morning, he'd improved on his standard one-liner. "Hey, Yank," he had yelled after the national security adviser, "I bet the only way you get laid in that suit is to get laid out."

Naturalized twenty-three years before, Yankovich had retained traces of a Serbian accent and was uncomfortable with locker-room repartee. So he had smiled wanly and hurried on. His resentment against Cobb was deepened by the fact that he suspected Cobb had leaked material to the *New York World* for a story that portrayed Yankovich as a "closet hawk" who had become a frenzied cold-warrior since Yugoslavia rejoined the Warsaw Pact after Tito. A gossip item in a Washington paper claimed that Yankovich was now referred to as "Mad Dog" by the President's closest advisers.

On top of that, Yankovich had found that his Raleigh bicycle, which he kept in the pool at the White House, had two flat tires again. After the latest price squeeze by the oil producers' cartel, Billy Connor had decreed that his aides should set an example of energy conservation by riding bicycles to work. The President had silenced their guffaws of derision by reminding them that Britain's naval chiefs had cycled to the Admiralty during World War II. Yankovich knew that Cobb was letting the air out of his tires, because every time he began to pump them up, White House press photographers and TV cameramen would appear from nowhere, and he would wind up on the front pages and the evening news. He now assigned the job to his secretary.

"Mr. President," Yankovich said, reminding him. "You have fifteen minutes left to get dressed and get ready for the press conference."

"Anything hot abroad I might be asked about?"

"There are signs of instability on the Yemeni border, Mr. President. There are unconfirmed news agency reports that an armored column from Aden has penetrated twenty-five miles into North Yemen, and that South Yemeni planes are bombing Sanaa."

"What's Sanaa?" asked the President.

"Sounds like a Swedish bath to me," Timmy contributed.

"Sanaa, Mr. President," Yankovich enunciated carefully, "is the capital of North Yemen."

"You think the Soviets might retaliate on behalf of their friends down there?" the President queried. He had taken his feet off the desk and was leafing through an atlas.

"You mean in North Yemen?"

"Yeah."

"It's the other way round, Mr. President."

"What's the other way round?"

"The—uh—guys in North Yemen are our friends. The guys in South Yemen are the Soviets' friends."

"Oh."

Yankovich rose to help the President locate the places on the map. Timmy Hicks, still clutching his beer, said, "Dr. Yanko means you've got it ass-backwards, Billy."

2

THE REPORTERS gathered in the White House auditorium noted that the President had made his contribution to St. Patrick's Day by wearing a green tie with his beige suit and sporting a green plastic carnation in his lapel.

"I have no opening statement," Billy Connor began. "Let's get straight to the questions."

The first six questions were all on domestic issues. The new crash program on solar energy, the lifting of restrictions on Mexican immigrants in return for guaranteed oil, and the President's tax returns for 1978–1979 while he was campaigning for the White House—all prompted reporters' questions. Billy Connor, as usual, proved himself the master of the casual putdown.

Bob Hockney got to his feet. When the Russian defector Barisov was safely in the hands of British intelligence, Hockney had returned to Washington with a new assignment from the *Reader's Companion* to write a piece on the Connor Administration's foreign policy. This was not a project that had seized his imagination until the Saudi crisis had started to blow up. But he needed to fill in time while Chris Campbell's friends carried out their debriefings of Barisov—after which he had been promised exclusive access to the defector.

"Is it correct, Mr. President," he began, "that there is an international Communist brigade of some twenty thousand Russians, East Germans, Cubans, and Ethiopians in South Yemen? Is it also correct that elements of this brigade are taking part in the invasion of North Yemen, whose regime is pro-Western?"

"I am not aware of any evidence of Soviet involvement in the conflict between these two small Arab countries," the President pronounced.

Hockney remained standing. As a dozen hands shot up, he said, "Follow-up question please, sir."

The President nodded.

"The Sultan of Oman issued a statement this morning in which he said that the attack on North Yemen was part of an international plot to grab control of the entire Arabian peninsula and the free world's biggest reserves of oil."

"What is your question?" said President Connor.

"Well, sir, in view of French news agency reports that Soviet pilots in MIG fighters are taking part in the assault on Sanaa, would you agree with the Sultan of Oman's assessment?"

Billy Connor tried to summon up a mental picture of the map he had been studying in his office. He didn't want to insult a friendly Arab ruler.

"The King of Amman," said the President, picking his words with care, "is entitled to his own view. It is not the view of this administration. I would suggest that the media keep its eye on the ball." The President paused for effect. "That means the SALT IV negotiations. If we fumble this one, we could find ourselves back in the cold war."

Hockney was still on his feet. President Connor recognized another questioner, but before the reporter had opened his mouth Connor swung back, pointing an accusing finger at Hockney. "Mark this. I'm dealing with the Soviet leadership every week. I know they want peace as much as we do. I also know that the greatest threat to mutual understanding is the kind of cold war rhetoric implied in your questions."

Hockney scribbled furiously. So did everyone else.

The next questioner was a middle-aged woman from the *Boise Bugle*, an out-of-town visitor plainly excited to be attending her first White House press conference. President Connor bestowed on her his celebrated papier-mâché grin.

"Mr. President," she said, reading from prepared notes, "I would like to know if you feel that the constant playing of our national anthem at each and every major sporting event debases and devalues our patriotic song."

Without a second's hesitation, the President replied, "With all due respect, I don't agree. I am a patriot, and I never tire of hearing our national anthem. It makes me feel proud to be an American, a citizen of the greatest country the world has ever known. But I have issued instructions that the playing of 'Hail to the Chief' should be the exception rather than the rule. It was beginning to sound like 'Hi to the Chief.' "

As reporters chuckled politely, the dean of the White House press corps rose and said, "Thank you, Mr. President"—the ritual cutoff. The thirty minutes allotted for the press conference were up.

Yankovich hovered at the door of the auditorium. As the President left, he thrust a message into his hand that had just been sent up from the code room.

"East German paratroops have just occupied the presidential palace in Sanaa," the national security adviser summarized. "The president and his family are believed to have been executed. We're also getting reports of military activity along the Saudi border. One of our advisers on the Saudi side says that the Soviets are airlifting Cuban troops and armored personnel carriers over the mountains and into the southwest corner of Saudi Arabia. There's another message being decoded right now from King Ahmed."

"The King's worried, huh? Well, we've sure given the Saudis enough hardware to look after themselves, what with those F-fifteens Carter sent them."

"With your permission, Mr. President," said Yankovich,

"I'd like to set up a crisis meeting right here in the Oval Office and get the head of the Joint Chiefs and the CIA director in immediately."

"Uh-huh." President Connor nodded reluctantly. "Guess you're right. But let's play it low-key. Tell everyone to use unmarked cars. We don't want a crisis atmosphere around here."

"Come on, Billy." Timmy Hicks butted in. "Time to shake ass."

"For what?"

"Don't tell me you've forgotten. We got the Paddlesteamers waiting for us in the East Room. The cameras are all set up."

The Paddlesteamers were Mississippi's number-one electronic pop group.

"Sheeeat," said the President, looking down at his beige suit. "I can't go in like this. Whaddya think I should wear?"

"No worries, Billy-boy. Keep the pants on, get rid of the tie, and we got a real nice shiny green vinyl jacket for you. Keep the zip open, and you'll look like a real Paddlesteamer."

President Connor turned to Yankovich, who was still hovering.

"We better hold this meeting over dinner."

Yankovich cantered off to his corner office, straightening his tie. As he heard Timmy Hicks screech with laughter behind him, he shook his head in disbelief. How could he function as national security adviser to a President who gave as much time to a Mississippi pop group as he did to what was bound, by the end of the day, to be a war council?

Yankovich was intercepted in the corridor by his CIA liaison man from the NSC, a bruised survivor of the great purges of the mid-1970s.

"What's the latest?" Yankovich could almost read the answer in the man's haggard face.

"Doesn't look good, Doctor," he reported. "Whoever's flying those Russian MIGs has done a fucking good job. The whole goddamn Saudi air force has been destroyed on the ground."

369

"Is that confirmed?"

"The KH-nineteen doesn't lie, sir. The Saudis made it easy by lining those F-fifteens up wingtip to wingtip." The KH-19 was the latest all-seeing eye in the sky.

As Yankovich rushed into his office, a great fear welled up inside him. The Soviets were moving into Saudi Arabia, and the President of the United States was trying on a green vinyl jacket. Yankovich, the liberal academic, realized that he would have to take charge. He also realized he could count on little backup from his own staff, several of whom, like his own deputy, Perry Cummings, had close associations with the Foundation for Progressive Reform. The staff had been handpicked by Vice President Milligan; Yankovich had not even been allowed the freedom to choose his own assistants. He knew he was no Kissinger. He dreaded the next few hours, when he would somehow have to assume real power in the White House and practice brinkmanship with the Russians. Kissinger would have been in his element.

Yankovich had to start somewhere. He picked up the phone, insisted on speaking to Billy Connor, and said evenly, "Mr. President, you will have to cancel your pop concert."

3

THE CRISIS TEAM that assembled in the Oval Office at the end of the afternoon had been kept deliberately small. President Connor looked at each of the seven men sitting around his desk: the Vice President, the Secretaries of State and Defense, the CIA director, General Smith of the Joint Chiefs of Staff, Yankovich, and the ever-present Jonah Cobb. Bill Crawford had recently been brought out of retirement and given his old job as CIA director after a series of debacles at Langley under the stewardship of military men whose grasp of intelligence was confined to computer printouts. Vice President Edward Milligan had pressed for another candidate to head the agency: the man who had pushed through the SALT III deal with the Russians and was now a trustee of the Foundation for Progressive Reform. But it had been agreed that his nomination would never be confirmed by the Senate.

Milligan had raised no objections to the reappointment of Crawford, who had taken special trouble to cultivate liberal senators and the media in the past. The Vice President had been especially impressed by Crawford's memoirs, which contained an unusually frank account of CIA wrongdoing. The book had not mentioned the KGB once in its 623 pages. During his years of retirement, Crawford had based himself at his old law firm, but had spent most of his time on the lecture circuit denouncing his former colleagues. At the last OSS annual reunion dinner, several veteran intelligence professionals had walked out when he got up to speak.

President Connor listened in silence while Crawford ran through the latest satellite reconnaissance reports. The commander of the North Yemeni army had surrendered his troops and thrown in his lot with the invaders. A people's republic had been declared in Sanaa and had announced in its first communiqué, that it had joined South Yemen in a federal state to be known as the People's Democratic Federation of Yemen.

"What do we have from our embassy in Sanaa?" the President inquired.

"Nothing, sir," Crawford said. "The embassy's communications appear to have been blacked out."

"How about the Saudi front?"

Director Crawford explained that the giant Soviet crane helicopters had flown back to bases on the South Yemeni side of the border. American monitoring had picked up the pilot's radio chatter. They were talking in Russian.

"But the Russians are out of it now," said the President, searching for reassurance.

General James Smith, the Air Force man who was now head of the Joint Chiefs, cut in icily. "I don't see how the Russians can be out of it, sir, since this seems to have been

371

their operation from the start. And it's not finished yet, since they've left three battalions with armor inside the Saudi border."

"But those troops aren't Russian," said President Connor.

"Near as doesn't make any difference, sir. They appear to be South Yemenis under Cuban command. The question is, what do we do about it?"

Vice President Milligan pounced on the General. "I don't see why we have to do anything at this stage. I thought we'd learned to avoid knee-jerk reflexes. Let's wait till the dust settles. Hell, we don't even know if this guy we're backing in Riyadh will be there tomorrow."

Crawford, looking at the presidential seal on the rug to avoid the others' gaze, nodded imperceptibly.

"That guy in Riyadh," Yankovich began, but then stopped sharply, appalled to hear himself using the Vice President's language. "The King," he tried again, "has sent us a message, urgently requesting the dispatch of two airborne divisions to secure the oil fields."

"What does he think we are, Israelis?" Jonah Cobb heckled. No one laughed.

"General," the President said to Smith, "do we have two airborne divisions?"

"No, sir."

"Well, how long would it take us to get whatever adds up to two airborne divisions to Saudi?"

The General rubbed his four-o'clock shadow. "I'd say anywhere from one to three weeks—unless we denude NATO Europe of U.S. troops. And the West Germans might have something to say about that. In fact, the way things are drifting backstage in Bonn, I'll bet the Germans would even object to our using our own bases there to support an airlift from the states."

"Why would the West Germans object?" the President queried, uncomprehending.

"For the same reason I would oppose this harebrained suggestion," Milligan intervened. He glared at Yankovich with pure hate. "We've been backing a corrupt, feudal monarchy that was bound to become unstuck. Didn't Iran teach us anything?"

Yankovich's Serbian accent thickened when he got angry. "Mr. President," he said, avoiding Milligan's stare, "we are not dealing with a revolution in Saudi; we are dealing with a Soviet bloc invasion. You read the post-mortem prepared by the NSC a couple of years ago on how the trouble really started in Iran. The report contained the facts on Soviet involvement that the CIA claimed it did not have at the time."

"That was a very unconvincing document," Crawford interjected. "Mostly hand-me-downs from the European services."

"But they got it first hand," Yankovich countered.

"For Chrissake," General Smith exploded, "we're not here to rehash Iran. It's the rest of the Gulf that's up for grabs."

"Our capability is on the line everywhere, Mr. President," the national security adviser resumed. "If we let Saudi go by default, you can forget about NATO. There'll be nothing left to salvage. If we allow a pro-Soviet takeover in Riyadh, I predict that within one year West Germany will pull out of the NATO alliance and make a security deal with the Soviet Union, guaranteeing its neutrality. Western Europe as a whole would be Finlandized."

"Yank's speeches on linkage all sound the same," Vice President Milligan complained. "The kneebone is linked to the thighbone is linked to the collarbone."

"You left out the backbone," said Yankovich, with a heavy attempt at American humor. Somber again, he continued. "Mr. President, I strongly recommend that we take three immediate steps. One, we send a letter to the Soviet leadership, couched in the strongest possible language, stating that we regard any threat to Saudi Arabia as a threat to our own security—and we make that letter public. Two, you authorize General Smith to prepare to send one combat-ready division to Saudi within a week. Three, we consult with our NATO allies and other friendly governments to determine whether any of them are ready to participate in a joint save-the-oil operation."

The President was jotting down key words in large letters on a yellow legal pad. He knew that if he said the wrong thing, Milligan would make sure it wound up on the front page of the *New York World*, where Milligan had several close friends. It was better to let others do the talking.

"Anyone object to Yank's proposal?"

"I do," said Milligan, abandoning formality. He glanced sideways at the CIA director, as if expecting support from that quarter. Crawford stared fixedly at the chandelier. "I say let it fester. It is not our problem. It is Europe's problem. Remember when Qaddafi took over Libya? The Europeans went along with that one very nicely. The French sold the Libyans over one hundred Mirage fighter-bombers. Let them watch their ass and we'll watch ours. We don't need Saudi oil ficlds. We've got another gulf in the world—the Gulf of Mexico."

His speech completed, Milligan pushed back his chair, propped his right ankle over his left knee, swayed gently back and forth, and displayed his better profile to an imaginary camera with a look of invincible self-awareness that had become familiar to millions of television viewers.

The President thought about his press secretary, Sam Cody, who was cooling his heels outside, waiting to be advised on what to say to the media. It occurred to him that if Saudi fell apart fast enough, the media wouldn't have time to attack him for failing to react.

"Hey, Billy." Jonah Cobb joined the discussion. He was the only one in the White House, apart from his old pal Timmy Hicks, who called the President by his first name during meetings. "We could strike it rich. We could give the taxpayer a bonus."

"Come again, Jonah?"

"Listen to this, Billy," Cobb went on, sweating with excitement. "The bad guys take over in Riyadh. So we confiscate their assets over here. Must be worth around a hundred billion. We'd have us a ball. We could wipe out the budget deficit and give the voters a big tax cut before the midterm elections. How does that grab you?"

Yankovich buried his head in his hands.

The Secretary of State coughed politely and spoke for

the first time. "I concur in the Vice President's assessment of the situation."

"What I wanna know," said President Connor, "is what kind of flak I can expect in the media tomorrow."

4

THE PRESIDENT was pleasantly surprised as he scanned the morning headlines. The fighting in Yemen was barely reported. The *New York World* carried brief excerpts from an official South Yemeni statement, claiming that an invasion attempt by North Yemeni and Saudi forces had been repelled, that a spontaneous people's uprising had taken place in Sanaa, and that elements of the Saudi air force had mutinied and blown up their planes. An unidentified State Department spokesman was quoted as saying that there were confirmed reports of border clashes. In response to a question on possible Soviet bloc involvement, he commented, "We have no concrete evidence on that at all. It wouldn't make sense to me in the context of the progress we're making on the SALT IV agreement."

The main picture on the front page of the *World* was of demonstrators outside the Saudi embassy in Washington, many of them wearing masks. It accompanied a sensational exposé of the private lives of King Ahmed and other members of the Saudi royal house. The piece alleged that King Ahmed had a private fortune in excess of $35 billion outside his country. The reporter had interviewed a call girl, a former member of Madame Claude's exclusive agency in Paris. She described how scores of girls had been shuttled from one capital to another in the wake of King Ahmed and his entourage. She recounted a wild night in London when one prince had dropped $600,000 at a gambling club and then gone on to Annabel's, where he had polished off a bottle of scotch in the company of a spectacular blonde. According to the *World*'s source, the blonde was an agent of the Mossad, the Israeli secret service.

President Connor tuned in to one of the morning talk

375

shows on TV. Senator Harmon was nodding approval on screen as a bearded expert explained that the conservative rulers of the Gulf were in trouble because Moslems believed that they had violated the precepts of the Koran through their high-jinks in Western capitals. The talk show host turned to Harmon.

"Senator," he said, "what do you think the United States should do about this upheaval in the Arabian peninsula?"

"I say it's none of our business," Harmon replied.

"But don't we have a mutual defense understanding with Saudi Arabia?"

"That might apply in the event of invasion by a foreign power. We're dealing with a different problem here."

"What about these reports of Cuban activity?"

"Aw, that old chestnut." Harmon shrugged.

"Well, what about this statement from the new Libyan ruler that King Ahmed is a heretic and must be overthrown?"

"Now, hold it right there." Harmon leaned forward. "We've got to understand, as your guest from the Foundation for Progressive Reform was saying, that a very profound process of change, of revolutionary change, is taking place in the world of Islam. It's an inevitable reaction to our misguided policies of propping up unpopular dictators. We should have learned that lesson in Iran. Here we have another reactionary tyrant whose time is up, and soon I suppose we'll start hearing suggestions that we should be sending in the Marines."

President Connor watched Harmon scything the air with his ballpoint pen as he worked up to his *coup de grâce*. "Vietnam," said Harmon. He paused to let the word sink in. Glaring into the eye of the camera, he continued. "The people out there have not forgotten. Nor have I. As long as I am chairman of the Senate Foreign Relations Committee, I can tell you that there is no way the Pentagon or the oil companies or the CIA is going to drag this country into another Vietnam for the sake of a ruler who is looting his people and suppressing human rights. If you don't believe me, read this." The Senator held up a copy of the morning's *New York World*.

"I'm sorry, gentlemen," said the interviewer, "we must pause for a station break."

Billy Connor switched off the set on his remote control and buzzed the Vice President.

"Did you catch the NOW show?" the President asked.

"Yep," said Milligan.

"Did you tell Harmon about the Saudi request for U.S. troops?"

"No," Milligan lied. The President knew he was lying, but didn't mind. Senator Harmon's preemptive strike had gotten him off the hook. He could now tell Yank and the generals that the military option was out because Congress wouldn't stand for it.

Yankovich was not easily pacified.

When the crisis team reassembled in the Oval Office, the national security adviser announced that he had received a call from the Chinese ambassador. "Ambassador Teng," he related, "says that his Chairman insists on an immediate response to this new act of Soviet aggression and that the relationship between Peking and Washington will be in jeopardy failing such a response."

Milligan cut him off. "I suppose Ambassador Teng also told you that the Chinese are ready to fight to the last American soldier," he said acidly.

Yankovich ignored the Vice President. "The very least we can do," he insisted, "is to issue a statement of support for King Ahmed and order a carrier task force to sea."

"What's the news on those Cubes on the border?" the President asked.

"They seem to be staying put," Yankovich replied. "But there are reports of street demonstrations in Riyadh and Jeddah. Yemeni workers tried to storm the American embassy in Jeddah but were stopped by the Saudi police. The CIA also has something on a mutiny in one army barracks, led by a colonel who served with the Syrian peacekeeping force in Lebanon."

"Well, this doesn't sound like a foreign invasion to me." Milligan interrupted again. "Sounds like King Ahmed's getting what he had coming to him from his own people. It's the Iranian thing all over again. We wouldn't want to make the same mistakes Jimmy Carter made with the Shah. I say let's tell the CIA to get on the winning side for a change. Let's disengage from King Ahmed—fast."

Only one thing was agreed at the meeting: President Connor would issue a bland statement that the United States had no intention of intervening in the Arabian crisis and counted on other powers to show similar restraint. Yankovich left the room fuming.

Jonah Cobb slapped him on the back and said, "You can't win 'em all."

"Jeeze," said Timmy Hicks as the meeting broke up, "Old King Ahmed's a lucky sonofabitch. Did you read about all his fancy hookers? Maybe I can get the spooks to gimme some of his phone numbers before he bites the sand."

Director Crawford had managed a watery smile. He wondered how long it would take before they started blaming the CIA for another intelligence failure. Thank God he had had the foresight to have an assessment prepared, following the collapse of the Shah, that predicted a fifty–fifty chance of a leftist coup in Saudi Arabia within two years.

Cobb followed Yankovich along the corridor. "Hey, Yank," he shouted after him. "Cheer up. It's not going to hurt us in the primaries."

Yankovich found urgent messages waiting on his desk from the Israeli, British, and Chinese ambassadors and from the head of the SDECE—the French secret service—who had arrived in Washington from Riyadh. He wondered who to call first.

Yankovich stayed in his office until after midnight. By the end of Day Two of the Arabian crisis, CIA reports had confirmed that the military revolt was spreading throughout the Hejaz and now included several American-educated princes in the Saudi royal house. Street violence in the major towns had increased dramatically. Stores selling Western goods had been looted and burned. Revolutionary messages were being broadcast from the minarets. Army and police units were panicking and were shooting at random into the crowds. King Ahmed and his immediate family had retreated to Taif, in the mountains near the Red Sea. The airports were closed. It looked like no foreign correspondents were getting in. That, he thought bitterly, would make the President happy.

5

ON DAY THREE, Yankovich was woken by the dawn arrival at his home in Chevy Chase of his friend Gideon Sharon, chief of the Mossad network in the United States. Yank was not surprised to see the Israeli. He had been a frequent traveler to Israel in his academic days, and his ties with the Israelis had become intimate since President Connor appointed him national security adviser. The Mossad preferred to talk directly with Yankovich on important issues. The Israelis' relationship with the CIA had been poor for years, ever since the abrupt dismissal of the counterintelligence chief, Nick Flower. The Israelis refused absolutely to have direct dealings with Bill Crawford. They were convinced that the CIA had been penetrated and viewed Crawford himself as a prime suspect. Though wary of some of the Israelis' conspiracy theories, Yankovich regarded much of the information they gave him as priceless.

In the wan light of the kitchen, Yank poured steaming water on the instant coffee. Gideon Sharon laid a thin file on the breakfast bar.

"I think you'll be needing this today."

Yankovich opened the cover. He found a seven-page biography of a Saudi colonel whose name he had never heard of—Colonel Mustafa. According to the Mossad dossier, Mustafa had gotten his military training in the U.S. He had been recruited by the Iraqi intelligence service on behalf of the KGB while serving with the Arab peacekeeping force in Lebanon in 1978. The Israelis had bugged Mustafa's house in Beirut and had taped conversations with

379

his Iraqi control agent. Mustafa was now the man heading the military revolt in the Hejaz.

Before Sharon slipped away, he reminded Yankovich that Israel could offer a solution to the Saudi collapse. The Israelis had contingency plans for occupying the Saudi oil fields and setting up a secure defensive perimeter, all within the space of thirty-two hours. All they needed was a green light from Washington and the pledge of strategic backup in case of attempted Soviet intervention.

Yankovich promised to take the Israeli offer up with the President at their next crisis meeting at 9:30 A.M.

The national security adviser had another date before the meeting. He stopped off at the Jefferson Hotel, where he went straight to room 408 to breakfast with another old friend from the secret world, the Count de Montrose, chief of the SDECE. The French and Israeli services, it was often said, were the only ones left in the West that behaved as if spies had a license to kill. The Count de Montrose was a giant of a man with a martial bearing and an encyclopedic memory. Montrose had been in Riyadh a few days before, and much of his information tallied with Sharon's.

"Who can we count on in Europe?" Yankovich asked the French spy chief.

"Unless you act, no one."

They spent part of their time discussing the morning's news reports. Despite the absence of Western correspondents in Saudi Arabia, there was no lack of purportedly eyewitness accounts of what was going on. They were all datelined Sanaa or Aden. The accounts were heavily loaded in favor of the Saudi revolutionaries and dwelled in graphic detail on the slaughter of the innocents by royalist troops. The *New York World* again led with a Washington-based story, this time on links between the CIA and the Saudi secret police. The bulk of the piece consisted of a telephone interview with Phil Kreps in Brussels. It did not mention that the CIA detractor had never set foot in the Middle East, or that he had left the Agency more than a decade before, or that he was a Marxist.

"Chapeau," commented the Count, with unfeigned admiration. "Hats off to Directorate A. Someone should be getting a promotion."

"Directorate A?" queried Yankovich, puzzled.

"But, *mon cher docteur,* you must know all about it. Soviet disinformation appears to be steering your country's foreign policy."

As national security adviser, Yankovich felt obliged to make a disclaimer. His heart wasn't in it.

The Day Three crisis meeting had barely begun when Yankovich's assistant burst into the Oval Office, ashen-faced, with an immediate action message.

Yank read it hastily and then said slowly, his Serbian accent almost overwhelming the English, "Mr. President, a new revolutionary government has been proclaimed in Riyadh. It appears to have decided not to abolish the monarchy, but to make a constitutional one, headed by a nephew of King Ahmed who was educated at Stanford. The new prime minister is a certain Colonel Mustafa. The government's first communiqué says that Saudi Arabia will henceforth be nonaligned and will continue to supply oil to all interested customers at a twenty percent markup. All outstanding contracts with Western firms will be reviewed. Private holdings, including those of the royal family, will be investigated."

"Where's King Ahmed?" the President demanded.

"Preparing to leave the country, sir."

Vice President Milligan looked triumphant. "I guess that answers his appeal for American troops."

There was a momentary hush in the Oval Office. Then the President looked at Crawford and said, "What do we have on this guy Mustafa?"

Crawford took off his glasses, waved them a couple of times, and put them on again. He cleared his throat and said, "I went through the files this morning, sir. Colonel Mustafa recorded an average performance at Fort Bragg. On his way home, he chalked up a few gambling debts in London. Apart from that we have no negative reports on him. There's no profile on his time with the Arab peacekeeping force in Lebanon. I guess he's one of those born-again Moslems."

Yankovich's nostrils flared. He smelled blood. Coughing to regain the President's attention, he said, "Sir, I have different information. I have reason to believe that Mustafa is a Soviet agent of influence, recruited through the Iraqis."

Milligan snorted. Crawford said, "That is not this Agency's understanding. So where'd you get it, Yank?"

The door opened and slammed shut as Timmy Hicks straggled in, late, and flopped onto a couch.

"Hey, Mr. Chief Spook," Timmy burped, impervious to the conversation that was taking place, "did ya get me those phone numbers yet?"

Yankovich leaped out of his chair and strode to the President's desk. He gripped the edge, his thumbs pointing upward. Billy Connor's foot, resting on the desk, was only inches away from his nose.

"Mr. President," he urged, "can anyone here doubt the gravity of the hour? This may be our last chance to prevent Moscow from gaining control of the world's biggest oil reservoir—the lifeblood of our friends in Europe and Japan."

"Let's stick to the point, Yank." Milligan did not let him finish. "You haven't answered the CIA director's question. Colonel Mustafa hasn't said anything anti-American. Why should we push him into Russia's arms? We did that with Castro, Ho Chi Minh, and Khomeini. What's your source for saying this guy's a Soviet agent?"

"Two friendly services, sir," said Yankovich, contemplating the sole of the President's shoe. He swiveled to face Crawford as he explained, "The Israelis and the French."

The CIA chief said, "If that's what they think, they haven't had the courtesy to tell me."

Milligan's lip curled into a sneer. "Dixieland disinformation," he pronounced.

"We never tell lies in Dixie," said Billy Connor.

"That's how the American community in Beirut used to refer to Israel," Yankovich snapped, unamused.

"Zionist propaganda, then," Timmy Hicks contributed from the couch.

382

"I don't see why we can't have the wisdom to accept that Colonel Mustafa might actually do what he says he is going to do, instead of relying on suspect undercover tidbits," Milligan intervened.

"On this point, sir," Yankovich resumed, "I have complete confidence in what the Israelis and the French have told me. I have seen Mustafa's file. In my view, the United States cannot afford to permit this man to consolidate his power."

"What other options do we have?" asked the President.

"There's a fairly easy one," said the national security adviser. He recounted the Israeli plan to occupy the oil fields. General Smith voiced enthusiastic approval.

"Insane," said Milligan. "The Israelis rushing in to prop up the crumbling feudal citadel of anti-Zionism? Tell me another. What the Israelis want is to grab the oil fields for themselves. If we help them do it, we'll have the entire Arab world against us. And what do you think the Russians are going to do in the meantime? The Soviets won't just sit on their hands."

The Secretary of State, a former Wall Street investment broker, had adopted his standard practice of keeping silent until he was clear on who was winning the argument. A Washington columnist had written of him, "Deep down, he's shallow." The President's personal secretary had just slipped in to hand him a message. Now confident that, yet again, the Vice President was about to checkmate Yankovich, the Secretary of State spoke up.

"I think this clinches it," he said. "The Soviets have just recognized the new regime in Riyadh. If we don't want to get left behind, we should follow suit immediately."

"I just wish we'd been first," said Milligan.

East Grinstead-Evreux

1

AFTER THEY HAD GOTTEN THROUGH East Grinstead, Bob Hockney had trouble following Chris Campbell's car. The taillights kept disappearing into the thick Sussex fog. Just before the village of Warbleton, Campbell swung left down a narrow side road. Hockney followed in his rented Ford Cortina.

They drove beside a high wall topped with spikes. Round a bend in the road, Hockney lost Campbell's lights again. When the road straightened, Campbell's car was gone. Hockney reversed, searching for the gap in the wall. He found it a few yards back. Campbell was waiting inside an open gate barely the width of his car. As Hockney drove onto the ragged, bumpy driveway, he glimpsed winged beasts—griffins or wyverns—on top of the stone pillars.

When they reached the courtyard, the Georgian country house seemed to be in darkness. The place looked abandoned. Weeds were sprouting from the gravel, and through the fog Hockney could see molehills on the edge of the lawn. He killed his engine and turned off the car lights, as Campbell had instructed him to do.

Campbell flashed his headlights—two shorts, one long. The prearranged signal. Before the light above the entrance came on, Hockney was startled to find his car door being opened by a stocky man in tweeds.

"Good evening, sir," said the guard.

Rural Sussex seemed an odd setting for Viktor Barisov— or rather, Vernon Barton, as they now called him. There had been many times, since their last meeting in Geneva, when Hockney had doubted that he would ever see Barisov again. He was still surprised that Campbell's superiors had agreed to his scheme to take Barisov to Washington to testify before the Senate Intelligence Committee. After all,

Barisov was the most important KGB defector the West had ever acquired, and the British had had only six months to debrief him. To milk Barisov of all his secrets would take years.

Britain's Socialist Prime Minister had been worried about the political impact of Barisov's disclosures about Soviet penetration of Western governments, including his own. What had finally persuaded him to give the clearance for Barisov to testify in Washington was the Saudi debacle. "Either we wake the Americans up," the Prime Minister had told the chief of SIS, "or we sign a security pact with the Russians, as you tell me the Germans have already secretly agreed to do."

Barisov gave Chris Campbell a warm handshake and then clasped Hockney in a bear hug. "Bob," the Russian exclaimed, "come and see my new dacha."

Hockney caught sight of Campbell turning a key in the wall beside the front door. The light above the keyhole switched from green to red.

"Just locking us in for the night," Campbell explained with a grin.

"He wants to make sure I don't slip off to visit the girls in London," said Barisov. "If we try to open any door or window while that thing is on, we'll trigger a siren, floodlights, a warning bell at the local police station, and a signal at SIS headquarters. I also have two armed guards upstairs with infrared telescopic gunsights."

"Her Majesty's Government takes care of her guests," Cambell observed.

Hockney knew there was a reason for these elaborate precautions. Campbell had told him in London that the Soviet Politburo had ordered the KGB's sinister Department V, responsible for wet operations, to kidnap or silence Barisov at whatever cost. Department V had sent a special man to London, and his instructions were to stay in Britain until the job was finished. He was using a cover name. The British had let him in, hoping that his movements would lead them to the hit squad the KGB had recruited to kill Barisov.

By the fire in the library, as Barisov poured drinks from the well-stocked bar, Hockney said, "They say that Sussex is the loveliest part of England, Viktor. Have you been enjoying yourself down here?"

"Do you want the honest answer or the diplomatic one?"

"The bottom line, as usual." Hockney glanced sideways at Campbell, who remained impassive, contemplating a tumbler of scotch.

"Well, living down here is like going to a disco and dancing all night with your mother. All I do here is answer questions and look at cows."

Hockney knew that Barisov was exaggerating. During the weekend breaks between interrogations, SIS had kept the Russian amply supplied with female company. Campbell had warned Hockney not to ask after Olga and the boys. The KGB had lured Barisov's wife back to Moscow. Olga's sister had turned up in London and given an emotional press conference, pleading for access to the defector's family. Overruling SIS objections, the British government had agreed. Olga's sister had told her that their father, having been stripped of his rank as KGB major general because of Barisov's defection, was now dying of cancer and that his last wish was to see his grandchildren. The sister even produced a picture of the old man in a hospital bed with a drip-feed in his arm. Viktor had argued that this was a standard KGB fake, but Olga had insisted on taking the boys home. Back in Moscow, she found her father in perfect health. She now wrote Barisov tear-jerking letters that the SIS carefully put on file without showing him. Barisov was not overly distressed about losing his wife; what disturbed him was the fear he would never see the boys again.

They agreed to turn in early, since Campbell had planned a 5:00 A.M. departure.

Barisov's last question was, "What happens after the testimony?"

"Fame and fortune," said Hockney. "With all the publicity you'll get, your book rights alone should be worth a million bucks."

"Steady on, you two," Campbell said as he set down his

glass on the mantelpiece. "The theory is that Viktor is going to Washington as a free agent. But let's not confuse theory with fact. Viktor is still HMG's property."

Hockney tossed and turned on his lumpy mattress. He dreamed they were all on Capitol Hill—himself, Julia, Barisov—being hunted through the basement of the Senate Office Building by a masked army of assassins. They jumped onto the miniature subway, but their pursuers caught up with them before it reached the end of the platform. They were dragged violently from the open carriage. Julia ripped one of her assailants' masks away. It was her brother. Hockney lunged at Cummings, but another man moved to intercept him. Before he could take a swing at him, Hockney was gripped from behind, his elbows pinioned . . .

"Morning tea, sir." It was the British guard, not Cummings, who spoke.

Hockney was drenched in sweat, as if he had been in a real fight.

"We're leaving in forty-five minutes, sir. Breakfast in the dining room when you're ready."

2

THE FOG was even thicker than the night before. Barisov climbed into the back seat of Campbell's car, and a guard slid in beside him. Campbell took the wheel, with a second guard next to him. A third guard rode with Hockney. Two security men in a third car that must have arrived overnight took the lead as the small convoy wound through the country lanes. The man beside Hockney had a walkie-talkie, which he used to keep in touch with the other cars.

Before they reached the first turn, barely half a mile from the house, a big orange tractor towing a hay cart drove across the narrow road in front of Campbell's car and stopped. There was no way around it. Campbell braked sharply, barely avoiding a collision. Hockney did not brake fast enough. His Cortina rammed into the back of Campbell's Rover. Glass shattered, and his headlights went out. Hockney could hardly see ahead of him.

Campbell grabbed his walkie-talkie to alert the lead car, which had driven on for a few hundred yards beyond the tractor.

"Back out," he ordered Hockney.

"We're stuck," Hockney's guard replied.

Looking over his shoulder, Hockney saw that a Land Rover had pulled up behind them. The road, bordered by a ditch and hedges on both sides, was not wide enough for him to turn.

Campbell was halfway out of his door, yelling "What the fuck are you doing?" to the tractor driver, when he was silhouetted in the glare of a floodlight. The light seemed to be mounted on the hay cart behind the tractor.

Shielding his eyes with one arm, Campbell pulled out his gun.

"You're surrounded," a voice boomed through a megaphone. "Give him up."

Campbell jumped back into his car and slammed the door.

He assumed that there were a couple of sharpshooters in the hay, and more behind both hedgerows. There was more firepower in the rear as well. If the hit men were Russian, he could take a calculated risk that they were bluffing; it was unlikely the Russians would dare to take on a British intelligence team in the heart of the English countryside. But Campbell had to assume they were hired killers—Palestinians, IRA, or London underworld—who were ready to shoot. He reasoned that their orders were to take Barisov alive, if possible. That might give him a few seconds to play with. In any case, there was really only one option.

"Eric," Campbell whispered over the walkie-talkie to the guard sitting beside Hockney. "When I say 'now,' I want you to run to the left and try to take out that floodlight."

The voice came over the megaphone again. "You have ten seconds to come out with your hands up." Hockney decided that the man behind the megaphone had a cockney accent.

"Give me a gun, Chris," Barisov pleaded over Campbell's shoulder. "Or at least one of those pills. You can't let them take me alive."

Wordless, Campbell reached for the spare automatic in the glove compartment and handed it back to Barisov.

"Now this is what we do," Campbell said quickly. "The minute Eric shoots, you, Jack"—he motioned to the guard sitting next to him on the front seat—"will jump out and draw their fire. Everyone else will jump from the right and run for the hedge. We'll try to catch up with the other car. Do you follow me, Bob?"

Hockney leaned over his guard's walkie-talkie. "Roger," he murmured.

"Your ten seconds are up," announced the voice from the megaphone. "At the count of one, we'll open fire. Ten-nine-eight . . ."

"*Now*," commanded Campbell.

Eric leaped out of Hockney's car, and emptied his magazine in the direction of the light. He was immediately answered by the chatter of machine gun fire. Hockney saw the guard fall, but as he fell, the light went out. The second guard, Jack, was already lying in the ditch, shooting into the hay, where he could see the gun flashes as the concealed hit men opened up.

Hockney flung his door open and hurled himself at the hedge. He bounced straight off it and fell into the ditch. The hedge seemed impenetrable. A few yards further up the ditch, Campbell was expertly shouldering his way through. Barisov followed at his heels, crouched low, with the third guard covering his back. Most of the shooting seemed to be happening on the other side of the cars. Hockney crawled up the ditch to the gap in the hedge that Campbell had made.

It was still dark, and the fog cut visibility to twenty or thirty feet. Now through the hedge, Campbell ran along the edge of the field, with Barisov and Hockney close behind. He physically collided with the masked man before

391

he saw him. The man tried to aim his submachine gun, but Campbell was faster. Campbell felled him with a single shot from his Walther P-38.

Campbell ticked off the moments in his mind, reckoning that it would take them twenty to thirty seconds over the rough terrain to come abreast of the third car on the other side of the hedgerow.

"Hijo de puta!" Hockney heard one of the attackers swear in Spanish, presumably hit.

Clawing his way through the hedge, Campbell saw that his mental reckoning was right. They were almost opposite the car. One of the security men was crouched in the ditch, his revolver poised. The other was still in the car, with the engine humming. All four doors of the car were open.

"Get in the car," Campbell ordered.

The car was already moving when Campbell threw himself in, after the others. He did a quick head count. Two men were missing. Eric had been shot. Jack, hopefully, was crawling his way across the fields.

"I've been onto control," the driver said. "Local police are closing in, and they're sending in the SIS."

"Tell control we're on our way to our original destination."

"I'm glad you didn't have any cyanide pills," said Barisov. "I might have taken one back there."

The driver sped through the fog as if the KGB hit squad was still on their trail. They narrowly missed a slow-moving milk truck as they turned onto the main road to the Channel coast.

"Slow down," said Campbell, cramped next to Hockney on the back seat. "We're clear. Put on some music. That might help everyone's nerves."

The driver switched on Capitol Radio, one of London's pop stations. They were playing an oldie from *Grease*, the rock film sensation of 1978.

"You're the one that I want, baby, ooh-hoo-hoo," the singer crooned.

"Well, you're not getting me," Barisov mimicked the singer's voice. "At least, not this time."

3

THE FOG had cleared a little and sunlight was struggling through as the car raced past a sign reading "Littlehampton." They came to a halt at the end of a wooden jetty. It was low tide, and Hockney did not spot the jetfoil until he got out of the car.

"There's your boat," said Campbell. "You two are on your own now."

Barisov was already on deck, his eyes level with the edge of the jetty. As Hockney lowered himself after the Russian, he shouted back at Campbell, "Not quite on our own, Chris."

"Well, this is where SIS bows out—for now. I must say, I never thought I'd see the Suez alliance revived."

The crew of the jetfoil had started the engine, and one of the security men on the jetty made ready to cast off.

As the jet engine hummed to life, Hockney yelled into the wind, "Chris! Suez alliance. What's that?"

"I think Viktor can fill you in," Campbell called back, with a crooked grin. "Once upon a time, dear boy, we Brits got together with the French and the Israelis to get rid of Nasser. That try failed, thanks to you Americans. Let's hope this one works, despite some Americans."

The car was gone long before the jetfoil had nosed its way out of the harbor. Sucking water in the front end and pumping it out the back, the jetfoil was much quieter than a hydrofoil, and was soon knifing across the Channel at 50 knots. As they forked southwest toward Arromanches, on the Normandy coast, Hockney brooded on the irony of the alliance that had made Barisov's trip to Washington possible. SIS distrusted the French SDECE because they thought it was full of double agents, and both were profoundly suspicious of the Mossad—especially when it came to dealing with the Soviet Union. One of Israel's major concerns was to get several million Jews out of Russia, so fighting the KGB was not the Mossad's principal priority. Yet SIS, the SDECE, and the Mossad had agreed to consolidate their resources to get Viktor Barisov onto Capitol Hill.

Britain's Prime Minister had taken the unprecedented step of approving a combined operation to get Barisov to Washington without the direct involvement of the CIA. But given the intimate personal relations between the SIS chiefs and the CIA over many years, there was no way that the operation could be kept secret from key Americans. The point was that the British government would deal directly with the national security adviser, not with the director of the CIA. Insofar as possible, Director Crawford was to be left in the dark.

Hence the devious three-stage plan. The British service had supplied the defector with a passport in the name of Vernon Barton, along with travel expenses, and had undertaken to ensure his security as far as the port of Littlehampton. The French SDECE had agreed to protect him between Arromanches and the air base at Evreux. With some misgivings, the European services had accepted Dr. Yankovich's advice that the Mossad was best equipped both to provide for Barisov's physical safety in the United States and to pull the right strings in Congress and the American media. An old ally of the Israelis, a Franco-Jewish entrepreneur named Cahen d'Enjeux—who had remade a dwindling family fortune by manufacturing forty-seven varieties of cocktail dips—had undertaken to provide the cross-Channel jetfoil and a Mystère-20 to fly Barisov across the Atlantic. Under normal circumstances, a Soviet defector would have been flown on the RAF plane direct to Andrews Air Force base, near Washington, to be delivered into the safekeeping of the CIA. But these were not normal circumstances.

This was why all three services, contrary to the rules, had also agreed that Hockney's presence might be useful. It would help to reinforce the cover story that Barisov was now a private citizen, working as consultant to an American author writing a major story for the *Reader's Companion.*

A couple of hours after leaving Littlehampton, Hockney and Barisov were bundled into a black Citroën waiting by the docks at Arromanches by two Frenchmen who did not introduce themselves.

When they arrived at the Evreux air base, halfway to Paris, the guard checked the car's license plate and waved them through. The Citroën drove onto the tarmac, and pulled up next to the waiting Mystère-20.

A huge man with a homburg and a bristling mustache inspected Hockney and Barisov as they emerged from the car. He stuck out his hand to the Russian.

"*Montrose. Très heureux, Monsieur Barisov.*" The French spy chief introduced himself. "What an amusing way to meet an old adversary."

"I'm glad that we're now on the same side," said Barisov in perfect French. He felt the words were not quite adequate to the extraordinary occasion. He was about to add something when a short, less courteous Frenchman marched up to the small group on the tarmac.

"Monsieur Barisov?" the new arrival asked, of no one in particular. Fixing his gaze on the Russian, he said, "I hope you're not planning to leave today. I have orders to escort you to security headquarters in Paris to discuss the murder of my colleague, Inspector Jaworski, in 1968."

"What's this?" Hockney challenged Montrose. "I thought we had everything arranged."

Montrose's first words were drowned out by the roar of a Transall transport plane taking off. The Count de Montrose bellowed to make himself audible. As the noise of the turbojets died away, his voice reverberated like that of a drill sergeant across the tarmac.

"Do I know you?" Montrose was booming at the unknown Frenchman.

"Inspector Uxkull of the DST. *A votre service.*" The inspector bobbed his head.

"Do you know who I am?"

Watching the two men, Hockney thought that if the

395

giant Montrose were to sit on top of the little DST inspector, he would be squashed flat like a goatskin.

"I have seen your photograph, monsieur. You are the director of the SDECE."

"On whose authority are you interfering with my business?"

As the two Frenchmen argued, Barisov inched his way slowly backward toward the landing steps of the plane.

"My orders came from the Minister of the Interior."

"My orders come from the President of the Republic," Montrose bluffed. "Step aside, monsieur, you have no business here."

The Count turned his back on the DST inspector, who was protesting helplessly, caught up with Barisov, and walked with him to the plane. As the Russian began to mount the gangway, Montrose said to him, "There are many things I'd like to ask you. But I'll confine myself to the one that interests my colleagues in the DST also. That pile-up on the expressway near Fontainebleau in 1968, when Jaworski was killed. You do remember, don't you?"

Barisov looked blank.

"We all know you were stationed in Paris at the time. We know you were at the house Jaworski went to visit."

The Russian remained poker-faced.

"You have just seen, Monsieur Barisov," the Count pressed, "that I have no interest whatsoever in having you charged today for some ancient crime. It is merely that, as one professional to another, this affair excites my curiosity. Am I not right in thinking that accident was a fake? A KGB fake?"

Barisov glanced from the Count's soldierly mustache to the open door of the plane at the top of the steps. Montrose guessed what was running through the Russian's mind.

"You have my word as a French officer," Montrose persisted. "All debts are canceled."

"I think you know it was us," Barisov conceded, mounting another step.

"Yes, yes," said the Count, impatiently. "But was it you personally?"

Barisov nodded. He was almost inside the plane.

"Most extraordinary." The Count put his foot on the first step. "I have never heard of a Soviet officer of your rank who executed wet operations in person. I had also been led to believe that contracts of this kind are issued only at the highest political level in Moscow."

Hockney climbed briskly past the Count to join Barisov at the top of the gangway. Montrose rose another step, as if about to follow.

"What you say is generally true," Barisov said, volunteering the minimum amount of information. "The occasion you mention was unusual. An emergency."

Montrose peered upward, into the assassin's face. It remained expressionless.

"Chapeau," said the Count. "A professional job. A pity you can't stay a few days with us here." He paused, as if about to urge the point. *"Bonne chance en Amérique,"* he said at last, wistfully.

When they were strapped in, Hockney said, "So you did kill people yourself."

Barisov gave the same nod. "Unlike newspaper work," the Russian observed, "my former profession was not a spectator sport."

It was the first time that Hockney had flown on a private plane. Cahen d'Enjeux's cocktail dips had enabled him to fit out his Mystère in the style of an oil shiek. There were two beds with fresh sheets, turned down ready for the night. There was a big TV screen with a library of video cassettes, including most of the James Bond films. While the Mossad guard who doubled as steward was serving Hockney and Barisov with smoked salmon and champagne, they agreed to put on *The Spy Who Loved Me.* They went to bed after the refueling stop at Shannon. Six hours later, as the plane cruised over snow-covered Maine, Boston harbor, and Long Island, Hockney pointed out the sights enthusiastically to Barisov, forgetting that the Russian had once been a KGB officer in America. When they landed at Newark, New Jersey, Gideon Sharon was waiting with an immigration officer.

Barisov seemed less than pleased with the safe house Sharon had found for him. It was a log cabin on a brackish creek that flowed into Chesapeake Bay, half a mile off a country road.

"After Sussex, I thought I might get a chance to see the bright lights," he complained, half-joking.

"I'm more concerned about keeping you alive," Sharon said, unsmiling.

The nearest small community was four miles away. The area was heavily wooded. The house was accessible only along a single, narrow dirt strip—or by water.

"Don't go wandering off into the woods," Sharon warned. "They're laced with trip wires, and there are booby traps close to the house, although we're more likely to catch foxes with them than men."

Washington

1

DR. MILORAD YANKOVICH, the national security adviser, was suffering from a weak disk. He was writing in longhand at a standup desk. Jonah Cobb had advised him to try pushups. Yankovich replied that the President's own doctor had counseled that that would be the worst possible treatment. "Yeah," said Cobb, "but did he tell you to try it with someone underneath?"

Yankovich, the former professor, still preferred to rough out his ideas on really important issues laboriously, by hand, before dictating. He was working on a draft of PRM-93, a presidential review memorandum that addressed itself to the changed strategic equation following the fall of Saudi Arabia and the creation of an independent Palestinian state in Kuwait. Yankovich's prime purpose was to produce some devastating arguments against the signing of the SALT IV treaty with Moscow, which was now almost in the bag. The treaty provided for the withdrawal of half the U.S. theater nuclear weapons deployed in Western Europe, in return for insignificant cuts in Soviet forces stationed in Poland and East Germany. The conservative swing in Congress since the midterm elections made it unlikely that the administration would get the SALT IV treaty through the Senate. But Yankovich knew that the mere knowledge that President Connor was ready to jettison vital European interests, following the abandonment of pro-American governments elsewhere, had placed seismic strain on America's remaining alliances.

Yank had found little support for his assessment in the East Coast editorials. That morning, the *New York World* had run a page-length editorial entitled "Moscow's Migraine." The piece argued that by getting involved all over the globe the Russians were creating more problems for themselves than they could handle, and that the wisest course for the United States would be to stand aside and let them create their own Vietnams. According to the *World*'s editorial writer, Soviet expansion in the Gulf would stoke up the Moslem problem inside the USSR, where centrifugal forces would eventually prevail. The Soviet leadership was depicted as a team of tired chess players who were used to concentrating on only one game at a time and were bound to be outsmarted on most of the boards they had rashly occupied.

In preparing his assessments for the President, Yankovich was well aware that he was debating with the media more than with his colleagues. An article in the *New York World* was accorded infinitely more respect in the Connor White House than a memo from the National Security Council. It seemed to be the view of Billy Connor and his Mississippi Mafia that if something wasn't reported in the major East Coast dailies, it hadn't happened. Yankovich often wished he had developed Vice President Milligan's talent for selective leakage, which had been such a formidable bureaucratic weapon throughout the White House in-fighting.

Yankovich began to list the most dangerous effects of America's acceptance of strategic inferiority:

1 The Soviets' capacity to seize critical areas under the umbrella of nuclear blackmail.
2 A West German move to withdraw from NATO's integrated command structure within the next three months. The French secret service had obtained a copy of a draft of a nonaggression pact between Moscow and Bonn.
3 Secret exchanges between Moscow and Peking, following repeated Chinese warnings to Washington about the dangers of acquiescence to Soviet strategic designs—all of which had been dismissed by the Connor administration.

Yankovich paused, considering how to say it all in language that President Connor could instantly grasp. People want to be on the winning side. Yes, that about summed it up. Even your best friends will drop you if you look like a loser. Yes, but the words lacked the dignity required for a presidential review memorandum—and for future historians. Yankovich did not want what might be his terminal philippic against the Soviet threat to be read, decades later, as an example of linguistic decadence.

Yank's secretary came on the intercom. "Mr. Crawford on the line."

Yankovich was shocked by the CIA director's tone and vocabulary. Normally soft-spoken to the point of being inaudible, Crawford sounded almost apoplectic with rage.

"Barisov!" Crawford yelled. It was the only word that Yankovich could make out apart from a stream of expletives.

"Now slow down, Bill," Yank soothed. "What's your problem? And who is Barisov?"

"Don't give me that shit, Yank. You know fucking well who he is."

"Oh. You mean that Russian defector in Britain?"

"Not in Britain, Yank. Right here. In the United States."

Yankovich flipped a switch and started recording the conversation. Tapes were strictly forbidden under the rules of the Connor White House, but he sensed that this could be a case of what was known in Washington parlance as CYA—cover your ass.

"Where is Barisov? Is he here in Washington?"

"We don't know. I thought maybe you might, Yank. The CIA has not been consulted."

"Isn't that a little unusual? I thought the British were our friends. What does SIS tell you?"

"They say he's a free agent and was last seen in France, on his way to consultations with the SDECE."

"What do the French say?"

"They say they never saw him, and referred us to the Mossad. That's why I'm calling you."

Yankovich ignored the innuendo. "Sounds like another American intelligence failure to me. Can't the FBI help you out?"

The question was barbed. Yankovich knew that Crawford and the FBI chief, a former federal circuit judge named Joe Hawkins—universally known as the Judge—hated each other's guts.

"If they know something, they aren't talking to me," Crawford admitted. "I suppose you'll never guess why Barisov's over here," he continued, sarcasm dripping from his voice.

"Not a clue."

"He's being groomed to appear at the Senate Intelligence Committee hearings that wild Irishman O'Reilly has set up."

"Well, if Barisov's role in the KGB was as important as I've been told, he should be able to make a distinctly positive contribution," said Yank in a professional tone.

"I don't know whether you would call it positive to have some Russian defector who has not been checked by the CIA shooting his mouth off about alleged Soviet agents in this administration before a Senate committee. The whole thing stinks of disinformation."

"I still can't figure out why you weren't allowed to get your teeth into Barisov after the British were finished with him. Does this mean the friendly services aren't quite so friendly? Who's supposed to be handling the Russian over here?"

"I can tell you who's been coaching him for his Senate debut. Nick Flower—that demented right-wing psychopath who used to tell us every Soviet defector was a plant. Now he accepts this one, without CIA screening, because Barisov is saying what he wants to hear. He thinks he can use Barisov to screw his old bureaucratic enemies."

The vicious feud that had raged between Crawford and Nick Flower before Flower was sacked from the CIA, as a result of Hockney's exposure of his illegal mail intercept program, was no secret in the White House. Even with Flower in retirement, Crawford was convinced that his old opponent was waging covert warfare against him.

"I think we should keep personal feuds out of this, Bill," Yankovich said in his silkiest voice, knowing it would goad Crawford even further. "But I'm fascinated that you've made a connection with Nick Flower. If you know about that, you must surely know where Barisov is hiding out. By the way, how did you find out about Flower?"

"Uh—routine surveillance."

"You mean bugging."

"Uh—"

"I hope you got a court order." Yankovich twisted the knife. "But tell me, Bill, if you've been bugging your old friend Flower, how come you couldn't tail him to the Russians?"

"Our former chief of counterintelligence may have retired some years back, but he hasn't forgotten his craft. Even in downtown Washington, he seems to change taxis every few blocks."

Crawford had also been reading intercepts of Flower's transatlantic phone calls. For a retired man, Flower kept in remarkably close touch with top-level contacts in Western secret services.

"Bill, I'd love to listen to you talk all day about these occult vendettas within the spy world, but I've got something more pressing to prepare for the President. So what do you expect me to do about all this?"

"You could begin by telling your Israeli friends that unless we get a first crack at Barisov, I'm going to go before the Senate Intelligence Committee in person and testify that he is a Soviet deception agent who is being used to discredit the American administration after suckering the Europeans."

"There's just one small hole in that, Bill."

"What's that?"

"I find it hard to think of one good reason why the Soviets should busy themselves trying to discredit this administration."

Crawford sucked in his breath. "I'm going to have to make a full report of this conversation to the President," he said.

"Help yourself."

Yankovich hung up. It had been imprudent to push the CIA director as far as he had done, but he was pleased he had. It was now an open race to see who would draw first blood. Crawford held most of the cards. But Yank's friends held Barisov. He returned to the standup desk and the problem of finding a more felicitous way to explain to the President that people don't like to be on the losing side.

Yankovich had still not found the right phrasing when Perry Cummings, his deputy, stuck his head in the door.

"I hear Crawford called you," Cummings said. "I've been getting flak from Langley all morning."

"What's the problem?" asked Yankovich, noncommittal.

"Oh, this Soviet defector, Barisov. Crawford's now on the blower to the President. And he had a long breakfast meeting with the Vice President on the same subject. Ed Milligan called me personally to mention that."

Yankovich grimaced. His young, cocksure deputy was always dropping the Vice President's name to reinforce his position. Cummings was Milligan's favorite protégé in the Connor administration. Yankovich had strenuously opposed his appointment as deputy director of the NSC, especially after he was informed that the FBI opposed the choice on security grounds. When he called for specifics, however, he was told that the FBI file on Perry Cummings had been destroyed by court order because the information it contained had been obtained illegally. He had not dared raise the matter with Cummings for fear of laying himself open to the charge of witchhunting.

It was all the more surprising, therefore, that over the past few months Cummings had frequently sided with Yankovich in interagency disputes. But come to think of it, Yank reflected, whenever Cummings backed his hard-line positions, he somehow knew that his boss was going to lose.

"So?" Yankovich challenged his young deputy.

"So the Vice President feels strongly that, until we know what this Russian is planning to say to the Senate Intelligence Committee, we should try to keep him on ice. I'm sure we still have enough friends on the committee to do that."

"But he could still blab to the press." Yankovich instantly regretted saying that, since it could provide a clue to the link he had recently established with Robert Hockney, the reporter he remembered dimly as one of his brighter students at Berkeley. Yankovich remained astonished by the activist role that a journalist was playing in what promised to be the biggest crisis between the Connor Administration and Moscow.

"Oh," said Cummings airily, "we can cope with the media. No problem. What we need is to get hold of this defector now. Once we get him into the hands of the CIA, we can stonewall indefinitely. These debriefings often take a couple of years. Think of Nosenko. That took three years, and in the end no one could decide whether to believe the guy or not."

Yankovich eyed his snappily dressed deputy, wondering why a tailored suit looked immaculate on Cummings, but as if the seams were about to burst on him. Cummings's intervention brought it home to him that he was facing a possibly unbeatable coalition. The Vice President. The director of the CIA. His own deputy. Senator Harmon. The Secretary of State. And all their media and congressional friends. All had their own reasons for wanting to see Barisov's testimony spiked. And, to judge by Crawford's phone call, Yankovich had already been identified unfairly, perhaps, as one of the men responsible for smuggling Barisov into the United States.

When Bob Hockney had approached him with his secret proposal for bringing the Russian to Washington, Yank had listened to the highlights of what Barisov intended to say to the Senate and then put Hockney in touch with Gideon Sharon. In different times, the exchange might have been considered tantamount to treason. But Yankovich believed he was fully justified. Still, for the sake of bringing the whole plan to fruition, Yankovich knew he had at all costs to avoid overidentification with Senator O'Reilly's gathering campaign. He risked losing his job either way. But if Barisov were blown, the national security adviser knew he could spend several years in jail on charges of conspiring with foreign intelligence services against the CIA.

He thought back for a second to that day in Sproul Plaza when Hockney had helped his former professor avoid an angry mob of antiwar demonstrators. Whatever positions he had adopted, Hockney had always shown guts. It was now up to Yankovich to do the same.

"I have complete confidence in your ability to arrange whatever may be necessary," Yankovich said to his deputy. And left it at that.

The Foundation for Progressive Reform held its war council in the Merchant family house on Cathedral Avenue, just above Georgetown. Alexia had inherited the big graystone mansion when her grandfather died the year before. It had the warm opulence of old wealth—even though the late Vladimir Merchant's fortune dated only from 1939.

The meeting was confined to the inner circle of FPR and its most influential alumni: Alexia herself, Perry Cummings, Rick Adams—whose longstanding friendship with Castro had not prevented him from becoming chief of staff to the Senate Intelligence Committee as Senator Harmon's top aide—and Hyde Lewis, deputy director of the Arms Control Agency, who had prepared a doctoral thesis at Cambridge on the wartime powers of the presidency. Adams and Senator Harmon's man were generally recognized as among the ten most powerful staffers on Capitol Hill—part of an army of 18,500 nonelected bureaucrats who had more influence on legislation than their supposed bosses. Over the past ten years, Adams had been the key liaison man not only between Congress and the Foundation but also between leading Democratic senators and radical regimes abroad, especially Cuba. He had made no less than eight visits to Havana, sometimes as escort for Harmon and other congressional figures.

For security reasons, Alexia had asked her guests to come by taxi and to stop at least a block away.

Rick Adams kicked off the meeting. "I've met him," he announced.

"How'd you manage it?" Alexia asked. A cigarette ash

407

toppled over her black knit dress, and she brushed it carefully from her breasts.

"Simple," said Adams. "We told O'Reilly there was no way that Barisov would be allowed to appear at the committee's public hearings unless key staffers were permitted to interview him first."

"Did you find out what he intends to say?" demanded Hyde Lewis, visibly anxious.

"It doesn't look as bad as we'd feared," Adams replied. "Barisov wants to deliver some long dissertation on Soviet deception techniques in the Western media."

"Was he leveling with you?" Alexia probed.

"Hard to say."

"I say no," Perry Cummings intervened. Everyone hung on his next words. But they took the form of a question. "Where'd you meet Barisov?" he asked Adams.

"In a hotel room at the Watergate."

"Did you follow him after the meeting?"

"Couldn't. We tried to tail him, but he was well covered. Our car was spotted, and bracketed by two other cars. We couldn't get out until he was well away."

"It doesn't matter," said Cummings. "I can tell you where Viktor Barisov is staying."

The others leaned forward in their chairs simultaneously.

"How'd you find him, Perry?" Alexia asked, admiringly.

"A friend called from the National Press Club. Guess who's in town? Our old buddy Bob Hockney. Since that piece Hockney published in the *Reader's Companion*, it wasn't hard to put two and two together. I figured that if Hockney was here, he had to be in touch with the Russian. Anyway, I thought it would be a nice idea to ask the CIA to do our job for us. I called Bill Crawford and suggested that he put Bob Hockney under round-the-clock surveillance. Get this. At first Crawford said it would be illegal. So he called in a private detective agency. We tracked Hockney's rented car to a secluded spot on the Maryland shore. There's plenty of security around. The detectives couldn't get to within a mile of the place. Crawford said he can't swear to it, but he'd bet the Israelis have taken over."

Alexia Merchant flushed. "Zionists," she muttered.

2

THERE WAS STANDING ROOM ONLY as the senators filed into the committee room. The front-page story in the *New York World* that morning, by Peter Lawry, the Washington bureau chief, had guaranteed total media coverage for the testimony of Viktor Barisov, alias Vernon Barton. Bill Crawford had testified in the O'Reilly Committee's public hearings on American intelligence failures the day before. The *World* had run Crawford's stunning allegation—that the KGB had sent a phony defector to Washington in an attempt to discredit key figures in the Connor administration—as its lead story. Crawford had given Barisov's real name, and the *World* carried an old picture of the defector from CIA files. But its main picture showed the scene in the Senate committee room as the excitable O'Reilly shook his fist at the CIA director after Crawford had charged that it was "frivolous" for the Senate Intelligence Committee to provide a platform for a former Soviet spy who had not been vetted by the Agency. Crawford warned that Barisov's appearance was designed to sow confusion and to convince America's friends and allies that the Connor administration was unreliable. Senator O'Reilly had commented acidly that there was little the committee's hearings could do to heighten these perceptions.

Pete Lawry's story claimed that, following Crawford's allegations, Senator Frank Mahee, the junior Democrat from California, had moved that the committee reverse its earlier vote to allow Barisov to testify in public hearings. Mahee was quoted as saying, "O'Reilly is a publicity seeker who is using this committee to promote his presidential aspirations."

The other main news story in the papers was about a new exodus of boat people from Vietnam. Under the leadership of a former South Vietnamese ranger captain, a group of refugees had managed to hijack a merchant freighter and were heading toward Hong Kong.

Almost a hundred reporters were jammed into an area of the Senate Caucus Room designed for half that number. Bob Hockney acknowledged the frosty greetings from the *World*'s bureau chief. He knew there were rumors all over town that he had traveled with Barisov; he was relieved that none of the reporters asked him questions. He kept himself busy and avoided conversation with his colleagues by jotting down the great historical hearings that had taken place in the Caucus Room—the Teapot Dome scandal . . . McCarthy's inquisition . . . Watergate. As he looked up at the ornate chandeliers and high ceilings supported by massive columns, Hockney also remembered that this was where two of his idols as a teenager—Jack and Bobby Kennedy—had announced their candidacy for the presidency.

He winked at Julia, who was sitting in one of the seats behind O'Reilly. Steadying the thick manila folder on her knee, she brought her hand to her lips and blew him an imperceptible kiss.

At two seconds after ten, there was a whir of camera motors as the photographers shot entire film rolls of Barisov being shoehorned into the committee room by Senate security guards. Behind him came a crush of newsmen who had been lying in wait at the entrance to the Russell Building and had dogged him all the way up to the Caucus Room on the third floor.

Hockney could make out the purple welt on one side of Barisov's face; his left arm was in a sling.

"What happened to your arm?" someone shouted.

"No comment," rasped Barisov's counsel, a flamboyant trial lawyer named Leroy Schein, who had lost only three cases in his twenty-five-year career. With earnings running into seven figures, Schein had agreed to act as counsel for the defector for a token fee of one dollar: he knew the TV publicity alone would be worth millions to him. Moreover, a man of his prominence in the United Jewish Appeal did not refuse a favor to the Mossad man, Gideon Sharon.

Even under O'Reilly's colorful chairmanship, it was hard

to get much drama into the first twenty minutes of the committee hearings. Only one thing struck an unusual chord in the exchange of routine introductions.

Looking toward the witness table where Barisov was seated beside his counsel, O'Reilly said, "We had agreed to protect your identity under the pseudonym of Vernon Barton. In view of this morning's media publicity, I think we should dispense with that fiction. Welcome, Colonel Barisov."

"Ex-colonel," Barisov breathed into the microphone in front of him.

"Point of order, Mr. Chairman," Senator Mahee interjected. "In light of the testimony of Director Crawford yesterday, we have not established the bona fides of this witness. I move that we suspend these hearings and turn the witness over to the Central Intelligence Agency for further investigation."

There was a murmur of approval from a section of the audience, some two hundred strong, among which Hockney recognized several faces from the Foundation. Rick Adams, the committee's chief staffer, who was sitting just behind O'Reilly, looked triumphant.

"Send him back to Moscow, where he belongs," someone yelled.

O'Reilly banged his gavel for silence and ordered the Senate security men to remove the heckler, who let out a stream of invective as he was lifted bodily and carried out.

"Mr. Chairman," Barisov's counsel spoke up. "I wish to point out that neither this committee nor the CIA has any jurisdiction over my client, who is now a British citizen, traveling on a British passport, with a valid U.S. visa."

"Thank you, Mr. Schein," said O'Reilly. "I trust the gentleman from California will wait to hear Colonel Barisov's prepared statement before raising any further points of order."

Barisov opened a blue folder and lifted the top sheet. The TV cameras zoomed in on him. The paper trembled gently in his hands.

"I am Viktor Barisov," he began to read. "I was an

officer of the Committee of State Security, the KGB, for twenty-eight years. For seven years, I served as deputy director of Directorate A, which is responsible for deception operations against Western countries. As a junior officer, I served in Accra, Ghana. I held later foreign posts in Paris, Washington, and Geneva. I served in Washington under the cover of embassy counselor. I reported directly to Kramar, the heart and brains of Moscow Center. Through my position and my family connections, I have had access to a great deal of information on Soviet agents of influence in politics and in the media. I am prepared to reveal to this committee the identities of key Soviet agents who have achieved positions of influence in Washington."

At the other end of Pennsylvania Avenue, Yankovich and his deputy, Perry Cummings, were standing in front of the TV set in the national security adviser's office. Yankovich glanced sideways at Cummings without moving his head.

"Can you believe this is happening?" Cummings burst out as the defector announced his intention to name names.

Yank shook his head. "No, I can't." He wondered how much Cummings had to fear, remembering those mysteriously sanitized security files on his deputy. If the Barisov thing came off, Yank reflected, it would bring down the Connor administration, himself included. If it failed to come off, it would bring only him down. Either way, there was no profit in it for him personally. But the country stood to gain.

Back in the Caucus Room, Barisov began to outline some of the main themes of Soviet disinformation. "The primary function of Directorate A," he explained, "is to deceive Western governments, and the Western public, about the real intentions of the Soviet Union. That was our essential brief. You must understand that, unlike you, we have a totally controlled press in the Soviet Union; even weather reports are subject to censorship. The Soviet leadership recognized many years ago that this gave them a decisive advantage in promoting their goals against an opponent who is inhibited, at every turn, by media criticism. The role of Soviet disinformation has been to anesthetize Western opinion into accepting our policies, while at the same time casting doubt and discredit on your own policies. Our success is apparent from the many speeches and articles appearing in the West that depict Soviet objectives as precisely the opposite of what they really are. Unrelenting conflict between East and West is a permanent premise of Soviet thought—that is, until the Soviet Union triumphs in the international class struggle. Yet we have helped to create such a mood of wishful thinking in the West that anyone who draws attention to our real objectives is quickly dismissed as a cold-warrior."

"Nothing new in this shit," a wire service reporter sitting behind Hockney complained audibly. "Sounds like one of those old sour grapes interviews that Kissinger gave after he lost his grip. I thought the guy was going to name names." Most of the newsmen stopped taking notes.

Rick Adams stretched out his arms and yawned theatrically. A network producer spotted the yawn from his control booth and switched the picture on the viewers' TV screens from Barisov to Rick Adams.

Barisov's counsel poured him some water, and he went on with his prepared statement. Ostentatiously, Senator Mahee picked up the *New York World* and started rustling the pages. Once again, the TV cameras zoomed in on an image of bored disinterest.

"When I worked for Directorate A," Barisov resumed, "I was part of the team that decided that we should hammer away at the following themes until they became conventional wisdom for the Western media. That our military buildup was inspired by the fear of encirclement by China. That a military conflict between Russia and America is unthinkable for either side, since there could be no winners in a nuclear exchange—when, in fact, our strategic doctrine has always maintained that it is possible to fight and win a thermonuclear war. That it is morally unacceptable for a democracy to tolerate covert intelligence operations."

Hockney had begun to worry that Barisov was losing his audience. Much of what the defector was saying could easily be dismissed by his media colleagues as cold war rhetoric, even though it came from a KGB renegade. Many of the spectators were openly chatting among themselves.

Sensing the need to recapture attention, Barisov looked up from his written text. "I suppose that many of you will question how it is possible for the KGB to get such things into print," he said. "Let me give you a few specific examples. The name of Laurie Pritchard is known to many of you. In fact, I saw a long article by him in one of your newspapers only this week, justifying Vietnam's support for Communist guerrillas in Thailand. That article identified Pritchard only as an Australian journalist living in Paris. In fact, he has been a lifelong Soviet agent, and has been openly identified as such by a previous KGB defector. Despite that, he has shown remarkable durability. His output—or rather, that of his ghost writers—continues to be phenomenal, and he has no difficulty in getting his books and articles printed. If Pritchard, who has been publicly identified as a KGB agent, can achieve this, it is not difficult for you to imagine how easy it is for our dozens of media assets who have remained under deep cover all over the Western world."

"Oh, Pritchard," Hockney heard the *World*'s Peter Lawry say to someone beside him. "That old fart's been pushing the party line for years. If that's all he's got, we've got no story."

"Pritchard's that guy who used to run the escort service to Hanoi during the Vietnam war," said another reporter. "Yeah, he's old hat."

Hockney thought of the first time he had laid eyes on Tessa, at the New York fund-raising party at which she had arrived fresh from a Hanoi junket hosted by the veteran Australian Communist Laurie Pritchard. Hockney had been outraged to read a piece by Pritchard on the op-ed page of that morning's *World* that identified him as a "liberal Australian journalist living in Paris." Hockey swiveled on his seat and was about to say "Stick around" to the restive reporters. He thought better of it.

"Permit me to cite a more recent example of Directorate A operations," Barisov continued. "You all know the name of Phil Kreps, a former CIA officer."

There was a collective groan from the reporters' desks. Mahee noisily turned another page of the *New York World*.

Several spectators started chatting loudly among themselves. Chairman O'Reilly gaveled for silence. Counsel Schein, putting one hand over the microphone, whispered into Barisov's ear, urging him to ignore the attempt to psyche him.

Barisov took another gulp of water, and plunged on. "Phil Kreps," he said, "has been the source of some of the most damaging allegations against the CIA. But I have first-hand knowledge that he has been a KGB agent, controlled via the Cubans, for at least fifteen years."

He paused for effect. "Phil Kreps's career," he continued, "like that of many other Soviet disinformation agents in the United States, has been greatly facilitated by an organization in Washington called the Foundation for Progressive Reform. This institute was created under the auspices of the KGB. Its founder-president, Mr. Vladimir Merchant, was one of the main conduits for covert Soviet funding in the United States. How do you describe that over here? Laundered money?"

The audience was now completely silent. Rick Adams loosened his collar, scribbled a note on a pad, ripped it off, and passed it along to Senator Mahee.

After glancing at the note, Mahee raised his hand and said, "Point of order, Mr. Chairman."

"I am not aware of any point of order," said O'Reilly.

"Mr. Phil Kreps, the subject of a grave accusation by this so-called defector, is due to appear before this committee in the near future," Mahee stated. "This is an attempt to discredit another committee witness before he is given the chance of a fair hearing. Furthermore, aspersions have been cast on the good name of the Foundation for Progressive Reform, a body which I and many of my colleagues in this house view with the highest respect."

"That point of order is out of order," O'Reilly snapped. "You may proceed, Colonel Barisov."

"The Foundation for Progressive Reform," explained Barisov, "was organized along lines similar to the Institute of Pacific Relations, which was the hub of a Soviet espionage network in Washington back in the nineteen-forties. However, the range of operations of the new Foundation soon exceeded by far whatever we might have expected of the earlier version. Under careful management, the Foundation became the controlling center for a network of Soviet agents of influence who fanned out into Congress, the media, the academic world, and even the White House. Many of those agents are in prominent positions today."

"Scurrilous," Senator Mahee exclaimed. "What are you trying to do," he directed his shaft at O'Reilly, "revive the McCarthy hearings?"

O'Reilly adjusted his leonine head to catch the best camera angle and raised his gavel as the audience erupted into a general brouhaha.

"I think we should have the decency," O'Reilly said, "to give Colonel Barisov the courtesy of a proper hearing."

"I'll second that," said Luther Bolt, the black Republican senator from South Carolina.

"I would remind you," O'Reilly boomed above the uproar, "that we are privileged to have present today a man who has risked his life to tell us what his former colleagues are plotting against us. There have been three known assassination attempts against Colonel Barisov since he made his escape to the West. One of them took place yesterday. It was clearly intended to prevent him from testifying before this committee. I do not intend to allow anyone in this room to silence what an assassin's bullet could not."

"Irish blarney," Mahee muttered, and went back to reading his newspaper.

Over at the White House, Cummings told Yankovich he was going to the bathroom. While the networks' live coverage of the Barisov testimony was interrupted for a commercial break, Cummings slipped into his office and phoned the Vice President.

"It's serious. Looks as if Barisov's about ready to name names," Cummings said to Milligan without ceremony. He assumed that the Vice President, like most other people in the White House, had been watching the hearings on TV.

416

"It can be contained," the Vice President assured him. "Frank Mahee has gone for the jugular already. The media have got O'Reilly's number. They think he's just out for publicity. Stay cool, Perry. The editorials will be on our side tomorrow."

"I hope you're right." The receiver in Cummings's hand was damp with sweat as he put it down.

In the Caucus Room, Rick Adams was passing the latest in a series of scribbled notes to Mahee.

"Colonel Barisov?" O'Reilly queried.

"That concludes my prepared statement, Mr. Chairman."

"We are indebted to you, sir. Questions."

The slack-jawed senior Democratic senator from Wyoming was first. He read his question from one of Rick Adams's notes that Mahee had passed along to him.

"Mr.—uh—Barisov," he started. "I find your allegations so preposterous that I would like to know what documents you have brought to substantiate them."

There was scattered applause from some members of the audience.

Barisov consulted his counsel. Leroy Schein again covered the microphone with his hand.

"You must understand," said Barisov, "that I defected from the Geneva station in a hurry, and that I did not have access there to the files of Moscow Center."

"In other words, you have no evidence," the Wyoming senator pursued.

"With due respect, sir," said Barisov, "I would have thought that my personal experience as a senior KGB officer rated as important evidence. But if you are asking for documentary proof, I can say that I was able to bring a few interesting pieces of paper with me. One of them is a copy of a memorandum of a conversation I had in Washington several years ago with a man who is now a senior official of the National Security Council staff. At the time this memorandum was composed, I was serving as this man's KGB case officer. I have further documents relating to media operations organized through Phil Kreps."

Rick Adams stooped behind O'Reilly, whispering into his ear. The committee chairman looked ready to swat the staff director like a fly.

Down the other end of Pennsylvania Avenue, the White House switchboard lit up like a Christmas tree. The battery of secretaries who worked for Sam Cody, President Connor's press assistant, could not cope with the swarm of reporters who were calling in from all over the country, demanding instant comment on the Barisov testimony to date. Phyllis, the veteran senior White House switchboard operator, got so fed up with the stream of abuse that she connected two irate callers and let them howl at each other.

Sam Cody declined official comment, pending the end of the day's hearings.

In the Caucus Room, it was Senator Mahee's turn to interrogate the witness.

"Why have you refused to be interrogated by the CIA?" Mahee challenged.

Barisov's counsel intervened. "There is no reason why Mr. Barisov should respond to that question," said Schein. "Members of this committee are already aware that he has been thoroughly vetted by Allied intelligence services, and that his bona fides are not in doubt. The ground rules for his appearance here were fully understood by the committee staff."

Rick Adams passed another note to Mahee. The Senator read it and nodded.

"Is it not true, Mr. Barisov," said Mahee, his voice rising accusingly, "that foreign intelligence services arranged for your trip to the United States, and that you are still under their control? *At this very moment.*" He underlined his accusation.

Schein, guarding his mouth with his hand, whispered into Barisov's ear.

O'Reilly spoke, his voice like thunder. "I would be grateful if the gentleman from California would cease wasting the time of this committee by reopening questions that have already been resolved."

418

"I am reopening this question, Mr. Chairman," Mahee countered, "because I have been informed that Mr. Barisov is under the control of the Israeli secret service. My information comes from none other than the director of the CIA. Now it is well known that the Israelis and also some of the Europeans are hostile to this administration because at long last the United States has accepted the new realities of the world situation and is liberated from its inordinate fear of communism. What concerns me is that Mr. Barisov, who is described as a specialist in deception, has been deployed here by foreign secret services to deceive us."

Mahee beamed into the camera, to the applause of the claque from the Foundation in the audience.

The man from the *World* tapped Hockney's shoulder. "They seem to have your boy's number," Lawry gloated.

O'Reilly, a purple vein throbbing on his forehead, pounded the table with his gavel. "If there are any more demonstrations," he threatened, "I will have the public removed from these hearings."

"Mr. Chairman," said Barisov, "I would like to say something that may help clarify the situation. In the KGB schools today, recruits are lectured on the strengths and weaknesses of the Western intelligence services they will have to combat. For a long time, my former colleagues found it hard to believe that our main enemy, the United States, had really emasculated the CIA. When we heard that the CIA had appointed a director of public information on covert operations, we thought this must be deception, plotted by someone with a sense of humor. We were convinced that, behind the smokescreen, there must be a new, really secret CIA that we had not yet managed to identify. Today, the KGB has concluded that there is nothing behind the smokescreen except smoke. KGB trainees are now taught that the CIA is indeed emasculated, that the British SIS is a cunning old fox that has lost most of its teeth, that the French are still dangerous, and that our deadliest opponents are the Israelis."

The liberal Jewish senator from Connecticut, who had voted for S4949, the law that required the CIA to report all contacts with foreign intelligence services to Congress, shifted uncomfortably in his chair.

"Thank you for that excellent clarification, Mr. Barisov," Senator Mahee said with a flourish, his gaze fixed on one of the TV cameras. "I think what you have said has confirmed my earlier statement that foreign intelligence services are trying to revive the cold war."

O'Reilly again stepped into the breach. "Do I need to remind anyone," he said "that Colonel Barisov is being hunted by KGB killers? He would not be alive today without help from certain quarters. If we have succeeded in castrating our intelligence services, would the gentleman from California seriously blame our friends abroad for trying to do our job for us? Would he blame Colonel Barisov for entrusting his life to friends who are more reliable than we have shown ourselves to be?"

Senator Mahee waved his hand dismissively.

"The gentleman's time is up," O'Reilly announced. "The gentleman from South Carolina now has the floor."

Luther Bolt looked up from his notes. "I think it would help us get back to the theme of disinformation that Colonel Barisov is here to tell us about if he could explain how his former department might have been involved in the Saudi takeover," the Senator began.

"The Saudi collapse came after my defection from the KGB," Barisov replied, "so I cannot speak with firsthand knowledge of the part my former colleagues played there. However, I was directly involved in the Iranian revolution, and I can see that some media techniques used there were duplicated in the case of Saudi Arabia."

"I'm interested in specifics, Mr. Barisov, not generalities."

From the press area, Hockney watched the black senator intently. He felt grateful to Luther Bolt. At last, Barisov was being given an opening to explain what had almost wrecked Hockney's journalistic career. He was confirming the substance of what Hockney had had to say in his celebrated *Reader's Companion* piece—and the Russian could speak with an authority no Westerner could rival.

"As you remember," Barisov continued, "the campaign

to isolate the Shah of Iran from Western support was conducted over many years. It was masterminded by Directorate A. We succeeded in having the Shah depicted as a uniquely bloodthirsty tyrant, when in fact his regime was mild compared with some of those in neighboring countries. Since our campaign to undermine the Shah was conducted so effectively through the Western media, there was no need for us to attack him directly. On the contrary, we succeeded in maintaining the image of cordial relations until his overthrow was certain.

"The Senator has asked for specific cases. One example of how my old department may have applied the Iranian experience to Saudi Arabia is the voice-tape of King Ahmed plotting civil war with the CIA agent soon after his retreat to the mountains that has been broadcast over American networks. This recording was very similar to a voice-tape of the Shah plotting counterrevolution with his generals that was faked on my personal instructions."

"How'd you get that false tape of the Shah broadcast over the U.S. networks?" Bolt queried. The Iranian tape had been a three-day sensation in America. By the time the top voice experts had pronounced it a fraud, the damage had already been done.

"It wasn't difficult," Barisov responded. "We passed it via the Tudeh party in East Berlin to Iranian students in Texas. They gave it to a local TV station, claiming it had come from a defector from SAVAK, the Shah's secret police. The networks picked it up. The denials and disclaimers didn't bother us. It's the initial shock that shapes people's minds, not what's said afterward."

"You said you were going to name names," the black senator reminded Barisov.

"Certainly," said the Russian. "But I think I should remind the committee, Mr. Chairman, about the sheer scale of KGB deception operations. When I, uh, left my service" —Barisov, like other Russians who had fled to the West, did not like the harsh term "defected"—"Directorate A was running between five hundred and six hunded operations a year."

"That's almost two a day," Luther Bolt observed, incredulous. "Was there any overall plan within which all those operations were conceived and executed?" he asked.

"Certainly. My instructions came from Kramar in Moscow Center."

One of the committee staffers whispered in O'Reilly's ear.

"Kramar," Barisov explained, "occupied, and still occupies, a unique position inside Moscow Center. He is responsible not only for deception operations in the broadest sense—for what is called, in our official terminology, 'active measures'—but for a number of critically important penetration operations. Penetration was the core of the long-term plan for the defeat of the West that is code-named Plan Azev, after the notorious czarist double agent."

"Tell us about Plan Azev," said Senator Bolt.

"The Soviet Union has been operating on parallel tracks in its efforts to establish a position of superiority over the Western alliance. One has been the breakneck expansion of Russia's war machine. Another has been the systematic effort to deprive the West of automatic access to its sources of fuel and cheap raw materials. The latest example of this element in the overall strategy, by the way, has been the unopposed conquest of Saudi Arabia by pro-Soviet forces. A third line of endeavor has been to insinuate agents and others who are subject to Soviet control into positions of influence in Western societies, including positions in the media."

"You mean a Soviet fifth column?" Senator Bolt sought clarification.

"Something along those lines. Now, if you asked me to specify the single most important operation—in terms of both deception and penetration—in which I was personally involved during the time I was stationed in the United States, I would have to nominate the work of the Foundation for Progressive Reform, here in Washington. Through this foundation, Directorate A has been able to influence media and congressional reflexes to Soviet policy moves. It has also served as our most important recruitment base for agents of influence in Washington under the last three administrations."

"Mr. Chairman," Rick Adams shouted, breaking the rules. He calculated it was better to create pandemonium than to let Barisov continue with his testimony on live television. Adams was on his feet.

"You're out of order, Mr. Adams," O'Reilly bellowed into his microphone. "Please sit down." The second phrase was lost in the catcalls from the audience.

"Mr. Chairman," Adams shouted louder.

"Mr. Chairman," Senator Mahee chimed in.

"Mr. Chairman!" Adams brandished his fist in the air. "Several members of the staff of this committee, including myself, are associated with the Foundation."

O'Reilly gaveled like a jackhammer. "I said, you're out of order."

"Senator Harmon," Adams shrieked, unheeding, "was a founding member of the Foundation."

"Sit down or leave the Caucus Room," O'Reilly ordered.

"Mr. Chairman." Adams's voice rose a few decibels more. "The Vice President of the United States has been a patron of the Foundation since its inception. Are we going to allow an unknown Soviet agent under Zionist control to go on telling these lies to the people out there?" Adams gestured theatrically toward the TV cameras.

"Mr. Chairman." Abe Zwislocki, the liberal Jewish senator from Connecticut, spoke up for the first time. "I object to the language of this committee's staff director. I move that Mr. Adams be asked to leave these hearings."

"Seconded," snapped Luther Bolt.

"Mr. Adams," said O'Reilly. "I am giving you your final warning. Either you sit down and hold silence or you will be evicted."

Adams sat down. As he did so, the clamor from the audience subsided.

"Mr. Chairman," Luther Bolt resumed. "Do I still have the floor?"

O'Reilly nodded, mopping his brow.

"Mr. Barisov," said the black senator. "Perhaps you

423

would now inform this committee of the names of the Soviet agents in Washington who have been controlled through the Foundation."

Barisov waited until there was complete silence in the room. "Directorate A maintained direct relations with a number of associates and former associates of the Foundation, including, of course, its founder and primary funder, Vladimir Merchant. We were able to control other members of the Foundation through proxies, notably the Cubans. For example, I received frequent reports in Moscow, forwarded from the DGI station in New York, from one of our most valuable agents, code named Ricardo, who was recruited by the Cubans. He had a top security clearance and had access to all the secret materials passing through the hands of the Senate Intelligence Committee."

Rick Adams was muttering urgently into Senator Mahee's ear.

Mahee raised his arm. "Point of order, Mr. Chairman," he insisted.

"There is no point of order." O'Reilly overruled him. "The gentleman from South Carolina still has the floor."

Luther Bolt leaned into the microphone and said in a low baritone, "Mr. Barisov, who is this Ricardo who has access to the secrets of this committee?"

Smoothing the wiry gray hair at the back of his head, Bolt looked a decade younger than his fifty-five years. It was odd, Hockney reflected, that Luther Bolt should be the man with all the right questions. The grandson of a slave, a former civil rights activist who had marched with Martin Luther King, Bolt had parted company with the black caucus in Congress. This was after Andy Young had rationalized the massacre of missionaries in Rhodesia and declared that Iran's fanatical Moslem leader, Ayatollah Khomeini, was some kind of saint. "By which church?" Bolt had publicly demanded. "Not by my church." Bolt was an enthusiastic lay preacher.

"The agent code-named Ricardo," Barisov began, "is in this committee room." Arm outstretched, Barisov's finger described a slow arc from right to left. Pointing directly at Rick Adams, he said, "That is the man."

Bolt leaned forward to see who Barisov was pointing at. White-faced, Rick Adams half rose to his feet.

"You mean Mr. Adams?" Bolt demanded confirmation. Barisov nodded.

Lips trembling, Adams yelled, "You goddamn liar."

There was a hush before the audience exploded again. A wild-haired young man ran forward and tried to grab Barisov from behind. The security guards wrestled him to the floor and carried him out of the committee room.

3

PRESIDENT CONNOR watched the instant replay of the wrestling scene on the TV in the Oval Office, flanked by his closest advisers.

"We got trouble, Billy. Big trouble," Jonah Cobb observed.

"Slow down, Jonah," said Timmy Hicks. "This isn't our trouble. This is Congress eating up its own tail."

"Shut up, Timmy," the President ordered. "You don't know anything about it."

It was the first time that any of the others present had heard President Connor slap down his old crony from Mississippi. Timmy was so startled that he spilled some of the Schlitz from the can he was holding.

All heads swiveled back to the TV screen. Rich Adams was nowhere to be seen in the Caucus Room. O'Reilly was struggling to reestablish order. His gavel could barely be heard. Barisov was flattening his hair. He looked as if he had been jostled.

"This committee has not been recessed," O'Reilly was shouting. "I recognize the gentleman from Connecticut."

Senator Zwislocki, an old-line liberal who had fallen out with the radical wing of his party, could barely make himself heard above the continuing din. "More names" was the only phrase that was audible from Zwislocki's question.

Names poured out of Barisov staccato fashion, as if he were afraid of being cut off at any moment.

"Turn up the volume," the President commanded. Jonah Cobb pushed a button on the remote control and crouched down beside the TV set in the Oval Office, anxious to catch every word.

"Phil Kreps," Barisov was saying.

"He's that renegade from the CIA," Cobb reminded the President.

"Hyde Lewis, deputy director of the Arms Control Agency."

Barisov's voice was drowned out again by a barrage of insults from the public seats.

The President, mouth agape, was sitting on the edge of his chair. He had just heard a Soviet defector name the deputy director of the Arms Control Agency, one of the key negotiators in the Salt IV deal—which Billy Connor had declared to be the linchpin of his administration's foreign policy—as a KGB agent.

"Jonah," the President ordered his chief of staff, "get Yank in here."

Jonah Cobb pressed the buzzer on the President's desk.

As Yankovich hurried into the Oval Office a couple of minutes later, the President demanded, "What next? You know this Russian. Who's he going to name next?"

The TV displayed a scene of complete pandemonium. O'Reilly was struggling to restore order as impromptu demonstrators shook their fists in Barisov's direction, shouting "McCarthy" and "Fascist."

Yankovich shrugged his shoulders.

"What are we going to do?" the President pressed.

"In your shoes, Mr. President," said the national security adviser, "I would get Senator O'Reilly on the phone immediately and see whether I could make a deal. For the sake of national security, we need to have these hearings suspended."

"Ssssh," said Billy Connor. The Russian was talking again, but his words were almost inaudible above the uproar in the committee room.

"What'd he say?" demanded the President. "What was that name he gave?"

"Couldn't get it," said Cobb.

"I think Colonel Barisov named my deputy, Perry Cummings," Yankovich contributed.

A nervous titter ran around the room. Yankovich remained stonefaced. The titter stopped.

"Are you serious, Yank?" the President asked.

Yankovich nodded.

"Jonah," Billy Connor said, "try to get through to O'Reilly in the committee room. We've gotta cut this thing off at the knees."

Within minutes, the President was watching the Senator reading the note that told him the White House was on the line. So, presumably, were tens of millions of TV viewers.

O'Reilly folded the White House note and banged his gavel.

"We'll take a recess until ten o'clock tomorrow morning," the Senator announced. "In view of the systematic disruption of today's proceedings, the public will not be admitted to tomorrow's hearings."

There was general bewilderment in Washington, bordering on incredulity, after the telecast of Barisov's first string of allegations. Why, in the last quarter of the twentieth century, would Americans of prominent social and political standing agree to serve the Soviet Union, a country that had lost its ideological appeal even for most of the world's Communists? If Barisov had been an American citizen making the same allegations, he would have been instantly dismissed as a crude McCarthyite. What made it impossible to shut out what he was saying was that he was a man from the inner circle of the KGB, one of the elite corps that Kramar had selected to execute his Plan Azev. All the same, Hockney realized, the public that had been reading the same liberal columnists he himself had formerly revered for the past two decades would demand—and deserve—a lot more explanation.

Hockney had learned that it is easiest to commit treason if you do not recognize it as such. The goal of the operation directed by Kramar from Moscow Center had not been merely to recruit agents who would penetrate high positions in Western societies; it was to blind and mislead others—many others—so they would serve Soviet policy interests without being remotely aware of what they were doing. The KGB was adept, too, at recruiting under a "false flag." Rick Adams had been drawn into the net by the lure of third-world radicalism, a cause that had recovered the glamour that Soviet communism lost when Stalin's crimes became too public. Hockney wondered whether Adams had experienced any crisis of conscience when he realized that Cuba, far from representing an independent model of revolution, had been converted into a surrogate for the Russians. By the time he discovered that, Adams had probably been in too deep to extricate himself.

What was hardest to understand was why a man like Perry Cummings should consciously and cold-bloodedly enter Kramar's network. How did a potential pillar of the WASP establishment become transformed into agent Coyote? As far as Hockney—or Barisov—knew, there had been no blackmail factor. Cummings had no need for money, and little visible interest in it. His affair with Alexia Merchant might have provided an initial point of contact with Kramar's ring, but it was hard to believe that her influence had been enough, in itself, to explain Cummings's treachery.

Nor could Cummings's actions be explained by the tide of antiwar radicalism that had swept over the country in the late 1960s. Thinking back to the cropped, gray-suited Perry Cummings who had worked for the Pentagon in the years before the Tet offensive, Hockney believed that his former friend's antipathy to the antiwar demonstrators had not been feigned. Cummings was no friend of disorder. On the contrary, he might be almost a clinical case of the reverse: a man whose attraction to power and social discipline was so great that it led him to reject the values of a society that was turning its back on both and transfer his allegiance to a hostile power whose leaders ruled without self-doubt.

And then there were all the frightened men. Hockney's friends on the *World* used to discuss how Hoover's FBI had dug up dirt on the members of the director's "hate list" in order to discredit them or control their behavior. But

428

even Hoover was a novice compared with the KGB. What was clear was that somehow Kramar's people had gained access to a huge quantity of documentation on scandals involving campaign funding and sexual exploits (not only in Moscow) that had been used systematically against key opinion formers in Washington—up to and including the Vice President.

It was not until twenty minutes after O'Reilly suspended the committee hearing that his call came through to the Oval Office.

"Sure, Shame, I understand. That's okay." The President oozed charm down the receiver. His aides gathered that O'Reilly had been tied up in taking care of the Soviet defector's security arrangements as he was smuggled out of the Russell Building, past the press.

"We need a heart-to-heart, Shame," the President said. There was a long pause, while the Senator talked on the other end of the line. The President grunted intermittently.

"The Russian too?" the President exclaimed. "Is that necessary?" O'Reilly's Irish burr sounded insistent. "I wanted a one-on-one," the President continued. "You want someone else?" his aides heard him say. "What's the name? Hockney? Oh. That reporter."

The President listened to O'Reilly for a few more minutes. Finally, he grimaced and said, "Okay, we'll do it as you want."

The President hung up and explained to his aides, "O'Reilly seems to think he's moving into the White House. He refuses to see me alone. He's going to bring the Russian and that shitass reporter, Robert Hockney. He says the Russian won't go anywhere without Hockney. He even tells me that the only man on my team he'll allow to be present is you, Yank. He wants us to meet at Camp David, under maximum security wraps. He asked for a guarantee that our conversation won't be taped. The only thing he didn't ask me for is my job."

Yankovich's lips curled. It was the closest thing to a smile that the dour Yugoslav could manage.

"What are you grinning at, Yank?" demanded Connor.

"I think we may have been shown the way out of this predicament, Mr. President," replied the national security adviser.

"What are we going to do about the newsies?" asked Cobb. "Sam Cody's waiting outside."

"Okay," said the President. "Let's try to work out a press statement that will limit the damage before we take off for Camp David to meet O'Reilly and his pals."

The White House press secretary came in with the late edition of the Washington afternoon newspaper. It carried a six-column banner: "Red Spy Chief Fingers Top White House Officials."

"Don't look at me," said Timmy Hicks. No one did.

The President's personal secretary buzzed him impatiently. "Sir, the Secretary of Defense has called several times," she told him. "Mr. Hyde Lewis of the Arms Control Agency has offered his resignation. The Vice President wants to see you immediately, sir, and I have Director Crawford on hold."

"Okay," said the President, "put Crawford through. Meantime, get me the Judge."

Judge Hawkins had been appointed director of the FBI after his predecessor, the Bureau's last professional boss, had been jailed for illegal phone taps of a Marxist urban guerrilla group. In his opening press conference, the Judge, a former civil rights attorney, had declared that he intended to close a sinister chapter in American history, when Americans spied on other Americans.

The President made a point of never drinking in the Oval Office. Now he asked Jonah Cobb to bring him a bourbon and branch water. Timmy Hicks popped open another beer. Everyone in the Oval Office had a drink except Yankovich, who sidled closer to the President's desk to catch his conversation with the CIA director.

"What do we do now?" the President asked Crawford.

"We try to limit the damage." The CIA director's voice came over the line.

"How?"

"I suggest, sir, that you put out a statement reiterating my testimony of yesterday, that the Russian's motives are not what he says they are. That he is not a genuine defector."

The President swigged his bourbon. "Look, a grenade just blew up in my face and you're offering me a bandaid. In fact, it's worse than a grenade. An ICBM just hit the White House. My SALT IV negotiator just resigned after being accused by this defector of working for the Soviets. What's the public going to make of that when it gets into tomorrow's papers? The public's going to demand some sort of investigation."

"That's not the province of the CIA," Crawford said curtly.

"It does look like we're up shit creek," Timmy Hicks volunteered. "But we've still got a paddle."

"What's that?" the President snapped. Yankovich turned on his heel impatiently, expecting a standard Timmyism. He was astonished to hear the President's buddy say what he himself had been about to advise.

"Instead of denying everything, Billy-boy," Timmy suggested, "you should get the Judge to round up everyone this Bar-ee-sov named and put them under protective custody. That way, we get ahead of the pack."

The White House press secretary, Sam Cody, hovered expectantly at the door.

"Later," the President grunted.

"I gotta tell them something," Cody protested. "The entire White House press corps is waiting to be briefed. I got network presidents calling me. The owner of the *New York World* insists on talking to you personally."

"Tell him I'll get back to him."

"What about all the others?"

"Refer them to Crawford's testimony yesterday. Say we're withholding comment until the Russian's allegations can be properly checked."

President Connor's personal secretary buzzed again. "The Democratic National Committee chairman is throwing a fit," she warned him. "Senator O'Reilly's office phoned to confirm that he will be at Camp David at eight-thirty. Shall I cancel your dinner?"

The President was scheduled to attend a private dinner

with the first independent Palestinian chief of state, the Chairman of the Kuwaiti Palestinian People's Republic, who had requested U.S. military aid as a test of "the new foundations of détente" that Billy Connor was given to talking about in his foreign policy statements.

"Yeah," Connor replied. "Ask the Vice President to host the dinner. Tell the Chairman I'm suffering from the Hormuz trots."

"What's that, Mr. President?" queried his secretary, puzzled.

"Aw, forget it. Just tell him I'm not feeling well."

"I have Judge Hawkins waiting on the line."

"Put him on."

The aging judge suffered from a permanent frog in his throat that he tried to clear once or twice in every sentence. The President interrupted him in the middle of a cough. "We've got to do something right away, Judge. Crawford says it's all crap. What do you say?"

"We have no way of knowing, sir," the Judge croaked.

"Well, I want to know what you've got in your files on the people this Russian has named."

"Sir, most of our personal files have been delivered up under the Freedom of Information Act, or destroyed to avoid further prosecutions of FBI personnel for using illegal methods to gather intelligence."

"Listen, I'm under a lot of heat here," the President said, louder. "You must have something on your computers over there."

"Sir, we don't have much of an institutional memory anymore. Anyone whose file has been destroyed will have to be taken off the computer."

"I'm not sure you understand the urgency that's involved here, Judge. I need checks run on the people Barisov has named, and I need them now. I don't care how you do it, but I want those names checked out. Now do you read me?" The President was flushed with anger.

"You mean wiretaps, sir? We'll have to get a court order."

"No time for that," the President growled.

"You mean raids, house searches?"

"Yeah."

"We can't do that without a court order either, sir."

"Well, find a tame judge!"

"With all due respect, Mr. President." The Judge coughed repeatedly. "I did take an oath. You know that under the laws of this country, there is no justification for any of these measures unless we have clear evidence that the subject has committed a criminal offense. The FBI hasn't had a single request for a wiretap on security grounds in the past two years."

"So what the hell has your counterintelligence division been doing?"

There was a lull in the Oval Office while the Judge coughed uncontrollably on the other end of the line.

"Mr. President," he said at last, "we just don't have the staff to cover all the bases. Since you took office, four thousand agents have retired or been dismissed. It's almost impossible to attract good new recruits."

"Screw all that," said the President. "I want a report on the people Barisov named on my desk before midnight. Do you hear me, Judge?"

"All I can say, Mr. President, is that I do hear you. I'm not sure that the Bureau can produce anything very useful. We can try to talk to the people concerned, if they're willing to talk to us." The Judge cleared his throat again. "But I would beg to inform you, sir," he resumed, "that the executive branch no longer has the authority in these matters that it used to abuse. May I suggest that's a good thing too."

The President slammed down the receiver without saying good-by.

"Damn," said Billy Connor, pounding the desk with his fist in a rare show of emotion. "Back in the mid-seventies, people said this country was becoming a police state. Now I can't even get the FBI to investigate an espionage case."

"What it means, Mr. President," Yankovich observed, "is that you are going to have to make a deal with Senator O'Reilly."

433

4

BIG DAN MACDONALD was the last of the old guard at the FBI, one of the few top professionals who had survived the chainsaw massacres under the Carter administration. He had survived by knowing more than most of his colleagues. As a deputy director in charge of counterintelligence, he had been stripped of almost all the assets his division used to dispose of. He didn't even have the manpower to have identified KGB officers shadowed in Washington on weekends. His informants had dwindled to a handful, scared off by the risks of exposure. Capitol Hill and much of official Washington was off limits to his division. MacDonald had carefully locked up in his safe at home xerox copies of security waivers that the White House had requested for officials appointed to top positions. Those were the only things he kept in his safe.

When the FBI had started making a bonfire of its personal files, MacDonald and a couple of trusted colleagues had microfilmed as much as they could. Big Dan now believed that, given six months and the manpower his department used to have available, he could nail 1,400 Soviet agents in the United States—including people with key positions in the administration, in Congress, and in high-technology industries. While most of his contemporaries, disgusted with life under the new regime of the civil libertarians, had accepted early retirement, MacDonald had held on, hoping that his time would come again. And now it had.

Big Dan MacDonald towered, tall and wide, over the diminutive Judge Hawkins in the FBI director's office. Stooped over his desk, he seemed to shrivel up in Big Dan's presence, looking almost like a hunchback.

"I've never heard the President so upset." The Judge reported on his call from the White House. Clearing his throat a couple of times, the Judge asked, "What can you produce by midnight, Dan?"

"Well," said MacDonald, "I've got Phil Kreps's number. I had to deal with that slippery renegade in Mexico City when he took a plane to visit the Cubans. I hear Kreps is in town, waiting to testify in the O'Reilly hearings. I can handle him okay."

"What about the others? What about the deputy director of the NSC?"

MacDonald glowered at the Judge. "I saw the file on Perry Cummings before it was destroyed, Judge. He's in with the Soviets up to his neck. In fact, I'm sure it was Cummings who stole the KH-19 blueprints."

"Why wasn't I informed of this?" The FBI director coughed.

"But you were, Judge," MacDonald boomed. "For a start, Cummings was listed in a report that my division prepared for you when you were appointed to head the Bureau—a report on officials in the Connor administration who had received security waivers. In Cummings's case, the security waiver was the result of the personal intervention of Vice President Milligan."

The Judge looked horrified. "You're not suggesting that the Vice President is implicated in all this?"

MacDonald shrugged his heavy shoulders. "Listen, Judge," he said, "this isn't the time for speculation." He glanced at the clock on the wall. "We got just over three hours to carry out the President's request. Do I have a free hand?"

The Judge spread his arms helplessly.

Big Dan MacDonald nodded. "I understand, Judge. It's my neck."

He loped out of the director's office and back to his own room, six doors away. It took him five phone calls to roust out the men he needed—a dozen FBI agents, reinforced by forty men he wrestled out of the Washington police chief. He made two more calls, to old friends, recently retired from the Bureau, who had shared in the battles he had lost in previous years. He didn't want them to be left out of this one. Before leaving his office, MacDonald strapped on his favorite Browning.

"I just hope we're not too late," MacDonald said as he

ran to his car. They had lost four and a half hours since Barisov had named the first names in public. They had lost nearly seven months since the Russian had defected and the Soviets had presumably issued a general alert—plenty of time for their agents to get rid of incriminating evidence. It could now turn out to be a case of Barisov's word against that of the people he was accusing.

5

THE THREE OUTSIDERS who were ushered into the President's private quarters at Camp David at 8:30 were slow to sit down. They stood awkwardly, accusing, while Jonah Cobb fixed drinks. The President had dismissed the servants and arranged a cold buffet dinner of chicken, ham, and roast beef. Only Yankovich, uncharacteristically, seemed relaxed.

"Please sit down," President Connor urged his three unwanted visitors—Seamus O'Reilly, Viktor Barisov, and Robert Hockney.

"I got you your own brand of vodka, Colonel Barisov." The President tried to play the genial host. "The real stuff. Stolichnaya."

"I gave that up along with my Soviet citizenship, sir." Barisov knew how to put people on the defensive. "I am now a Black Label man."

The President's celebrated papier-mâché grin came unstuck.

"Let's come right to the point, Mr. President," said Senator O'Reilly as soon as he had gotten his fist around a tumbler of bourbon on the rocks. "What's staring you in the face is something bigger than Watergate. You are facing the biggest crisis that any American President has had to confront in peacetime."

"Let's not go overboard, Shame," the President parried. "In fact, let's not even start talking until we agree on the ground rules. I don't understand what Mr. Hockney is doing here tonight."

"Mr. President." O'Reilly sprang to Hockney's defense. "If it weren't for Bob Hockney and his help in bringing Colonel Barisov to these shores, we might never have known—until it was too late—to what extent the foreign policy of your administration is being manipulated by the Soviet government."

Hockney had learned the reporter's trick of masking his emotions behind a cocked eyebrow. But beneath his detached, skeptical facade, he was exhilarated. He was not merely a witness with an incredible ringside seat. He, Robert Hockney, was helping to change world history. He felt like a surfer riding, mastering, a tidal wave.

The President glared malevolently at Hockney.

"Well, if Mr. Hockney's presence is really necessary to these proceedings," the President said, "I would like his word of honor that no part of this conversation will appear in print."

"I'm not sure that I understand, sir," said Hockney. "Are you saying you don't want any of this to be published while you are still in office?"

"What you put in your memoirs is your business."

"Then I accept."

"Do I have your word that nothing on this will appear in the media?" the President insisted.

"Yes, sir."

Hockney was not surprised at the President's insistence, although the rules on off-the-record conversations had been cheerfully and successfully violated time and again by the *World* and the rest of the media.

"Shame," said the President, addressing Senator O'Reilly, "while I respect your motives I hope you can respect mine."

The President was about to rest his feet on the coffee table, but stopped himself, realizing that the Russian might take it amiss.

"I hope you understand," Connor continued, "the disastrous effect that Colonel Barisov's testimony is having on public morale and the image of the United States abroad. Let me assure you that I am guided only by national security considerations. Now the Colonel is making some

437

very serious allegations about Soviet penetration of this administration, not to mention the news media. I'm having these allegations checked out by the appropriate official agencies at this very moment. But I would suggest that if we are going to take this business seriously, the way to proceed is through a serious investigation, not a TV extravaganza. What I saw on TV this afternoon was a national disgrace."

"Yes, Mr. President," O'Reilly countered, "the situation is a national disgrace. The paralysis of our law enforcement agencies, the corruption of our institutions, the wanton failure of this administration to clean its own house—*that*, not the public airing, is the national disgrace."

Hockney studied the President's face. Billy Connor looked ten years older than the last picture he had seen in the papers. He looked deflated, shriveled, like one of the toy balloons Hockney used to blow up as a boy and then release, letting the air escape with a rude noise.

"How much further are you planning to go, Shame?" demanded the President.

"I think that Viktor should be allowed to answer that one for himself," the Senator responded, gesturing toward Barisov. "After all, it's his evidence, not mine."

"Colonel Barisov," the President asked, "are there any more members of my administration that you propose to name in these hearings?"

"I'm afraid I have very bad news for you, Mr. President," said the Russian.

The President gulped his bourbon and held out the glass for Jonah Cobb to refill.

"Perhaps you will permit me to begin by making some technical distinctions, sir," the Russian continued. "The KGB makes use of many different types of agents and informants, many of whom are not fully aware—and may, in fact, be completely unaware—of what interests they are serving. We call a valuable source who has an intimate relationship with the KGB a principal agent, or *osnovny agent*. This is the kind of man who may be running a network of lesser agents, or providing vital secrets, and who has been consciously recruited and trained by the KGB. The deputy director of the NSC, Perry Cummings, known to the KGB under the cryptonym Coyote, is an example of an *osnovny agent*."

The President seemed to sink lower into his chair, sipping his bourbon.

"Another type of KGB contact," Barisov went on, "is the trusted person, or *doveryonnoe litso*. We use that term to apply to people who are totally reliable politically and will knowingly carry out Soviet instructions but who have not been formally recruited as KGB agents. They are often especially useful as talent spotters who will help KGB case officers identify valuable potential agents. The late Vlad Merchant, who founded the Foundation for Progressive Reform, was an example of a *doveryonnoe litso*. His granddaughter, Alexia, who controls the Foundation's finances today, is another."

President Connor nervously pulled up both socks. Cobb belched and did not excuse himself. Hockney wondered how much of the dialogue he would be able to reconstruct on the drive back to Washington from Camp David.

"A third kind of KGB contact," Barisov continued, impervious to Cobb's deliberate vulgarity, "is an unconscious source, or *tyomhaya verboura*. This type of person serves Soviet interests and works under KGB control without realizing what he is doing. Lenin used to call such people useful idiots. Without being conscious KGB agents, they are often in a position to accomplish far more for the Soviet Union than the people who are knowingly working for us."

A red light flashed on the white phone on a rustic wooden table at the President's right hand. The light was accompanied by a low, intermittent purr.

"Excuse me, Colonel Bar-r." The President stumbled over the defector's name. He picked up the phone.

"Yeah, Judge," Connor soon was saying. "What's that? You've issued an order for the arrest of Perry Cummings? You found what at the Foundation?"

Then, aware of the eyes fixed on him in the lodge, the

President realized he had said too much. He listened in silence as the FBI director explained that Dan MacDonald's team had raided the office Cummings still maintained at the Foundation and found a loose brick in the fireplace. It was one of the specially adapted tape recorders that could send out twenty minutes of recorded conversation in a twenty-second burst.

"Send it where?" Hockney heard the President ask.

To a passing car, the Judge explained.

"What the hell do they need that for?" the President demanded, trying to understand.

The Judge gave the details of instant-burst transmission.

"Where'd they get that piece of equipment?" the President said into the phone.

To find the answer to that, said the FBI director, would take a little more time. But there was something more. They had found an unusually large collection of postcards in Cummings's apartment and were examining them to see whether they contained microdots—a method of clandestine communication greatly favored by the KGB.

"Where is Cummings now?"

Running, said the Judge, or gone to ground.

"I doubt you'll find him alive," Barisov observed when the President had hung up.

"Tell me one thing, Colonel," said the President. "If you knew that Cummings was a Soviet agent, your former KGB friends must have assumed you would tell the British and they would tell us. So why didn't they move to get Cummings out after you defected?"

"I think the answer to that must lie in Washington, Mr. President," said Barisov. "You may find it if you consider the possible reasons why no investigation of Cummings has been authorized before today."

President Connor held out his glass to Cobb for another refill.

"Okay, Colonel," the President said. "You were talking about a third type of KGB agent, the unconscious source. You didn't give any examples. Are you saying there are some of these people in my administration?"

Barisov nodded.

"Give me the names," the President commanded, raising his voice.

Barisov looked at O'Reilly. The Senator nodded.

"This will come as a shock to you, Mr. President," said Barisov. "While I was stationed in Washington, the KGB resident told me that two of your close friends were being handled by my service and the International Department of the Soviet Communist Party as unconscious sources. One was Mr. Harmon, the Senator. The other was Mr. Milligan, the Vice President of the United States. This was later confirmed to me by Kramar in Moscow."

The President burst into shrill laughter. Hysterical, Hockney thought. Billy Connor laughed so hard that his drink, raised halfway to his lips, spilled over his red tie. Uncertainly Cobb joined in.

"This is preposterous," the President exclaimed. "The KGB resident in Washington must be smoking hash if that's what he's been reporting to Moscow. Do you have a single shred of evidence to back up what you've just said?"

"An unconscious source," Barisov said carefully, "is subject to control by a variety of other people who do not declare themselves to be Soviet agents. In the case of Senator Harmon, the guiding influence was Rick Adams, who was under the direct control of the Cubans. In the case of the Vice President, it was Perry Cummings."

The President mopped his tie with a Kleenex that Cobb handed him. "Okay," Billy Connor said in a subdued voice, "then tell me how you think the policies of my administration have been shaped by the Soviets?"

Yankovich, who had sat throughout the conversation transfixed, without so much as crossing or uncrossing his legs, now intervened to answer the question for the Russian.

"The Soviets," the national security adviser said, "have succeeded, by drawing on vice presidential patronage, in planting people we know to be agents of influence in the middle echelons of your administration. But their biggest accomplishment has been to make us deaf and blind to what they themselves are doing."

"That is exactly right." Barisov approved Yankovich's summation.

The President pondered for a moment, then got to his feet.

"Shame," he said to O'Reilly, "I'd like to have a few minutes with you alone outside."

6

THE AIR was chill as the President and Seamus O'Reilly walked under the trees around Dogwood Lodge. It was early fall. President Connor swung his feet nervously through the dry leaves as he strolled, as if kicking an imaginary football.

"What are you after, Shame?" he probed.

"You know I've got enough to bring down your administration," said O'Reilly, confident. "The crash would be bigger than Watergate."

The President paused under a poplar. He folded his arms, shivering slightly.

"All right," said Billy Connor. "Go ahead. Deal."

"If you want to stay in office for the rest of your term," said O'Reilly, "the script writes itself. A cleanup of this administration from top to bottom. First, you'll have to fire Perry Cummings and the others and announce that a criminal investigation is under way. By the way, there are lots of other people, in Congress and the media, that Barisov has got the goods on. They'll have to be checked out too. If they can't be prosecuted, they can at least be exposed for what they really are."

"That sounds to me like your job, Shame."

O'Reilly nodded his burly head. "Okay. But we're also going to bring in a few new laws through Congress to put some teeth back into our internal security setup. We'll need full White House backing."

"No problem so far, Shame," said the President, letting his arms fall loosely to his side. "Anything else?"

"I think it's about time you got yourself a new CIA director. Crawford's shown his true colors in this business. We need a ballsy professional who's not going to tailor his national intelligence estimates to your foreign policy line—which I also assume will be changing."

"I don't see that there's anything wrong with our foreign policy." The President defended himself. "We've kept this country out of every war since Vietnam. We haven't shed a drop of American blood. We got sixteen conflicts going in the world right now, and we're not involved in a single one. That makes me very proud, Shame."

"Yes, that's very true, Mr. President. And what's the end result? Most of our allies have already made their deals with Moscow and are allies only in name. Do you need another Pearl Harbor before you realize that we are about to be taken?"

"Okay, Shame. You're not on the floor of the Senate now. Let's save the foreign policy debate for some other time. Who did you have in mind for the CIA?"

The Senator mentioned the name of a veteran operations officer who had predicted with absolute precision what was going to happen in Saudi Arabia and Iran in the absence of a forceful American initiative. Perry Cummings had accused him of leaking secret material on Soviet violations of the SALT agreements to Senator O'Reilly's staff.

"I was planning to do a little spring cleaning anyway." The President lied in a futile attempt to save face. "I'll look into it."

"Of course, Vice President Milligan will have to go too." O'Reilly dropped his bombshell like a casual aside.

Wordless, the President shuffled on through the leaves.

"It wouldn't be the first time," O'Reilly said to the President's back. "Nixon dropped Agnew." It didn't soften the blow.

"It won't be that hard," O'Reilly pursued. "You'll have to announce that Milligan's resigning on health grounds."

The President's head sank between his shoulders.

Still with his back turned on O'Reilly, President Connor said, "What's in it for you, Shame?"

O'Reilly explained. He was going to be Vice President of the United States. It wasn't a job that would have interested him under normal circumstances.

"But after all, you won't be running again, Mr. President," O'Reilly concluded. "I will."

New York - Washington

1

XENOPHON PARRISH NUTTING was at his desk in the study of his triplex on Fifth Avenue, mulling over the extraordinary telephone conversation he had just had with the President of the United States. The surface of his desk was cluttered with ragged clippings from the first edition of the paper that he had torn out in the early hours of the morning. Following his customary practice, he had used a red grease pencil to score the various stories with a rating of zero to ten. The Barisov piece on the front page had rated a near-perfect nine.

Under the by-line of the paper's Washington bureau chief, the lead paragraph of the *World* story read:

In the O'Reilly hearings today, the alleged Soviet defector Viktor Barisov gave testimony on intelligence failures. He named several administration officials as Soviet agents. Senator Mahee commented, "I don't believe a word he says. This attempt at a frame-up is reminiscent of the McCarthy era, one of the darkest periods of our history." The CIA and the White House have charged this Barisov is a Soviet plant who has been assigned by the KGB to disrupt relations between the Connor administration and its European allies.

But that was before the phone call. After what the President had told him in great confidence over the line, Nutting realized that the story was wrong. Dreadfully wrong. Perhaps deliberately wrong.

The owner of the *World* tightened the surgical rubber gloves he always wore when handling newsprint, and pulled another copy of the morning edition off the stack beside his desk. He scored the Barisov story with three big zeros.

It was nearly 8:00 A.M.

Nutting rang for his butler. "Have the Washington papers arrived?" he said.

The butler brought them.

The lead story on Barisov in the *Tribune* also cast doubt on the defector's authenticity. But skimming it fast, Nutting's eye came to rest on two damning facts buried in the body of the piece that his own paper had failed to carry. The *Tribune* reported that the deputy director of the NSC, Perry Cummings, had vanished from his home and that not even the White House could reach him. There was speculation that Cummings might have been connected with the theft of the ultrasecret blueprints on the KH-19 satellite. The *Tribune* piece also reported that Hyde Lewis of the Arms Control Agency had tendered his resignation.

Now the President had confessed over the phone that the White House was in serious trouble. He had said the damage could be contained, given responsible news handling, but Billy Connor had also told the owner of the *World* that the Vice President would be resigning shortly, for reasons of health. Nutting did not believe this was unconnected with the Barisov affair, especially since pictures of Milligan water-skiing during a two-day break in the Bahamas had been published the previous weekend.

Xenophon Parrish Nutting reflected on how his father would have dealt with the problem. He then called for his limousine. He had decided to make one of his rare visits to the editorial offices of the family newspaper.

Nutting called his withered secretary on the radio phone in his car and instructed her to have all the senior editors waiting for him in his office on the top floor of the *World* building when he arrived. She pointed out that most of them would probably not show up until around 11:00. It was now just after 9:00.

"Then get them out of bed," he ordered. The edge in his voice suggested to his secretary that the boss was about to erupt. What was happening was unprecedented; she had never seen Nutting lose his composure in the many years she had worked for him. It could only mean something awesome was about to happen.

447

2

THE LAST TO STRAGGLE into the office of the owner's secretary was Ed Finkel, the national affairs editor.

Red-eyed and visibly hung over, Finkel said, "What's the flap? I had a heavy night."

"Bonus time, I guess," the foreign editor quipped.

"Don't hold your breath on bonuses, gentlemen," said Nutting's secretary, unsmiling. "Is everyone here now?"

Len Rourke glanced at the other men in the room: managing editor, editorial page director, national affairs editor, foreign editor. The assistant managing editor was absent, on a tour of the foreign bureaus.

"Yeah," Rourke said.

"You may go in."

As the editors filed into Nutting's private office, Rourke saw that the owner was already seated at the conference table. Nutting did not bother to acknowledge the chorus of good mornings. He was spraying the back of his throat with a wheezer. He had suffered from asthma since childhood.

Six copies of the *Tribune* were arranged around the table.

"Gentlemen," Nutting began, "we've been scooped. Worse than that, we have been humiliated. This is our worst reporting failure since the *Tribune* scooped us on Watergate. What have you got to say for yourselves?"

No one replied. The only noise in the room was the gnashing of Rourke's molars.

"Well," the owner demanded, "what are you planning for an encore?"

"It's a very confused picture, Zen," Rourke said lamely, "with a lot more conjecture and innuendo than fact."

"I'll give you some facts," the owner interposed, angrily. "The President's cleaning house. He seems to take Viktor Barisov seriously, so why don't we?"

"Because we know who's behind it," Finkel interjected.

"What do you mean?" snapped Nutting.

"This is Bob Hockney's revenge, not Barisov's defection."

"Hockney's defection is a very stale story," said Nutting. "This year's story is Barisov. In fact, it looks to me as if Robert Hockney has been vindicated."

"I think the picture is still awfully confused." Rourke repeated himself, hesitantly. "Ed"—he motioned to Finkel—"why don't you fill us in on what we've got planned for tomorrow?"

"Okay," said Finkel. "We've got some good lines out to Perry Cummings. We should be able to get hold of him today and report his side of the story. Phil Kreps is in Washington. He's supposed to testify before the O'Reilly Committee later this week. Pete Lawry is having lunch with him today. I understand Kreps should be good for some dirt on Hockney's role in all of this. And Bill Crawford has promised us the inside track on the rather peculiar part the European and Israeli services have played in this whole affair."

The owner looked balefully at his paper's national affairs editor. Ed Finkel had just been dragged out of bed. It seemed improbable that he had found time to coordinate the paper's news coverage at that hour of the day. More likely, Finkel and his friends had worked out a damage limitation scenario from the word go. Finkel seemed uninterested in whether what Barisov was saying was true or not.

"What I want," Nutting said firmly, "is to get this paper back on track. Our readers are interested in what is really going on, not what you gentlemen think is going on. I want the Washington bureau to get in touch with O'Reilly, and Yankovich, and the FBI. We might even run an interview with Robert Hockney."

Finkel bridled. "I'm not going to run an interview with that ratfink who walked out of this paper and has been sniping at us ever since," he protested.

"Are you saying you refuse to carry out my instructions?" the owner challenged.

Finkel looked blank. It was the first time Xenophon Parrish Nutting had interfered in an editorial decision.

"If you want the *World* to become the laughingstock of the trade, then run an interview with Hockney," Finkel said at last. "I'm just trying to protect the reputation of this paper."

"Goddamn it, so am I!" Nutting exclaimed. He brought his fist down on the table, but slowed its fall so that it merely brushed the top. Then he took a handkerchief out of his breast pocket and cleaned his hand with elaborate care.

"I'm not prepared to expose this paper to ridicule," Finkel said softly, glancing toward Len Rourke for support. Rourke sat silent, rubbing his chin.

"If that's the way you feel," the owner addressed Finkel, "you're fired."

Finkel sat openmouthed, disbelieving.

"With all respect, Zen." Rourke attempted to defend his national affairs editor. "I don't think we should do anything in haste."

"Len, I disagree with you on the need for haste," the owner said. "Seems to me we've spent years covering up for the Connor administration. That leaves us with a hell of a problem. In one word, it's credibility."

Finkel cleared his throat, about to speak.

"Mr. Finkel," the owner said with cold formality, "your presence is no longer required here."

Stunned, Finkel rose to his feet and walked out of the room. He looked ready to burst into tears.

"Sam," Nutting addressed the editorial page director, ignoring Finkel's departure, "about the lead editorial for tomorrow. I want you to know—but this must be kept between us in this room—that this thing reaches as high as the Vice President. President Connor has told me, in deepest confidence, that Milligan's resignation is about to be announced. The White House will say it's on health grounds. But I know better. What I would like to read tomorrow is an editorial that encourages the President to persevere with the investigations into the Barisov testimony. I think we ought to give some kudos both to Barisov and to Bob Hockney for their courage in bringing these matters to the light of day. And I think we should also raise the question of to what extent this country's foreign policy has been steered by Soviet agents of influence since Billy Connor's election."

Sam Vander Kamp, the editorial page director, had been reared on New Deal liberalism. He had rallied successively to Gene McCarthy, George McGovern, and Jimmy Carter. Vice President Milligan was one of his oldest friends. His impassioned anti-Vietnam editorials had taken him to the head of the page. Now he had the owner telling him what to write.

"What you're asking me to do, Zen, would violate one of my most sacred principles," Vander Kamp spluttered.

"And what, may I ask, is that?" Nutting's voice dripped sarcasm.

"I've spent most of my working life trying to defend people's rights to their own ideas against McCarthyite witchhunters and cold-warriors. Now you're asking me to lead the pack."

"What I am asking everyone on this paper to do," said the owner, "is to uphold the very same values they've always upheld against an invasion from a quarter which all of us, me included, have always refused to take seriously enough. I'd like a draft of that editorial on my desk by 2:00 P.M. I'll be here."

"Sorry," said Vander Kamp. "I'll have to pass on this one. I don't think I can write the kind of editorial you want."

Rourke's molars chattered as if he were in a blizzard.

"All right, Sam," Nutting said, "I'll write the editorial myself. Don't bother writing anything else for tomorrow either. I'll need the entire space."

The remaining editors looked at Rourke expectantly. To their surprise, the editor of the *World* still said nothing. Inwardly, Rourke felt a mixture of relief and triumph. He had been fighting and losing battles with Ed Finkel and Sam Vander Kamp for years. It was a pity that it had taken Nutting's personal intervention to turn things around. But then, Rourke confessed to himself, the owner had shown more guts than he had.

3

THE CALL from the owner of the *World* reached Bob Hockney in Washington via Senator Seamus O'Reilly's office. He was with Julia and Barisov in the Mossad's safe house near Leonardtown, poring over the morning papers. The O'Reilly hearings had been suspended for the day, while the Senator waited to see whether the President would keep his side of the deal agreed to at Camp David.

Hockney returned the call from Xenophon Parrish Nutting as soon as he got the message. Nutting's conversation was succinct. First, he offered profuse apologies for the way Hockney had been treated by the paper in the past. Next, he congratulated Hockney for his role in the Barisov affair, which he described as "the best piece of enterprise journalism since Woodward and Bernstein brought down Nixon."

Finally, Nutting said, "I want you back on the paper, Bob. I'm sorry for what happened back in seventy-six. You can write your own ticket, jobwise and salarywise. In fact, I need you back here today. I'd be grateful if you could get on the next shuttle."

"Well, it's a two-hour drive from where I am now to National airport," Hockney calculated. "I guess I could just make the two o'clock shuttle. But what's the rush?"

"The rush is tomorrow's editorial. I want you to write it for me."

"Bob," Julia said as he slammed down the phone. Moments later he was cramming a few essentials into an overnight bag. "I'm worried about Perry."

He took her head gently between his palms. "They'll track him down." Hockney tried to comfort her. "After that, it won't be easy. But Perry brought this on himself."

Hockney had just installed himself behind the IBM typewriter that had been set up for him inside the private office of the owner of the *World* when Nutting's secretary came in with a roll of wire service copy.

The first item was on Perry Cummings. His body had been found floating in the Potomac, five miles downstream from the city limits. He had been killed by a bullet fired through the mouth. Diving weights had been tied to his ankles, but they were not heavy enough to take him down to the riverbed. The police were still debating whether it was suicide. The FBI was convinced it was murder.

Hockney crumpled into his chair, badly shaken. He wondered how he could break the news to Julia—and whether, in some part of her subconscious, she would blame the tragedy on him. He could still barely fathom what had driven his friend and youthful mentor down a pathway that had ended with an assassin's bullet. He reflected mournfully that his career had been launched in blood—with the suicide of Bonpierre in Paris. Now it seemed Hockney the journalist was to be relaunched to the accompaniment of another death. Could he wash himself entirely of blame?

He read on through the wire service copy, trying to take his mind off the image of Perry Cummings floating face-down in the Potomac.

Hockney returned the wire service items to Nutting and started to discuss them. But a call from Lawry came through on Nutting's line, and he hung up after a couple of quick questions.

"Seems strange," the owner explained to Hockney. "Kreps didn't show up for the lunch. I thought the man was begging for publicity."

"We should run a trace on him," Hockney said. "Let me get hold of the FBI guy in charge of the investigation of the Barisov allegations. He should be able to help out."

"Are you in touch with him?"

"Oh, I can do it through O'Reilly's office," Hockney said vaguely.

It took Senator O'Reilly's executive aide Dick Roth barely ten minutes to relay the answer from Big Dan MacDonald of the FBI. Phil Kreps had been found dead in his hotel room. It looked like a cardiac arrest, but the FBI was skeptical, given Kreps's relative youth and the fact that he had no previous history of heart trouble. MacDonald thought that the Soviets had an obvious motive for liquidating Kreps now that their game was up in Washington— the fear that he might be erratic enough to crack and confess all under cross-examination in the O'Reilly hearings. Hockney wondered whether the FBI man's hunch was right. His British intelligence friend, Chris Campbell, had told him once that the Russians had developed an electronic beam that could be aimed from a window at a pedestrian in the street below, producing instant cardiac arrest and sudden death. Had Kreps died that way?

Hockney found it hard to visualize the man who had started out as his friend and best source and ended up as one of his most bitter adversaries laid out in the morgue. The KGB had tried to kill Hockney, just as they had tried to kill Barisov. Now it seemed they were trying to cut their losses by killing their own.

Hockney wound some paper into the IBM typewriter and began to hit the keys.

4

AFTER THE ENFORCED RESIGNATIONS of Vice President Milligan and CIA Director Crawford, there was a festive mood for days in the office of Dr. Milorad Yankovich, the national security adviser. Yank was now confident enough to tell Jonah Cobb, the White House chief of staff, that he did not have time to see him. He even told the President that his friend Timmy should be sent to a health farm in Arizona where alcoholics went to dry out. The President actually agreed; after that, Timmy Hicks and his can of Schlitz were no longer to be seen at sensitive discussions in the Oval Office. In fact, the President had taken to agreeing with almost everything Yankovich had to say. It was no longer Billy Connor's approval that Yankovich required for his foreign policy initiatives. It was the approval of the new Vice President, Seamus O'Reilly, who had become President in all but name. And O'Reilly and Yankovich had yet to disagree on anything.

After the great purge of the Connor administration, which finally claimed 171 officials, ranging from code clerks to two assistant secretaries of state and the Vice President, Yankovich and O'Reilly were ready to impose a new direction on U.S. foreign policy. They began by scrapping the SALT IV treaty—in diplomatic language, of course. The statement they compelled President Connor to put out reaffirmed the administration's commitment to arms control, but declared that because of new evidence of serious violations by the Russians of previous agreements, the SALT IV treaty would not be presented to the Senate for ratification in the foreseeable future.

Yankovich's next move, with the help of the tough-minded new CIA director, Ted Wittingham, who had been station chief in Paris back in the sixties, and with O'Reilly's continuing clout in the Senate, was to authorize massive funding for guerrilla resistance to the newly established Marxist regimes of the Middle East. Within a matter of days, a secret royalist guerrilla army in Saudi Arabia announced it had seized control of Abqaiq, the nerve center of the oil fields, and Ras Tanurah, the country's biggest oil terminal on the Gulf. Again at Yankovich's instigation, President Connor took the initiative in calling an emergency NATO conference to discuss two American proposals: first, to deploy hundreds of medium-range U.S. missiles in Western Europe to match the one thousand SS-20s the Soviets had positioned within striking distance of the Europeans, and, second, to expand the Atlantic alliance into a global defense structure for all countries threatened by Soviet expansion.

The Russians reacted cautiously at first. When the American government expelled sixty Soviet diplomats and trade officials who had been named by Barisov as spies, only ten American diplomats were expelled from Moscow in reprisal. When the Connor administration ditched SALT IV, the Russians retaliated merely by announcing that they

455

would expand their defense spending another five percent a year. The CIA analysts concluded that this was a hollow threat, since Soviet defense expenditures were already so colossal that a further increase would impose a devastating toll on the Soviet economy and the Russian consumer.

But the threat to Moscow's puppet regime in Saudi Arabia obliged the Russians to react in force, or risk losing credibility with their newfound Islamic Marxist friends throughout the Middle East. After the capture of Abqaiq, the CIA reported that the Russians had put five divisions equipped with hot-weather gear on full alert.

The Soviet President called his opposite number on the hot line in the Oval Office. But it was Vice President O'Reilly who took the call. The Soviet threat was blunt. Unless the United States withdrew support from the royalists who had occupied the Saudi oil fields, Soviet troops would retake them by force; the Saudi Islamic People's Republic would refuse to sell oil to America or its allies; and the Russians would ensure that the handful of Arabian emirates that had so far resisted the tide of Moslem revolution would also succumb. If the Americans attempted to airlift troops to Saudi Arabia via their bases in Europe, the Soviet President went on, peace-loving labor unions would paralyze the Continent and force the local governments to refuse to permit the planes to take off.

Vice President Seamus O'Reilly's reply was pithier still. "If you try to do that," he said, "your men will need their hot-weather gear, because they'll be diving into a sea of fire."

There was a pause for a few seconds while the simultaneous translation was completed.

"And what is that supposed to mean?" the voice of the Soviet leader crackled back over the hot line.

"We've put up with your sort of liberation movements around the world for quite a few years now, Mr. President," O'Reilly said. "It's about time you learned to put up with pro-Western guerrillas. What I am suggesting is that if you try to land your troops in the Saudi oil fields, our boys out there will set a match to them. That would be hell in a very small place."

456

Another pause. Then the Soviet leader said, "You are bluffing."

"Try me," said O'Reilly.

They didn't.

5

BOB HOCKNEY AND JULIA CUMMINGS had a quiet wedding at the First Unitarian Church in Arlington, Virginia. There were just a few invited guests—Hockney's parents, Dick Roth, Vice President O'Reilly, Nick Flower, and Gideon Sharon, the Israeli secret service chief. Julia's father had died two years before; Chris Campbell flew in from London. Julia's mother was in tears throughout the service. Viktor Barisov was Hockney's best man. The champagne reception at Sharon's home was quite unlike any that Hockney remembered. They wanted no publicity, and they got none. The minister who officiated at the ceremony did not even recognize Hockney's name. Hockney was relieved.

Afterward, Admiral Tennant Hockney said as he kissed the bride, "He doesn't deserve you, but he's made a few substantial down payments this year."

One of the last things Hockney did before embarking on his honeymoon was to send a cable to the American consulate in Hong Kong. It was a response to a personal message he had received from the *World* bureau in the British colony. The message said that among the Vietnamese refugees who had escaped in a hijacked merchant ship and reached Hong Kong was a woman named Nguyen Canh Lan who claimed to know him, and who was requesting his sponsorship for an American visa. Hockney agreed not only to sponsor her but to pay her fare to New York.

The revolution always consumes its own, he thought, remembering Lani's burning commitment to the Vietcong cause in the year of the Tet offensive. It was sad that the lovely young woman he remembered had also fallen victim to the war. But it was also a kind of vindication of his own

457

reassessment of the conflicts that had challenged and divided the Americans of his generation.

Hockney knew they had earned a proper honeymoon. In two weeks' time, he would have to face a barrage of paperwork and telephone calls as the new Washington bureau chief of the *World*. As his wedding gift, Chris Campbell solved the problem of how they would spend their first few days of married life.

The yacht was waiting for them in Rhodes.

"Not a very big boat," Campbell advised them. "Built for the North American lakes. Too much top and not enough bottom to ride well in choppy seas. But it's clear sailing for you two from now on. Anyway, there's a crew of eight and one of the best cellars afloat." Chris was a little vague about the ownership of the boat, and Hockney knew better than to ask.

As they sailed out of Rhodes harbor in brilliant sunshine two days later, Hockney pointed out twin pillars rising on either side of the channel. One was surmounted by an imposing bronze stag, the other by a doe.

"What do stags do?" Julia said coyly. She was already stripped to a skimpy bikini.

"They fight for their women."

"What do they do when they've won their battles?"

"They go below deck."

So they did.